Relinquished

Also by Pollyanna Porter

Rectified (2021)

Redeemed (2022)

From Foreword Magazine

"You can take the teacher out of school but you can't take her thirty-plus years of interacting and educating children out of the teacher. Or her understanding of the parent-child relationship. What say she put that knowledge to good use in fiction? And that's exactly what Pollyanna [Porter] did in the novels *Rectified* and *Redeemed* — at an astonishingly high level, according to *Foreword*'s Executive Editor Matt Sutherland. With art theft, childhood trauma, mother-son estrangement, and so much more..."

$$\bullet \bullet \bullet \bullet \bullet$$

About Relinquished

"Through their shared trauma, Porter examines loss, resilience, and the fragility of basic human rights, particularly for people of color and LGBTQIA+ individuals. The prose is compassionate and immersive, capturing the systemic failures that perpetuate cycles of bullying, societal rejection, familial neglect, and violence... Porter's narrative shines in its portrayal of quiet bravery. 'Sometimes, kids who are thinking of running just need more support,' the detective remarks, encapsulating the novel's wake-up call for accountability and action in the name of justice. With Sadie's unwavering empathy and faith, and Kate's fierce love for family, Relinquished leaves readers with a powerful message: healing begins not in escape, but in confronting the past — one truth, one choice, and one courageous step at a time." — *BookLife by Publishers Weekly*

"Readers will find this book engaging due to its many twists and turns, which will keep them on the edge of their seats." — *U. S. Review of Books*, Recommended, Book Review by Amanda Hanson

About Rectified

"With nuance and honesty, Porter develops a strong female protagonist with imperfections, independence, and the determination to right a horrific wrong." — *U.S. Review of Books*, Recommended, Book Review by Michelle Jacobs

"Written from the heart, this story may arouse your anger, and shock you in parts, but it will keep you reading as you experience hope, crave redemption and trust that there's a good outcome." — Kitty Boyes, *The Arina Perry Series*

• • • • •

About Redeemed

"This compelling family saga starts with a bang and keeps exploding like a string of fireworks...suspense, mystery... and just a touch of the supernatural." —Joseph A. Citro, *Passing Strange*

"Porter's novel is exceptionally well-written with beautiful descriptive language. Her book is a must-read for history buffs and romantics." — *U. S. Review of Books*, Recommended, Book Review by Kat Kennedy

Relinquished

Pollyanna Porter

2024 / *Vermont*

Book Design by Jennifer Payne,
Words by Jen (Branford, CT)

Printed in the USA

Library of Congress Control Number: 2024923773

ISBN: 979-8-218-55053-0

Copies of *Relinquished* may be purchased
from online retailers or by visiting:

www.pollyannaporter.com

Dedication

*To Andy, my husband — a good
man if ever there was,*

and

*To Pami and Posey — my sisters
who make me laugh,
hope and remember when...*

"Some of us think holding
on makes us strong: but
sometimes it is letting go."

Herman Hesse

BOOK ONE

Sadie, Winter 2015

Chapter 1

Tristan, please! If you don't take me home, I've got no other way to get there," I pleaded. His acne glowed in the flare of a match. The smell of sulfur was strong in the cab of the truck. He didn't look at me, instead he blew out the match and took a long drag from the cigarette. We were crawling down the Mountain Road; the driving conditions had become treacherous.

Should I have just done it and gone home right after? Begging him now was pathetic, but being left in town stranded for hours wasn't good either. The sleet was hitting the windshield even harder. It was cold in the truck. The heater barely worked.

"Nah, you had your chance," he answered, sneering at me. "What a big, fat fuckin' mistake this was." It was the only thing he'd said since picking me up that I could agree with him on.

Suddenly, we hit an icy patch and the old truck spun around, just missing the guardrail by inches before it came to a rest. Two loose cans of Budweiser rolled over my feet. His drinking and driving was scaring me — just like when the old man drove with his cans of Busch.

I leaned forward, looking out the window. "Let me out here!" My voice was tinged with fear.

He reached over, grabbed the door handle, and opened it. He reeked of beer. His hand was chapped, his knuckles red and raw. "Suit yourself!" he replied.

Cold air quickly filled the truck, and I instantly regretted saying I wanted out. "Okay, wait. Let's go someplace right now. I'll do it, really, I will." My legs were starting to shake. Was it the cold or my desperation to end this awful night with him?

"Too late," he replied.

I looked at him in disbelief. His neck was all blotchy above the collar of his Carhart jacket. Tristan always had an edge, a meanness about him. Everyone saw that, but this — dumping me here — was unbelievable.

With force, he yanked my purse from my shoulder and threw it out the door. I didn't have to think twice. I jumped out after it, hitting the pavement and falling down hard on one knee. My kneecap stung. *Was I bleeding?* My shoes had no tread and were slippery on the black ice. I looked back into the cab of the truck and tearfully asked, "Could I at least use your cell?"

"Nah, it's not my fault your old man's too poor to get you a phone." He threw his lit cigarette out, just inches from me.

He revved the engine, the over-sized tires spewing muck from the shoulder of the road as he backed up and left. The truck's rear lights grew smaller as he drove down the hill towards town.

Relief flooded me that he was gone, but now I was really stuck. The sleet hitting my face stung. *Get to the guard rail,* I thought as I started to fall again.

I held on to the cold steel all the way down the hill to the big sign at the entrance to The Mountain. My hands were freezing, my jeans were torn at the knee, and my moccasins were soaking wet. No one had passed by me. The road in all three directions was deserted.

A RESTAURANT SIGN, SHAY'S FINE DINING, was lit up above the parking lot down below the guard rail to my right. A ski equipment store, a bakery, and an antique shop were all closed up tight adjacent to it. A door, further down from the main entrance to Shay's, was wide open. Someone was taking garbage out to the dumpster just behind a lattice-covered fence.

I climbed down the embankment but ended up slipping and sliding the rest of the way on my bottom. Shuffling across the parking lot, I headed for the dumpster and that open door. I could hear people's voices and see figures crossing back and forth.

Despite the freezing rain, the restaurant was busy. Its lot was full of big SUVs with out-of-state license plates wedged in tight. The sleet was loud as it hit the tops of the cars.

I didn't know yet what I was going to do once I got to that door. There was no way to get ahold of my father, and Kate, my sister, still had hours left of her shift at the nursing home. I'd never once set foot in the restaurant, but staying out in this weather wasn't an option.

I opened up the screen door, hesitated, then stepped into a large kitchen. Cautiously, I moved further in and closed the screen behind me. I was near a big walk-in refrigerator and freezer. A man, not far from me, quickly glanced my way but then returned to what he was doing: filling three plates — two full of slimy things on half shells and one humongous shrimp cocktail. Yelling something I couldn't make out, he grabbed six more plates and lined them up. He reached into a silver container in front of him that was full of lemon wedges and then grabbed a squeeze bottle and squirted out a fancy design over the little fried cakes he'd just taken from the oven behind him.

A waiter walked up and reached for the first three plates, placing them on a black, oval tray. He hoisted the tray up over his shoulder and briefly looked at me before turning to leave. I took a step back, wanting to stay out of sight.

Somewhere to my left, another guy yelled, "Stephen, the twelve top has a shit load of apps — the slip is coming!"

"Jesus Christ!" the first guy — Stephen — responded in a pissed-off voice. He wiped his hands across a rag and walked past me into the big walk-in. On the way out, he gruffly said, "Shut the door." His hands were full of Tupperware containers. I quickly stepped forward and closed the door. I returned to my spot, hoping nobody else had noticed me.

My hands had stopped stinging. I held my arms tightly around my waist, feeling the warmth. The cooks were in short sleeves, sweating even. Everyone looked frantic — the guys behind the bank of metal shelves in front of the open flames, and the waiters and waitresses who were reaching for the plates below the bank of heating lamps on the other side of them.

Ms. Clark, one of my elementary teachers, yelled something to one of the guys at the humongous oven. He burst out laughing then nodded to another guy at the stove who was wearing a towel around his neck.

She took a dinner plate then called out, "Where's the parsley, Eugene?"

The guy with the towel quickly reached over and sprinkled something all over the food on the plate. "I'd like to parsley you all…"

But she cut him off and laughed, "Only in your dreams, darling." She carried the plate out a swinging door.

The heat of the kitchen and the smells were incredible. Mostly, I recognized garlic — that and steak sizzling.

No one seemed to be paying me any attention, even though I was making a puddle where I stood. Behind the open door was a bucket and mop. I debated reaching for the mop and wiping up the water.

Just then a woman approached me and, above the clamor of the kitchen, asked, "Who are you, and what are you doing?" She was all business-like, dressed in a fancy white shirt and black pants. She didn't look friendly at all — a lot like Kate did on a typical day. Her dark hair was up in a tight bun, and she wore blue eyeshadow. Her lipstick was deep red. She wasn't young, but she wasn't old, either.

Nervously, I replied, "Sorry. Can I hang for a minute? Please? And then I'll leave, I promise."

There was no reaction, just a cold stare. I quickly added, "This jerk was drinking and driving. I got out and walked here, to your back door."

One of the big cooks in front of the row of ovens suddenly yelled, "Eighty-six the sword!" and then, "For fuck's sake, where's that second dishwasher? We'll never get through the night!"

The woman looked over at the sink. I followed her gaze. It was filled to the brim with dirty pots and pans. Two trays were covered with bar glasses, and a busgirl was trying to find room to place another bucket. There were several other buckets filled with dishes heaped on the floor around the sink area. A tall, skinny kid I recognized from school was at a large dishwasher, opening its door. The steam covered his face, fogging up his glasses. The apron he wore over his jeans had splotches of food stains all over it.

I turned to the door, but I didn't want to go back out in the sleet and have to walk into town. I still had no plan for how to get home. I quickly glanced at the woman then back at the dishwasher. I heard my neighbor Karen's patient voice telling my dad, "Never hurts to put yourself out there, Jarod." I stood up straight and brushed the hair from my face. It felt good in here; warm, loud, chaotic, but like maybe this place could be my place, too.

"Um...." I cleared my throat and said, "I'm available. I'm willing to help out, you know, over there." I nodded to the overflowing sink area.

The woman raised her eyebrows and looked me squarely in the face. She started to say something, hesitated, then asked, "You at least fourteen?"

"Sixteen last week, and I know Corey." I nodded at the tall, skinny kid. "I'm fast as long as he shows me what to do."

"What's your name?" the woman asked.

"It's Sadie, Sadie Wade. I'm a sophomore, same as Corey."

"Do you need to ask your parents? You won't be home till late."

Thinking of my father, I paused, then replied, "Nah, besides, our phone's been turned off. It was either that or oil. It's fine. Maybe, though, I could get a ride home when I'm done? I live on Tabor Road."

For the first time, the woman kind of half-smiled and nodded. "I know where Tabor Road is." She paused again, searching my face.

"Really, I can make a difference." I wasn't sure where this new-found confidence of mine was coming from.

She nodded slightly, looking at my clothing. "I've got a dry sweatshirt you can wear. It'll be too big, but that one must be freezing. We also have some cook's pants — way too small for any of these guys, but I bet you can make them work. We'll get you a bar towel for your hair, your face. Your mascara's running." She motioned with one hand to her own face and added, "It's raw out there. Can't imagine what I'd look like with all this gook on. Then we'll get you started. We'll pay in cash, okay?"

I felt a sudden rush of excitement and asked, "Do you have a spot where I can put my purse?"

"Of course." We both turned and passed Corey. He glanced our way and looked surprised to see me. I gave him a little wave.

"Sadie's going to help us out tonight," the woman said, raising her voice loudly enough so he could hear her above the kitchen's clatter. His eyes grew big as he watched us go out the swinging kitchen door. We walked down a small hallway into an office. Within minutes, my purse was stowed away in a little locker and I was changing in the ladies' bathroom.

I rolled the black and white checkered cooks' pants over at the waist and used the big safety pin the woman had given me to pin them in place. The blue sweatshirt with the Harpoon logo was too big, but it was warm and soft inside. I tied the kitchen apron around my waist twice and wiped my face clean. I ruffled my hair with the towel. I quickly took off my socks and put paper towels in each of my shoes. Just as I was leaving, I wondered where I should put my wet clothes. I paused, wanting to throw them all in the trash, but I didn't. When I walked out, the woman was right there, holding a brown take-out bag with Shay's logo on the side.

"For your wet clothes. We'll put this bag in the office, too. And I'm Jeannie, the dining room manager here. Corey's going to show you everything."

I gave her my biggest smile and replied, "You won't be sorry, Jeannie. I promise." I couldn't believe my luck. Here I was — warm and dry and I had a ride home.

Back in the kitchen, the large clock above the walk-in read 8:30. Tristan was probably at the party, already telling lies about me. There'd be more stuff said to me at school on Monday. But for now, I pushed the thought aside. I was ready to work and prove myself.

Jeannie was talking to one of the guys behind the line, who was now looking my way. He shouted out, "Everybody, say hi to Sadie. She's here to help us out!" The kitchen kind of stopped for a split second, and everybody called out to me. I was embarrassed by the attention but managed to give another little wave. A second guy along the stove added, "Corey, you lucky dog!"

I followed Corey's directions on how to load the dishwasher, how to feed it the powdered soap, and then where to stack the clean dishes. For the most part, he replenished all the clean dinner plates, glasses, silverware, coffee cups, and saucers at the stations in the kitchen and out on the 'floor.' I filled the big sink with hot water and dish soap then placed the pots and pans in it. I put on long latex gloves and settled in to scrub. The pile was high, but I didn't mind. My hands were warm in the soapy water, and my moccasins were drying out.

As I stole glances around the kitchen, one tall and thin waitress came by and leaned against the wall near me. She was talking to herself as she frantically looked down at her pad. "God, I'm so in the weeds!" she exclaimed then added, "Shit, his scotch on the rocks!" She practically ran out the kitchen door.

A male server tried to catch her arm as she passed by, but she never stopped.

"Take these plates to her table twenty, then come right back for yours," a man said, looking at the paper slips spitting out of some sort of little printer. The male server seemed just as rattled. He looked like he was about to object, but then he loaded up the dinners and left.

Jeannie came back through carrying a dinner plate, and she asked one of the cooks to put a steak back on for another minute or so. The cook didn't look happy, and he held the steak with tongs up to the guy beside him. "It's fucking medium rare, just what he ordered."

We heard glass breaking just outside the swinging doors. In came Corey, announcing to no one in particular, "It's okay, two wine glasses, that's all." He grabbed a broom and dust pan and quickly exited through the 'out' door.

I dried all the pans then made two trips over to the cooks' area. It was even hotter closer to the stoves, and the guys were using tongs to lift stuff from the burners.

"We'll take 'em from here, Angel," one of the guys said as he winked at me. He had burn marks all over the back of his hands and up his arms.

The cook next to him spoke out, "Careful, Eugene, jail bait."

Eugene looked over at me and smiled. "You're about my niece's age... Just being nice, super cool, you know, uncle-like."

When I was finally all caught up with the pots and pans, I started to run the clean stuff out, too — mainly to the bus people and the bar. The first time I left the kitchen with a rack of clean wine glasses, I stopped in awe of the large dining room before me. Beautiful tables and booths with small cast iron lanterns and vases filled with fresh flowers filled the room. The tables were covered in rich, cream-colored tablecloths that draped over the sides, and there were cloth napkins in a pale powder blue over peoples' laps or folded in a fancy design at the few tables that weren't occupied. Framed paintings hung on the walls with little lights above each one. The paintings were all of The Mountain and the different ski runs. Wide plank floors reflected the glow of the lanterns, and four glistening chandeliers dropped down from the high ceiling. Two smaller dining rooms were off to the right. I didn't dare go and look in them.

Several servers, all dressed like Jeannie, were carrying trays over their shoulders, clearing tables, and speaking to the customers. It was loud but nice — glasses clinking, people talking and laughing as they ate. I stood, taking it all in. It felt surreal, yet very real, too, with all the noise and motion.

I had to keep moving, and I cut through the bar and placed the rack of clean wine glasses on the end, where it would be the most out of the way.

"What'll you have?" Ms. Clark asked a couple at the bar who had taken the two stools in front of her. She placed two napkins down and smiled at the woman — that same smile she'd given me back in the fourth grade. Another bartender stood behind her. He was squirting the soda gun into two glasses then topping them off with orange slices and cherries. In the corner was a large stone fireplace with a roaring fire. It was, by far, the biggest and prettiest fireplace I'd ever seen.

Two little girls were on the floor, coloring on what looked like children's placemats. Their father leaned over, placing those fruity drinks beside them.

One of the cooks — I think it was Eugene — came along the edge of the bar and looked out over the dining room. He

filled a glass with soda, whispered something in Ms. Clark's
ear as he passed by, and then disappeared through the side
door. She ignored him while she poured white wine into a
glass and placed it down in front of the woman. The man
draped their damp coats over the back of one of the bar-
stools. He briefly looked over at me and smiled.

As I turned to go back into the kitchen, Ms. Clark called
out, "Thanks, Sadie! We need more bar towels."

On my way back to the kitchen, Zoe, a bus girl I'd met
briefly in the kitchen, stopped me in the hallway and told
me to wash the ramekins as quickly as possible because they
were all out. I didn't know what ramekins were and told her
so. She smiled and pointed to a dirty one on the tray she
was carrying. "The little dishes we put the oil and garlic in
for dipping and the butter and, you know, the crème
brûlée."

I moved fast, trying to keep what everyone needed
straight and to remember where things went. It was plenty
warm, and I wished I had a t-shirt on under the sweatshirt.
At one point, I came around the corner of the wait station
with the clean ramekins. Corey and Jeannie were there.

"You know, Sadie Wade's a slut. She puts out for everybody," Corey said.

My stomach dropped, and I turned beet red. Stepping
back, I stood absolutely still, already dreading what else he
was going to say. But Jeannie, in that mean voice she'd used
with me at the door, asked, "Has she put out for you,
Corey?"

He didn't say anything back. Jeannie didn't let up,
though, and said more forcefully, "Come on, tell me, has
she put out for you?"

He stammered, "No, it's just that…well, everyone…"

But she cut him off. "So, you just lied. She doesn't put
out for everybody, does she?"

Corey scooted past me, his eyes fixed on the floor.

Jeannie nodded my way and said, "Let me help you with those, and Sadie, you're doing great."

"Thanks, I like it here. It's fun...and warm."

I grabbed the empty rack and intercepted Zoe, again in the hallway, carrying two empty glass racks back into the kitchen.

"Let me take those for you!" I called out, feeling incredibly happy. Except for my sister, Kate, nobody ever stood up for me.

Zoe was already turning around, heading back into the dining room. But she stopped and asked quickly, "You go to Langdon High?"

"Yeah, you?"

"I'm at Colton — a Junior."

"Sophomore, here," I told her, smiling.

SHAY'S GOT SLAMMED — what Zoe called it as we were closing. "It's the first major snow of the season, and everybody who skis The Mountain came up. It might be sleet in town, but up on the slopes it's pure gold."

Henry, the owner, asked Jeanie where she'd found me — said I was as good as Corey and the other "little shit no show" put together. He'd given me a couple of approving looks when I'd brought out the clean pots and dinner plates over to the cooks, and when I'd helped clear the last big table.

At 12:10 a.m., Corey and I came out to the bar. We'd mopped the kitchen floors, put every single dish away, emptied all the trash — including at the wait stations — and placed the linen bags near the back door, ready for the morning pick up. Jeannie was drinking a glass of red wine, and Henry was going through the slips of the night.

He looked up and smiled. "Sadie, want a job?"

"Yes," I replied and looked over at Jeannie. She didn't say anything right away.

Jeannie closed a little crossword book, grabbed her car keys, and said, "You're faster than Corey and Ted 'no show' put together. Isn't that so, Henry?"

He looked at Corey and replied, "Yeah, you're a worker, Sadie. This guy here — he's going to have to step up his game and shut his mouth if he wants to keep his job."

I glanced at Corey. I didn't want him to be mad at me. He hardly looked at any of us as he clocked out and turned to go back to the kitchen.

Jeannie opened the front door, and I followed her out. I waited while she locked the door. Suddenly the *Shay's Fine Dining* light went out.

"That's Henry in the kitchen at the switch," she said.

There were only two cars and one truck still parked near the back door by the lattice. The sleet had stopped, and the walkway and parking lot were covered in sand. A truck must have sanded the lot at some point, making it safer for the customers to leave.

Jeannie, walking ahead of me, called out, "Careful, Sadie, it's slippery in places. Karl does a good job, but still..."

She had turned out to be real nice, taking a chance on me. Tomorrow I'd tell Karen, our neighbor, about me *putting myself out there*. If my dad wasn't going to do it, it'd at least give her some satisfaction to know that *somebody* was listening to her.

We pulled out of the parking lot, and just before we turned northwest towards Tabor Road, I glanced up the hill. What story had Tristan told his friends at the party about our night together? If it was anything like Derek Reed's lies, it'd be a bunch of exaggerations and more grief in school on Monday. Derek had supposedly told his friends that he'd screwed me in every hole I had. *What does that even mean?* I wondered. When I'd googled it at school, the filter in place had shut down the question.

That week had been one of the worst weeks of my life. That's when '*Wanna get laid? Call Sadie Wade*' had started to show up on Snapchat, on the boys' bathroom stall doors, and scribbled across the tables in the library. What really hurt — it was written on my green notebook that I'd left by accident in math class. A girl I knew, and had considered kind of a friend, had held it out, smirking when I'd finally retrieved it from her.

The rumors were still going strong. I wasn't even sure why I'd said yes to going out with Tristan. Part of me had known it could be a mistake, but I'd also wanted a chance at being normal and accepted. If people at Langdon High could see me as more like them, instead of as a loser, then maybe they'd stop all their bashing of me.

Jeannie started to climb the hill out of Langdon. She looked over at me and said, "Now, tell me about that jerk you were with earlier."

I didn't want to be disrespectful, but telling her about Tristan wanting me to suck his dick would only spoil the night and embarrass me. The whole episode with him was so different from what I'd just experienced at the restaurant.

I glanced her way. "I don't want to really talk about it, just because…well, the rest of the night was so awesome. Is that okay with you?"

"Of course, it's okay. I've had my fair share of losers — guys who have to treat girls like crap to make them feel good about themselves."

I nodded as I looked at her profile. *She's about my mother's age, maybe 40.* Suddenly, I felt guilty I hadn't seen my mom lately.

We reached the turn off to Tabor Road. Jeannie put on her high beams, and suddenly, in the headlights, we saw a deer leap across the road.

"Whoa, time for me to slow down. There's usually a second or third deer close by."

I pointed to the thicket out my window and replied, "Last spring, a big bull moose was up around here." It was pitch black, but I knew every inch of this road; it was the only one I'd ever lived on, except for that short time in Tennessee.

Jeannie exclaimed, "I still haven't ever seen a moose!"

Her car dash was lit up like what I imagined the cockpit of a plane would look like. Blue and red lights outlined all the little instrument panels. A car freshener was clipped to one of the air vents. It smelled of vanilla and coconut, like sunscreen.

"Your car is nice," I said. "Is it brand new?"

"Yep. I fell in love with it. I'm done driving old shit boxes. Oops, I shouldn't swear," she said, glancing my way.

"It's okay," I replied, smiling. That was nothing compared to Kate.

Our road hadn't been touched since the earlier sleet storm. Up here, like on The Mountain, it was all snow because of the higher elevation. Our road was usually one of the last ones to get plowed.

"Tomorrow, if you can, stop by about four p.m.," Jeannie said. "We'll get your W-2 filled out. Any problem if you stay right through the dinner hours? It's Sunday and won't be anywhere near as late as tonight. I can give you a ride home again, too."

"Yes, I can do that. Should I bring a sandwich to eat for when I get hungry?"

"We'll feed you." Jeannie looked over at me and said, "Wait, didn't anybody offer you food tonight?"

"No, but it was pretty busy. Corey's shy. He didn't really say anything to me, except, you know, how to do stuff." I'd heard all he'd said about me, but that was because I'd been eavesdropping — not too cool on my part.

"Well, he should have told you that Stephen or Eugene would cook you something for dinner. There's no charge, and you can get a soda from the bartender, for free, whenever you want," Jeannie replied.

"Oh, okay." I grabbed my purse and the bag with my clothes. "We're the next turn off on the left. Be careful of the culvert — see the reflector? Well, you'd see it if it wasn't leaning so far over."

We pulled into the driveway, right up to the trailer. My dad had plowed, but the outside light wasn't on and no lights were on inside. It looked totally depressing in the car's lights, especially after all the glamour of Shay's dining room and bar. Even the new snow couldn't cover up the rust on the roof or the way the three front steps were sagging.

"My dad's asleep and my sister and her kid are here — that's her Honda over there." I pointed to the side of the trailer. "My mom and brothers live in Rutland." Jeannie nodded and I quickly added, "Thanks for the ride home, and thanks for giving me a chance tonight."

"You bet. The jerk you were with? You got the better end of the deal, right? A little spending money and a job." She smiled. "I'm just going to sit and wait until you're in the door."

"'Kay," I replied. As I walked toward the trailer, my feet were already feeling the cold again and my legs were tired from all the running around. But I'd never felt better.

Chapter 2

Once I was inside, Jeannie left. I poured a bowl of Rice Krispies and wolfed it down. I wanted another bowl, but there wasn't much left in the box and Carson had to have some in the morning.

I put the clothes Jeannie had given me into our laundry bag. Tomorrow we'd go to the laundromat down in Langdon. It was Sunday, our usual day to do laundry. We always tried to hit it when church services were starting between 9:00 and 11:00 a.m., because it was usually empty. It'd be good to bring these clothes back to Jeannie all clean and folded. It'd show my appreciation.

My father was snoring loudly just down the hallway. It was cold in the trailer, despite the recent oil delivery. We turned the heat down to 60 degrees at night to save on oil. I was sleeping on the couch because Kate and Carson were back — until she decided what to do about their 'situation,' as she called it.

We had limited cable, and nothing was on this late at night. My anthology from English class was in my bookbag near the couch. We were reading *Flowers for Algernon* in Mr. Banks' class. The main character, Charlie, was changing, getting smarter. I reached down for it, but I didn't open the book; my eyes were tired.

I hoped Carson had had a good night with Dad. Kate worried about leaving them alone sometimes, and I did, too, but Dad was trying hard. She had to work the second shift at the nursing home down in Colton. Carson hung with me most days and evenings, but Kate said my Saturday nights should be free for me to go out and have fun. Yeah, what fun — not!

The money Jeannie had paid me — sixty dollars in two twenties and two tens — was sitting on the coffee table. Tomorrow I'd go on the payroll. I couldn't wait to tell Kate about it and ask if she thought Dad could handle Carson more nights a week. In my notebook, I jotted: *November 14, 2015,* and then below it––*Shay's $60.00.* Below that I wrote, *Cell phone $60.00.* Getting my very own phone would be awesome.

It was tricky sleeping out here on the couch — I had to tuck the blanket in just the right way or my feet would freeze. Our trailer was crappy from the outside, but it was cozy and clean inside. Between us three — Kate, Dad, and me — we kept things tidy.

"One day we'll have a better place. Until then, we'll make do," my father sometimes said.

There were times I missed my mother and the twins, but leaving Dad all alone and not seeing Kate and Carson every day — that couldn't happen.

It was selfish to want the $60 all to myself, I realized, and quickly tore out the notebook page and wadded it up. Father Ray's words from the pulpit, when the baskets were being passed around, had been: "God loves a person who gives cheerfully." Kate always needed gas money; Dad, new reading glasses; and Carson deserved a little something extra.

Once, my father had placed several dollar bills into the basket of the tent church we'd attended down in Tennessee. Kate had seen the money and leaned over and whispered to me, "I'm meeting Brother Ron later. You come, too, and we'll ask to go for a ride and then stop at the diner. You can order a lot and take some food back to the camper. It'll be okay."

I smiled, remembering our time down in Tennessee. But I then stopped. I didn't like how it had ended, not at all. I had to change my thoughts quickly before those images of the boy came, before I remembered what those men did to him. They had no idea that a little girl — me — was in the back of the station wagon watching the whole thing.

Kate never wanted to talk about our four months there. I knew why. Carson's features were coming into view, and it was clear who his father was. All those times she'd been hanging with Brother Ron… They'd been doing a lot more than just taking rides. I wanted to reassure her and tell her not to worry. *"Dad won't see it, he's oblivious."* But just to say that much would make her uncomfortable since Brother Ron had been a married man and part of the tent church. I didn't want Kate to ever feel bad about Carson. They were the best part of my life.

Even though I was tired from working at the restaurant, my mind was alert. I turned on my side and looked across the living room to the paneling on the opposite wall. It was old and marked up, but our family pictures covered the worst spots. The picture of my brothers on the swings with Mom's pretty face turned toward the camera was one of my favorites. The twins were in their senior year now and big Rutland Raider football players. Mom had gotten married, and her husband was a decent guy. Football was their life.

Next to the twins' picture was a black and white photo of Dad in a Langdon baseball uniform. He was standing off of second base and grinning. It must have been taken when he was in tenth or eleventh grade. He was handsome. Sometimes, on his good days, that grin still came out.

My favorite picture of all, though, was one of me and Kate standing in front of Karen's house down the road. We'd just helped her plant a whole bunch of daffodil bulbs. I was looking up at Kate, and she stood there with a rare smile, her arm around me, protecting me — from what, I couldn't imagine. She was pretty when she smiled, which wasn't often. I was about 12 years old in the picture. That made her close to 20 and already a mother. Carson must have been sleeping on Karen's deck in his stroller, or he would have been in the picture.

Karen's daffodils bloomed every spring, and for the past four years, we'd walked down to see them and eaten out on her deck. Some springs, we still had to wear our winter coats. Big splotches of yellow covered the back banks that sloped down into her yard. Last spring, we'd had a bonfire at her house after dinner — Dad had carted the wood down the road in a wheelbarrow. He and Karen had grown up together on Tabor Road, and the path through the wild honeysuckle between our two places showed years of use. That time we'd planted the bulbs, Karen had praised us for working hard. But it hadn't really been work. Tonight, at the restaurant — that was work, and my first real job.

I replayed what Zoe had said to me. She'd smiled when I'd come out to the dining room carrying two buckets to help clear the last, big table. She'd grabbed my hand and said, "We're going to be good friends, Sadie, I just know it."

The bad stuff that had happened with Tristan was leaving me. My attempts to try and fit in with my classmates were over. The boys who'd asked me out had sick motives. And the girls who'd mentioned the parties coming up on the weekends — it was just their way of laughing at me and setting me up. I saw that clearly now.

"The Lord is my strength and my defense," Father Ray had preached often. In the cold, dark living room, I whispered those words.

Burrowing deep down into my blanket, my thoughts drifted to Charlie in *Flowers for Algernon*. How much he'd wanted to get smart to make new friends. *One new, true friend would be awesome.* The humming of the refrigerator and my father's snoring lulled me to sleep.

Chapter 3

Y ou came in late," my father said as he shuffled by the couch on the way to get his morning coffee. He opened the cupboard. The furnace had kicked on, and the trailer was warming up.

Kate, further down the hallway, called out as loudly as she dared, "Dad, can you pour me one and bring it to me, pretty please?"

I sat up and smiled over at him. "Something big happened last night, and I can't wait to tell you guys." I puffed up my pillow, rearranged the blanket, and leaned back.

"Oh, yeah?" He stopped pouring and turned to me. He had bedhead; his gray hair stood straight up in back. His beard was too long, and his t-shirt had a tear right below his collar bone, showing how skinny he was. At that moment, he looked much older than his 52 years. *Poor guy*, I thought.

Kate and I sometimes referred to him as 'the old man,' but never to his face.

"Come out here and drink your coffee, Kate. I've got to tell you something," I called out. Carson must still be asleep or else he'd already be tearing down the hallway and doing a big Spiderman leap onto the couch.

"What's the something, Sadie?" Kate asked as she came into the living room. She wore a Langdon sweatshirt over a pair of my flannel pjs. She was always borrowing my clothes, even though they were way too short on her. Half her things were here, the other half over at her boyfriend Drew's house. Carson had a backpack filled with clothes and his toothbrush, but his toys were here. Drew didn't want any of that 'shit' around his place anymore. Two weeks ago, after stepping on one of Carson's action figures at his place, he'd stumbled and banged his calf against a coffee table. Within minutes, he'd thrown all of Carson's toys out in the yard. That caused Carson to lash out and go after him. Kate, the momma bear she was, had sworn at Drew and left. Slowly though, Drew was winning her back. But Carson was firm that he wouldn't take any of his toys there ever again. It was real iffy if he'd sleep there again, too. This was Kate's present situation. Dad called Drew "the Royal Asshole," and the name stuck. We just had to be careful not to say it around Carson.

Kate wore her hair down in the mornings. By the time she was out the door, it'd be pulled back in a ponytail, usually with a ball cap on until she got to work. Her hair was long and dark, way thicker than my fine, straight blond hair. She was also athletic and strong, even though she'd never played any school sports. It suited her well for lifting elderly people at the nursing home. My slight build, she said, was ridiculous. "A strong wind could lift you up and carry you away for miles." While we shared the same father, our mothers were different.

We were hard pressed to see our father in either of us. Kate once said, "That's a good thing, Sadie Rose, believe me." We never dissed our dad to his face, but we'd seen him in the worst possible ways: either drunk and passed out or with us wishing he'd pass out. He suffered flashbacks from his time in the military. His helicopter unit was part of the invasion of Granada back in the early 80s. It was a short mission, but he'd seen fatalities, maybe even caused some. Once in a while, he'd get to crying and neither one of us ever knew what to do. Kate wondered if he was sad that both our mothers had left him.

Overall, he hardly went anywhere except to his buddy Chet's place or to the veteran's hospital up in White River. Or to do laundry sometimes — he found it relaxing. He hadn't worked a steady job in years. Mostly he puttered around in his tool shed, blasting Led Zeppelin and Aerosmith on old cassettes he'd turned into CDs.

With Carson, though, he played — a lot like an older kid would play. "Figure that one out," I heard Kate say to Karen once. Karen had replied, "He's coping, and at least that's a healthy way."

NOW, I PATTED THE END OF THE COUCH for Kate to sit down, and Dad gave her a cup of coffee. He took the chair closest to the door. They both looked at me expectantly. I hadn't quite worked out in my mind how I'd tell them about the Tristan part of last night. They didn't need to know the nitty gritty. If Kate heard the story, she might go find the jerk and make a scene. What would my father do? It was always a question as to how much things were registering with him.

Anyway, I had their attention, so I took a deep breath and began. "Last night I went into Shay's — you know, the fancy place at the bottom of The Mountain Road. I was going to call you at work, Kate, because things weren't going well at the party I'd gone to. Anyway, Shay's was minus a dishwasher and guess what? I said I'd help out. At the end of the night, the owner, Henry, asked if I wanted a position there. I'd done a good job keeping up with the other dishwasher who I know from school. They paid me cash and even gave me a ride home after."

I reached over. "Sixty-dollars, see." I fanned out the bills and looked at my dad then at Kate. My father smiled and looked over at Kate, too.

"I know I'm supposed to watch Carson after school, but maybe, you know, Dad could do a little more, and I could work there and help with stuff we need around here. We're always trying to get through the month. Those last few days are the hardest. This'll help, won't it?"

Kate took a sip of her coffee and slowly nodded. My dad spoke up. "For sure it'll help, Sadie. Do you know what they're thinking for a schedule?"

"I'll find out more today. Jeannie, the manager, said I have to fill out a W-2 form. Corey, the other dishwasher, works the weekends and two school nights. So that still leaves me two or three nights with Carson, and you can still have time with Drew, right?" I wanted this to work out, but I knew I needed to back off. Kate never liked surprises.

"But what about you going out, having fun?" Kate asked.

If she only knew what a complete lack of fun I'd had with Tristan.

Just then Carson came barreling down the hallway and did a flying leap onto the couch.

"Watch it, Carson, my coffee!" Kate glanced at me and started to stand. "Dad, are you willing to do a few more nights with Carson? My shifts are pretty locked in."

My father turned to the little guy lying across my lap and said, smiling, "That kid, why he's impossible, he's the devil incarnate!"

I started to tickle Carson, and he squirmed all over with laughter. I knew my father loved his time with Carson, but I still glanced towards Kate. She wasn't quite sold on this.

"I'll ask Jeannie more about the schedule," I said. "You know, like what they have in mind for nights. Can one of you get me there a little before four p.m. today?"

"I will." Kate started to say something more then stopped.

My father stood up and walked towards the bathroom. "I'm taking a shower. Everybody all set for the bathroom?"

I nudged Carson and said, "Go quick. I'll turn on *Paw Patrol*." He jumped down and skipped past his mother and grandfather.

My father called out, "Hey, ya little devil, there ya go, bargin' past me like you own the joint."

Kate whispered, "If Dad, you know, can't handle it or he starts up again, I've got nobody else but you."

I reached for her hand and squeezed it. "No question. I'd stop at the restaurant immediately."

She gave me her rare smile. Carson returned and hunkered down between us. Soon we were watching Ryder and his gang save the day.

Carson reached over for my hand then for his mother's. But Kate stood up, kissed the top of his head, and said, "French toast coming up! They were going to throw out a whole loaf of bread at work; it's expired, but I checked and it's fine. We've still got Chet's syrup in the fridge."

Just as she reached into the refrigerator for the eggs, she turned back around and asked, "What wasn't okay at the party? You can tell me — Carson's glued to the TV."

"Oh, you know, a lot of drinking and basically jerks being jerks."

"Okay, well, how did you get to the restaurant?"

"One of the guys dropped me off," I replied quickly.

That seemed to satisfy her and she turned back around, but it didn't feel good bending the truth like that.

Carson looked up at me and asked, "Which Paw Patrol are you today?"

He was always Ryder. "Um, today, I'll be, let's see… Marshall!"

"Yes!" he said, leaning into me. My heart was full. I glanced back at Kate as she sprinkled nutmeg and cinnamon over the French toast. I loved the smell, just like the garlic last night in the restaurant's kitchen. Four o'clock couldn't come soon enough.

Chapter 4

On Monday morning after the bus dropped us off in front of the gymnasium, I braced myself. I could avoid most everywhere but the hallways. They were tricky, and today, just like after my supposed night with Derek, everybody seemed to be turning in my direction as I entered the old school building. Just outside of Banks' classroom, one of the upper classman boys walked by me and coughed. A loud "Slut" was mixed in there with all his phlegm. Two girls laughed as they passed by. I opened the door and took my seat. *It was going to be a long day.*

At lunch, I slid in next to Estelle, a girl in our grade who had disabilities and needed a wheelchair. I ate lunch with her and Mrs. Hatch, her paraeducator, every day. Sometimes we were joined by two other students. Today, Estelle smiled over at me while Austin and Ty, also from the

Intensive Needs program, held up their hands. I quickly gave them each a high five. Mrs. Hatch smiled and said, "Hi Sadie, welcome to another Monday at Langdon High."

Mrs. Hatch was about 60 years old and was the kindest, most patient woman I'd ever met. Sometimes she brought me books to read that she thought I might like and fresh homemade desserts in little Tupperware containers. Her husband was one of our custodians, so she knew all about the '*Wanna get laid, call Sadie Wade*' graffiti.

Just as she was starting to tell me about who was coming to her house for Thanksgiving, Garrett Morse slipped in next to me.

He was a jerk, everybody knew that. Mrs. Hatch stopped talking, and we both turned to him as he said, smirking, "Here's a calendar, Sadie. It's got the next few weeks marked for who you're, you know, um… taking a ride with." He held up his fingers to make air quotes around the word *ride*.

I looked down at the crude calendar he'd drawn. My face stung as if I'd been slapped. Guys' names were written in boxes below the dates for the rest of November. First names — all in different writing — like each guy had jotted down his own name in a slot on a Super Bowl spread sheet. I knew exactly what this mean joke was implying. Tristan had lied and said I'd done it.

Mrs. Hatch snatched the paper up and said, in a voice I'd never heard from her before, "Get out of here, you mean, ugly little shit. Mr. Stevenson is going to see this. And I can't wait to see your father this afternoon. He's putting on my snow tires."

Garrett's face turned white, but then he curled back his lips and said, "You swore at me. You're a teacher. I'm gonna tell on you."

"You go right ahead. But don't think your documented sexual harassment right here is going to go away because of something you claim I called you." She imitated him and did air quotes around the word *claim.*

Out of the corner of my eye, I watched him return to one of the large tables where everybody laughed.

Mrs. Hatch held up the paper and said, "I'm going to go down to Stevenson's office just as soon as Estelle, Austin, and Ty are back in the room. I mean it. This is awful, Sadie, just awful."

But I knew nothing would happen after that. Mr. Stevenson meant well, but nothing ever changed. When Mrs. Hatch got up to take the trays to the bin, I glanced over at the table again. Nobody was paying me any more attention. But then I saw Corey sitting just off to the left of them. I bet he saw the whole thing.

When I walked in to the computer lab for my second-to-last class of the day, *"Blow me"* was scrolling across the screen saver on the computer where I always sat. I quickly deleted it and looked around. Ms. Denison was oblivious while the students closest to me exchanged knowing looks.

The final moment came when I climbed off the bus after wishing Ralph, my bus driver since kindergarten, a good night. Someone yelled "Whore!" from the last window of the bus. When I turned to look, one of the rotten little middle school boys who was always giving Ralph a hard time was putting up his window.

I turned towards the trailer. Tomorrow would be more of the same, but eventually things would die down like they usually did. Tomorrow I'd also be back at Shay's at four o'clock. *That* was something to look forward to.

Once I got inside the door, Kate called out from her bedroom, "Hey, I made goulash for everybody tonight. Even baked rolls!"

Walking to her closed door, I called back, "Sounds good." I moved across the hall and went into the bathroom and quietly locked the door. I turned on the sink's faucet and sat on the toilet. The tears came easily — I'd been holding them back all day. Kate knocked, and I quickly responded, "Sorry, got a tummy ache."

Soon I heard her go out the front door. I didn't have long before Dad and Carson would get home from pre-school. Standing up over the sink, in front of the mirror, I saw that my face was all red and blotchy and my mascara was smeared. *Why do they hate me so much?* As I reached for pieces of toilet paper to dry my tears, I started to cry again. This, right here, was the only time today where I'd have total privacy.

Chapter 5

"Who's got Sadie?" Jeannie called out. It was what she did every night I was on the schedule when Kate couldn't pick me up after her shift and I needed a ride. We'd be opening in a few minutes, and Jeannie had just gone over our specials for the evening.

Two of the waitresses conferred briefly with Ms. Clark — Julie. She answered, "It's me tonight."

Jeannie caught my eye and nodded. "Okay then, folks, let's go, and remember to push the Ahi Tuna!"

Eugene came by and leaned against the counter. "Like I said, my old Subaru is parked in the barn. It's got decent studded snows and insurance for another four, maybe five months. Ask your dad. You can drive it for the winter. No big deal."

He was completely bald, and his broad shoulders stretched the cotton t-shirt he wore, with a fringe of chest hairs poking up from his collar. He looked like Brutus from my father's old Popeye comic books, minus the hair.

"Yeah? Thanks, Eugene. It's just that once I took Driver's Ed and got my Junior Driver's License, I've never really gone out again. Didn't have a chance because my dad wouldn't be good at it and Kate is too busy."

"Let me drive it here this weekend. Come in early. We'll practice in the parking lot, then, as you get more confident, you can drive it up over The Mountain Road and down along the condos, past the big places. How's that sound?"

"You'd do that for me? Really?"

"Of course! You're our angel, Sadie Wade!"

Eugene tied a bandana around his head and walked through the kitchen door. He was heading to Ms. Clark — Julie — because he had a thing for her. The question was: Did she feel the same way about him? Sometimes, maybe, but then not so much at other times.

I followed and walked out to the wait station. It was December 14th, one month since I'd snuck into the kitchen. My work schedule was mostly the weekends and sometimes Tuesday and Wednesday nights. Vermont had strict working rules for minors, and Jeannie was a stickler about following them.

The servers who had eaten before we were open brought their dishes over to the tub I was holding. One of them, Bartholomew, was pretty funny — always talking with a British accent even though he was from Cuttingsville just up the road. He'd spent a year in London and wanted to go back there to live.

"Here you are, Sadie-girl!" he said as he placed his plate in the tub. The other servers rolled their eyes.

"You're not that convincing, Bart," someone said.

He looked over at me and asked, "Sadie, what do you think? Do I sound like a Brit to you?"

It was hard being put on the spot like that, but Bartholomew had been nice to me from that very first night. He'd glanced my way when I'd stood at the door but had never said anything. I appreciated that. Everyone was looking at me as I replied, "You sound more British than Peppa Pig!"

Everyone laughed. "Thanks, luv!" he called out to me.

"Ah, no fair asking Sadie. She wouldn't say a bad thing about anybody," Alice said.

I turned to her and shrugged. "Being mean sucks. Besides, you guys are the greatest."

The difference between my life here at Shay's and my life at school was huge.

The guys behind the line called me Angel. Eugene was the ringleader, and they all followed him. He was gruff, but he wasn't as ornery as Stephen, our sous-chef. Last week, Stephen had thrown a bag full of mussels against the kitchen wall, yelling, "Shit, they stink, they're past serving!"

Jeannie had been standing by me, looking at the mess — little black mussels scattered all over the floor of the kitchen, under the countertops, and behind the ovens. "I hope you know the kids aren't going to clean this up," she'd said, her hands on her hips.

"What do you take me for…a *complete asshole*?" Stephen had snarled. I'd started to laugh at that and tried to cover my mouth before anyone saw me. I couldn't help it. Stephen had looked over at me and slowly smiled. Then Eugene started to bang the pots with his tongs and yelled, "See that, everybody! Angel got Stephen to smile!"

Eugene's offer of his old Subaru was appealing. Jeannie or Henry gave me a ride home on our late Saturday nights, but otherwise either Kate swung by after work or one of the girls drove me home. Jeannie wouldn't let any of the kitchen guys take me. "Nope, that's not going to happen. They're all irresponsible," she said to me in the beginning. "You know how many paychecks I've had to re-issue because they put them through the wash or just plain lost them?"

I did notice that while the cooks worked hard each night, their lives were packed with drama. Sometimes they talked about their crazy 'after work' shenanigans in the kitchen. Usually they tried to keep it to coded comments or ribbing back and forth. Drugs and alcohol were almost always involved.

One time, recently, Henry got really mad at Stephen and reamed him out by the dumpster. Something about the police coming by and it involving his girlfriend. Later that afternoon, I'd met a policeman near the kitchen door. He'd asked me to get Stephen. A little while later, Stephen came back in from talking with him in the parking lot.

"Angel, get the cop a coffee to go, please," he'd said, opening the walk-in.

The policeman had thanked me and motioned towards Stephen. "He's got a rough exterior, but he's a decent guy, isn't he?"

"Oh yeah, he's awesome," I'd said, smiling.

Jeannie had a potty-mouth jar in the kitchen for all the times the guys behind the line swore, which was all the time. It wasn't much of a deterrent, that was for sure.

The kitchen was definitely its own world compared to the other parts of my life. Sometimes, though, I wondered if my sister's bad language when she was pissed was a match for the guys at Shay's. Once, not long ago, I'd asked her why she swore so much.

"It was the quickest way to you." That wasn't an answer I understood, but Kate hadn't said anything else.

"JULIE IS AT THE BAR whenever you're done." I looked up and nodded at Corey. We worked pretty well together; neither of us talked much, but it suited us. We were fast with the dishes. Eugene had taken the time to show me how the walk-in was organized, so that when they needed certain foods, they'd sometimes call on me. The bar staff also used me to fly down to the wine cellar and the storage area next to it for the imported beer. My memory was good, and that impressed Henry. Jeannie often called me out to help Zoe set up tables in a hurry. "Maybe, we should get you black pants and a white shirt," she said once, "and keep them in your locker."

It no longer felt like a big deal to go out into the big room or the two smaller dining rooms. Corey usually stayed back, manning the dishwasher. He liked that better than being out on the floor.

The thing he'd told Jeannie about me 'putting out' for everybody — he must have figured it was a lie, or if it had been true, I wasn't putting out any more because I spent most of my nights at work with him. At school, he was quiet, hanging with the kids nobody paid much attention to — the geeks and gaming fanatics. But now, whenever we saw each other in the halls, we'd wave or say something quick about the restaurant like, "New snow; we're gonna get slammed." The day I'd met the cop, Corey had come to my school locker to say, "Stephen got in trouble. My mother heard it on the scanner."

Corey always picked up the heavy, long 'no slip' mats behind the line so I could mop underneath them. And he shoveled the back walkway to the dumpster before the kitchen crew left so I didn't have to. In return, anytime I went to grab a soda from the bar, I always got him one, too. I also started to bring him cookies — whatever kind Carson wanted us to bake after school. Corey kept them out of sight, but he usually ate all of them before the night was over.

WHEN I WAS DONE MOPPING THE KITCHEN and Corey was taking the last of the garbage out to the dumpster, I went to the bar to clock out. Eugene and Julie were standing near the bar, while Henry and Jeannie were busy writing all our names out on small slips of paper.

"It's for our Secret Santa Christmas party. Can't spend more than ten bucks. We're thinking of having it on the twenty-third, in two weeks. We'll stop taking reservations and walk-ins after that," Henry said. He handed Jeannie more slips of paper he'd just cut.

I smiled, and replied, "That sounds like fun."

"Let's draw names tomorrow before we open. Most everybody will be on," Julie said as she walked out from behind the bar and grabbed her coat. "Ready, Sadie?"

"Yep. I'll meet you in the parking lot. My stuff's in the office." As I turned to leave, Jeannie reached over and handed me an envelope.

"What's this?" I asked.

"Happy one month here at Shay's! It's a little something we thought you'd like."

I looked at her, then at Henry, Eugene, and Julie. "Aw, thanks, guys. It's been the best month of my life!"

"That — that sweetness of yours is why we're all lucky to have you here. Open it!" Julie replied.

It was a gift certificate to Sephora for two makeup sessions and a gift card to Applebee's.

"Really, Jeannie? I mean, I'll ask Zoe to come with me, but are you sure?"

Jeannie smiled. "Yes, and I'm your chauffer."

I quickly hugged her and smiled at everybody. As I turned to go to the office, Eugene called out, "Talk to your father! This Saturday we'll practice driving — right out here in the parking lot!"

Chapter 6

My father reluctantly said "okay" to me using Eugene's car. "Just to the restaurant and back. You'll still take the bus to and from school, and no friends in the car."

I'd been blowing on Carson's hot chocolate and thought, *Is he crazy? I've never had anyone over, ever, or gone to anyone's house, ever.* Besides, I couldn't have anybody else in the car with a Junior Driver's License. But I didn't say any of this to him. Instead, I quickly hugged him and told him how nice it'd be not to have to ask for rides home anymore.

Eugene was a different guy as a driving instructor. He was very patient and gave me directions in a quiet, clear voice. The first time I got behind the wheel, he showed me how to adjust the seat, the side mirrors, and the rearview mirror. We were taking it slowly around the parking lot of

Shay's when he said, "Okay, this is ridiculous. We're going up The Mountain Road."

I quickly glanced at the guard rail where I'd jumped out of Tristan's truck. *Did that really happen?* So much had changed for me in five short weeks. At school, the insults had stopped, even if nobody was ever really friendly. I didn't care, though — Shay's was where I belonged. I felt it every day when I clocked in. Looking over at Eugene, I smiled and thanked him again.

He pointed ahead and replied, "Eyes on the road, Angel."

After the fourth time we drove out and about in town and the highway, we both felt I was ready to go solo. After all, it was a straight shot from Shay's to my road up Route 103. Eugene liked my father's terms about not cruising in the car with friends or driving outside of work.

"That's good, he laid down the law. My old man never did that."

I started to explain some of my dad's issues but then dropped it. He'd come through for me by watching Carson more nights.

THE FIRST TIME I DROVE HOME ALONE was no big deal; a clear, cold night with little traffic on the main road. Tabor Road was always quiet — nobody but the people who lived there ever drove down it. My second night, a Friday night, was not so smooth. About four miles out from Shay's as I was heading northwest on the highway, I ran into a road block. A terrible head-on collision between two cars had happened just minutes before I came through. Blue lights and ambulances were just getting there. The police — it was the same cop who had come to see Stephen — stopped me and the car behind me and told us that we'd be rerouted unless we were headed to Tabor Road. I sat with the heater going and the radio on and watched the other car turn around. There was a trail of lights in my rearview mirror. Most of the cars were turning around.

Within seconds, someone was banging on my driver's side window. At first, I couldn't tell who it was, and I quickly rolled the window down. Jeannie was standing there with Stephen beside her. I was confused and asked, "Hey guys, what are you doing? No one can get by yet."

Stephen ripped into me. "For fuck's sake, Sadie, you need a cell phone. We didn't, we couldn't, we thought..." He was worked up and didn't finish.

Jeannie said, much more calmly, "We thought it might be you in the accident. You just left the restaurant, and then we heard the sirens. There was no way to check if you were okay. So, guess what? I'm putting you on my cell plan tomorrow. I've got an old iPhone you can use. We can't worry every time you leave to go home and have no way to check on you."

"Aw, you guys, that's sweet but come on. See, I'm okay and..."

"The phone's old, but you can buy a cool case for it. It's settled. Now we've got to get back to the restaurant."

They turned and started to walk back to Jeannie's white RAV. I leaned out and said, "But Jeannie, I'm not sure my father will say yes to the phone."

She waved me off. Whatever I had to say didn't matter. It was settled.

THE SAME POLICEMAN finally walked over to my window and said, "I'm going to try and get you through so you can get home. What's your name again?" he asked.

"It's Sadie, Sadie Wade," I replied.

"Okay, Sadie from Shay's. You been driving long?"

"It's my second time solo, so, um...no."

He nodded and replied, "Just slowly drive along that shoulder and don't look at the accident."

Driving slowly past the broken glass and pieces of the wreck, I tried to avert my eyes and touched the Saint Christopher medal on the visor that Henry had given me. It was the patron saint of travelers. I prayed for the people in the accident and for their families, too.

KATE CAME IN QUIETLY ABOUT an hour later. As she hung up her coat and placed her boots on the rubber tray by the door she whispered, "Did you see the accident? I think maybe somebody died."

I hadn't been able to sleep. The blood — all over the road's surface — was bringing back memories of seeing the boy down in Tennessee get beaten up. He'd hit the pavement of the parking lot hard, and the blood had spilled out all over. The men who had been beating him still went after him, even when he couldn't fight back.

I didn't want to admit it — even to myself — but I'd been having dreams about it lately. Remembering the blood, the boy's fear. Things were good at Shay's and with Kate and Carson and Dad, but somewhere, in the back of my mind, the memories lingered. I could never quite seem to escape what I'd seen.

With the memory of the blood on the pavement in my mind, I did something I hadn't done for a long time. I reached out for Kate's arm as she walked past me and said, "Please, can we talk about that last night in Tennessee? You never want to, but I'm having bad memories of what happened. Maybe, if you let me talk 'em out — describe to you what I saw — it'd help me know what was real and what's just my imagination."

Kate extricated herself from me as she went into the kitchen and whispered, "How many times have I told you,

Sadie... By dawn the next morning, we drove out of there. No help from the old man — he slept for ten hours in the car as soon as we left. But you, you were fine. If there'd been a fight, it was long over."

Getting up quickly, I followed her to the refrigerator. She was rifling through the shelves. Kate stood at least five inches taller than me and weighed maybe thirty pounds more. I couldn't ever go toe-to-toe with her to make her listen, but sometimes, like now, I wanted to. Instead, I pleaded, "Please, listen. I need to get this out of me. If you won't talk to me about it, maybe someone else will."

She closed the refrigerator and stood up. In a quiet but firm voice, she replied, "Sadie, this is just another case of the shit Dad's drinking did to us. But I came and got you. I took over. It's been years now, and the best thing you can do is to forget about it. As for talking to someone else? We don't let other people know our business. It could be used against us."

"There you go again, shutting me down," I said in a pissed off tone I never used with her.

I didn't know why I was suddenly pushing it, after years of keeping it bottled up. But something about seeing that blood, wondering what happened... It was bringing up the memories again. And this time I didn't want to bury them.

Kate stopped eating the yogurt and looked at me with surprise and then tenderness. She whispered, "The accident tonight clearly rattled us both. And especially since you're a new driver. Come sleep with me like you used to."

I shook my head and turned to walk back to the couch. But Kate called out, "Okay, I'll move the coffee table and get my bedding and sleep on the floor right beside you."

Once we were both settled, Kate reached up to me on the couch and took my hand. "'Member when we used to sleep like this?" she whispered.

I squeezed her hand. No matter how hard I tried to talk about it, what I saw that last night in Tennessee was mine alone.

Chapter 7

T he boy tapped on the table and asked, "You okay if I sit down?" The school's library wasn't crowded. There were a couple of totally empty tables, but being rude wasn't in my nature, so I moved my math notebook and trig papers closer to me. "Sure," I replied and then kept trying to figure out the problem.

"I haven't done the assignment yet. Is it hard?" the boy asked, now sitting across from me. It was Tuesday, and the last day before our Christmas break. The restaurant's holiday party was tonight.

"No, not if you follow the book's examples." Glancing over at him, I added, "Cosines aren't bad."

"Good." The kid paused. "Man, I heard *all* about you this past weekend."

My heart sank and my stomach took a roll. The Tristan stuff had mostly died down, but I guess I'd been naïve to think it was all done with. Now this jerk — Michael Scott — was ready to fill me in. I braced myself and looked him squarely in the eyes. "Oh yeah, what are they saying, huh?"

Michael was opening up the same textbook as me, and he cocked his head to see the page number I was on. "Well, according to my aunt, you're like the greatest teenager who ever walked the planet. She couldn't stop going on about you. You've replaced me as her favorite."

"Your aunt? Who's your aunt?" I was all confused.

"Jeannie Ricco. She's not really my aunt. She's more like my mom's best friend. But, um, yeah."

I didn't know what to say.

"Shay's got great food. Do you get to eat for free?"

I nodded. He and I had a few teachers in common, but we never really talked much.

"My aunt said a lot of good things about you. We both had Ms. Clark in fourth grade, and we're in the same English class with Banks. That short story on the retar — whoops — mentally disabled guy was good, wasn't it?"

Again, I nodded slowly. A girl named Lexi walked by. Michael's attention turned to her. She sat two tables over, all alone. It was clear he was interested in her — he kept stealing glances. Lexi was in my Chemistry class and helped everybody with their labs.

"You should go over, sit down and start a conversation with her, just like you did with me. You're a natural."

Michael asked, "Really?"

"Definitely. Besides being smart, Lexi's really nice."

He still looked unsure.

"What have you got to lose? If she's not interested, she'll give you a blah response. But, if she's friendly, then you'll know."

"And what is it I'll know?"

Shrugging, I replied, "That she likes you, too."

He started to stand then looked down at me. "All the shit those assholes say about you? Nobody's going to say anything anymore. The line cook at Shay's — Stephen, I think his name is — his younger brother is Levi Sterns."

Levi Sterns was a crazy, scary kid in the 12th grade. Nobody messed with him.

"Aunt Jeannie said Stephen told Levi to go after anybody who said a shitty thing about you."

Michael slowly walked over to Lexi's table. They exchanged a few words, then she nodded and he sat down. As Michael took out his trig book, he glanced my way. He was smiling.

Chapter 8

That night at Shay's, I put all my gifts in a box and then put the box behind the large counter by the dishwasher. I had drawn Bart's name but had still made little gifts for everybody. Dad helped me out with a few of them. For Bart, I'd found a little Peppa Pig key chain at Walmart so he'd feel like a real Brit. Dad had burned a wood sign for Eugene that read: *"Look Both Ways!"* For Stephen, I'd painted a bullseye on a white cloth and had bought three little bean bags. It was for when he was pissed off in the kitchen about something — he could hang the bullseye on the wall in his station and then throw the bean bags really, really hard at it. Henry was getting a cut-out silhouette of three ballerinas, just like his daughters. Mrs. Meyers, the art teacher, had helped me find a picture after school. We'd projected the silhouettes up on the wall to trace. It came out really good. A big tin of assorted Christmas cookies had Corey's name on it. Teddy, the kid who'd never showed up the night I'd snuck into the kitchen but who still worked here a little bit, was getting a ribbon to pin on his apron. It read, *"No-Show Teddy Rocks."*

When it came to Julie — Ms. Clark — my dad had suggested a paperweight he already had. It was a four-leaf clover in a small, glass-like rock. "You could tell her how lucky you are that she's come back into your life."

"That's a great idea!"

Jeannie got one of my new poems, though it wasn't that good, so I also got her a little book of synonyms for when she did her crossword puzzles at the bar. Alice, my favorite server, once said she liked a scarf I'd crocheted. I washed it and wrapped it in tissue paper for her. I put little gifts in the box for all the other Shay people.

Zoe's gift was hardest of all. We'd just gone to Keene for our Sephora session, and we'd bought makeup and had eaten lunch out with my gift certificate from everybody. "What do you give a new best friend?" I'd questioned Kate one night.

She'd shrugged her shoulders and said, "Don't ask me."

It was Dad who'd replied, "Spend time with her, Sadie. That's what buddies do."

We couldn't wait to start the Secret Santa stuff. Until then, a wedding party was in one of the smaller banquet rooms and two tables were still eating in the big dining room.

All of our closing duties had to be done on the early side so we could enjoy the festivities. "Do you think it's too soon to do the bathrooms?" I asked Corey.

"Nah, I think it's good. I'm going to finish these pots and ask Eugene when we can start the floors."

HI, SORRY, just putting in more toilet paper and kind of tidying up," I said as I opened the first stall. A woman was standing in front of the mirror. Her auburn hair was pulled back in a pretty clip, and she was wearing a champagne-colored dress with beading down the back. She was beautiful. I glanced her way again as I moved to the second stall.

"A little old for a bride, don't you think?" She smiled at me through the mirror. She was reapplying her lipstick.

I stopped what I was doing and stood behind her, seeing my own face reflected in the mirror. "No, not at all. Your dress is beautiful. Congratulations."

She stopped applying lipstick and turned to me. "That's so sweet. Thank you." She turned back to the mirror but glanced at me through it and asked, "You go to Langdon High?"

"I do, I'm a sophomore." I quickly gathered up the plastic trash bag below the hand dryer and stood, ready to go out.

"My daughter is a junior. Do you know Amy Dunne?"

I nodded. I didn't *know* Amy, but knew who she was.

"We're in the second dining room. It's so festive with all the holiday decorations, and it's small, just like we wanted. The food and drink are delicious — and the service is the best! Do you like working here?"

I smiled. "Oh yeah. It's a great place. Karen, my neighbor, is at your reception."

At first, the woman seemed surprised and then maybe confused. I probably shouldn't have shared that. I glanced at the soap dispenser between the sinks. There was plenty of the pink stuff still in it. I gave her a little wave and turned to go out the door. I needed to get a clean plastic bag for the garbage can before anyone else came in.

"Wait! Are you Jarod's daughter, by chance?" she asked.

I never knew how to answer questions about my father. It was fine talking about my dad in passing, but I didn't like discussing him with people who knew him. I wasn't sure how much they knew about his issues. I stopped and answered, "Yes. His youngest. My name's Sadie Wade."

Now the woman turned fully towards me. She still wore a puzzled expression, and she seemed to be searching my face and tearing up. This was awkward.

"Sorry." She brushed away a tear and added, "I went to high school with your dad. He and my husband — " she caught herself — "my late husband were good buddies and baseball players. I have fond memories of your dad. In fact, Tabor Road was the place to go, back in the day."

That picture of my father in his baseball uniform came to mind, and Karen, our neighbor, laughing about the logging road just past her house. How it was a popular drinking spot. Now, it was all overgrown, used only as a place for the town snow plow to turn around — when they actually did plow.

"Ah." I smiled back at her. "Karen's told me a little bit."

Just then the door opened, and an older woman walked in. We moved to give her room, and Amy's mother motioned for us to go out. I needed to get that clean bag and get back to the kitchen, but I felt she wanted to say something else.

Once in the hallway, she said, "Please, tell your father I send my love. Rachel Blanchard was my name in high school, but today it's Rachel Sumner." She reached down and gave me a big hug. "That's for your dad." On her way back to the banquet room, she called out, "I'll tell Karen and Amy we just met!"

The linen closet was where we stored the plastic bags. As I opened it, I thought about my father and all he'd been through since high school: his service in the army, PTS, not being able to work a steady job, and his bouts with alcoholism.

I closed the closet door and was hit with another flashback of being in the station wagon outside the bar in Tennessee. But this one was after the fight. Dad had been sleeping off his second night of drinking after being sober for so long. His snoring had been loud, and he'd smelled horrible. I'd opened the back tailgate and climbed out. It had been daylight. I'd grabbed some rocks not far from the car for my Polly Pockets. I'd wanted to walk further, but I wasn't supposed to leave the car, so I'd turned back. Kate had shown up then, banging on the back tailgate and calling out, "This is bullshit, Sadie, you here with him like this." Then we'd left Tennessee for good.

Kate just recently reminded me about that last part. But the other flashbacks — of the boy running, the men grabbing for him, and him falling — weren't to be talked about and most definitely not shared with anybody else.

As I was putting the new plastic bag into the bin, it occurred to me that those rocks were probably still in that beater of a car parked out behind the trailer along with every other car and truck Dad had ever owned.

I walked through the swinging door of the kitchen. Zoe and Jeannie were placing the wedding cake and plates on the cart with wheels. The butter cream frosting was thick, with a beautiful design etched all along the sides.

"Grab the coffee, Sadie, and then come back for the cups and saucers, okay?" Jeannie said.

"Got it." I loved being here. *What I'd just told Rachel Sumner was the honest truth.*

As I made my way down the three stairs to the smaller dining room carrying the coffee carafe, it occurred to me that there might be a second reason that Kate dreaded any talk of that fight and Tennessee. The main one was to avoid any possible reveal of who Carson's father was. The second reason, though, could be guilt for not watching me those last two nights.

My own guilt — that I'd hid and done nothing to stop those men — was growing by the day.

Chapter 9

The party at Shay's was a blast. Everyone seemed to like the little gifts I gave out. Jeannie teared up reading my poem and then quickly put it away. She looked over at me and whispered, "Thank you."

Henry's wife, Marlene, hugged me, exclaiming she knew just the right place for the ballet dancers. I leaned in and confessed, "My art teacher did most of it."

And before the party was over, everybody was taking a turn at Stephen's bullseye. The kitchen guys had placed it on the back of one of the dining room chairs and marked off an area to whip the bean bags at it. Eugene hit it so hard that the chair flipped over.

That's when Jeannie called out, "Enough!"

Stephen came over and thanked me for the 'anger management' gift.

"It might help, right?" I joked.

"Yeah, Angel, and this." He reached into his pocket and held up a silver chip. I didn't know what it was.

"Twenty-four hours of sobriety — no booze. That cop hooked me up with a meeting. It's a start. Only you and Jeannie know, so let's keep it that way."

Corey had drawn my name and wrapped up a pizza box. Inside was a $20 coupon to the pizza place in town. "You spent twice as much as we were supposed to," I exclaimed.

He shrugged and replied, "I can eat a whole pizza, and I bet you can, too." It was the nicest thing he'd ever said to me.

There was an open bar, with all sorts of appetizers. We got our own sodas and raided the fruit tray. When Kate stopped to pick me up, Henry insisted she come in for a drink. She did, reluctantly and still in her scrubs from work. I hugged her and introduced her to everyone. I think she felt awkward, but a couple of the kitchen guys got her to smile. She was beautiful when she smiled.

ON THE WAY HOME from the party, I told Kate how I couldn't wait for Christmas morning. Carson was going to open up the new big box of Legos I'd gotten him. It'd been expensive but worth it for the amount of time he spent playing with Dad. Our Christmas tree was small and a little lopsided. We'd found it just off the road, between our place and Karen's. Tonight, though, it looked beautiful.

"Hey, look at the box Lynn dropped off this afternoon. She was really disappointed she missed you," Dad said as we hung up our coats and slipped off our boots.

A big box covered in pretty silver and gold wrapping paper and red bows was pressed against the wall. It was filled with gifts for all of us.

"The twins were with her. Everybody's good. Carson opened up that." Dad pointed to a race car track that was set up on the linoleum floor in the kitchen.

I had missed my mother's and brothers' yearly Christmas visit. "I'll definitely call her tomorrow and make a time to see her."

"You should, Sadie, she misses you," my father replied, smiling.

CHRISTMAS AFTERNOON WAS COLD, and the winter sky was a dark gray-blue. Our furnace was working hard to keep the place warm. Wrapping paper was strewn about, and boxes of assorted chocolates and nuts were opened on the coffee table. The plates from our Christmas brunch were piled in the sink.

I reached down to help Carson with his race track for the hundredth time when I heard a screaming sound from the bathroom. "What is it?" I asked, shooting up. More screaming. When I opened the door, Kate was doubled over, clutching her side…

"I'm dying, Sadie, call an ambulance — tell them to hurry!"

I dialed 911 then called Karen.

HURRY UP, GIRL, get your stuff on. We'll get there right after the ambulance," Karen said when she arrived. She wasn't smiling; she was worried. Her eyes wouldn't meet mine.

But I didn't move other than to shake my head and say, "No, I can't go yet. I've got to…" But I stopped. I didn't know how to explain to her what I needed to do.

Karen opened the door and said, "It's cold, but the roads are clear. Stay right here with your cell close by."

With that, the three of them left the trailer. I heard Carson, out on the steps, ask, "Why does Mommy hurt?"

And the old man's reply, meant to lessen his fears: "She's got a bad tummy ache — they'll make her better."

"All better?" he asked. The doors of the car slammed shut, then I heard them back out.

The last of the sun was coming through the window above the kitchen sink. It was going to be dark soon. I needed to hurry, and I reached for my own coat hanging on the peg by the door. I slipped into my boots and grabbed my scarf.

Walking quickly to the end of our property, I knew right where to go — to the old logging road. There was a spot right at the beginning where I could lay down.

My boots crunched on the snow-covered road, and I could see my breath. Karen's porch light was already turned on. *She doesn't think she'll be coming back soon.* I shivered, recalling Kate's pale face, her clutching her side and telling me to call an ambulance.

I WALKED EVEN FASTER with my eyes firmly glued to the spot I had to get to. Inside my pocket, I felt an old Kleenex and pulled it out. It was a cocktail napkin from Shay's. I wiped my nose and blew on my hands. I should have grabbed mittens.

The base of the old logging trail before it disappeared up into the woods was perfect. The plow truck had cleared a place to turn around in. I climbed up and over the snow-bank to the small clearing. The last bit of sun was peeking through, filtering the area with light. I needed to hurry.

Nobody had been around here; there were no snow shoe or snowmobile tracks anywhere. The snow was hard and crusty. My footsteps, breaking through the glazed layer of snow, was the only noise I heard. Little bits of ice slid down into my boots. I wasn't wearing socks.

The peacoat I wore was the one Dad had gotten me from the Salvation Army store in Rutland. It was dark blue wool and roomy. One of its buttons was loose and dangling by a thread. The lining was torn. I slipped it off and spread it out on top of the snow.

My thoughts were swirling around the tent church and all those people speaking in tongues, placing their hands on the sick and the needy, praying as if the world was coming to an end. All that had fascinated me. But now I understood their fanaticism. My world was ending; Kate was dying.

With my eyes focused toward the trees, I laid down on top of the coat. The sun seeped through the bare branches, like the altar inside the tent church with its cross and a painted sun behind it. I couldn't recall the exact words of the prayer Father Ray had recited when it was the start of healing time. Instead, I drew from other prayers I remembered and began with, "Lord, come to me, Holy Spirit, give me your grace and your healing power to save Sister Kate. You are my savior, and I believe in you, Lord Jesus. Please, hear my prayers, offered in faith, in the name of the Lord. Make my sister whole again…" I repeated the prayer, this time faster and with my hands firmly clasped. I closed my eyes.

Thoughts I'd had that I wasn't proud of came at me in rapid fire: wishing I could run away and leave Dad after his last bout of drinking, my jealousy over the twins being big shots at their school, wanting bad things to happen to Tristan — and before him to Derek, and all the other mean boys at Langdon — and hoping Kate would move out so I could have my own bedroom. Finally, I thought about the boy in Tennessee. The way he'd run and fallen and how the men kept hitting him over and over. How I'd watched and let it all happen and hadn't said a word. I cried and prayed for Jesus' forgiveness, my hands covering my face.

I opened my eyes and looked up through the trees. Their tippy tops swayed back and forth, but there was no wind down here on the cold, crusty snow.

While my memories of the tent church were mostly of the congregation moving all about, I remembered Hetty, from the campground, telling me to be still so the Lord could hear the prayers offered in faith and move through us and raise the sick up. "Do you feel it, my little healer?" she would say as she held my hand.

I wiped my nose with the sleeve of my shirt and concentrated on being still, not moving a single muscle. My breathing slowed. I imagined the thick layer of leaves and twigs underneath the snow and then below that the rich soil of the forest floor.

At first, it was just a faint sensation — a slight tingling in my feet. I wiggled my toes. Then a slow warmth started to spread up through my legs, into my groin and then further out, reaching all the way to my hands, my fingers. It was like warm water rippling through my blood stream. I lifted myself up off the coat and felt my arms, my face. I was hot to the touch, despite the cold. Rich colors — pinks and oranges, blues and purples — blanketed the branches of the trees, and the white bark of the birch trees seemed to glow. The whole forest was a prism with the sun at its center. I knelt down, and in one more burst of prayer, I asked Jesus to heal my sister through me, to use me to save the sick.

I stayed that way for seconds, murmuring the words, repeating them faster and faster. I wasn't making any sense at all, but I kept at it. The sun disappeared, and the frigid cold returned. I stood up, shook the coat out, and wrapped it around me before I climbed back over the snow bank. It was dusk, much darker on Tabor Road than down in

Langdon where the street lights would be coming on. I was feeling drained but determined to save Kate because I now was sure that the Holy Spirit was in me. Like the congregation in the tent church, I was full of purpose, and I knew what had to be done.

I GRABBED MY FATHER'S TRUCK KEYS and ran to it. I'd never driven it before, but I didn't hesitate and gunned the engine up over the bank near our culvert. It rattled down Tabor Road, but once it was out on the highway, it leveled out. I reached 50 mph and stayed there.

The text Karen had sent me said Room 212. Taking the stairs two at a time, I passed a nurse who smiled and called out, "Oh, I wish I had your knees."

Kate was on her side, turned away from the door. I quickly walked up to the bed, leaned over, and placed my hands on the part of her back that the gown didn't quite cover. "Lord, heal this child of yours, take the sickness…" I whispered.

She batted my hands away, thoroughly annoyed. "What are you doing, Sadie Rose? Stop that gibberish and keep your freezing hands off of me. I'm fine. It's a kidney stone. I've got to strain my pee."

"You're not dying?" I asked, searching her face.

"No, I'm not. Though it was worse than my labor pains with Carson. The thing is, I've got to pass it through my urine or they'll have to do something else. Look."

She reached over and held up a little strainer still in its plastic wrap. "It's a tiny stone, and this is supposed to catch it."

Just then, Karen and Carson walked in. Karen was carrying a tray while Carson sipped from a plastic cup with a straw. "Mommy, it's apple juice! And Karen got me mac and cheese."

Feeling starved myself, I asked Carson for a bite. He motioned for me to sit with him in the chair by the curtain. I looked at Karen then over to Kate. I kissed the top of Carson's head and smiled as my dad walked in. He'd been talking to the nurse and had two prescription slips in his hand.

"We need to get these filled," he said, holding them up.

Karen nodded, Kate closed her eyes, and Carson slurped his apple juice.

My world *wasn't* ending; it was, in fact, perfect. Christmas had turned out perfect.

Chapter 10

"Hey Sadie." Julie spoke quietly to me by the dishwasher. "Officer Sousa — you know, the cop who's been helping Stephen? He's out at the bar. He wants to give you his card to give to your father. Apparently, he was up at your place earlier, hoping to catch him. He came in now and mentioned Tabor Road and Jarod Wade. He asked if that was your father. I told him it was and that you were working right now." Julie paused then added, "Now, I think I shouldn't have volunteered all that. Yep, not cool of me."

"Really? He went to see my father?" I asked. It probably had something to do with his SSI disability check being stolen and his identity getting all screwed up in the state's system. That had happened not so long ago, and Kate had taken care of it. I wiped down the counter, wondering if I should get involved or just let Kate handle it.

"I can tell him you're super busy. Besides, he mentioned something about Tennessee. That's way back — right?" Julie asked.

"He said Tennessee?"

"Yeah, I'm pretty sure."

My stomach tightened the way it always did when I heard that word. I forced myself to nod and replied, "Can you tell him he can try my dad another time?"

"Of course!" She turned and blew Eugene a kiss. I think I was the only one to see it besides Eugene.

I always found that this time at work — before we were open and when everyone checked in with each other and had their specific jobs to do — was peaceful. But this time, I found myself distracted as I watched Eugene weigh portions of meat on a little scale and then wrap the ounces in saran wrap. Stephen was doing the same for the day's catch, and a third cook was standing right near Henry as he tasted the sauces for the night's special entrées.

Zoe came in and grabbed the clean water glasses and silverware stacked near me. The wait staff was setting up the dining room — putting fresh flowers and linens on the tables and folding the silverware into napkins. Jeannie had just left to run to the store for last minute things the bar needed.

"Not many reservations. It's going to be a slow night. Everybody's still home, enjoying their Christmas," Zoe said, leaning over the counter.

Opening the dishwasher's doors, I felt the steam settle over me. *Why would that officer want to talk to my father about Tennessee?* I moved to the swinging door that led into the bar from the kitchen and looked through its window. Julie was cutting up fruit.

As I turned to go back to my area, I froze. *What if it has something to do with Brother Ron, Carson's father? Or the boy, my boy, who got hurt?* Both possibilities made me shudder. I quickly turned back to the bar. I needed to find out.

When I came into the dining room, Julie nodded towards the cop at the very end of the bar. He was reading a newspaper. All I could see was his dark hair and hands holding the paper up in front of his face. I quickly grabbed a rag and made my way down to the end. He was drinking coffee and had a bite left of a piece of cheesecake on his plate.

I blurted out, "Sorry, I made Julie fib. I'm not that busy."

The officer lowered the paper and folded it onto the bar. "Ah, Sadie, how's the driving going?" He started to stand up and reach for his coat. He had that open, friendly face I remembered from that time I gave him coffee to go when he helped out Stephen.

Just then, Jeannie walked through the front door holding a small grocery bag. She looked surprised and said, "Oh, didn't realize we were open."

Julie quickly replied, "We're not yet, but, well…"

Officer Sousa interrupted her and said, "I actually stopped in to see if Sadie was here, then I asked about a cup of coffee. Julie was kind enough to let me sit and enjoy some cheesecake, too. Hope that's okay."

Jeannie smiled and that all-business look on her face disappeared. "It's fine." She turned her attention back to Julie and took out oranges and a jar of maraschino cherries from the bag. Julie slipped the officer a check.

As he handed her a twenty-dollar bill, he reached over to me and said, "Could you give this to your dad? It's my card. I'll go back up some time, but it'd be good to talk over the phone first."

I looked down at the card briefly then asked, "You're a detective?"

"Yes, for almost one whole week," he replied. "So I'm now officially Detective Sousa. But you can call me Dominic, okay?"

I nodded and asked, "If this is about Tennessee, does it have anything to do with my sister, Kate? Or maybe about a boy getting hurt?" I felt my hand start to shake, the card moving up and down.

Dominic hesitated for just a moment. We were all looking at him. "No, neither. Just a few questions for your father about his time down there. Tennessee authorities have asked us to do this. There was an investigation sometime back and they overlooked him as a witness. We're just wondering if he may know or remember seeing something. It's a common thing between law enforcement to help each other out. It's no big deal."

"Oh, okay." I put the card into my apron and briefly looked at Jeannie. She smiled at me. I turned and left the bar.

"Thank you!" he called out after me. I gave him a little wave.

As I filled the big sink up with the pots and pans the cooks had used for prep, Karen's words came back to me. *"It doesn't hurt to put yourself out there."* It was clear that I was never going to forget what I saw at The Diamondback, despite Kate wanting me to. Not knowing what had happened to the boy — if he had lived or died — was on me to find out.

Detective Sousa had just left. What if he could find out the truth? It was time for me to do the right thing and stop burying this inside. I quickly turned off the faucet and wiped my hands. I might be able to catch him.

The kitchen door was wide open despite the cold. Stephen was smoking a cigarette and talking on his cell. I ran out past him and stood, scanning the parking lot. Just then a Volvo backed out and turned towards me. It was the detective. I put my hand up and stepped across to the driver's side. Dominic rolled down the window.

"Hey, Sadie, what's up?" he asked.

"I was wondering if I could tell you about something that happened down in Tennessee. Maybe you could ask your Tennessee people about it?"

"Is it what you mentioned back there — something about your sister or a boy getting hurt?" he asked.

The mention of my sister made my bones run cold. *What am I thinking? Carson is at stake here — someone could connect the dots and figure out who his father really is. And then what would happen? What would we do if he took him away?*

I slowly backed up and replied, "Nah, never mind. Just forget I said anything."

Dominic Sousa glanced at the kitchen door and then back up at me. "Seems to me, from the way you came running out here in the cold, that this might be pretty important to you, Sadie. Maybe there's a place in the restaurant we could just talk — out of everyone's way?"

No one had ever encouraged me to talk about what I saw from the back of that station wagon. All the times I'd wanted to, I was either shot down by Kate or shown remorse but no real interest from my father. I was straining against six years' worth of holding it in. The detective was still looking up at me and waiting.

I replied, "It's about the boy, but my sister's kind of involved, too." I shivered and rubbed my arms then blew on my hands. "There aren't any reservations in the smallest dining room. We can go in there if I check with Jeannie."

"Good, and ask Jeannie if she can join us. You're a minor, and it's standard practice."

"Okay." Turning to go in, I felt my stomach knotting up. *Whatever happens, Kate can't find out.*

Chapter 11

T he fancy French doors were closed, which was a rare sight. I quickly glanced at Jeannie. She squeezed my hand as we both watched Dominic take out a small notebook and pen. I couldn't help it and said, "Oh wow! Just like on TV. That's cool."

He smiled and replied, "Some of the guys take notes on their phones, but I'm not good at that. And I don't think this is anything I need to record."

Jeannie spoke up and asked, "Is this okay? I'm not her parent or legal guardian."

"I think it's fine, but if Sadie tells me anything that I'm concerned about, we'll definitely stop and go from there. Does that make sense?" he asked.

Jeannie smiled and seemed to relax.

Dominic had a nice, calm way about him, and his eyes were kind. I took a deep breath, jumped in, and said,

"Basically, I saw a kid get beat up really badly one night a while ago, and I want to know if he was okay after. I was in the back of our station wagon, and I watched two guys run after him and punch him over and over. Is it possible to find out anything about him?" I'd rushed my words, but the relief in finally unloading was huge. Sitting back, I wiped my mouth and watched Dominic writing stuff down. Jeannie slid her Coke over to me and whispered, "Take some. I haven't touched it."

He stopped writing and asked, "When did this happen? And where exactly were you, Sadie?"

He was taking me seriously. I replied, "Okay, I was nine, and it was at the end of the summer or even a little past. I'm sixteen now, so it was back in two thousand and nine. We'd been staying at a campsite in Goodlettsville in someone's camper. I came back here and went into the fourth grade. Julie was my teacher."

Dominic finished writing that down and then motioned with his hand out towards the bar. "That Julie?"

I nodded.

He smiled and said, "Small world, small town, huh?"

Jeannie added, "Three of our wait staff are teachers."

I jumped back in and said, "It's been on my mind a lot lately. I think it's because he wasn't a whole lot older than I am now. The thing is…" I stopped. I'd already told the detective more than Kate would ever want me to tell anybody. But I couldn't help it and added, "The thing is, I did nothing to help him, and that's eating away at me."

Dominic Sousa closed his little notebook and put the pen down. "I can definitely ask my counterpart in Tennessee to check for any assault records around this time — late August through the first couple of weeks of September at a campground in Goodlettsville, in two thousand and nine. It may take a little while, but it's doable. And I'll get back to you."

I shook my head, "No, no, sorry. The fight didn't happen at the campground. It happened at a bar, in the parking lot of The Diamondback."

Suddenly, Dominic seemed to look at me differently — more focused. "You said The Diamondback?" He quickly reached for his notebook again.

"Yes, I know for sure because for two nights my father was drinking inside that bar. He'd been sober, but something must have snapped, because he pulled into that parking lot, right under its sign out back, and we didn't move for two days." I stopped talking, remembering how Dad had gotten me all sorts of coloring books and snacks, even new Polly Pockets. Told me he'd come out and check on me, but he really only had on that first day and night.

I added, "Anytime I had to go to the bathroom, I'd go up the ramp to the back of the bar and scoot into the girls' room. The cook, a nice lady, gave me fries with gravy and all the Cokes I wanted."

Dominic wrote this all down. I wasn't done talking, though.

"My sister, Kate, who's a lot older, finally found us in the station wagon on that second morning. She was ripping mad at the old man — my father. He was sleeping it off in the car. Kate got in, started up the station wagon, and we left Tennessee that very morning. I remember her saying, 'This is bullshit.'"

I finally stopped and glanced at Jeannie then Dominic. I took a sip of the Coke and added, "Seeing the boy get hit, over and over — it's bothered me. Those men were brutal. I keep getting flashbacks of it. If your people in Tennessee can find out but keep this all under wraps — not mention my name — I'd really, really appreciate it." One of my knees was shaking under the table. Jeannie could probably feel it.

Dominic gave me a quick nod and closed his notebook. We sat for a few seconds in silence, then we all stood and left the small dining room. Shay's was open now, and two tables were being seated. Zoe was pouring water at the first table. I turned to head to the kitchen, but needed to ask Jeannie a quick question about the schedule. When I backtracked, I saw that she and Dominic had stepped back into the small dining room.

I heard Dominic ask, "You know her father, Jarod Wade?"

Jeannie replied, "A vet, some PTS and alcoholism, but gosh, he's raised a wonderful child."

Dominic added, "This time period and locale is exactly what I'm supposed to ask him about. A girl went missing around that time, and it's still an unsolved case. It feels too coincidental not to be connected in some way."

"Well, it sounds like he won't be much help. Shitfaced for two days."

"Yeah, that's interesting," he replied.

"What about the fight Sadie saw?" Jeannie asked.

"You know how many hundreds, if not thousands, of fights there are out in the parking lots of roadhouses?" Dominic Sousa replied.

I quickly turned and headed to the kitchen, my heart sinking. *Maybe he wasn't going to be able to help me after all.*

Chapter 12

T wo nights later, Shay's was having another slow night, but Henry didn't seem to mind. He went up to everybody to show them a video on his cell phone of his youngest daughter at her first dance recital. Daisy was just 4. "Look at her hold that position!" he exclaimed over and over.

Julie came to the back of the kitchen and started to cut out big red letters for a new bulletin board for her fourth graders. "Valentine's Day is just around the corner," she said, smiling.

Eugene was experimenting with sauces for the beef tenderloin and wanted us to try them. "Too much shallot?" he asked me as I held the ramekin and tasted it.

I shook my head. "No, love it, and all those bits of mushrooms — yummy!"

Alice quickly came over and said, "The creamy parmesan is my favorite."

Jeannie asked Zoe and Corey, "What 'five letter word for a man's hat starts with a T?'" They stared blankly at her, then Zoe laughed and told her to go find smarter people.

Karl, the snow plow guy, came through the kitchen door. He had his son, Logan, with him. They were hoping for some hot chocolate. I quickly started to make it from scratch — it'd become my specialty. I asked Logan if he wanted some cake, too. He looked at his father, who nodded.

We sat at the back counter to enjoy the cocoa and watched all the happenings in the kitchen. I was glad it was slow, and I could dote on the boy. He was in kindergarten, and his teacher's name was Mrs. Coughlin.

"Come on, Superman, time to fly!" his father finally called out from the back door.

"Superman?" My eyes grew big. "You mean I've been sitting next to Superman this whole time and I didn't know it?!"

Logan quickly unzipped his coat and flashed me his shirt with a big 'S' in Superman colors.

"Superman needs a cape so we can tell!" Julie said.

Shortly after that, I was replenishing cups and saucers in the smallest dining room when Jeannie walked by and paused. "Hey, I'm sorry about that whole Tennessee thing with your dad, Sadie. I'm sorry you had to go through that."

I wanted to change her perception because it wasn't quite right, so I quickly replied, "Those last two nights — they were the only bad nights down there, really. I spent my days at the campground with other nice kids my age. A woman named Hetty was watching me, and I felt safe with her. Every night, we gathered at the tent church and worshipped. Well, except for Kate. She didn't believe in any of that. That last night *was* awful, but Kate came, my dad sobered up, and we made it home."

Jeannie nodded and replied, "I'm glad to hear it wasn't all bad, like what you described. And I hope Dominic 'what's his name' will find something out for you."

"Sousa is his last name. He was nice." We both turned to leave, but I reached out and touched Jeannie's sleeve. "I've kept those nights from my mother. Any bad stuff about my dad would make her want me to live with her even more. But I belong with Kate. Please keep this confidential, okay?"

Jeannie responded quietly, "Of course, I will, Sadie."

When it was time for me to clock out, I heard Julie and Jeannie talking about Dominic Sousa. Apparently, he'd come back for dessert again. "Right? I know. His eyes… they're incredible — big pools of my favorite dark chocolate!" Julie exclaimed.

Backing out of my spot near the restaurant's kitchen door, I stopped. Today, with Jeannie, I'd talked openly about Tennessee again. That would never have happened before. But I knew that she was there for me, just like everybody else at Shay's. Things had definitely changed; plenty more people were in my corner now.

I carefully pulled out onto Route 103. The roads were clear. I checked my side mirrors and turned up the heater. An uneasy feeling started to take hold of me. *What if the boy hadn't turned out okay?*

I tried to tune into a station on the radio, but the reception leaving Langdon sucked. It was nothing but static, and I snapped the radio off in frustration. A new worry came: *What if talking so openly about those nights to Dominic Sousa and Jeannie wasn't the best thing for my family? What if Kate was right, and it was better to keep our secrets to ourselves?*

It was a starry night; the Big Dipper and the North Star were visible, but I didn't care. The fact that Dominic wanted to question my old man about a missing girl only added to my uneasiness.

Chapter 13

In Cuttingsville, I filled Kate's tank in the Honda. The best part of the whole dishwashing job was that I could contribute. No more sitting there as Dad and Kate talked about the bills. Each paycheck of mine made a difference.

My mother had invited me up to her house in Rutland that morning, just days after Kate's Christmas trip to the ER and after I'd spoken to Detective Sousa.

Kate was home from work hoping to pass the stone. I'd left her watching a movie with Carson and holding a gallon of water. "Drink, Strain, Repeat!" I'd chimed as I left. She had not looked happy and had stuck out her tongue. Dad had been off somewhere, maybe out in his tool shed.

When I was younger, I'd spend two weekends a month with my mother. Their house was a modern ranch they'd bought in a subdivision not far from the high school. Even back then, the twins were already stand outs in Peewee football. My mother had met her husband, Aaron, through Parks and Rec when my brothers had been 8, maybe 9. She'd been working as a bank teller at one of the larger credit unions in the city. Aaron was the head mechanic at the Saab-Volvo dealership across the street from the credit union.

To hear Mom tell it, he'd fallen in love with her the moment he'd watched the twins play ball. He said that wasn't true at all; it was when she'd taken his paycheck week after week at the credit union and never cracked a smile, even though he'd tried to get her to. Their relationship seemed solid and easy going, although during the fall season they were pretty intense. The boys and football dominated their schedule.

There was a time when she and Aaron put pressure on my father to have me come live with them. I think it might have been the spring before fifth grade, after Julie had me as a student. But, by then, their lives were completely centered on the boys. My father and Kate had thought I was doing fine, and I'd told my mother a flat out "no." Carson was about to be born.

My mother and father had made the decision for me to stay put. Dad had told her that while Tabor Road wasn't the ideal place to grow up, I was the center of his and Kate's universe. Kate had stood her ground, very pregnant, and told Lynn that there was no way I was leaving, that we were sisters, most of all. Lynn couldn't argue with that. She knew her boys were all-consuming. She also knew how bored and disengaged I had been all those weekends I'd visited, watching the twins play ball. Often times I'd be coloring or crocheting on those beginner patterns. What I'd really wanted to do was play on the playground at whatever school their football games were held at. But then she or Aaron wouldn't have been able to watch the twins play ball. My monthly visits had started to taper off.

After the rumors about me started up at Langdon, I wondered if a different school would be better — if being the Donovan twins' younger sister would help me socially. It'd been a passing thought, and one that made me feel guilty.

AS I TURNED ONTO THEIR STREET, I saw that the twins were out in the road throwing the football around. When I parked, they came over, and Joel instantly picked me up like a sack of potatoes and yelled to his brother, "Get ready for a lateral reverse." I started to kick him, but I was enjoying the attention.

"Put her down *now,* Joel!" It was Aaron, my stepdad, already walking toward us. He gave me a big bear hug. "I've never seen you look so much like your beautiful mother!"

My mother was standing in the breezeway, not looking especially happy. She never liked how physical my brothers were with me.

"Hey Mom, what do you think?" I called to her. I posed like a model. I was wearing the new coat she'd given me. It was a little too dressy for my taste, but it fit perfectly. It was from Hollister, the expensive place in the mall. She motioned for me to come up and in.

The kitchen was where the Donovan family gathered most of the time. The boys ate constantly, and the big island with the stools was the perfect spot for today's brunch. A plate full of assorted danishes was already out, next to a large pitcher of orange juice. I could smell bacon and sausage in the oven, and I noticed two cartons of eggs on the counter ready to go.

Mom asked me to turn around, and I did, twirling a bit for show. Aaron started to walk into the kitchen, but she shook her head and said, "Give us a few minutes alone, and keep them out." She'd nodded toward the window, indicating the boys.

I resembled my mother: petite and blond, with green eyes. She was just 39 years old. Sometimes, I tried to remember what she was like when she was younger, but mostly, I remembered Kate. Still, to this day, I couldn't understand how she and my father had hooked up. They'd met when she was already pregnant with the boys, and then I'd come along two years later.

All these half-brothers and sisters were confusing to anyone outside our base. I hadn't fully explained it to Jeannie or Zoe, yet, other than to say, "We're a family of halves, but it's Dad, Kate, Carson and me who make a whole."

My mother wore her hair in a shorter than usual cut. It was styled like those cuts you can pick out in the books at hair salons. Hers would be in the 'short hair' section, and I bet a lot of women picked that look out. Her teller's position had grown into a manager's spot at the credit union, and she always looked her best. I think Aaron loved that about her, especially after working all day in the big, noisy garage with the other mechanics.

We hugged, and when I let go, she still hung on. She searched my face and said, "You're driving, that's great. And you've got a job. That's so awesome. And you like it? I mean you're not doing it because you have to, right?"

My mother's serious look and voice came out in every visit. It was like she had to know that how she thought things were going for me were really how things were going for me.

"I wish you wouldn't do that — look at me with such worry in your eyes." I'd never said it that bluntly before.

She turned away, and that made me feel horrible.

"I'm sorry, that was rude of me, Mom," I said and touched her sleeve. "No, I don't have to work there, but the money is good. I mean, I'm only a dishwasher, but I can buy my own shampoo and makeup, so that's cool, right?"

"If your dad needs more money in our monthly agreement, he can just say so."

"No, Mom. Dad is doing fine, and as soon as Kate passes that kidney stone, she'll be good as new. We're all fine."

I draped my coat over the stool and sat down. The kitchen was bright, with pops of yellow. Our fridge paled in comparison to their big stainless steel one. Part of her worry was guilt over me living in the trailer, still, after all these years.

But you know what, I thought as I looked through to the living room, *this house is just average*. Kate's pride, or maybe it was her defensiveness, was rubbing off on me. I shouldn't feel that way, I knew.

Aaron poked his head back in and asked, "We good to come in?"

I stood up quickly and put my arms back around my mom. "Yes!" I smiled. "Send those monsters in!"

She pulled me even closer and kissed my temple and whispered, "Remember all those times they scared you, pretending to be monsters?"

"That and putting me places I couldn't get down from or out of like Aaron's work table in the basement or up in the cedar chest in your bedroom."

The boys came bouncing in. They weren't boys really; they had facial hair, deep voices, and stood over six feet tall. They weren't hard to tell apart. Joel was taller and thinner while Jack seemed broader and stockier. They'd inherited their biological dad's dark hair and olive complexion.

"Hey Mom, Sadie may be taller than you!" Jack called out.

"That's not saying much!" replied Joel as he poured a glass of orange juice. We all sat down at the island and started to call out how we wanted our eggs done. Aaron was our short order cook as he cracked the eggs on the big range.

There was discussion between the boys about what gifts needed to be returned and exchanged or refunded totally.

"Can I have the money if I don't want to exchange it for something else?" Jack asked.

Aaron delivered scrambled eggs to me then to Joel. He glanced at Jack and said, "No, we know you. You'll send everything back to load up on new video games."

My mother said quietly to me, "I love the calendar you gave me. Did you do that online — download the pictures and choose a different one for each month?"

"Yes, on Shutterfly. A girl from the restaurant, Alice, showed me how to scan them to her account. I wish some of the photos of you and me were just a little bit clearer."

"It's beautiful, Sadie. Thank you," she replied.

I assured her and Aaron that everything Dad, Kate, and I had gotten from them was great and that Carson's little race track was a huge hit.

"No exchanges, no refunds?" Aaron asked. "Like your rotten, spoiled big bro here."

Jack stood up and moved to his father, bumping his chest into Aaron. "Oh yeah, wanna go at it, old man?"

"We're not starting any of that in here, guys," Mom said, raising her eyebrows as she looked over at me.

AT THE END OF THEIR STREET, I pulled the Honda over and stopped. My mother had given me a Christmas cookie tin, and I wanted to eat one of the cookies with the red cinnamon dots. As I ate, looking out at the different houses with their holiday decorations, I was glad I'd driven up to see everyone. It wasn't a betrayal to my dad or to Kate to have had a great time with this other side of my family. Sometimes I felt that way, but not today.

I thought about the clearing just past the turn-around. Things I'd felt bad about — like the twins being hot shots — I needed to work on. Jealousy wasn't cool. When you were envious, it meant you weren't thankful for your own blessings. But me praying to save Kate? It had worked; she wasn't dying.

One night in the camper in Tennessee, Kate had tried to tell me that all the healing going on in the tent church was a scam. Once, a kid about my age now had stood up without his crutches and walked just fine after Father Ray and the others had laid hands on him and prayed. I'd sat, dumbfounded, as the boy had passed by me and left the tent.

Kate had asked me, "Have you ever seen that kid before? In the congregation? No! Because he was a fake, paid to do all that shit."

My father had told Kate to stop talking like that, but she'd been determined to set me straight. "From now on, during healing time, anyone who's a regular member of the congregation who has like arthritis, or I don't know, a hangnail... They'll be invited up as we pray. But any of the dramatic stuff — we won't recognize those people because they're actors, Sadie, actooooooors."

She'd said that last part in a long, drawn-out, exaggerated voice that had set my father off.

"Don't be so disrespectful!" he'd told her.

"You know it's true, Dad!" She'd gone out the camper's door, disgusted. "What a crock of bull."

WHEN I ARRIVED HOME after visiting my mom, I parked next to Dad's old truck. Carson swung the door wide open and yelled, "Sadie, Mommy's rock came out!"

Kate had passed her stone.

Chapter 14

I stood just beneath the overhang. We were in a lean-to out in the woods off one of Colton's back roads. Zoe had driven slowly, zig-zagging over the ruts, confident her grandfather's old Jeep could handle it.

Big, fat snowflakes fell onto the edge of the floor of the lean-to then disappeared into its planks. Standing next to Zoe, I watched her high school buddies setting up for the party. I knew no one but her, and I had no idea where we actually were. If, for some reason, we got separated, could I find my way out of the woods? That thought was a little scary, and I moved closer to Zoe. She must have read my mind, because she leaned in and whispered, "We're hanging together, bestie."

Curious looks came my way. Zoe had told me to be ready for them because I looked "so damn good." We'd gotten ready at her house. Her parents were away for the weekend, and we'd experimented with our Sephora makeup.

"Party of the Year," she'd said when we'd realized that Jeannie had given us both Friday night off from Shay's. It was her way of thanking us for working so hard during our Christmas break.

Colton was our arch rival in most sports. In football, they beat us 49 to 7. Some Colton kids had painted our water tower green — their school color — after our loss. I didn't know where we stood against them in basketball. Now that I worked at Shay's, I never went to any games. But I never really went before, either.

"Where are all the girls?" I asked. I'd only seen a few others so far.

"Oh, they'll be here. Still getting ready. Bet they won't be as warm as us." Zoe smiled at me, shaking the snow from her wavy, red hair as it tumbled out from under her hat.

I reached over and smoothed out a spot of foundation along Zoe's cheek. She didn't like her freckles and was always trying to cover them up.

Tonight, we'd raided her brother's long underwear drawer and each of us wore one of his hunting jackets. Mine was red and black checkered, while Zoe's was a bright orange. For once, I had on mittens and heavy socks. The black Carhart hat I was wearing was Zoe's father's.

Our plan was to spend the night out here. The jeep was full of blankets and pillows. I was excited and nervous, too. Zoe said her friends would like me, although I wasn't so sure. My track record at Langdon sucked, so why would this be any different? While the rumors had died down and I was being left alone at school, I knew that could change at any moment. Stephen's little brother, Levi, was protecting me for now, but he was graduating in the spring.

A big guy with mammoth hands was placing firewood into the firepit while another guy crumpled up old newspapers. A can of lighter fluid rested against a red cooler. Another kid was stacking wood, telling them, "There's still a shitload in my truck."

Other guys were hauling beer and wine to the snowbank to the right of the lean-to. They were hollowing out a hole in the snow then laying six-packs and wine coolers carefully around the hollowed-out space. They definitely knew what they were doing.

"Have we got everything?" A guy wearing a green and white Colton sweatshirt called out.

"No, the hard stuff isn't here yet. Brett's bringing that."

He nodded and carefully put a few pieces of wood along the edge of the area, delineating the booze in the snow.

The really big guy smiled over at me and said, "My bet is you're from Peddan, no, maybe Langdon."

Zoe reached over and put her arm around me. "Wouldn't you like to know, Sam!"

"Oh, I plan on finding out, Zoe."

I gave him a little wave and said, "Hi. It's Langdon."

"That's not the only thing I want to know." He had a wide, open face.

"Calm down Sammy-boy," Zoe quipped. The kid with the newspaper laughed as he smiled over at me, too.

Zoe squeezed my hand and whispered, "Sam's a good guy. Mark, next to him, not so nice."

Just then we heard people coming through the woods, down the path we'd walked earlier. A big group, mostly girls, were laughing loudly and carrying bags of chips and Solo cups.

Zoe called out, "Carley, did you bring the s'mores?"

Two girls held up boxes of graham crackers and bags of marshmallows. One of them called out, "We'll need to find sticks!"

"Hey, Sadie, this is Carley, my friend from way back," Zoe said.

Carley held up the Hershey bars in a plastic bag and smiled.

More people made their way down the path to our spot. Suddenly, long benches appeared from somewhere and the guys arranged them around the firepit. I heard someone say there was one more long bench behind the last lean-to if we needed it.

Zoe promised she wouldn't leave me. I leaned into her and whispered, "Remember, I don't know anyone but you."

"I know, don't worry," she whispered back.

Despite her assurance, I was a little uneasy. "Bears are hibernating, right?" I asked, smiling.

Zoe nodded and replied, "Let's hope so!"

THE FIRE WAS WARM, and at times, I had to move away because I was too hot. Each time I walked around the outer circle, I kept an eye on Zoe. She was right, though — her classmates were friendly, and a few of the guys had even come over to talk to me. The big guy, Sam, seemed to be hovering; he'd gotten me two beers and when I needed to pee, he'd found a girl who knew where to go. Her name was Dede, short for Denise, she told me. We giggled as we walked down a trail in the woods that led to an old root cellar that offered us some privacy. We used our cell phone lights to see. Someone had brought a roll of toilet paper. There was no reception up here — wherever here was. Dede was a senior and loved Zoe. They both played on the intramural volleyball team.

"I wonder if she's going to hook up with Ryan. She's been in love with him since the summer," Dede said as she threw the toilet paper roll over to me, and I caught it.

Zoe hoped that, too. I didn't know what that meant for me tonight if they did, though.

"Is he here?" I asked. We turned to head back to the fire.

"Haven't seen him yet. He delivers pizza for Domino's, so he'll probably be here soon."

DEDE HOOKED HER ARM IN MINE as we started back down the trail. I could hear laughter and see the fire and its sparks through the woods. Someone was calling out, "More s'mores!"

I'd been fake drinking the beer; it tasted gross. Zoe didn't drink either, and she'd told me she always faked it. There were a couple of joints being passed around but neither of us did anything other than to pass it on to the next person. Most everybody planned on staying, some camping in their cars further back from the turn off or in the lean-tos that were scattered around. Already there were couples who had left the fire and drifted elsewhere. I needed to figure out what to do if Zoe did go off with Ryan.

Suddenly, Sam stepped out and grabbed my arm and asked, "Want to take a walk, Sadie?"

Dede looked up at him and smiled, then she saw my face. "Sam, we're hanging for a bit so fuck off."

We moved past him and made our way back to a spot on the bench. I looked over at Dede and quietly said, "Thanks. I'm, um…it's just that I've had some guys lie about being with me. That I've put out for them, and school's been hard because of it. The truth is, I've never done anything with them. When he just grabbed me like that, well, I don't want things to start up again."

Dede nodded knowingly and replied, "I've been around jerks, too, who can't wait to lie to their buddies about how far they got with a girl. But just so you know, Sam's a great guy. He's not like that."

Dede was more mature than a lot of the kids here. I nodded and watched the fire. Two guys were telling a story about one of the teachers at Colton. Everybody seemed amused until a girl yelled out, "Stop it! He's a good teacher. You guys are too hard on him." An argument started, with other kids weighing in. I stayed quiet and thought about what Dede had just said.

I shouldn't ever hang with a guy just to fit in, to look normal. Tristan was mean and had only wanted a blow job. That shouldn't have come as a surprise. And then I'd actually told him I'd give him one for a ride home. *That was pathetic on so many levels.*

Ryan, the boy Zoe liked, appeared from somewhere behind the fire and scooted in next to her. She looked over and smiled at him but neither one spoke. She was happy, I could tell.

Sometime, a little later, I felt the bench move and looked to my right. Sam had taken a seat about two spots over. No one was between us. Had I pissed him off by not taking a walk with him?

"Hey, Sadie, sorry about back there," he said.

"It's okay." I looked at him and quickly then back at the fire. It was making loud, popping noises.

"Can we talk?" he asked.

"Only if I can I ask you a question first — like, how tall are you?"

Laughing, he replied, "That's always the question. To a few of the schools scouting me out, I'm six five and two sixty. But really, I think I'm only six four and a half, maybe two forty-five."

"Wow!" I didn't know what else to say and just nodded at him.

"Now, it's my turn." He stretched his legs out toward the fire. "So, you're from Langdon. What year are you in school and how do you know Zoe?"

I answered him briefly, then from somewhere his name was called and a football came sailing past me. He caught it with one hand and effortlessly passed it back to someone beyond the fire. He asked me to place my hand in his to compare our difference in size, so I slid over next to him. His hand was warm and rough with callouses, and it was at least twice as big as mine. I withdrew after a minute.

In an exaggerated, fake-hurt voice, he said, "Aw, don't take it away, that felt nice."

I smiled but kept my hand on the bench. I mentioned my brothers played football for Rutland.

"The Donovan brothers? Really? I bet they're headed to Division One schools."

We could hear a girl getting sick just past the lean-to closest to us. Sam gave me a look like 'poor kid.' She was crying between throwing up. Someone yelled, "Get a towel or something!"

Sam asked about my family and if I had a boyfriend. I was honest with him, even though I didn't want to be.

"No boyfriend, and I'm not popular, at all. I live outside of Langdon, and my dad's a vet — not the animal vet, the veteran vet. He's got issues."

None of it seemed to faze Sam. He leaned over to stoke the fire and said, "I don't believe that, about you not being popular."

"It's true."

At one point, a kid came by and sat down close to us.

Sam looked over at him and said, "Beat it." The kid got up and left.

"You know the big farm on the left as you start to come into Colton? Right before the turn off for Zoe's road? That's my family's farm. My dad and uncle still work it. It's smaller than it used to be. My mom teaches first grade in Colton."

I'd held my nose when we'd passed the farm just this afternoon. Zoe had laughed and said, "Chicken manure is the worst." That was Sam's place.

A few times, I looked over at Zoe and Ryan. Once they were kissing. It was kind of sweet.

Sam saw it, too, and whispered, "About time."

Sam's nose looked like a fighter's nose — a little dented — and his neck, like his hands, was massive. He seemed to be self-conscious about his nose, because he ran his finger down it a lot.

"Did you break your nose or…" I asked then stopped suddenly. I felt my heart begin to race. Looking away from Sam and into the fire, *I saw the boy at The Diamondback. Was his nose broken, right there in front of me, when the bigger man had struck him? In slow motion, I replayed the boy turning toward me, his eyes wide with disbelief, his mouth twisted in pain. A streak of blood had splattered across the side window of the station wagon. He'd laid there, blinking slowly and looking my way. I'd hidden in horror under my blanket, watching, until his eyes had closed.*

"Yeah, twice. Once as a kid I fell off a tractor, then last spring, one of our horses knocked me flat. I'll probably break it again playing college ball."

I wasn't listening to Sam anymore. Instead, I was reliving that moment, each frame freezing slowly. My hands were sweaty, and my breathing had become shallow.

Sam stopped talking and asked, "Hey, are you okay?" He touched my shoulder.

The touch was just enough to startle me back. "I need water. Can you get me some?"

He got up quickly and returned a moment later with a water bottle. I opened it and took a long sip of the icy cold water. "Could we maybe take a walk?" I asked, wanting to get away from the fire and everybody there.

"Sure," he replied. As we made our way along the same trail I'd taken with Dede, Sam talked. He loved math and was thinking of studying architecture. But where he was going to end up at college was anybody's guess. "It's all about who offers me a football scholarship and financial aid. Lots of variables, as my mom says."

We passed some girls laughing. One of them had fallen and was trying to get up. Sam reached down and helped her, which set the other two girls into another fit of laughter. After they started back towards the benches, Sam looked down at me and asked, "You feel better? You look better."

The anxiousness I'd felt in my body just minutes ago was leaving. The water and his steady voice had helped with that. I answered, "Sorry, I was just remembering something." We'd made a loop walking and were back near the bonfire.

A guy let out a few loud f-bombs not far from us. Sam shook his head. "The language of kids these days."

I'd never had anybody talk to me like this before — saying all this personal stuff out loud, like he actually cared what I thought.

We sat back down, and he threw a few sticks into the fire then asked, "Have you always lived in Langdon?"

The images of the boy were gone. Taking the last sip of water, I shook my head and started to tell Sam a little bit about our time down in Tennessee and how the tent church had shaped me and my beliefs around God. I avoided all talk about The Diamondback. Sam nodded as I spoke. He definitely believed in God, too. Living on the farm was not 'cool' to a lot of kids at Colton High, but he liked it and wasn't embarrassed. "Farming is God's work — my grandmother says that."

People must have been walking all around us, but we paid them no attention. At one point, Sam reached over for my hand and asked, "Is it okay?"

This time I liked it when he held it, and I smiled.

Finally, one of his friends came over and asked if they should get going. He nodded and said, "I gotta go, pretty girl. We're helping my father first thing. He needs the truck."

When he stood, I stood, too. I was at least a foot shorter, even more. "Maybe we'll meet up again," I said, looking up at him.

He smiled. "Maybe? Just a maybe, Sadie Wade?" He touched the tip of my nose then kissed me. It wasn't long or deep, but I felt it.

Nobody had ever kissed me, called me pretty, or said my name in that way.

He hoisted the cooler up on his shoulder and held his ax. He looked like the lumber jack in one of Carson's fairy tale books.

I gave him a little wave but didn't smile. I didn't want any of this to end.

Zoe was watching me, her own eyes seeming to mirror exactly how I felt in that magical moment.

Chapter 15

Basically, my life had changed totally, again, in one night. I tried to tell Kate about the party and Zoe's friends in between her ruffling the sheets as we changed the beds. She listened as we did Dad's bed first and then hers and Carson's.

When I got to the part about Sam — that he'd called me pretty and had wanted to know all about me and that he lived on the farm on the way into Colton — she asked, "The farm that smells like shit?" She drove down to Colton every day around 2:30 to work the second shift at the nursing home. She went right by it.

I nodded and kept on talking, telling her his height and weight, that his hands were the size of a tennis racket. Kate usually didn't smile much, but she was smiling now.

"Can't think of a better first boyfriend for you than a big farm boy who spreads cow shit all over his place," Kate laughed.

"It's actually chicken manure, and he loves his farm. He's not embarrassed by it at all."

"And that's why — " Kate grinned, as she put the last pillow case on — "you'll have no problem bringing him here to meet us."

Just the thought of that — him coming up here to Tabor Road — made me nervous. This was all so new.

Kate left to go drag more of the clean laundry in from the backseat of her car. I thought about telling her of the flashback I'd had at the bonfire, but it wouldn't do any good — she wouldn't listen.

Standing at the front door, I watched as she closed the car door with her hip while holding on to a large garbage bag full of clean clothes. A burst of cold air came in with her as she said, "We've got about three weeks' worth of folding, so let's get started."

I reached down for a pair of blue jeans. I had hoped that after talking to Dominic Sousa, these feelings of guilt would go away. But now I just felt guilty twice — for betraying Kate and opening up our business, and for not helping that boy when I had the chance. *I know I was only a little kid, but I should have screamed for help.* I thought about that moment at the party, and how I'd suddenly been there, watching the boy get beaten again. Sam had been so kind, but what would I do if the memories just kept coming? If they wouldn't stop? The pants felt damp still, so I draped them over the kitchen chair and glanced out the window above the sink. The old station wagon seemed to be staring back at me. *What if Dominic Sousa can't find out anything? Will I go crazy?*

I had Jeannie's old cell phone and I was on her plan, but I didn't use it much. Like the car, my father had accepted it under the condition that, *"It's only for emergencies."* But that afternoon, after our marathon folding, I texted Zoe and asked her to give Sam my number.

Twenty minutes later, I got a *'Hey, how r u? Been thinking about u.'*

'I'm good, thx.' I texted back.

'What r u doing now? Wanna FaceTime?' he texted back.

But I didn't reply. Instead, I grabbed my coat and called out to my father and Kate, "I'm taking a walk. I'll be home before it's dark."

Walking towards Karen's, I reread his text messages. If he only knew how much I'd been thinking of him.

I knocked on Karen's door. She opened it, smiled, and said, "Sadie Rose, Happy New Year!"

I blurted out, "I think I have a boyfriend!" and stepped in.

BACK AT SCHOOL, things were different. It was hard to pinpoint what was going on because it wasn't the same as before. After Banks' class, I walked down the hallway and knew I was being stared at, but this time the seniors weren't hurling insults at me. Instead, they were talking quietly amongst themselves while watching me.

Amy Dunne came up as I closed my locker and said, "Hey, Sadie, do me a favor. Walk with me while all these assholes stare."

I turned to her and asked, "What's going on?"

"You're the talk right now. It's not horrible what they're saying, it's just so childish. Like girls are possessions, not people." She nodded towards the end of the hallway where the upperclassman guys were congregating.

"Okay, thanks." I quickly added, "I met your mom."

"I heard. Now, let's walk through this hallway like we own it — because we do own it."

I glanced up at her. She was big and bold and beautiful. With her beside me, I felt different, like I could be okay with being me.

I found out later that the Langdon guys were hearing from the Colton guys that Sam Pelton had dibs on me. Sam, the number one player from Colton, the guy headed for college football, was interested in me, the girl from Tabor Road.

Chapter 16

y the end of the week, we were hit with a cold, hard
rain. Up at the higher elevations, ice was forming on
the trees, the power lines, and across the roadways. I
could hear snapping — limbs breaking off in the woods
outside the trailer. My father and Carson stayed put,
content to build one of the new Lego ships from the Christmas Lego package.

I had to go to work and crawled down Tabor Road. Once
I got to the main road, the salt trucks were the only vehicles
I came upon.

The restaurant was slow that night. I clocked out at 9:10
p.m. Henry was concerned about a possible power outage
and decided to close early. Areas all around us already had
downed power lines.

When I walked up to the Subaru in the parking lot, someone in the car beside it lowered their window. "Hey, Sadie. Remember me? From the party out at the lean-tos?"

It wasn't Sam, I knew that right away. I came over to the car and looked in. "Yeah, sure, I do. How are you?" I asked, holding my coat up over my head, trying to keep dry.

"My name's Mark, just in case you forgot."

I smiled and replied, "From the fire pit. What are you doing up here in Langdon on a bad night like this?"

"I was bored. Thought I'd play around on the back roads. Get in, we'll take a drive. It's still early," he said, watching me closely.

I didn't like how that sounded or how he was looking at me.

I was suddenly hit with a memory of a creep asking Kate to go for a ride. We'd been coming out of the movie theater up in Rutland. A crowd was waiting to go in to the next show. As we crossed the parking lot, some guy in a muscle car had slowly driven by. He'd said something like, "Hey gorgeous, let me take you for a ride. Your little sister can come and watch."

Kate had said loudly, "Fuck off."

Now, it was my turn to say "fuck off," but I didn't. Instead, I leaned over and said, "Nah, Sam's calling me in twenty minutes." It was a lie, but I thought he'd back off hearing Sam's name.

Mark didn't look too happy and started to get out of his car. I quickly looked back at the restaurant. Henry was the only one still there, and the kitchen door was opened. Would he be able to hear me if I needed him?

"So, um, Sadie, boys up here tell me you put out real easy," he said as he stood, leaning against the door he'd just closed. "How 'bout you let me be your first official Colton guy, 'kay?"

It was strange; I didn't feel scared, and while the rain was uncomfortable, I wasn't cold. What I felt was anger. "You're a jerk, and you're making me mad," I replied.

"Come on, my back seat's real comfortable." He grabbed my hand and opened the door behind the driver's seat.

From someplace inside my head, I heard Kate again. *"You gotta hit 'em where it counts."* I moved quickly, twisting his hand off of my wrist. I lifted my leg up fast and kneed him hard in the groin. I don't think I'd ever used that much force on anything. He looked surprised as he bent over, his hands covering his privates. Then he stood up, clearly embarrassed and pissed. His hair was dripping wet, and the Colton sweatshirt he wore stuck to him.

"Get out of here!" I yelled and then quickly added, "Or I'll call the police and tell them you tried to force me into your car. That's fricking kidnapping!"

I stepped back and watched him get in behind the wheel.

"Don't fool yourself. Sam's all about getting into your pants, too. Langdon guys told him plenty," he yelled back.

He took off but not before spinning out in the parking lot.

Just then Henry called out from the back of the kitchen, "Sadie, are you okay?"

I waved to him and walked back to my car. *How dumb was I to think that Sam wouldn't hear about 'Wanna get laid, call Sadie Wade.'*

Totally drenched now, I was going to pull out of the parking lot, but a plow truck pulled in and stopped. It was Jackson Larson. We both rolled down our windows.

"Hey, cuz," he called out. "It's all black ice on the roads at the higher elevations. We're going through a ton of salt. Wait till you see a town plow go by, then get in right behind it."

I nodded and replied, "Okay, I will. Thanks, Jackson." My father and his mother were somehow related from way back when.

I didn't have to wait long before a town plow went by. The salt swirled out of the back — little, white crystals scattering all over the road as we started the climb towards the turn off to Tabor Road. The rain hitting the windshield was icing up. I turned the blades on faster.

Sam's different. But was he really, though? He'd first grabbed my arm when I was walking with Dede. I hadn't forgotten that.

Pulling up to the trailer, I turned the car off. My father stood in the window — clearly relieved that I was home. But the thing that just happened with Mark had rattled me. Sitting there, hearing the ice pellets hit the top and sides of the car reminded me of the night I'd first walked to Shay's. Were the lies and ugliness of the Langdon boys — now along with this Colton guy — the norm? How about the violence I'd seen from the men chasing down the boy in Tennessee?

Yet, as my father called out to me from the steps, "Come in, get warm!" I thought of all the guys at the restaurant and now Dominic Sousa. They were completely different. *Maybe I'm just too young or dumb to figure it out.*

Chapter 17

I t snowed after the ice storm, and the slopes were packed again. All the inns and hotels were filled to capacity. Jeannie had me out front bussing tables. It was my first time.

Alice's father took my hand when I reached in to clear his salad plate. Now he stood and slightly bowed. Alice looked up at me and said, "Oh no, so sorry, Sadie."

I smiled and shook my head, "It's okay."

His wife explained, "He taught dance in New York. You may be in for a lesson."

"Like this?" I asked as he arranged our hands. The old man nodded silently, then stepped back and to the side as he led me around.

People at the other tables nearby were watching us. It was apparent that Mr. Chasen was reliving a dance class and I was one of his pupils.

Jeannie appeared and tapped Mr. Chasen's shoulder. Seamlessly, he let go of me and took her hands. Jeannie was able to guide him back to his seat and say, "Mr. Chasen, our lesson is over, your food has arrived."

Alice, her boyfriend, and her parents settled in to enjoy their wedding anniversary dinner.

Jeannie leaned into me and said, "You were sweet with him. Dementia's so hard."

I took the tray of salad plates and walked into the kitchen. *How does Kate deal with this kind of stuff at the nursing home? It's so sad!*

Before the night was over, I had to run a credit card out to a couple who'd accidentally left it and then search underneath several banquettes for a lost retainer. Besides all of that, Zoe's dad came to pick her up. She'd been sick in the bathroom and needed my help to walk out the back door.

"Oh, poor girl, let's get you settled in the back seat." Zoe's dad spoke to her like she was a little girl. He thanked me and drove away.

Washing dishes is way more predictable. I walked back into Shay's. Plus, I liked the control I had back there in the kitchen. School and my flashbacks — along with all the other recent stuff — made me feel like I had no control at all.

Chapter 18

I thought about calling Sam to find out how he felt about me, especially after what that loser, Mark, had said. That definitely would be me putting myself out there. But for right now, ignoring Sam's text messages and not picking up when he called was easier. It was my way of keeping that night from being spoiled by all the usual lies swirling about me. I hadn't told anybody about Mark, and I didn't plan to. I did decide to open up to Kate about Tristan and Derek and the rumors about me at Langdon High. She was pissed off.

"What were you thinking, Sadie, keeping all this from me? That I didn't care? Are you crazy? We're sisters, most of all."

We were shoveling the front stoop and the path to where she always parked the Honda. Underneath the snow was a layer of ice, and we were trying to chip away at it before spreading sand. It was a mess.

"I know you care. It's just that I didn't want you to make things worse." I wiped my nose and looked over at her. Kate was using the edge of the shovel like a pick ax and getting nowhere. Her frustration was growing, especially now with what I'd just told her.

"Jesus Christ, if one more *'Wanna get laid? call Sadie Wade'* turns up, I'm going to blast that school and everyone in it, I swear."

"Kate! Don't take the Lord's name in vain! Or threaten the school like that. It could land you in jail."

She turned back to the path and attacked the ice with all her might. But she finally gave up and said, "All this is bullshit. Let's stop and go pick up Carson then get pizza. You still have that gift certificate?"

I smiled and replied, "Only if we can play foosball while we wait."

THE NEXT NIGHT AT WORK, Stephen called over to me with impatience, "There's a version of Gronk outside the goddamn door, Sadie, go!"

His prep area had six plates lined up with garnishes. The restaurant was hopping.

"What are you saying, Stephen? Please, in English and without the swearing." I held my own with him. For some reason, he took it from me and nobody else.

"Okay, Angel, there's a monster of a dude outside wearing a Colton football jacket. He wants you to come out."

Sam must be here, out near the dumpster. I'd ignored over a week's worth of his messages and now he'd driven up from Colton. I looked over at where Corey was loading the big dishwasher. He nodded and said, "Go, I'm good."

I grabbed my sweatshirt from the peg by the walk-in and stuck my tongue out at Stephen. As the screen door banged shut, I heard him say, "Little Angel-ass bitch."

Sam was standing there, looking even bigger than I remembered. I gave him a wave and searched his face for traces of that sweet guy back on the bench, holding my hand at the fire.

He took a step back when I reached him, and we both turned towards the parking lot. People were climbing out of a big SUV in front of Shay's front door. The driver then pulled up into an open space not far from us. We waited for the man to pass by.

"Hi," I said, awkwardly. The cold air felt good to me, but the dumpster smelled. "Want to come in, maybe, and…" My voice trailed off. This was about the only semi-private place at Shay's right now.

He shook his head and said, "I've been texting and calling you, but I got nothing back. What's up, Sadie? I kind of thought we had something going on."

All the magic I'd felt that night at the fire, along with how I'd described him to Kate and Karen, flooded me. "We do have something, but I know you've heard some things about me from the guys in Langdon."

"That's why I came. Are they true?" he asked, his eyes focused on me.

In my mind, in that place where I held our night safe from all the bull about me, I'd imagined Sam defending me against any lies he heard because he'd know they couldn't be true. He would know based on the fire that I wasn't like that at all.

"No, it's not true. None of it is!" I replied in alarm.

"Come on, Sadie, shit like that doesn't just come out of nowhere. Something you did or maybe you do with guys when you're alone with them…" He paused and looked at me intently. "They had a lot to say."

In that moment, I realized I had nothing to lose because I didn't have anything 'special' with him after all. In a pissed-off voice, I replied, "Oh, I get it. You're not here to see me, really. You're just here to back up what those jerks told you."

I turned to go back into the kitchen.

"Sadie, tell me the truth!" he called out.

"I just did!" I paused before stepping back into the kitchen. "Now go, I'm working." But I wasn't quite done and walked back to him. "Don't you get it, Sam? If you're asking me if '*Wanna get laid, call Sadie Wade,*' is true, then that night and how we spent our time TALKING meant nothing…to either of us."

I left him standing there and slammed the kitchen screen door.

Eugene turned, and asked, "What the hell's wrong?"

Stephen looked up then glanced out the door.

"Nothing," I replied.

"Did that asshole out there do something to her?" Eugene asked Stephen.

Stephen nodded and wiped his hands on his apron.

"I'm gonna kick the living shit out of that bastard," Eugene said as he put down his tongs and started for the door.

But Stephen held him back. "It's got to be both of us, and we need Bart. Shit, the kid's as big as Gronk."

"No!" I yelled. They both looked over at me. "Let him go."

Corey asked, "Are you okay?"

"Yeah, but I don't want to go out on the floor tonight. Will you?"

He nodded and reached for the Tupperware of cookies I'd brought him earlier. "Want one?"

I grabbed two, took off my sweatshirt, and hung it up. *This is my place, and these are my people.*

Jeannie came through the door and walked over, ready to tell us what she needed. But she stopped. She could see something was up with me and asked, "Hey, what's wrong?"

I took a bite of the cookie and wiped my mouth. "Guys aren't really worth it. It's like you said — they have to make you feel bad for them to feel good, right?"

Jeannie hesitated for a moment and replied, "Some guys, yes, Sadie, but not all guys."

I left Shay's that night feeling empty. It was an old feeling I hadn't felt in a while. It was hard to see the road through my tears but I knew my way. Sam asking me if those things were true was just as hurtful as him believing them.

Chapter 19

The very next day, Kate and I were on Tabor Road, heading down to the grocery store in Langdon, when I saw Dominic Sousa's Volvo driving toward us.

All that stuff with Sam and Mark had occupied a lot of my thoughts recently. I wasn't ready for this.

I looked over at Kate and said, "Oh, boy. I know this guy. Please pull over." I put my hand out, and Dominic stopped.

"Be right back." I quickly got out, ran over to his driver's side window, and said, "That's Kate, my sister. I haven't told her anything, and, I guess, now's the time. She's going to blow. Be ready."

Kate watched us talk then motioned for me to get back in the car. "What's going on Sadie? Make it quick."

"Okay. This guy is a Vermont detective, investigating a missing girl from Goodlettsville. He wants to talk to the old man because he was at The Diamondback where, I think — I do not know for sure — this girl disappeared from."

"That's no big deal, Dad won't have anything to offer. It's fine," she said, ready to go.

"He's working with the Tennessee police." I took a deep breath. "But Kate, I also told him about my time in the station wagon and how I saw those men beat up the boy." At her alarmed expression, I looked away. "I had to! I'm just as guilty as people who leave the scene of a crime. This detective said he'd find out what he could. We talked about it at the restaurant. " I'd been spitting out my words and gesturing with my hands. I wiped my mouth and waited.

Her explosion didn't disappoint. Kate started to open her mouth then shut it. Instead, she opened the Honda's car door.

Before she went at him, she turned back to me and asked, in an alarming voice, "So, you told him about us being down there, too?"

"Yes, but..." She turned towards Dominic. I yelled, "It was all about the boy, the boy who got beat up! I never mentioned Carson, Kate! I knew enough not to mention Carson!"

Immediately, Kate pounced on Dominic Sousa. "You interviewed my sister? She's a minor. Who the hell do you think you are?" she yelled.

Dominic climbed out of the car and held up his hands. "Whoa. I didn't interview her at all. She asked me to find out some information with my counterpart in Tennessee. That's all. It was no big deal."

Kate glanced back at me and then turned to Dominic and replied, "No big deal, you say? I got a four-year-old son who is not, I repeat, IS NOT going to get taken away by his father who is a real asshole and predator. If he gets wind that he got me pregnant and he's got a boy up here, so help me God. Whatever business you have with my father, it better not involve my kid or us." She pointed at me then tapped her chest.

Dominic looked over at me and then back at Kate. He was, I think, trying to read the situation. He replied, "The statute of limitations is on your side, especially if you were a minor. You can still press charges."

Kate took a deep breath, winding up. Her face was completely red as she yelled, "You idiot! I wasn't a minor, and it wasn't rape. I fucked him for all the necessary stuff, you know, like food — " she was shouting at him from three feet away — "and for goddamn car parts so we could get the hell out of Bible land!"

Kate abruptly left him and came back to the car. She threw open her door and bent down. "Do not speak to him ever again, got it? No more Tennessee bullshit, okay, Sadie?"

I nodded, unsure if Dominic Sousa would ever want to speak to me again, anyway.

We started to pull away, but not before I heard her yell to him, "Don't fuck with me!"

I tried to turn around just long enough to see what he was doing. I think, but wasn't sure, Dominic Sousa did a K-turn right there in the middle of Tabor Road. Who could blame him?

Kate was a fighter, but just now she'd been over the top. I was sure, too, that any chance I had that the detective would want to help me was gone.

Chapter 20

It was just past 2:30 p.m. My book bag was where I'd left it, near the couch, tucked under the coffee table. I reached in and felt for his card. *'Dominic Sousa, Detective, Bureau of Criminal Investigation.'* I laid the card on the table and sat down. I remembered all the times Father Ray had preached about honesty and temptation and lies. How the Lord knew what was inside each of us at all times and how, no matter what, he would forgive us. There was a verse from Proverbs he often recited: *"Whoever speaks the truth gives honest evidence, but a false witness utters deceit."*

Last night, Carson had stood outside in the cold, calling for a stray cat he'd seen. He'd been worried and had kept asking all of us, "Where's the pussy cat?" My father had gotten a box and put a blanket and an open can of tuna in it.

"If the pussy cat is still around, it'll find the box on the steps and climb in. We'll check first thing when we wake up." Dad had finally carried Carson down the hall to his little bed.

WHEN I WOKE UP TODAY, the cat was my first thought. I went to our door and looked out. There was no sign — the tuna hadn't been touched. I called out, "Where are you, pussy cat, where?" Nothing.

At school, in my morning class with Mr. Banks, I was doodling while he was reading aloud in his deep, rich voice. He asked us a question — to define what a hyperbole was, because the short story he was reading was chock full of them. I raised my hand, and he called on me. But I froze, my brain like mush. He gave me time, but I drew a blank. He then called on someone else. Defining literary terms and using the vocabulary words he introduced weekly was one of my strengths. If you used the words correctly in conversation, he'd give you extra credit. I had lots of extra credit.

Today's new "R" word — he was making his way through the alphabet — was up on the board. I wrote it and its definition down, but then I spaced out again and started to draw random stuff on my notepad. I looked down at the pathetic kitty I'd just sketched. Beside the kitty, I'd written, *"Where's your pussy?"* I wrote that again — this time my pen pressing down hard into the paper, causing it to tear. I was becoming agitated. *Why had I written that?* I knew I didn't mean pussy, as in cat, at all.

I quickly put the paper in my notebook because it was time to move on to 4th period. As I was leaving class, two idiots grabbed Paige McNally from behind. She had something they wanted. While she was laughing, they tried to grab her again. But I imagined all sorts of things, like she wasn't laughing at all but trying to get away. Suddenly, I felt

light-headed and my chest was tightening up. The girls'
bathroom was just down the hallway. I ran to it.

Once inside, I moved to the sink and turned on the
water. The cold water on my face helped, and I drank,
cupping the water from the faucet. A girl walked out from
the stall and said, matter of factly, "Looks like an anxiety
attack. You have to breathe. Do the box."

I had no idea what she was talking about, but I watched
her. "Here, I'll do it with you. Ready, let's go… See the box,
we're inhaling as we go up one side, hold it as we go across,
then exhale as we come down the other side and hold once
more." She put her hands down and looked at me expectantly. I hadn't done it with her, only watched.

"It's corny, but it works, at least for me. Come on, you
look a little better, but this will help."

This time I did it with her. I smiled when we were done.
"It did kind of help."

"I get anxiety attacks a lot. It's not fun. See you around."
She scooted out.

I never went on to 4th period. Instead, I hunkered down
in the furthest stall and took out the paper. I replayed that
last night in Tennessee in slow motion, but this time with
the words I'd heard. I then went to the office and called
Kate to tell her I didn't feel well and that I needed her to
come get me. It was a lie, but then, it really wasn't a lie.

On the way home in her car, I wanted to open up about
what I'd just remembered. But I held back, because Kate
had made her position clear. As we passed Shay's on the
left, Jeannie and Henry were outside working together to
replace a bulb in the lantern near the front door.

I glanced over at Kate as we started the climb towards
home. What just happened was too significant to bury.
Doing nothing about the boy was over. It was time to act.

Kate dropped me at home and left for the nursing home. Carson would be at preschool for another hour or so. Dad was at Chet's, probably smoking weed since I didn't have to work tonight and I was the one babysitting Carson. The trailer was quiet. I sat down on the couch.

The right thing would be to call Dominic. But the right thing would make things more complicated for all of us. I recited part of the verse again in the quiet of the kitchen. "Whoever speaks the truth gives honest evidence…" I picked up his card and moved to the sink where our cell reception was the strongest. I dialed his number.

"Hello Dominic, It's me, Sadie Wade from the restaurant. I remembered something else about that night in Tennessee with the boy."

"Hey Sadie. I've been wanting to talk to you. I'm sorry, but I can't give you any information on him. There just wasn't anything they could find. It's been some time since you asked and…"

I interrupted him. "I think what I remembered today, at school, might be important." My heart began pounding. This was the first time I was saying it all out loud.

"Oh, okay."

"You got your trusty little notebook with you?" I asked.

"Yep, I do. I'm just not sure if any of this new information you're giving me will make a difference. Like I told you — no assaults with the criteria you gave me were reported."

"Please, just listen to me. You might be…" I turned back to face the kitchen table. The box for the stray cat was on top of it. I took a deep breath and started, "Before those men were starting to hit the boy, they were going after him and he was trying to push them away. I could see him and them down on the bottom of the ramp, off the back of the bar. They were making their way towards our car. He wasn't very big, compared to them, and he was skinny.

Anyway, both of the guys were grabbing him from behind. The boy fell, got up, and tried to run, again. That's when they started to hit him.

"Today, I suddenly remembered that one of the guys was saying, '*Where's your pussy?*' over and over to the kid. I must have fallen asleep under my blanket not long after that, because I don't remember much else until later, when they were long gone."

"Okay, Sadie, I've written this down, but honestly..."

I interrupted him again and said, "Dominic, don't you see... What if that girl you're looking for is that boy, my boy? The man kept saying '*Where's your pussy?*' It wasn't '*You're a pussy.*' There's a big difference." I paused and walked to the front door and then back again, touching the top of the box as I passed. "Could your missing girl and my boy be the same person?"

Dominic replied slowly, sounding cautious, "It might be possible, and it could be the connection, Sadie. I never showed you a picture of Lucia Alvarez. I can text you one right now. Maybe you'd recognize..."

"Or you could check the station wagon out back here — it's a nineteen-eighty-eight Chevy Caprice. I think there's some stuff in there from that night that might be..." I looked out at the junk cars and the two trucks lined up in the yard. I could see my footprints in the snow from a few minutes ago. "Well, it could prove a whole lot if the DNA lasts."

"Wait. I'm not following you."

I slowed down, trying to remember that morning after the fight. "When I woke up after it all happened with the men and the boy, my father was snoring in the car and it smelled really bad. It was just starting to be daylight, and I could see fog above the swamp at the other end of the parking lot. I wanted to get out and go look for rocks and feathers. I had my Polly Pockets, and I was into building little fairy stuff for them. I climbed out and found some rocks. But one rock I picked up had stuff on it. That's when I saw a bandana under the front tire. I grabbed it and covered the rock with it. I still got yucky stuff on me. I think now it could have been blood."

Dominic's voice changed. He sounded excited and asked, "And that's still in the station wagon?"

"Yes. We've never driven the car since getting back from Tennessee. It's a piece of junk, and it's like a glaring reminder of my father's fall from grace. It's right here, I'm looking at it now." I moved the little curtain above the sink aside. "I came home early today, and while Kate was getting ready for work, I went out to it. I didn't touch anything. I knew I shouldn't. But, yeah, a few rocks, the bandana, and my blanket are still in the backseat. I must have taken my Polly Pockets out when we got home."

"Holy shit," Dominic whispered. "Excuse me, Sadie, but this could be huge. What can you tell me about the two men? Would you be able to identify them?"

"Nah, never. But I do remember they weren't dressed like the tent church men."

"How so?"

"They wore dark shirts, not the usual light or white-collared shirts. I remember one of the men pulled a hankie from his pocket — maybe it's the one out in the car — and wrapped it around his knuckles after he hit the boy. The other guy had really short hair, like a new hair cut because I could see how white the back of his neck was along his hair line. At one point, he came close to the side of the car. I want to say his shirt had some writing on it."

"Were they White men? And how old would you say?

"Yes, White, and I'd say old, but I don't know."

"The age of your father?"

"At least."

"Let me finish writing this down and sit with it for a second."

"Yeah, sure." I moved the frying pan on the stove over into the sink and turned on the hot water. I put my cell on speaker and placed it on the windowsill between Carson's little cactus plants.

Suddenly, I said, "You need to leave me and Kate out of it. You promise, Dominic?"

Kate reaming out Dominic was still fresh in my mind, and I was sure it was still in his mind, too. She'd told him more about Carson's father, in the middle of Tabor Road, than she'd ever told us.

"I'll do whatever it takes to protect you, but this, what you've just told me today? This takes it to a whole new level. First thing, we'll want to dust the car, run finger prints and DNA analysis, and see what comes up. You'll all have to be a part of that — prints and DNA swabs. We'll need to discount all family members."

I hoisted myself up onto the countertop and replied, "The car is a piece of junk, that won't bother any of us. Carson wasn't even born, so there's no need to do him. That's good. The problem is Kate. She told me to never talk to you again. I've gone against her." The weight of my betrayal hit me. *What have I done?*

It seemed like Dominic understood what I was feeling because he replied, "You've done the right thing here, Sadie. You alone may have given a cold, missing child's case a new direction. I understand what's at stake with Kate. I get that. She's a mother, protecting her child. There will be a way to do this and keep her and Carson out of it. I'll make it a priority."

His words were reassuring and made me feel better.

"Is Kate there now?" he asked.

"No, at work. Nobody's here."

"Just so I get it straight, Kate and Carson live with you and your father?"

"Well, sometimes Kate stays at her boyfriend Drew's place, but not always."

"Got it. They're pretty serious?"

I laughed for the first time all day. "No, no, I wouldn't say that. He's a 'Royal Asshole.' But, you know, I think she gets lonely and he's around."

"Ah, got it. Okay, so here's what has to happen. No one can get near the station wagon, at all. Can you make sure of that?"

"Yes. No one's been near it for a long time, and there's no reason to go in it now."

"Good, that's good. I'd like to meet with your father and Kate as soon as possible to tell them what needs to happen. You can be there, or, if you'd rather not be, that's okay, too. I'll be with a couple of other detectives, and we'll lay out what the procedure will be. It'll be strictly by the book, and I'll reassure them that keeping Carson out of this is very important."

"Okay, Dominic. It just gets even more complicated because Kate hasn't ever told my father or me that Brother Ron from Tennessee is Carson's father. So, yeah, it's going to be an awful mess. Plus, if there's one thing Kate despises, it's surprises. She's not good with them."

Chapter 21

I was growing anxious by the hour, waiting for Dominic Sousa to come to the trailer with the other police and tell my father and Kate all about the station wagon and what may be in it. I'd hardly slept since we'd last spoken.

Kate had come in last night feeling pretty good. "My car's at Drew's. One of you is going to have to give me a ride to get it in the morning."

My father whispered to me, "She's been drinking some."

Kate was washing up and brushing her teeth. I debated going into the bathroom and telling her about Dominic Sousa. But I chickened out.

LATER, AT THE RESTAURANT, I worried about it even more. So much so that I forgot things — like where the Belgian beer and the Guinness Stout were stored in the basement. It took me forever to bring it up to Julie. And then I'd stood in the office, trying to remember what Jeannie had just told me to get for the ladies' bathroom.

She'd gone by and peeked in. "What am I getting, Jeannie?"

"Paper towel roll!"

A LITTLE GIRL LOOKED UP AT ME when I entered the bathroom. "Hi there. Just adding paper towels." I smiled down at her as I unlocked the cabinet.

A woman from one of the stalls called out, "Lilly, why don't I hear you washing your hands right now?"

Raising my eyebrows at the girl, I asked, "You need a little help?"

She nodded as she stood on her tippy toes trying to reach the basin.

I turned on the faucet and tested the water. I also squirted some pink soap into her palm. "Here you go. Tell me when you're done, and I'll turn on the water again for you to rinse."

Lilly was small, maybe just a year or two older than Carson. Something was off about her, though. I watched her soap up. She was being very thorough, washing in between her fingers and over the back of each hand.

It was her eyebrows. She had none and her hat, a bright yellow knitted cap, was pulled down, completely covering her head. *She's sick,* I thought.

At that moment, she smiled up at me, and I asked, "Ready to rinse?"

She nodded again.

When she was done, I grabbed some paper towels off of the new roll I'd just installed and reached for her hands. "Here, Lilly — that's your name, isn't it? Let's dry your hands."

From the stall, the woman — her mother — I think, called out, "Oh, thank you so much. I have new leggings I'm trying to put on and I've twisted my skirt all around. Lilly, say thank you!"

I knelt down on the bathroom floor and held Lilly's hands in mine, the paper towel growing wet from her hands. Our eyes met. She had green eyes just like mine.

Just then the woman opened the stall door and asked, "Everything okay?"

I withdrew my hands and stood up. The little girl said, "Mommy, can I have dessert?"

Her mother seemed to hesitate, then replied, "Not until you've thanked this nice girl for helping you."

Lilly suddenly wrapped her arms around my waist and hugged me tight.

"Wow! This is definitely a big thank you!" I said and lightly touched her hat.

We all left the bathroom. I stood and watched Lilly walk down the hallway into the big dining room. Her mother briefly turned back and smiled at me.

ON THE DRIVE HOME, I didn't like how I felt, at all. Dread about Dominic Sousa and lack of sleep made my body ache and my chest feel tight. It hurt to take deep breaths. My hands felt shaky, like how I imagined those big energy drinks made you feel. I turned on to Tabor Road.

LILLY HAD COME BACK TO SEE ME before the night was over. Once again, Stephen had said, "Somebody's out there for you."

I'd known it wasn't Sam. We hadn't spoken since that night, and no matter what Zoe said to try and get me to reconsider, I wasn't interested. Kate thought it showed good judgment on my part. Now, I was scared of what she would think of my judgment in trusting Dominic Sousa.

When I'd walked outside, a man had been holding Lilly in his arms just past the dumpster. He'd looked uncomfortable when I'd walked up to them. Lilly had been wearing pjs under her winter coat, and she had a stuffie in her arms — a brown dog with floppy ears. The bright yellow cap had been on her head.

"Lilly, hi! What's going on?" I'd asked and lightly took hold of one of her pink, footie-pajama-covered feet. I'd looked at the man, questioningly.

He'd smiled briefly and said, "Well, Lilly couldn't quite go to sleep until she had you, um, well, she wants you to bless her stuffie, right, Lilly?"

"No, Daddy, that's not what I said. I said…" She'd grown shy and leaned into her father. She'd looked smaller in his arms. "I said I wanted you to pray over my puppy like you prayed over me and get the bad stuff out."

I'd shaken my head. "I don't know what you mean?"

"'Member when you held my hands and I heard your prayer in the bathroom? Puppy is sick too." She'd held the puppy out to me. Her father had glanced at me nervously.

Just then I remembered Father Ray's exact words, the ones I couldn't remember in the clearing on Christmas day. I'd reached over and put my left hand on top of her stuffie and the other hand on Lilly's arm. Closing my eyes, I'd said, "This prayer, offered in faith, will make the sick person…" I'd paused. "And puppy-dog — well, the Lord will raise them up."

Lilly had quickly brought the doggie up to her mouth and kissed it. "Yay, Puppy!" Lilly's father had reached into his pocket and asked, "Can I give you something for your time?" He'd seemed unsure of what to do.

I'd shaken my head. "No, please. Lilly is a doll, I'm so glad we met!"

THE TRAILER WAS QUIET and, for once, not so cold when I came in and got ready for bed. I was restless, though, and couldn't sleep. I was positive I hadn't said a prayer to Lilly in the bathroom when I'd dried her hands. *I thought it,* but I hadn't said it out in the open like that. Besides, wouldn't her mother have heard it, too, and said something?

It had been fear, I thought, on the father's face as he'd held Lilly in the back of the restaurant. Sitting up on the couch, I tried to imagine the magnitude of fear a parent would have for their sick child. But it was impossible. I hoped, like the tent church days, that my laying on of hands would add to all the other prayers out there and heal her. Lilly deserved a good life.

I stood up and poured myself a glass of water. I sipped it at the sink, leaning against the counter. My own fears were plenty lately. The biggest one that had consumed me on Christmas day had been the fear that Kate was dying. I also remembered the fear I'd felt outside of Tristan's truck — being helpless and stranded. I wouldn't wish that kind of fear on anybody. The recent flashbacks of the boy's fear were having an effect on me, too — like nearly paralyzing me at the party with Sam.

Getting back on the couch and rearranging the pillow and blanket, it occurred to me that at the time, I hadn't been afraid of Sam believing all that bad stuff about me. I'd ended up being totally wrong on that.

Kate's fears — they were front and center. Her fears over Carson made her so tough, so guarded, that it cut her off from doing things and meeting new people. Then there was Dad. I felt like his fears were legit because he'd seen bad stuff firsthand. Did Karen have fears? I didn't think so, but I'd never asked her.

How about Jeannie? She'd once told me she was waiting to meet the right man to start a family with and that she'd had a lot of false starts with the guys she'd dated. She had worries that maybe the right one wouldn't come along.

I wondered how it felt to live without fear. Sam and my twin brothers came to mind, because they each seemed fearless. But were they really without fear? I bet right now all three of them were scared that the college they most wanted to play football for wasn't going to come through.

That brought me to my mom. Her biggest fear, at least from what I could tell when I was around her, was that she shouldn't have left me here on Tabor Road. I think that's what fed her guilt.

Turning onto my side, I tried to sleep again, but all I did was toss and turn some more. Jeannie told me I needed to stop drinking so much soda because of all that sugar. She'd die if she saw the amount of sugar I'd put in the sauce pan for the hot chocolate tonight. Maybe that was why I couldn't sleep and my hands shook.

I wrote all these thoughts down in my notebook and then tried to sketch Lilly in her footie pajamas, holding the stuffed animal. Above her little head, I drew hands — lots of them.

The clock on the stove read 2:00 a.m. I tucked my notebook back in my bookbag and rearranged the pillow and blanket. Right before sleep finally came, I thought back to Kate and my own fears. That she was going to hate me for getting in touch with Dominic Sousa again.

Chapter 22

Kate and my father tried to wake me for school, but I wouldn't budge. Finally, around 11:00 a.m., I managed to go to the bathroom. There was a note on the kitchen table: *Up in White River at Dad's appointment. Carson has all day pre-k. Karen's going to check on you.* This time I climbed into Kate's bed and fell back to sleep.

"HELLO...? IT'S ONLY ME. Sadie! You awake?" I'd been in and out of sleep for some time. I shuffled out to the living room. There was Karen, holding a saucepan of something.

"Homemade broccoli and cheddar soup, baby, your favorite. You don't feel well, huh?"

"Yeah, it's weird — all I've done is sleep. Now I'm starved. Thank you for making this."

I reached to take it from her, but Karen said, "I'll put it on the stove for you. It just needs a couple of minutes to warm up. Go sit."

I turned and watched her reach for a bowl and a spoon. She started to stir the soup.

Karen's full name was Karen Bobar. It appeared on a banner in the school gym since she had scored a thousand points for Langdon's basketball team. I couldn't remember what year she'd accomplished that, but my father would know it exactly. He told us how she used to glide over the court, the best player he'd ever seen in person, male or female. She'd gone on to play college basketball, but I didn't remember where. She was tall and thin and graceful, towering over a lot of men, especially my dad.

"Can I ask you something?"

Glancing my way, Karen replied, "Sure, baby, what is it?"

"Well, I've been thinking about what people are afraid of, you know, the bigger things than just spiders or like running out of gas."

Karen took off her coat and draped it over the back of one of the kitchen chairs. "Yeah? That sounds like some pretty heavy duty thinking going on."

"Like my mom. She's always been afraid that her decision to leave me here wasn't a good one. Do you remember that about her?" I asked.

Karen stopped stirring and turned off the stove. She put the lid on the pan and leaned against the counter, giving me her full attention. "I was still living in Chicago when Lynn was here. It wasn't until you were in kindergarten and she was already gone that I came home. What a hard decision she had to make, huh?"

I nodded and replied, "I think she'll always have that fear, you know, that she made a mistake. Even though I've told her it wasn't a mistake."

"Maybe, Sadie, you're just going to have to show her it was the right decision by doing well — in school, and outside in the real world, with whatever you decide to do after you graduate."

"Yeah, I know what you mean." I moved my father's weekly swap pages off of the placemat and brushed some crumbs into my hand. I quickly got up and threw them into the garbage bin.

When I sat back down, I asked Karen, "Are there things you, I mean, do you have any fears?" I laughed. "Besides those skunks that come sashaying across your yard every spring!"

She picked up the bowl and ladled some soup into it. She'd already found some saltines in the cupboard. Walking the bowl and crackers over to me, she replied, "I'll tell you, Sadie, when my parents died — my very White, adoptive parents — and I came back here to where I grew up, totally sheltered, I had some fears. I thought, 'What's a Black woman doing, living all alone on a remote, dead-end road in the Whitest state there is. Was I crazy?' But, as I settled back in, making changes to the house, getting a good job, and having one of my high school buddies, Jarod Wade, still living out here, raising not one, but two beautiful daughters, I let go of that fear."

I nodded and said, "So, you're not afraid of anything, anymore?"

She walked back to the stove and lifted the saucepan, moving it to the sink. She turned back to me.

"Oh, there's always the fear of dying — for most every-body, I think. That's the ultimate fear. But I have to tell you, after my mother died and my father was on his death-bed, he said to me, more than once, 'All my fear is gone, all of it.'"

"Did that make it easier for you when he died?" I asked.

"I wouldn't say easier for me, but for him, I know it did." Karen stood up and reached for her coat. "I'll get my pan tomorrow. For now, have your soup and curl up on the couch. Watch some funny cartoons. Jarod and Kate will be home soon."

I reached over and grabbed her hand. "I'd hug you, Karen, but my breath is really, really bad."

She held on to my hand and gave it a squeeze. "Feel better, beautiful girl. Call me if you need anything."

As I heard her back out of the driveway, I ate a spoonful of the cheesy soup. I couldn't taste it at all.

Chapter 23

T wo of the detectives took a seat on our couch. The third one was Dominic Sousa. He grabbed a straight-back chair from the kitchen table and turned it towards us.

When the cars first pulled up, I had quickly gone out onto the steps to tell them that my sister might get really mad that they were there. Dominic and I exchanged glances, remembering how she yelled holy hell at him not long ago.

Now Dominic started to speak, looking right at Kate. "Your sister has vital information and possibly direct evidence for the FBI — these gentlemen here with me. They're federal agents from the Tennessee branch office. They're here to further their investigation into the disappearance of Lucia Alvarez, a sixteen-year-old who went missing in two thousand and six. There's a possibility that

the boy Sadie witnessed getting beat up, is, in fact, her. We
appreciate Sadie's courage in coming forward, even though
her family may be upset. Mr. Wade, thank you for agreeing
to this."

As introductions were being made all around, I watched
Kate. She was standing to the left of the door, her arms
crossed tightly at her chest. Red blotches were appearing
along her neck. She looked over at Dad and me, wide-eyed,
like we were traitors. One of her legs started to shake, and
she reached down to stop it.

My father gently touched my knee and whispered, "It's
going to be okay." Dominic stopped speaking and looked at
the other two detectives.

The older one with gray hair and a goatee said, "Ms.
Wade, I understand it's important that your son, Carson
Wade, not be mentioned in any of our investigative work
here. Your father made that very clear. This can be done, as
long as we have your absolute assurance that your son has
never been in that Chevy or touched the evidence we're
taking for further forensic analysis. One of our first steps
will be to eliminate all family members."

Kate asked, shaking her shoulders, "Evidence? From the
station wagon out back? I have no idea what's going on. I
can't tell you one way or another because I'm totally clue-
less. Sadie? Dad?"

Dad looked at her in a way I'd forgotten he could look;
like he was in charge, and there was nothing to worry about.
"There are a few things in the back of the station wagon
that Sadie remembers putting there when I left her in the
car at The Diamondback. When Detective Sousa called, I
told him about Carson, how we have to keep him out of all
this. But we can still help. Sadie wants to, needs to see this
through."

I listened to Dad from where I was sitting on the floor with one of my knees tucked up under my chin. When he stopped speaking, I shifted my leg and looked straight at Kate. The shock of our betrayal was written across her face. I wanted to scream out that this was the right thing to do. In a shaky voice, I said, "That night and what I witnessed has been eating away at me. I know you said…that you didn't want any of this to come out, but I couldn't forget it and I shouldn't forget him!" In a much stronger voice, I pleaded, "Please, Kate, don't be mad. That boy was somebody, and he mattered!" A floodgate of emotions spilled out of me — part anger that it had taken me this long to stand up to her but part fear, too. Would she ever forgive me? Lastly, I felt relief. *Finally, something was being done for the boy. I could let go of the guilt.*

My father handed me his hankie; I wiped my eyes and blew my nose. Dominic gave me a slight nod.

Kate wasn't happy. She leaned back and hit her head slowly against the paneling — one, two, three times. She was winding up, getting ready to blow. She looked around at everybody, clearly trying to figure out who to go after, who was responsible for risking her life with Carson.

My father moved quickly out of his chair to stand at her side. His voice was urgent as he said, "There's no way Carson is in jeopardy, Kate. No one will ever find out, because there's never been any reason for anyone to think he exists. Carson is ours."

The way he said, 'Carson is ours,' was strong and clear. My father repeated it again, this time in a whisper, "He's ours."

"You're sure about this?" she asked.

"Yes." He returned to his seat near me.

Dominic started to talk, and for some reason, his voice and overall calmness helped bring the tension down. "A van is due here shortly from the Vermont Forensic Laboratory up in Waterbury. With your permission, they'll get the three of you swabbed. It's a long Q-tip that's brushed against the inside of your cheek. The swabs will be sent to the folks down in Tennessee, along with the forensic evidence gathered from the car. This way we'll be able to eliminate you and narrow our focus on the items that Sadie gathered in the parking lot of The Diamondback and then brought into the car.

"Tomorrow morning, we have you scheduled to give depositions at the Rockingham Barracks and get finger printed. Each of you will be interviewed about the events surrounding those two days and nights." He looked at Kate and repeated, "We'll only ask you about the last night and the following morning of the assault that Sadie witnessed. I've left the times of the depositions somewhat open, knowing that your son has school. Before we leave this afternoon, we'll firm up what time is best for you, okay?"

Kate didn't respond. This was a lot to take in.

The gray-haired FBI agent spoke up. "We'd like to have your son swabbed — though his involvement will remain confidential — in case his prints and DNA are in that wagon. I mean, it's pretty close to the trailer, and kids like to explore."

Kate glanced at me and asked, "I've never seen Carson in the car or near it, have you?"

I shook my head. Her voice didn't sound angry or accusatory. Yet, I'd gone behind her back with all this. *It was the right thing to do,* I told myself again.

Dominic Sousa stood up and nodded at my father. "Mr. Wade's told me his grandson hasn't been out there either. He's only four. The car's been locked. I don't think any kid that young can get the keys and unlock a car door with that much snow and branches all around it. There's no reason to have his DNA uploaded into the data base or his name and age documented anywhere in the investigation."

He turned around and opened one of the kitchen cupboards. "Sadie, I'm getting you a glass of water."

Just then we heard a van pull into our driveway. The FBI men stood up to leave, and the older one said, "We'll head to the station wagon and get started. I have to say that you've jump-started a missing child's case from years ago. Thank you, Mr. Wade, Sadie." He reached over and shook my father's hand. When he started to reach down for mine, I quickly stood and shook his hand.

The same agent turned to Kate, but she gave him an icy stare and said, "Make sure all this stays confidential — like our address, names, and whatever else you have that can identify us. There'd better not be any rogue cop down there giving out our information."

He didn't respond and simply left, holding the door open for a man and woman who were coming in.

Dominic, still standing by the kitchen sink, started to put on his coat. "I'm just going to head out and make sure…" His voice trailed off.

Kate replied, "Thanks for shutting them down about Carson." She looked beat. All this had come as a shock, and I suddenly felt as if we'd ambushed her.

He began to say something back, but the woman called out, "This will only take a minute to do."

Chapter 24

After the man and woman had left, Kate closed the door and turned to us. "I need to tell you some things. It's past time, I know." She sighed and moved towards me.

But before Kate began, she picked up my water glass and filled it at the kitchen sink. As she handed it back to me, she bent down and kissed the top of my head and gently placed her hand on the back of my hair, just like she used to do when I was little.

"I'm not mad at you, Sadie. I'm sorry. I should have listened to you all those times you tried to tell me about your memories of the bad men in Tennessee."

She sat down on the floor near me and leaned her back against the chair.

I shrugged my shoulders and replied, "It's okay." Despite downplaying it, I was relieved. My worst fear —

that she wouldn't love me because of what I'd done — was gone.

"But it's not okay," she replied, turning to me. "I want you both to understand why I've been so guarded." She glanced at the old man and asked, "Dad, do you remember that on the way down to Goodlettsville, I turned eighteen on the road?"

Of course, he doesn't remember, I thought. He'd packed us up here in the trailer in two hours, telling us we were going on a road trip. I'd been jumping up and down with excitement, asking him, "Where? Where we going?" until I'd heard Kate say she had a shift that afternoon, waitressing at the Friendly's down in Peddan.

"Call 'em and tell them you're not coming in. We're out of here, heading to Tennessee," Dad had called out, filling a garbage bag of food from the refrigerator. He'd been separating what we could take in the car and what needed to be thrown out in the trash.

Kate had been mad and left the trailer upset. It was her birthday the next day, too, but it had been clear that her job and birthday didn't factor into my father's decision to leave suddenly. I'd found her outside, up behind the tool shed. She'd been crying but had tried to hide it from me.

"Maybe you don't have to come, Kate. It'll be okay if it's just me and Dad," I'd said as she'd wiped away her tears.

"No, Sadie, I'm coming. If I stay home, all I'll do is worry about you."

The next day, somewhere in southern Ohio, we'd bought Twinkies and Kate and I had sung 'Happy Birthday' as Dad filled the gas tank in the station wagon.

I COULD TELL THAT MY FATHER was uncomfortable, but Kate continued, finally ready to tell it all. "Once we got to Tennessee, it wasn't long before your friend got us that fifth wheel to stay in. And I got work at the car wash once we knew Sadie had Hetty to watch her. Dad — your buddy from your unit set you up at that construction site, remember? What were you guys building again?"

"A gun shop in front, and a place for his wife and girls out back," he replied.

"Oh yeah, I remember those girls, they were nice," I said, sitting up and sipping my water.

Kate glanced at me and continued, "You missed the last three, maybe four weeks of school in Vermont, but the schools down there were already out for the summer. We started to go to the tent church, and you guys got right into it. It became the new social thing at the time. But it wasn't my thing at all. It was all pretty boring to me. The abstinence from booze and smoking — that part suited you, Dad, didn't it? It was where your head was at, right?"

My father spoke up. "Benjamin invited me down. He knew I had rolled the truck in that ice storm and was off the wagon. He offered me a chance to get sober, get healthy in my mind and body, and give you girls an opportunity to follow the Lord. Plus, he had work for me. He needed me right away or some other bloke was going to step in."

Kate rolled her eyes and repeated, "A chance at clean living and following the Lord...hmm...not quite the case from what I saw. Father Ray's son, Brother Ron, and a couple of the other so-called deacons were jerks. Basically, those guys were drinking and fooling around with 'outside the tent church women' when it suited them. Brother Ron's wife, Darlene — remember her? She had those two little girls they'd just adopted. She was always running around, deliriously happy because they finally had children.

"The only thing was, Brother Ron thought I looked pretty good in my halter top and cut-off blue jeans washing all those souped-up trucks at the car wash. He started in on me right after I began working there." Kate stopped and stood up. "I need water now."

I watched as she filled a glass at the sink and glanced out the kitchen window. The crime lab people and detectives were still there; we could hear their voices.

She picked up right where she'd left off, looking over at Dad. "Brother Ron took Sadie and me out to the diner over in Hendersonville more than a few times to eat because we needed better food than hot dogs and peanut butter and jelly sandwiches every day. And he paid for the universal joint that you fixed on the station wagon. I said it was me who bought it, but I lied. It was him.

"He told me that he and Darlene couldn't have kids, that he was 'shooting blanks,' so we never used anything. Then the two nights at The Diamondback happened. I finally found you guys and we left. Carson, as far as I'm concerned, is the only good thing that came out of our time down there. But I get it, Sadie, you loved it, except for how it ended. And Dad, you were sober…until you weren't."

The old man stood, smoothed back his hair, and did that thing with his beard when he was uncomfortable — combing through it with his fingers.

I looked back to Kate and said, "And you've been afraid that if Brother Ron finds out he has a kid of his own blood, he'll be up here to take Carson."

Kate nodded, her eyes suddenly tearing up. "He'd have no problem yanking him from me, from us."

My father walked around the kitchen table, appearing agitated. He picked up his coffee cup and rinsed it at the sink then turned and said, "Ron and a couple of those guys he hung with were a bunch of hypocrites, but they were the exception, not like most of the good folks we met."

Now he sat back down and leaned forward. "Here's the thing, Kate. I thought about our time down there right after Detective Sousa called me wanting to come out here. Except for Benjamin, nobody else knew much about us. Before we drove down, I switched out our license plate to one Chet had — from New Jersey — on account of my tickets. Once down there, I got paid in cash, under the table. You did, too, and Sadie was never enrolled in school, so we left no records down there. And Benjamin — he only knew the phone number to the landline that's been turned off for months, right? Hell, all he knew was that we were from the northeast."

Dominic Sousa knocked and opened the trailer's front door. "Sorry to interrupt, but they're done out back. I'm not sure of the turn-around time for the crime lab down in Tennessee. The state's got a real problem with missing teens. I'm sorry I can't be more specific or positive."

Kate walked over to the door and said, "We'll show up in Rockingham about nine a.m. to answer your questions. That's what works best for getting my son to school."

Dominic nodded and looked over at me. "You're a brave girl, Sadie. Thank you, again."

He closed the door. I didn't feel brave, I felt relieved. Everything — about the boy possibly being the girl and who Carson's father was — was now out in the open. Plus, we'd managed to protect Carson from it all.

Both Dad and I started to stand up, but Kate held up her hand and said, "Just so you know, I mentioned Vermont to Brother Ron lots of times and the town of Langdon by name. Told him more than once that I wanted to go home. Carson's not safe, at all."

WHEN KATE GOT HOME THAT NIGHT, I was on the couch still awake. Kate whispered, "Everything good tonight?"

I quietly replied, "Carson, me, and Dad had an arm-wrestling contest. I think Carson may have won. Like legitimately."

Kate moved over to the couch and whispered, "Dad and his wiry arms, you and your skinny ones."

I sat up and said, "Two things happened today that I want to tell you about."

Kate moved my blanket aside and sat. "Are you kidding me, Sadie? Everything happened today."

"No, no, two other things happened beside the obvious that were kind of big, too, at least, I think so."

"Yeah?" Kate asked, now interested.

I smoothed out the blanket and looked directly at her. "The old man took charge for a few minutes there. You noticed it, too, I could tell. He was really in the present and had a clear position on what was going on. He wasn't passive, like he most always is."

Kate nodded, "Yes, I saw that. Maybe it's the new meds he's on. I'll tell them about it at his next appointment at the Veteran's hospital. And the second thing today?"

I turned to her and reached for her hands. Looking directly at her, I said, "The whole time we were down in Tennessee — the whole four months — I was forming the basis of what I believe. The tent church and its teachings did that."

"That's cool," Kate replied, pulling her hands away. "You know, though, that I'm not a convert."

She started to get up, but I held on. "No, don't go, this is the second thing that happened today. Please, hear me out."

She sat back down. "Okay, I'm listening."

"It's right here, feel it." I laid her hand just above my chest, near the hollow of my throat. In a strong voice, I said, "I believe in the Holy Spirit and in God's gift of Salvation. If anything were to happen, I'd spend an eternity in Heaven because I believe in Jesus Christ, the Lord, our Savior. I haven't proclaimed this to anybody, Kate, in a very long time, but I am now to you. I'm recommitting to my faith."

We sat for a moment. Kate didn't tell me I was being ridiculous or that she didn't have time to hear me out. Instead, we listened to the sound of our breathing and she stayed that way, feeling the rise and fall of my chest. I closed my eyes, at total peace within the renewal of my faith.

Chapter 25

The school nurse is wondering if it's mono. She says I need to get tested. Has Dad even gone into the doctor's office, yet? Because we could call Jeannie. She'd come pick me up and keep me at her place until you're back."

"Let me call her. Stay put," Kate replied.

"Don't worry. Not feeling good enough to go anywhere." I turned away from the nurse and lowered my voice. "I might have to take the mono test before I can come back."

I hung up the phone and sat back down, glad that I was the only one in the nurse's office. I felt horrible — tired and achy. My temperature was 101 and maybe going up. Hopefully, Jeannie was home and Kate would reach her.

Within minutes, Jeannie was at the nurse's door, acting like I was near death and the most important person in the world. As soon as we got to her place, she took off my coat and bent down for my boots. I laughed, even though I felt lousy, and said, "Jeannie, I'm sixteen, not three. I can take them off."

"You're all set up in the second bedroom off the kitchen. There are flannel sheets and a big comforter on the bed. Your next Tylenol dose is at noon, which is in three hours. You should drink something. How about some Gatorade? I bought three different kinds as well as orange juice." Jeannie was looking at me expectantly.

I glanced around her place. It was just as I imagined it would be — beautiful, with splashes of color and big, cool furniture. I replied, "Maybe a little something later. Sleep's what I need most."

She nodded, and I followed her into the bedroom. She pulled the shades down and closed the curtains. An over-sized Minnie Mouse t-shirt was laid across the comforter. I looked over at Jeannie and smiled. "Aw, for me to sleep in?"

"Can you believe my father still buys me Minnie Mouse stuff because I loved Disney World so much as a kid? That was thirty years ago!"

"Thanks for all this, Jeannie."

"I'm just glad I was available. Kate has no idea how long they'll be, so get comfortable." She moved to the door and started to close it but then stopped and said, "I want to be able to hear you if you need me, so I'm not closing it all the way."

The bed was big and soft and warm — so different than the couch in the trailer with the thermostat turned down to 60 degrees every night. I stretched out and turned on my side. No matter what I did, my toes stayed fully covered.

When Jeannie had come to the nurse's office, she'd reminded me of Hetty, the woman at the campground in Tennessee. It was the way she'd fussed over me. Hetty used to do that when we'd get ready to walk through the fields to the tent church to meet my dad after his day of work. She'd redo my hair into a braid down the middle of my back and wash my face. Sometimes, if my knees were dirty from playing, she'd wash them, too — all with a purple, lavender-smelling soap. My church dresses were hand-sewn and made out of colorful paisley and Indian prints. I looked different than the other little girls but nobody said a thing. Hetty was as close to God as anyone could be.

She had crystals and read palms and often said, "True believers keep all options open." Once she told me a man had been struck down in the middle of the last field we walked through on the way to the tent church. He'd been denouncing his faith and a bolt of lightning had stopped him in his tracks. Sometimes Hetty would point to a patch of ground in the last field where nothing was ever growing. "I think it was there, doll. Right there." I had looked at it in awe each time, worried that Kate was going to be struck down for not believing. "Oh, folks have to find out what they believe through their own journey. Some people can't be fed what to believe. Kate's got time," Hetty would say.

JEANNIE TURNED THE TV ON LOW. It was nice here in her place. I hoped Kate wouldn't come too soon. I drifted off, remembering one more thing Hetty used to say to me: "Doll, I think you've got the touch, I really do."

I SWALLOWED AND OPENED MY EYES, unsure of where I was. But then I remembered it was Jeannie's place and that I'd had a temperature at school. I was here until Kate could come.

But Kate was already here. She and Jeannie were talking quietly in the kitchen, just beyond my door.

"My trip to Sephora with Sadie and Zoe was a riot! We had a blast. But I'm probably going back to my usual makeup. These new colors aren't me," Jeannie said, laughing.

Kate, in a quiet voice, replied, "I should wear makeup, but I never have. I think it's something you learn how to do like in middle school with your friends. My middle school years were filled with a lot of behavior issues. Kids and teachers were afraid of me."

I was surprised by how honest she was being.

"Why so?" Jeannie asked.

"I needed to be with Sadie, so I learned early on that a well-placed 'fuck you' to a teacher or the principal was my ticket home. My father was struggling with PTS. I was worried about Sadie. While he did his best, sometimes I had visions of Sadie wandering down Tabor Road. It didn't happen, thank God. He kept it together more in my absence than I gave him credit for. He does okay with Carson, too."

"What about your mother? Where's she?" Jeannie asked.

It was wrong to eavesdrop like this, but my energy level was low and it was nice to hear them getting along. Kate hadn't liked the whole phone and car deal. She'd said, more than once, *"And when you don't work at Shay's anymore? What then?"* Plus, she saw it as a hand-out, and she had too much pride to accept it easily.

Kate answered, "Sadie and I don't have the same mother. Mine took off when I was pretty young. She was an addict. My father and I have no idea where she ended up — I think she wanted it that way. My dad 'took in' Sadie's mom, Lynn, sometime after. He literally welcomed her into our trailer when she was four, five months pregnant. The father of the twins she was carrying was abusive, and she had nowhere else to go. My father has a rough exterior, but he's got a kind heart."

Someone in a car out on the street beeped its horn. Jeannie asked, "What's Sadie's mom like?"

"Oh, Lynn? She's sweet and was wonderful to me, but she and my father didn't ever really become a couple. Well, that's not entirely true because along came Sadie. When she was born, the twins were two. Lynn left with all of them months later, but she brought Sadie back. It was way too much — three little ones — for her to handle on her own."

I turned on my side, away from the door. *Should I get up and get dressed so we can go home or sleep a little longer?*

As I was deciding, I heard Kate say, "It was mostly me who took care of Sadie, except when I had to be in school. That's when my anxiety would kick in. I was always trying to get in trouble, trying to be sent home to make sure she was safe."

The memory of Kate crying up behind the tool shed the day we took off for Tennessee came back to me. She'd been almost 18 then. *But s*he'd already been taking care of me way before that — almost her whole life.*

"Listen, nothing against Eugene, but him letting Sadie use his car and you putting her on a phone plan…"

Here it comes, I thought.

"There's no way she can afford those things until she's out of high school and working full-time," Kate said pointedly.

Jeannie walked near my door. "Wait, so going to college isn't an option for her?"

I didn't want Kate to have to answer that, so I called out, "Hey guys, I'm awake." When I sat up, my body hurt, my mouth was dry, and my head ached, but I still smiled.

Both of them appeared at the door. "How you feeling, Sadie?" Jeannie asked.

"Oh, you know, maybe a little better." I stood up slowly and moved to Kate. I leaned into her. "No, I really feel horrible," I whispered.

Kate wrapped her strong arms around me and said, "We'll get you tested and on meds."

I needed help getting dressed and then into the Honda. After I was settled, Kate went quickly back into Jeannie's.

"What did you have to do?" I asked when she came back out.

"Just thanked her for getting you from school and apologized for all the times I've been shitty to her."

I leaned against the window as Kate drove through Langdon. Looking down at my hands, I knew it wasn't mono. *I'm way sicker than that.*

Chapter 26

Sadie, you need to wake up." Kate reached over and gently shook my shoulder. "Remember, you're having blood work done this morning. Since you're negative for mono, this is the next step." She lightly stroked my hair and whispered, "Time to wake up, sleeping beauty."

I stretched and turned over, opening my eyes. "I fasted last night just like you told me. It was hard not to have the orange sherbet Dad and Carson were eating."

"The sooner you get up and dressed, the sooner we can come back and have breakfast. I wouldn't even shower — throw your sweats on and let's go. But be quiet. Carson and Dad are still sleeping."

She nodded toward the bathroom down the hallway and said, "I'll fold this stuff up while you brush your teeth. We'll stop at the bagel shop after."

On the way down Route 103 to the Health Center, she kept glancing over at me while she drove.

"Did you sleep okay?" Kate asked.

"Yeah, that melatonin Dad bought at Rite Aid last month really works. It's funny, it's hard to actually fall asleep, but I'm tired all the time. This isn't going to hurt, is it?" I asked.

"No, just a little prick, but it's better if you don't watch. They'll draw enough blood for a couple of vials then put a band-aid on it."

I nodded. "I might go to school for half a day after. I counted. I've missed nine days in the last three weeks — that's more than half. It's hard to keep up with all the missed assignments. Jeannie doesn't want me working tonight. Teddy's coming in."

As we entered Langdon and turned up onto Vernon Street, Kate said, "Hopefully, this blood test will pick up what you're missing, like from your diet. If you're anemic, they'll put you on iron pills. There's other stuff, too, that can show up — infections or problems with your immune system."

We turned into the parking lot of the Health Center, across from the emergency room of the hospital. It served Langdon but also neighboring towns like Colton and Peddan. Most everybody's doctor had offices here.

Kate parked and started to climb out of the Honda, but I stopped her and said, "I can go in alone — just need my insurance card, right?"

Fishing into her wallet, she handed it over to me, and I opened the car door. But in one swift move, I closed it and hunkered down onto the floor of the passenger's side.

"Kate, that's Sam coming out — oh my God!"

She looked at the entrance and asked, "The big kid in a Colton sweatshirt, wearing baggy gray sweats and huge shit-kicker boots?"

"Yes!" I stole a quick glance and saw that they were walking right towards the car next to ours.

Realizing Sam might be able to see me, I whispered urgently, "Grab Carson's backpack and snowsuit from the back and cover me. Hurry!"

Kate grunted as she reached for them and threw them onto me. "He's right here. Do not move, Sadie," she said.

I watched Kate glance out the window and smile.

"He's gone. You can get up."

I moved Carson's stuff off of me and sat up. "That was so close!" I exclaimed.

"He's big, like really big. He's got a great smile, just saying," Kate replied.

I picked the insurance card up off of the floor and left. As I walked to the Health Center, I considered how I felt about Sam. I didn't know what to think. It'd been weeks since he came to Shay's.

Fifteen minutes later, I climbed back into the car and told Kate I was going to try a latte this morning.

"Did they tell you when we'd get the results?" she asked.

I shook my head and buckled in. I had walked right past the door to the lab and gone into the bathroom further down the hallway to wait it out. There was no use in getting my blood drawn, because it wouldn't matter what they found.

We left and drove to the bagel shop. Just as I reached for the door handle, Kate touched my arm and said, "You know, it's okay if you still like Sam, if you want to give him a second chance."

I shook my head and slowly replied, "Sometimes, there's much bigger stuff than just who you like and who likes you back."

Kate glanced at me. "Yeah? Like what?"

"Maybe, some of us, like me, aren't meant to…" But I paused and said, "God is the one who ultimately decides what will happen. That's from Proverbs, and I believe it."

A man came out of the bagel place and climbed into a utility truck. Someone else parked next to us.

"Okay," Kate said, smiling at me tenderly.

I grew even more serious and replied, "I don't understand everything. Just know that whatever…"

But she cut me off and said, "Let's get you a latte!" This was getting way too serious for Kate.

"It's March first. Can you believe it?" I said as she opened the shop's door for me.

We left with a half a dozen bagels, and my latte was flavored with enough junk to sink a ship. All the way home, though, I hardly took a sip of the drink.

"You've got to eat a bagel when we get home, Sadie. You're too thin. A strong wind could…"

"I know, I know…could lift me up and carry me away for miles."

"Remember, I switched with Darcy today. Want me to drop you off at school?" Kate asked, searching my face.

"Maybe tomorrow. I'm feeling lousy again," I replied, slumping down in my seat. We turned onto Tabor Road, and it started to snow. *What a bummer.*

Kate read my mind and said, "March in Vermont sucks, doesn't it?"

Chapter 27

Kate asked me once more if I wanted to try school, but I shook my head. My father and Carson were already gone — Carson to pre-school and Dad to Chet's. Sugaring season was finally here, and Chet and Dad took tapping the trees, collecting the sap, and boiling it very seriously. Kate left, and I had the trailer all to myself. I climbed into her bed.

Things were going on inside of me. I felt it — like my body was breaking down. It hurt to move, to breathe, but my mind was alert. Whatever was happening, it was God's will — intentional and full of purpose. I prayed for guidance.

Fitful sleep with strange dreams kept waking me up. In one dream, I was at Shay's and Hetty was there, and so was the little girl, Lilly, from the bathroom. They were joining the boy from The Diamondback at the round-top, table 14.

At one point, the pregnant woman I had talked to outside the drug store not so long ago walked over to the table. In the dream, I touched her big belly just like I had that night while I'd waited for Dad. In the next dream, the same lady was trying to tell me something urgent, but I couldn't make out what it was.

I slept on and off for most of the day until Dad and Carson came home. We ate tomato soup and crackers for dinner and watched cartoons. My fever was back, and I took more Tylenol. Now, I tried to crochet the hat I was making, waiting for the Tylenol to work and bring my fever down.

When my father closed the bathroom door to give Carson his bath, there was a noise outside. I opened the front door, but no one was there. The tops of the trees were swaying along Tabor Road. The wind sounded strange as it howled down past our place, making its way to Karen's and then beyond, to the turn-around. I closed the door.

Sitting back down on the couch, I picked up the little hat. But my hands began to shake. I felt my forehead and then my face. I was burning up. It was way too hot in the trailer. I needed to cool down.

Stepping back outside, I watched the trees sway some more, snow falling from their branches and blanketing the just-plowed road. The air felt good — a relief from the suffocating heat of the trailer. I pictured the fresh snow at the turn-around. It would be good to lay down on it, to bring my temperature back to normal.

I walked down the steps and turned away from the trailer. My body felt lighter and didn't ache as much. My lungs were filling up with clean cold air. I began to run. It was dark, but I knew the way by heart.

Yellow blinking lights turned toward me. I looked down at my bare feet on the snow-covered road and smiled. I hadn't run like this since I was little, in the fields surrounding the tent church.

Hurry, hurry, get to the snow to stop this inferno raging inside my body.

I looked up just as the lights were upon me. There was a loud, deafening noise, and suddenly I was airborne. Somewhere far off, I heard a baby cry.

BOOK TWO
Kate, Spring & Summer 2016

Chapter 1

Mrs. Lake, my favorite resident, and four of the other ladies loved the daytime soaps. In between shows, Darcy always made them stand up and stretch then do a lap down the corridor and back. But today they were taking advantage of me — especially Mrs. Lake, the ringleader. "We'll miss the recap of yesterday, Kit. You don't want that, do you?" she asked.

I never watched soap operas, so didn't know if recaps were even a thing. She was probably pulling a fast one on me. But the snow was back, coming down even harder, and the ladies all looked comfy in their shawls and afghans.

"All right, but I want you to know — I'm taking detailed notes for Darcy, with names!" They hardly looked over at me as I sat at the table in front of the large picture window. Their next show had begun.

There were gusts of wind creating white-outs in the courtyard. The Pines Nursing Home tended to be too warm most days, but today it felt good, the building solid against the weather. I wondered if Sadie was curled up in my bed, maybe crocheting or sleeping again. The results of the blood test couldn't come back soon enough.

Carson was at pre-school, and today, Tuesday, they were having two dogs come from the Humane Society. The dog lady was going to talk about the proper care of dogs and let the children play with one puppy and an older, very gentle dog. "Very, very old, Mommy; he has a white face."

My father was going to pick up Carson after school. I hoped his old truck could make it down into town and back in this snow. There was no back up plan, but my father would find a way.

I looked down at the charts for when medications needed to be dispensed. My usual shift was three to eleven, covering dinner and the evening hours. The turnover rate for employees was high at The Pines. Except for Darcy, our cook, and me, most everybody had two years or less working here. It could sometimes be a hard job — getting close to a resident, only to have them pass on, or dealing with a few whose health needs were complicated and difficult. There was a time I thought about working on the other end of the spectrum in a day care. But The Pines was where I'd landed once we'd gotten back from Tennessee.

I held my breath every time I got a text, thinking it could be Sadie telling me she was feeling worse. I wondered if I should call Sadie's mom, Lynn, and fill her in. Sadie tried to downplay how bad she really felt, like with Jeannie at her house. But as soon as she was near me, she crumbled like most kids did when they were with a parent.

A long-ago memory of Sadie suddenly came to me. She wasn't crawling or walking yet. But what she loved to do was grab her toes and bring them to her mouth, babbling the whole time. I remembered how she would suddenly kick at me and I'd exclaim, "You kicked me!" and she'd giggle loudly. On one of those mornings, Lynn had come out all sleepy-eyed to watch us. I remembered her saying, "No one loves her more than you, Kate!" But then Lynn had corrected herself and said, "No one's love means more to her than yours, Kate."

AT THE END OF MY SHIFT, I ran out to my Honda with a container of soup. Cheryl, the cook, had made a hearty creamed chicken and veggie soup for dinner. I thought Sadie might like it and that she'd finally eat something. I started the car and grabbed the brush to clear the snow from the windows. About five inches had fallen in all. That wasn't so bad.

Suddenly, Dominic Sousa, the detective, appeared at my side and said, "Here, let me help you."

I was surprised, but then I looked at him with apprehension and some suspicion. He must have read my mind, because he quickly said, "I'm here to visit my grandmother. She lives at The Pines. My mother's mother — Violet Lake?"

Stepping back, I hesitated then asked, "Are you the Nicky who brings bagels and watches *Good Morning America* with her?"

"That would be me a couple of times a week. I also balance her checkbook." He reached over and lifted my driver's side windshield wiper, clearing the ice from it. "It took me a little while to figure out where I'd seen you before. I finally got that it was from here. But my grandmother doesn't call you Kate. It's Kit, right?"

"Yep, Kit. It's got something to do with Katherine Hepburn. Supposedly, I'm headstrong and independent just like her."

He raised his eyebrows ever so slightly.

"Yeah, well…" I thought we were both remembering my 'headstrong' vocabulary on Tabor Road. I put my hood up, moved to the back window, and started brushing it off. He moved with me.

"I've got to get home with soup for Sadie. She's been sick."

"That's too bad. There's nothing new on any of the Tennessee stuff. I'll definitely let you know when there is."

Just then a big snow plow went by, and I pointed to it. "The plows are finally out, I'm going." I got into the Honda and rolled down my window. He was still there. "You know, I've seen you naked." It felt good to say that, for me to have something over on him.

He gave me a sliver of a smile and replied, "That picture of me, about four, in the bath tub… I hope she's not showing it all around."

"No. But she did have it enlarged and framed. It's on her dresser, now." I rolled my window up and backed out.

On the slow drive home, I found it interesting that Dominic Sousa was Mrs. Lake's 'Nicky.' There were a lot of little stories, anecdotes I'd heard through the conversations she and I often had in the early evening hours. Now that I knew he was 'Nicky,' it diminished his authority in my eyes. I tended not to do well with authority.

Driving up through Langdon, I went over what he and the other detectives had said about the missing girl and Sadie's theory that the girl might be 'her boy' from the parking lot at The Diamondback. They were going to upload our DNA and the DNA found on the items inside the car to CODIS, the national DNA database, to see if there was a match . It was pretty farfetched, but as long as it wasn't costing us anything and it satisfied Sadie's need to do something, I was okay with letting it play out.

The old man's assurance that no one would find out about Carson, least of all Brother Ron, was bullshit. I didn't believe that for a minute.

That's why I kept $1,741 squirreled away in the trailer — all cash, in an envelope taped to the wall behind the headboard in my room. I'd been saving it for a long time. A small duffle bag full of clothes was under my bed, too. If Carson's father ever came to Langdon, I had a plan.

A second state trooper went whizzing by me on Route 103, just past Shay's. I couldn't believe how fast he was going. The roads were okay but not *that* okay.

As I made the turn onto Tabor Road and passed the thicket of dense brush where the bull moose had been, I felt that something wasn't right. I slowed way down as I rounded the last curve before the straight away to our place. Blaring blue lights were in front of me. I stopped. An ambulance, its siren quiet with no flashing lights, drove past me towards the main road. I turned and looked back. An EMT was outlined in the light of the back door. He was sitting down.

"Miss, we're not allowing anyone further up the road," a policeman said as he approached my window.

"I live here, in the trailer. What's happened?" I replied anxiously.

He turned slightly to speak into his radio. "Send Officer Mack. Resident of the trailer is here."

The way he said that jarred me, and I swiftly got out of the car. He put up his hands like he was trying to corral a horse about to run. "Wait here, please!"

I side-stepped him easily and started to run towards our driveway, yelling, "Carson, where are you? Carson!" But our trailer was quiet and dark. The cars were further down, toward Karen's. Big lights were on at the turn-around. I could see the town snowplow lights and other, stronger lights magnifying the area.

Two police cars were turned towards me, but it was confusing…they were on the wrong side of the road. Their engines were running, their blue lights swirling. Suddenly, Officer Mack stepped out and grabbed hold of my arm. I didn't know where he'd come from. "Let me go, I've got to find Carson!" I demanded.

But he held on and replied, "He's okay. He's in the second car back, Karen's got him. Your father is in this car." He pointed to the cruiser just a little further down, in front of us. "Kate, there's been a terrible accident at the turn-around."

I looked at the cruisers, their headlights blinding me, then back at him, trying to understand. He'd mentioned Carson, Karen, and my father, but not Sadie.

"Fuck you!" I yelled, practically spitting on him as I broke away from his hold. I was in middle school all over again; I had to get to Sadie to make sure she was safe.

I ran and was gaining speed until I hit a patch of ice underneath the new fallen snow. I fell hard, the right side of my body taking the brunt of the fall. Within moments, I felt Karen's strong arms reach out and pull me up. She held me and smoothed back my hair. It was the look in her eyes that told me, that made me understand — I hadn't come in time.

I folded into her. She tried to hold me up but slipped, falling down to her knees. "Oh baby, baby, baby." She rocked me as we cried. Officer Mack's boots were less than a yard from my face. *The ambulance didn't have its lights on because I didn't get to Sadie in time.*

Officer Mack helped both of us up and carried Carson from the patrol car into Karen's house. My father was adamant that we leave — get away from all the flashing lights, the static of the radios back and forth between officers, and the eeriness of being out in the cold, dark night.

I gave him a blank stare and then nodded. I followed Karen, who was following Officer Mack and Carson.

The last thing my father said to me was, "Sadie's mother is coming. You've got Carson, and Karen has you." He looked how I felt — helpless, scared, and on the edge of panic.

"WHAT DO YOU KNOW, KAREN?" I asked once we were inside and Carson was occupied with his shelf of toys designated for him when we visited.

"Oh boy, Kate, this is tough," she replied quietly. She was starting to make a pot of coffee. I looked up at her, but it was hard to focus and my legs were starting to go numb. Karen stopped scooping coffee into the basket. Her hands were shaking.

Suddenly, one of the officers who I'd seen sitting with Dad in the cruiser walked into the house. She shook off her boots and walked over to us with authority. "Here, let me make the coffee, Karen. You sit down with Jarod's daughter."

I didn't know her, had never seen her before.

"Tell us what's happened, please," I whispered, glancing back at Carson.

The officer hesitated then asked, "Are you sure you're ready to hear it?" Her kind eyes took both of us in.

"Yes, I want to know," I whispered back, holding my right wrist and flexing my fingers.

"Okay, then." She finished pouring the water into the back of the coffee maker and turned off the static on her radio. She turned to us and began talking. "The medical examiner didn't speak to your father, but one of our officers — an ass, if you ask me — did. He said that blunt force trauma from the plow seems to be the initial cause of Sadie's fatal injury. The markings on the plow indicate that she was out in front of it, not to the side, as first thought. She was thrown in the air and…" The officer stopped, sighed deeply, and continued, "She was thrown maybe twenty yards and impaled on one of the broken branches of a deadwood tree in the small clearing before the logging trail.

"The regional medical examiner declared Sadie dead at six fifty-four p.m. He's got a call into the State's Attorney's office to release her. They have to get that before they're able to move her. Then she'll go to Gibson's Funeral Home down in town. The funeral people should arrive any minute if they haven't already.

"It'll be up to the medical examiner as to whether there will be an autopsy. But no final decisions have to be made right now, at least not until her mother gets here and her parents have had a chance to talk."

This was all surreal. I stood up and moved aimlessly about Karen's kitchen. I felt sick, nauseous, and stopped before the blue light on the coffee maker. Karen moved around me, seemingly lost, too.

"Sadie's still out there, in the cold?" I whispered as the officer placed two cups of coffee on the table. She motioned for us to come back and sit. It read 7:38 p.m. on Karen's kitchen clock.

Karen put her hand gently on the back of my shoulder and said, "No, baby, our Sadie Rose, our baby girl, is already gone."

We both began to cry; it was too much to take in, too much to process.

Officer Mack knocked and opened Karen's door. "They're taking the body…" He looked at Karen and then over to me and said, "They're taking Sadie into town now. Jarod and Lynn are together, following Gibson's car. We'll be out here for a while. Wondering if you'll want some lights on, heat turned up in the trailer, Kate? It's pretty dark down that way."

Karen replied, "Thanks Mackie, but Kate and her son will be spending the night with me. We'll let Jarod and Lynn have that space."

I spoke up. "Could someone drive my Honda down here? I have to get the backpack in the back seat. It has…" I couldn't finish, though, remembering covering Sadie with it just that morning.

"We'll drive it down here." Officer Mack replied as he nodded to the other officer. Just as he was about to close the door, he turned back to us and added, "Haven't been out this way in years, Karen."

Chapter 2

Voices were coming from downstairs…I was rising to the top, almost ready to open my eyes… *Don't! Something horrible has happened.* I rolled over and fell back to sleep.

The next time I woke, Dad and Karen were talking, but she wasn't mad, she wasn't telling him to get his shit together. Her voice sounded sad and tender. I heard Lynn, too. Was Lynn back? *It's because Sadie's dead.* I burrowed deep into the covers. *Sadie is dead!* No. I drifted away once more.

I finally opened my eyes. The sunlight streamed in from the window. Carson's breathing next to me was raspy; he'd caught a cold.

Lying there, not moving, I remembered a night years ago when we'd walked here to Karen's house… My

*father had been drinking and had fallen through the front
door of the trailer. We'd stepped over him and left.
Carson — barely two months old, Sadie — just 11. In
the dark of the night, we'd made our way down the road.
Sadie had asked me if we had enough bottles, should she
run back for another can of formula. That time Karen
had kept us for a whole week.*

*"Don't say anything to Lynn," I had whispered to
Sadie back then before Karen opened her door. "Remember, we have to stay together, most of all."*

*Then, two years ago, my father had stopped taking
his meds and sat motionless for long stretches of time. I'd
run down to get Karen. She'd stood big and ballsy as
shit, telling him to"Fucking grow a pair — be there for
your daughters and grandson."*

*That time, Karen had looked at me and said, "Grab
your things, you don't need to put up with this." I don't
remember how long we'd stayed, but eventually he got
better. There'd been no relapses since, but we knew things
could turn on a dime.*

CARSON STRETCHED and whacked me across the face.
I lifted the down comforter and slowly slid from the bed
onto the braided rug. I curled up into a ball. An overwhelming sense of dread and fear flooded me. The sunlight
through the white, lacy curtains touched the hardwood
floors and landed across the comforter covering Carson. I
watched him sleeping. *Sadie is dead.* I laid there on the floor,
my legs drawn up, my arms hugging my sides. *She's gone.*

I finally walked to the bathroom just down the hallway
and glanced out the window. It was high enough to see
down the road, to the turn-around and the start of the old
logging trail. A yellow tape was draped from one side of the

road to the other and then along the snowbanks, forming a rectangle. There was a police cruiser parked nearby. I couldn't tell if anyone was inside. It seemed wrong that the morning was bright and the new snow glistened.

What I'd been told last night was hard to wrap my head around — that Sadie had stepped out in front of the plow just after it had made the turn. She'd been thrown some 50 feet until she'd hit a tree. That it had been dark and hard to see that far down on Tabor Road, away from any house or barn lights. The driver, Karl Ogden, had radioed the town garage and the garage had called 911. I knew Karl from school and remembered Sadie saying that he had a little boy now. He had passed a breathalyzer test.

According to my father, Sadie had walked out of the trailer without his knowledge. He'd been busy giving Carson a bath. The sirens had brought him out to the living room and that's when he'd seen the police cars go shooting past. It was at that point he'd realized Sadie wasn't inside, was nowhere to be found.

"She had a temperature," he'd told Karen, between his bouts of incomprehension that his daughter had been hit and killed. The police had gotten all three of them — Dad, Karen, and Carson into the two cruisers, and had called Lynn in Rutland. They'd tried my cell but I hadn't answered. Dad had told Officer Mack that I was due home soon and they should be on the lookout for me.

THE SLEEPING PILL Karen had given me was still making me feel groggy. Right before I'd swallowed it last night, I'd asked her to call Jeannie at the restaurant and tell her what had happened.

This morning, between moments of trying to wake up and then falling back to sleep, I'd kept wondering if the minutes on the drive home last night would haunt me forever. That, once again, my consuming thoughts had been about that asshole, Brother Ron, taking Carson from me, and not about Sadie and her sickness. I wasn't with her when she needed me the most.

Leaning against the bathroom window, I heard different voices below. I pulled my hair back and washed my face. Karen had put out a new toothbrush for me. Her guest room dresser held some of her clothes. I quietly rifled through it and grabbed one of her sweaters, pulling it on over the nightie she'd given me. I picked a pair of heavy socks from the basket in the corner of her bedroom. Carson was still sound asleep. I closed the door and tiptoed downstairs.

I paused on the stairway and looked at the photographs on the wall. Many of them were of Karen, her parents, and her high school basketball days. Some were of us. There was one photograph in a matted frame of Karen and her high school buddies posing in front of an old Camaro, stuck deep in the muddy springtime ruts of Tabor Road. The spot was just across from here — her parents' home. Everyone in the picture had this 'tough as hell' look. I easily recognized my father, and of course, Karen, then Officer Mack, 'Mackie,' Tommy Dunne's dad, who'd died of cancer a while back, and Tommy's mother. The picture was dated 1981, their senior year.

The voices below stopped. I took a deep breath and made my way down into the living room and then turned towards the kitchen. Sitting at the kitchen table were Jeannie and Dominic Sousa. They both stood up. With alarm, I asked, "Where's Karen? We...we...need her." Jeannie walked over to me and pulled me close. She started to cry, her tears falling into my hair and onto the sweater I wore.

Dominic quietly said, "I'm so sorry." His eyes were a deep brown, sad, and full of concern. "I came to see if you needed anything, anything at all."

Jeannie, holding my hands in hers, said, "Karen is with your dad and Lynn, but she's coming back to check on you and Carson."

Moving to the couch, I sat down heavily and faced the door to wait for Karen. "We need her," I repeated. It was the first time I realized that the 'we' in my 'we' was forever altered.

Chapter 3

"Shut up, Drew. Leave me alone." I glanced at him, standing at the bar beside me. The place was practically deserted. The music had been turned off. A woman was putting chairs up on the tables.

"Come on, you've had enough for tonight," he whined and shook his head at the bartender. The guy slid the pint he'd just poured for me over to Sullivan, the town drunk.

"Cheers to you, Sullivan," I said, holding up an imaginary glass. I slowly climbed off of the bar stool and reached for my coat. As Drew was helping me on with it, I leaned into him and burped loudly in his face.

"Nice, Kate, real nice," he said. He reached for my hand and turned toward the door.

I started to sway, realizing just how shitfaced I was.

Once we were in his truck and pulling out of Pete's Bar, I asked, "Why you turning towards Tabor Road?"

"Because you're too far gone to come to my place. I don't want you getting sick all over it again. These past two months have been nothing but this shit. It's getting old, Kate. Believe me, it's getting old," Drew said as he glanced my way.

"Um, not quite sure what you want me to say, Sir Drewski. Let's see how you'd do if your kid brother..." But I stopped.

"Unreal," Drew said, pressing down on the gas.

"Royal asshole," I muttered, my head spinning as we passed Shay's.

"KATE, YOU OKAY IN THERE?" my father called to me between my heaving.

"Leave me alone, go away!" I yelled, grabbing the edge of the toilet bowl and puking again.

"I'm out here if you need me."

Eventually, I laid down on the linoleum, the cold floor feeling good against my face. My eyes were level with the gap between the vanity and the floor. There were dust balls and a few Q-tips underneath and something shiny. I reached in. It was one of Sadie's little heart-shaped stud earrings. When she'd turned 10, she'd gotten her ears pierced and had picked out these studs. I blew the dust off and closed my eyes. My head was spinning.

We'd been back for a while from our time down in Tennessee, and I'd just gotten the job at The Pines. Dad had been sober again, and Sadie had worn the studs as we'd celebrated her birthday and my new job. We'd eaten at The Weathervane up in Rutland. It was Sadie's first time tasting lobster. She'd grimaced, and Dad and I had shared the rest of the lobster tail while she'd waited for a grilled cheese sandwich.

*I hadn't known then that I was pregnant with Carson
— wouldn't know for another five weeks. It wasn't until
I'd felt a strange, little fluttering inside my belly that I'd
gone to the clinic to find out what was wrong. The doctor
said it was 'quickening,' common at the 16-week mark.
Shocked, I'd asked him to test me again. "We'll do even
better than that, let's get you an ultrasound." I was
carrying a boy.*

THERE WAS A TOWEL HANGING on the bar above
me. I reached for it and draped it over my shoulders. I
managed to put a corner of it underneath my head. The
baseboard my feet were touching was cold, but soon it'd be
spitting out heat. The bathroom floor was as good a place as
any to sleep off my hangover. Besides, I wasn't sure I was
done throwing up. My father coughed on the other side of
the door. "Go back to bed, Dad. I'm not moving."

"Suit yourself," he said. "But get up before Carson
wakes up."

CARSON WAS PRACTICALLY STANDING on me
while he washed his hands. My mouth was dry and tasted
awful; my head was pounding and my back ached from
sleeping on the floor.

"What's going on?' I mumbled.

He reached for the towel still draped over me and wiped
his hands. "Cereal," was all he said.

No "Hi Mommy" or hug. He was pretty fed up with me,
just like most everybody else these days.

"Kate, I gotta use the bathroom now, so get up and get
out." My father's patience was clearly shot.

I walked past him into the bedroom and quickly took off
my clothes and threw them into a corner of the room. More

clothes were piled onto the unmade bed, but I didn't care, I climbed in anyway.

The earring was still in my hand. The backing was gone. I began to slowly jab the post into the palm of my hand. It hurt, but I did it again and then again until, finally, there was blood. I turned on my side and placed the earring on the nightstand next to me. My hand hurt, but it didn't hurt bad enough. I reached for the pillow and covered my face to keep from screaming. Carson's cartoons were loud and annoying.

LATER THAT DAY, I parked and walked across the street, surprised the kids weren't out on the playground. It was chilly, but they came out to play in all sorts of weather. Cynthia saw me through the window and waved. I didn't ring the buzzer, instead I just waited for her.

"Hi, Kate. What's up?" she asked.

That seemed like an odd thing to say, and I raised my eyebrows. "Um, picking up Carson. It's early, but we're going to go get a cookie." All day I'd felt bad about the way Carson had found me this morning, and I wanted to make it up to him.

Cynthia paused and then replied, "Remember, it's their big field day trip to Billings Farms to see the baby lambs. Your dad went, too; he's one of the chaperones. You signed the permission slip. Did you forget?"

"Totally, sorry." I shrugged my shoulders.

"I'm surprised Carson didn't remind you, especially this morning. His class has been counting down the days since April first. But, Kate, I'm glad you're here. Can we talk for a few minutes?"

She motioned to the two chairs just past the sign-in area. I nodded and walked to the closest chair and sat down.

The Center was quiet. I'd never been here when it was like this. Glancing around the big room, I noticed various drawings on one stretch of the wall. The title, "Animals of Vermont," was placed over the pictures. A drawing of a big brown moose might be Carson's — it was one of his favorite things to draw.

Cynthia sat down across from me. She had been Carson's pre-school teacher when he'd started at 3. Last year, she became the director — a very hands-on one. She smiled then leaned forward and said, "Carson has been mostly keeping it together since Sadie's death. But now I think he's getting into the angry phase of grief. He's been pushing others, and yesterday he yanked a toy from one of his best buds and then hit him with it. He's been our model little guy for so long. It's understandable, and we're all being extra attentive to him, like I'm sure you're doing at home. For however long he needs the extra support, we'll be there for him. I just wanted you to know this."

The full extent of how absent I'd been hit me. There hadn't been a moment since Sadie's death where Carson had had my full attention. In the past two months, I was either at work, sleeping, or out. My father was there for him, but I hadn't been.

Touching my arm, Cynthia said, "It must be extremely hard for you, Kate. I remember you coming here to the Center way back in middle school. You were so good with the little ones — you shined. And I know what you did for Sadie. You were parentified, making sure she was taken care of and safe."

Tears sprang to my eyes. I immediately wiped them away and stood up. This was getting uncomfortable. She was reminding me of a school counselor I'd had — kind and caring, but way too personal.

"Lately, my father has been spending more time with Carson than I have since Sadie…since the accident. But I'll be better." I moved toward the door.

"Are you getting counseling to help you through this?" Cynthia asked, her eyes searching mine.

"Nah, not necessary. It'll be okay." I put my hand on the door handle and looked back. "Thanks for telling me about Carson. We'll have a talk."

Walking across the street, back to my car, I regretted not checking out the drawing of the moose to see if it had been Carson's.

Later, when he and Dad got home, I had dinner ready — homemade mac and cheese. We ate, hearing about the baby lambs and all the other animals on the farm. Carson also told me how, in the olden days, people had to make their own butter. He was happy; his eyes were bright, his voice animated. At one point, Dad told him that he was going to start the bath, but I quickly said, "I'll do it tonight."

Things were going good until Carson went to the bookshelf and pulled out *The Giving Tree* for me to read with him. It had been one of Sadie's favorite books; she even wrote about it for Mr. Banks' class just last Thanksgiving. There were notecards with her writing still inside the jacket. I asked Carson to choose a different book and tucked *The Giving Tree* under my leg.

But he wasn't having any of it. "No! I want that book, the green book. Give it to me!" He yanked on it.

I tried to redirect him, even suggesting we go watch a cartoon — something we usually didn't do right before bed.

"Give it to me, now!" he yelled and reached up and took a swipe at me. I covered my face.

"Carson, do not hit!" I quickly got up and grabbed hold of his hands. My father came to the door. Carson ran to him, crying. I walked past them and grabbed my wallet and car keys. I couldn't get to Pete's Bar soon enough.

Chapter 4

Jeannie had left a voicemail letting me know that she had Sadie's last paycheck from way back in February. *"Do you want me to put it in the mail, or can you stop by the restaurant?"*

I hadn't answered her, but now, two days after the terrible night with Carson, I turned onto her street. She was out front, digging up a patch of dirt near the walkway to her house. The mid-morning sun was bright, and the air smelled of spring.

Jeannie stopped when she saw me pull up. I turned off the Honda and climbed out. I gave her a tentative smile, but she didn't respond. Instead, she turned and motioned for me to join her up on the porch. On the ground where she'd been digging were a couple of little bags of seed.

I leaned against the post near the front stoop while she sat on the railing. Her porch was bare; it was way too early to put out porch furniture. We weren't done with frosts yet, and a freak snowstorm in Vermont was still possible. "Sorry I never got back to you about the check. I haven't been on top of things," I said.

Jeannie took off her gloves and held them. "I get that, Kate. It's been a tough couple of months. It still blows me away that she's gone. If it's hard for me — I can't imagine what you're going through."

I nodded and replied, "I'm not religious — never had a strong opinion of what happens to us when we die. But now, honestly, that's what I think about the most. Where she is and why she doesn't give me a sign." I glanced over at her.

"Well, Sadie had an unwavering belief in God and Heaven. Maybe you could find comfort in that — in what she believed."

"A sign would be better," I replied, knowing Jeannie was just trying to make me feel better.

"The pastor who spoke? I liked what she had to say," Jeannie added.

The wake and the gathering after, at Shay's, had been one big blur to me. I'd gone through the motions but couldn't remember much of anything except that a shitload of people came. People who hadn't really known and certainly hadn't cared about Sadie. They were just curious. Sadie's death had been a freak accident, and people were drawn to it like moths to a flame. Even now, Tabor Road had traffic late at night heading to the turn-around.

Jeannie looked thoughtful and added, "I grew up Catholic, but I don't practice anymore except Midnight Mass on Christmas Eve and Easter morning. But I swear, Kate, if ever there was someone bound for Heaven, it was Sadie. The poem she gave me at Christmas? It was beautiful."

We sat for a minute or two, then I replied quietly, "She loved all you guys at Shay's. I'm glad she had that — a group of people who supported her."

Jeannie nodded. Hesitantly, she said, "I was at Pete's the other night after the restaurant closed. Drew was with you."

"Yeah, Drew…that man deserves a medal, huh?" I was making light of it, but inside I was feeling defensive and embarrassed. Since Sadie's death, any love interest I'd had in him had evaporated. He'd become my glorified designated driver and not much else. "Drew's a royal asshole. I tend to gravitate toward assholes. Carson's father was one, too. I keep looking over my shoulder, half expecting him to try and snag Carson from me."

She replied, "That must be hard for you, to have to worry like that."

I stood up and started to walk down her steps.

Jeannie joined me on her walkway and pointed to the area she'd just been scraping at with a shovel. "You know anything about zinnias?"

"To plant those now, before we're done with frosts?" I shook my head and added, "They won't take. Wait another month. To plant zinnias from seed, all you need to do is loosen up the soil then scatter the seeds." I looked up at the big maple in front of her house. "It might not be sunny enough for them right here. They need lots of hours of sunlight. Just saying."

Jeannie smiled. "I was feeling springy today and remembered these packets of seed I got in the mail. I didn't bother with the fine print." She moved her arms to encompass the shovel and the overturned dirt.

I turned towards my car, admiring the houses all up and down the street. Sadie used to draw little neighborhoods she wanted to live in. Jeannie's street reminded me of one of those pictures.

Just as I opened the driver's side door of my Honda, Jeannie called out, "Crazy that Sadie's hunch about the boy proved right, isn't it? His DNA matching the missing girl they were all looking for. Dominic Sousa said it was Sadie who came up with that."

"Wait, what?" I asked, now turning back. I wanted to make sure I'd heard her right.

"The detective who Sadie talked to…remember him? He told me," Jeannie replied.

"I know who you mean. When did he tell you that?" I was abrupt, instantly regretting the tone of my voice, but I couldn't help it.

"Not so long ago. He sometimes stops in at the restaurant to grab coffee and dessert before we're technically open. He was on his way to your place to tell you and your father. He said the Tennessee authorities still don't know where the boy is, but now that they know he was the missing girl, they have more to go on."

Jeannie reached my car and touched my arm lightly. "I was with Sadie when she first asked Dominic to check on the boy, to see if the Tennessee police could find out if he was okay. I'm sure that's why he told me."

We both turned to the house on the left when a man called out, "Hello, Jeannie!" He was helping a little boy get on a bicycle with training wheels. *Carson needs a bike like that, but Tabor Road sucks for bike riding.*

"What a big boy!" Jeannie yelled and then turned back to me. "Dominic and I had been talking about Sadie and how Shay's was coping with her death, and then he told me."

The neighbor and his boy turned down the sidewalk. Vaguely, I remembered something about Dominic Sousa being at the trailer. But I'd been in my room, trying to sleep. I'd blown him off at The Pines, too. One evening he'd stopped in and asked if I had a minute. "I'd like to update you," he'd said. But I'd been curt and had told him there was too much going on and I couldn't chat, that I was working. I'd been snippy and had left him there, in the hallway, outside Mrs. Lake's room.

"He did tell my father, now that I think about it. But I'm sure you saw at Pete's — I've been mostly out of it, not coping at all. My life has basically imploded."

Jeannie looked over at me with eyes full of concern and understanding. For just a moment, I wondered what it would be like to have a friend, someone to unload to. But the thought passed, and I quickly walked around the Honda to the driver's side door. "Google hydrangeas. They'd look good — one on each side of your walkway, just under your railings. They come in all sorts of colors." I looked back up at the Maple tree and added, "Partial shade is fine for them."

WHEN I GOT TO PETE'S THAT NIGHT, Drew was already there, hanging with some chick from Rutland. Did I care? Nah, not really. We weren't ever exclusive. There were plenty of other guys who wanted to buy me beers. I stopped drinking before midnight — I didn't have a designated driver. When I climbed into the Honda, I knew I was a little impaired, but I could make it home — it was just a straight shot out of Langdon up to Tabor Road.

Just past the bull moose thicket on that final curve before the straightaway to home, I took the curve too wide. I tried to correct it but overcompensated, and suddenly the car shot off the road. I was now traveling down the left side culvert and hitting every heave and dip in the bank. I tried to turn the steering wheel hard right, but that didn't work. I slammed on my brakes, and the Honda spun around. Soon,

I was straddling the culvert, but at least the car was partially back up on the road.

I'd hit my forehead, maybe on the steering wheel. It was bleeding, though the airbag hadn't gone off. My heart was racing as I sat taking inventory. Finally, I opened the car door and climbed out. My knee was banged up; it hurt to walk. My cell's flashlight showed chunks of dirty snow and grass hanging from the front bumper. I shined the flashlight behind me, clearly seeing the trail of gouges from the front of the car scraping along the culvert. But my tires were all okay, and the frame didn't appear damaged.

Turning the camera on me, I took a selfie and then looked at it. The cut was small, just under my hairline. Standing in the dark, I knew I'd been terribly lucky after losing control like that.

Lights were coming from the direction of the trailer. It was Chet, my father's buddy, leaving. He'd dropped off a load of scrap metal earlier, and Dad had invited him back over for dinner and cards. Chet had no family, and he found Carson highly entertaining.

I waved my arms, and he pulled up. I nodded, but the way Chet was looking at me sobered me up even more.

"What the hell, Katie. Did you and your old man trade places? Is that what's happened? He puts the kid to bed, and you're out here, driving drunk and landing in the ditch?"

"I'm not that drunk…" I replied, taken aback by his scorn.

"Jesus, you're just like him, the way he used to be. That ain't good."

He started to pull away, but I called out, "Wait! Help me, Chet, help get me back up onto the road."

Revving his engine and taking off was his answer. I was on my own.

Climbing back into the Honda, I started it up and began to rock the car back and forth, from park to drive, then drive to reverse. Back and forth until I gunned it and the rear tires caught and the car finally moved up and out of the ditch. Back on the road, I turned it around and started for home.

A light was still on in the trailer. *Let this please be my wake-up call,* I whispered. Somehow, I wasn't entirely convinced it was.

Chapter 5

T he days were getting longer. Something about having more light during the afternoon hours gave me hope that Sadie, wherever she was, was all right. But there was a constant ache, a big gaping hole where she had been in my life.

Karen, like Cynthia, suggested I see someone to deal with the grief, but that wasn't for me. I only needed to remember how, in my eighth-grade year, the school had me evaluated. Some guy asked me absurd personal questions and then followed me into a couple of classes. The diagnosis had come back that I was 'emotionally disturbed.' *No kidding.* It wasn't hard to see how the school's authority disturbed me greatly. That being under their thumb every minute, with no way to check on things at home, was never going to work. I had laughed out loud in the middle of that meeting while the school principal looked at me disapprovingly and my father tried to shush me. I'd walked out then and climbed into his truck, vowing I was done with them all.

The next day, I'd refused to go back into the building. One day of refusal became three and then two full weeks. Finally, they'd set up an alternative program for me, and I'd gone to the Langdon town library to be tutored. A college kid had met with me, and she and I had exchanged what our anxiety looked and felt like. I remembered her name was Gertie. We'd finish early on most days — the work was pathetically easy — then walk around town, sometimes stopping to grab a Coke from the laundromat. She wasn't going back to college; instead, she thought she'd head west, maybe to Colorado. The next two years after that, I went to the high school, going through the motions and getting suspended often. It'd been spring, like now, when I'd turned 16 and had finally quit.

The garden center, further down Route 103 from the turn off to Tabor Road, had hired me for four mornings a week. It'd been perfect, and every day I'd breathe a sigh of relief that I was outside, in the sun, and even, at times, the rain. I was no longer in school, a place that had caused my anxiety to go sky high. Sadie was finishing up the first grade at the time, and Dad was Dad — trying to do his best.

I PULLED INTO THE PINES to start my shift. The building was getting a face lift, with scaffolding set up all along the west side near the courtyard. Two guys were just beginning to scrape off the old paint. I parked and walked by them.

"Hey there, Kate. How's it going?" one of the guys called out. He stopped scraping and lit a cigarette. I looked

up at him. His name was John, a frequent flyer at Pete's bar
— same as me now. He was one of the guys who'd kept my
glass filled the other night. No one knew, not even the old
man, that my night had ended up in the ditch. It seemed
like Chet had decided to keep it quiet.

"Hanging in there. Starting my shift." I smiled and
added, "Good day to be working outside." Their radio was
turned to a country western station, and a Luke Bryan song
was just starting.

"If you ever want a good, steady guy around, I'm
available," he called down from the scaffolding.

"Oh yeah, Johnny-oh? I'll keep that in mind," I replied,
laughing.

His partner chuckled, and I walked on.

Right at the entrance, I froze. An SUV bearing a
Tennessee license plate was parked out front. With Sadie's
death, my worries about Brother Ron had receded to the
back of my mind. But now, fear flooded me. I walked closer.
'Davidson' was written across the bottom of the plate.
That's the county Goodlettsville is in. My hands started to
shake. I could turn around now, get back to the trailer for
the cash, and then to the Center to pick up Carson. *But
would he even come with me?* Carson didn't like me much
these days.

I looked back at John and his partner then to my car
further down in the parking lot. I was hit by a sudden
flashback of Brother Ron telling me I looked "pretty damn
good, good enough to eat." It'd been at the car wash. He'd
smirked and the other guy with him had looked at me in the
same creepy way. But that had been six years ago, and I
wasn't that girl anymore. I turned back to the entrance, still
unsure of what to do.

Just then a man came out carrying an opened box with
'Samsung' written across its side. He looked over at me and

smiled. He lifted the back of the SUV and put the box in. I walked around the car and stood there. I didn't know him. I managed to take a few deep breaths, slowing down my heart rate.

"Afternoon," he said as he put the back tailgate down. "Vermont has beautiful spring weather, eh?"

I hesitated then replied, "We've gotten snow this late before."

"My wife and I drove up to enjoy the New England scenery. I'm Elsa Whitt's nephew. She's a resident here."

I nodded. Just as I turned to go in, the man quickly reached for the front door and held it open.

"Thanks," I responded, already feeling completely drained before I'd even started my eight-hour shift.

THE NEXT DAY, I walked down Tabor Road in the opposite direction of where I'd driven into the ditch. Here, in the higher elevation, spring came slower than in places further down in town. The snow was melting slowly as the spring run-off from the mountains filled the culvert. By August, it'd be all dried up, but right now the water was rushing by.

A memory hit me… I was running along this side of the road, keeping my eyes on a stick boat I'd made for the twins. Lynn had called for me to stop running, to come back and take the baby so she could hold onto both of the boys' hands. The twins were two and a half and a handful.

Sadie had been a beautiful little baby with clear, bright eyes. I'd loved to hold her, feed her, and rock her to sleep. I'd been her momma more than her real momma some days, but that was okay with me. When Lynn had moved out with the boys and Sadie, I'd been lost until Sadie had come back.

"She wants you, Kate. She cries for you every day. The boys are rough, too, around her. I'm overwhelmed."

Dad and Lynn had walked and talked while I'd held my breath, watching them come to a stop in the driveway. It wasn't until I saw Dad lift the port-a-crib from the trunk of her car that I'd known Sadie was staying. I'd hugged her tight, twirling her around in my arms. "We're sisters, most of all," I'd sang to her.

Lynn had stood in our doorway, crying. "I'll check on her all the time, okay?" And I'd watched the old man hug Lynn, tears in his own eyes because he knew how hard it was for her.

I WONDERED, for the first time, if all my fears over Brother Ron taking Carson were rooted deep in that core memory of seeing the anguish on Lynn's face as she climbed back into her car without her baby girl.

The black flies weren't as bothersome as long as I kept up a steady pace. Just as I approached the turn-around at the end of the road, I saw something: a blue and yellow object poking out from one of the snowbanks along the side of Taber Road that didn't get much sun.

Something about it seemed vaguely familiar. Keeping my feet firmly planted on the side of the bank and holding onto a clump of samplings, I leaned down and grabbed at what appeared to be a piece of clothing. It didn't budge.

The force of the water was carving out a chunk of the bank. The culvert couldn't be more than two feet deep if I were to slip in. *But don't slip in.* I tried again to pull up on the cloth, but it was frozen and matted in there good. I needed both hands to free it.

My determination grew, and I scooted even further down, precariously close to the water. I suddenly didn't care if I got wet or how muddy my boots and the bottom of my jeans were getting. With both hands, I grabbed and pulled hard. It came up much easier than I thought it would, throwing me off balance. My left foot slid down into the culvert, shocking me at the sudden cold. I quickly scrambled out of the water and up the bank. I was breathless and soaking wet all the way up to my left thigh.

I held the object, wiping away the mud. It was a child's hat, crocheted in blue and yellow — with an 'S' for Superman on the front. I held it against my chest, my heart racing. It was what Sadie had been making for Karl Ogden's little boy.

This was why she'd run down the road to stop him when she saw the plow. She'd finally finished it while she was home sick from school and the restaurant and had wanted Karl to take it. No one, not even me, could figure out why she'd stepped out in front of that plow. The little hat must have fallen out of her hand when she'd been hit and thrown almost twenty yards before being impaled. It was too deep in the culvert for the police to find.

They'd gotten it all wrong — concluding she'd run out, delirious with fever and unaware of what she was doing and where she was going. Like she was practically blind. The police had come out and had told my father, weeks later, that it was Sadie who had been found negligent in the accident. She'd failed to act with 'reasonable care' by stepping out in front of the plow.

The old man had shut the door on them and turned my way, his face full of pain and sadness. People were speculating about whether or not he was going to try and sue

Langdon Public Works. But he had no plans to and probably never even heard any of the talk. He was going out even less these days.

Sadie's time of death was 6:54 p.m. But that was wrong, too. Karl's wife, Ellie, had told me that Karl's phone, broken in the accident, had stopped at 6:50 p.m., the exact time of impact. He'd sat for a full four minutes before radioing the town garage. He'd been stunned, in shock, and not sure if he'd really even seen Sadie. But I wasn't going to tell anyone about that. Just like I wouldn't tell them about the phone's cracked screen with the time frozen on it and now the hat, literally frozen. The Langdon police were done looking into the death of Sadie Wade.

The wind was picking up, and the light, filtering through the branches of the trees, stretched my shadow across the road. It reminded me of the tent church and how, one afternoon, Sadie had held up her hand, making a rabbit and then a dog, and the folks all along our wooden bench had looked over and smiled at her, pointing to her hand puppet shadows against the tent's white wall. She'd grown embarrassed by all the attention and had hidden her face in my shoulder. But, just as soon as Father Ray's deep voice had reverberated throughout the tent, she'd sat up straight, ready to listen and hear how to be an even better child of God.

I counted the new batches of flowers, candles, and handmade crosses left at the turn-around. They were the new little offerings this week. Sadie would be embarrassed, barely able to look at me, knowing her classmates were attracted to the gore of her accident, the graphic description of her impalement going all around social media.

Feeling totally hopeless and defeated, I started to cry. But then I stopped for the hundredth time, because I knew, was absolutely certain, that in the last months of her life, she'd met the best people and she'd been her happiest since our tent church days. "I hope you scare the shit out of the assholes, Sadie," I said out loud as I kicked a fat candle and three cigarette butts away. They were out here, at night, having seances and taking pictures. "Make 'em shit their pants," I added defiantly.

A car was slowly coming down the road. Karen passed her driveway and kept driving my way. She pulled up alongside me. "Hey, baby, you doing better?"

I held back from showing her the hat and kept it out of sight. I wasn't ready to share it with anyone, just yet. "Yeah, you know, trying to clear all this stuff." I looked at her and smiled. Karen was always telling us to be positive, to remember our glass was always at least half full and some-times it was spilling over. But I knew Sadie's death had hit her hard. I saw it on her face every time we spoke.

"I've cried every night about Sadie Rose. The best thing we can do, Kate, is spend time together, keep talking about her, and remember her. Why don't you come have some chili I made for lunch?"

"Nah, I'm good, but thanks." I squeezed her hand and let go. She turned the car around.

The clouds were starting to roll out, replaced by sun-shine. I began to walk back. The trailer was stark, the last bit of snow in front of it turning to mud. Depression and hopelessness descended on me again. I was suddenly hit by everything: drinking too much after Sadie's death, driving drunk, my piss-poor way of handling Carson lately, and the renewed fear I'd felt yesterday at The Pines when I'd seen that Tennessee license plate. *Something has to give or else I'm going to be stuck like this forever.*

Once inside, I quickly changed out of my jeans and socks and into drier clothes. Then I put the hat into the kitchen sink and filled it with hot water, squirting dish soap over it.

I kneaded the hat, watching the water turn dirty and feeling the chunks of ice start to dissolve. I held up the hat while I let out the water then refilled the sink. "I found the hat, Sadie. It came out really good. He'll love it," I whispered.

Kneading it again, trying to soften it up even more, I heard a clink in the sink. It made me look at it closer. A small crochet hook was still attached. Maybe she hadn't quite finished it, after all. Once the hat was rinsed out, I placed it on a bath towel near the baseboard in the bathroom.

It was too nice outside to stay in the dark trailer, and I had no place to be until Carson was done with pre-school. Slipping on an old pair of my father's boots, I left, choosing to go out the back door.

The hill behind our place had a trail further up, into the woods. I hadn't walked it in a long time. When I passed the station wagon, I thought of Sadie's obsession with the boy from Tennessee. How she wouldn't let it go and had finally done something about it by telling Dominic Sousa. Even when she'd known it would upset me, her need to do the right thing had been greater.

I kept walking and making my way up through the gnarly vines and over fallen trees. Once in the forest, it was quiet, but signs of spring were everywhere. I had to duck under white pine needles and sidestep pools of standing water on the trail. My boots made sucking noises as I straddled the low-level spots of the fields I crossed. Little birds — sparrows — darted in and out of the rows of old corn stalks and grew noisy, sounding the alarm when I got too close to their ground nests.

With each step I took, I realized that Sadie, unlike me, had started to live beyond the confines of Tabor Road. But I hadn't ever dared to think that was a possibility for me. The weight of my father, the responsibility of Sadie, and then the scare of losing Carson had eclipsed everything. Our lack of money fed into my belief that there were no other options for me. It was enough just to get through each day.

At the edge of the last field, I stood and looked out over at the garden center's outbuildings. Mr. Heaton was on the tractor, moving a pile of mulch from one spot to another one under a wide lean-to. Someone else was mending the plastic sheeting along the closest greenhouse that faced me.

It was dumb that I had quit school. That my anxiety around Sadie had caused me to act in the ways that I did. The old man was the adult; I'd just been a kid. What had Cynthia at Carson's pre-school called it? *Being parentified.* Quitting had limited my options as I'd grown older. But my father had let me call the shots. What did I know? I'd never admit what a mistake it had been to anyone, but it was true. I'd been sealing the deal, the mindset, to not expect much else from that point on.

But for Sadie, things were starting to be different. She'd gotten the job at Shay's and had allowed herself to see and experience what my fears, my insecurities, and, to some extent, my pride, wouldn't allow me to see.

The afternoon sun felt warm on my face. *What if I could live differently?* My baggage — the paralyzing fear that I could lose my son — determined most, if not all, of my actions. It held me back, in fear and anger. If I didn't do something about it, I would become Carson's baggage — carrying the weight of his mother and her issues.

Mrs. Heaton and her two retrievers came out of the back door of their old farmhouse near the garden center. She'd been the nicest woman to me back then, when I was just 16. We'd worked side by side in the greenhouses, getting the annuals unloaded and set up, placing the pots of perennials along the east side of the garden center, and arranging the decorative garden items in the small pavilion. After Sadie's death, she'd brought us food.

"You were the best big sister," she'd said as she handed me a casserole while Mr. Heaton had sat in his pickup, watching us. I knew it wasn't true, but I'd thanked her all the same.

The two lab retrievers, one chocolate, one yellow, came bounding up the hill towards me. I waved down to Mrs. Heaton. The dogs ran around me then flew back down the hill.

I turned to go back home but stopped. *What if I finally did something?* I stood absolutely still. A thought, an idea, was trying to make its way to me. I inhaled deeply and let my breath out slowly. *What if I confronted Brother Ron head-on and told him he had a son? Could I get him to give up his rights to Carson? What if I threatened to tell his father and wife about us that summer if he refused?* I started to walk again, slowly, my eyes scanning the ground, my thoughts focused in on this idea. *I could even check on Sadie's boy once I was down there in Tennessee. It'd be a chance to make up for all the times I'd blown her off.*

The sparrows sounded the alarm again, but I hardly noticed, concentrating instead on these new possibilities. The library was open for at least another hour.

I felt myself slipping down the hill behind the trailer, but I managed to grab hold of some vines to catch myself from falling. Just as I rounded the tool shed, my sweatshirt caught on a piece of scrap metal my father had piled there. Quickly, I tore it away, not caring about the rip, and kept moving.

Once inside the Honda, I grabbed an old shopping list in the console and scribbled on the back of it: '*Signing away parental rights,*' and below that, '*Lucia Alvarez, missing child.*'

Chapter 6

After a restless night of little sleep, I drove to The Pines the next morning. Mrs. Lake's room was the third door down on the left. I looked in. Dominic Sousa was taking a big bite out of a bagel while his grandmother was turning up the volume on *Good Morning America*. He looked surprised to see me and put the bagel down. Mrs. Lake turned to me and smiled.

"Can I borrow Nicky for a minute?" I asked her, speaking loudly over the TV.

"Of course you can, Kit."

Dominic wiped his mouth and then his hands on a napkin and walked to the door.

"Can we talk?" I asked.

"Sure," he replied. "But please, call me Dominic."

"Maybe in the community room?" I pointed down the hallway.

Once there, I moved to the table in front of the large picture window and sat down. Dominic followed me. He looked unsure, and I was unsure of what, exactly, I was about to say. No one else was in the room; it was way too early.

He smiled, and it made me less nervous.

"I'm going to Tennessee to confront Carson's dad and tell him he has a son. It's time. If the shit hits the fan, well, so be it. At least I'll have a say in it. I've been too passive, too scared to find out if he knows or what he'd do if he did," I said, sounding more sure than I really felt.

Dominic nodded and said, "Okay. What can I do to help?"

"Nothing when it comes to Carson's father, but…" I hesitated. Sadie had been upset at my reaction around the detectives, yet her need to find out about the boy had been greater than her worry over me. I brought my hands up and rested them on the table in front of me. "I'm also going to try and find out about the boy, once and for all. I owe it to Sadie."

Dominic looked surprised and replied, "The Tennessee Bureau of Investigation still hasn't had any new developments after they matched Lucia Alvarez's DNA to the things inside your station wagon. All the information on the case and the missing children's website was updated to reflect that he identifies as a male. The last time I read the file, no new leads had come in. Also, the other DNA we found inside the station wagon hasn't had any new hits in CODIS — the national database for DNA profiles. In other words, the two men Sadie saw beating him up are still unidentified since their DNA isn't in the system."

I squared my shoulders. "I know it's a stretch, but while I'm down there dealing with Carson's father, I'm going to find out what I can. For years, I squashed all of Sadie's talk about him and those men. All I did was blow her off."

Dominic paused then replied, "Sadie was really rattled by the beating. If the kid survived, he could be living somewhere else, finally, as who he wants to be. He probably doesn't want to be found. What's it been — six years?"

I quickly replied, "And that would be great." Looking out the picture window, I watched two squirrels zig-zag across the courtyard. "I'm not going to do anything other than ask around. He was about my age, and there's a possibility we hung out at some of the same places. The Diamondback was just a stone's throw from the tent church, and our campground was close by, too. There was a bar that a lot of young people went to besides The Diamond-back. Look, it's all kind of like this." I quickly grabbed a bingo card and a pencil from the table next to us, and I scooped up some bingo markers.

"This is how close we were to things." I turned over the bingo card and put five chips around it. Lightly, I drew a line on the table from one marker to the next, finally connecting them all. "The bingo card is the city block around Fifth and Sixth Street. Sorry, I can't remember the cross streets. We were definitely in a less desirable part of Goodlettsville. Our campground was mostly just old campers on cement slabs off Fifth Street. There was a motel here, an autobody shop here, the car wash I worked at was near the corner of Sixth Street, and these wavy lines I'm drawing were the fields to the tent church." I quickly got up to grab two more chips. "Here, past the tent church, was The Diamondback. And my last marker back on Sixth — that was a bar called Rita's. They'd serve anybody, including me, even though I was underage." I sat back, surveying my little Goodlettsville map. "The boy Sadie saw get hurt was here. If I focus on this area, who knows, maybe something will come up."

"And where would you connect with your son's father? Somewhere in here?" Dominic moved his hand over the card and chips.

"I think the best way to connect with him is away from the tent church but around his old hangouts. That'd be the autobody shop here. He was big into old trucks, and the guys at the autobody place were friends of his. They'd bring their newly restored vehicles over to the car wash because their place didn't have the space to wash 'em. He also fished a lot, way out here, on Old Hickory Lake." I drew a circle with a fish in it. "He had a boat in a slip there. He couldn't drink out in the bars; it went against the tent church. But he drank and smoked when he was on his boat."

Dominic looked down at the table with the markers and then up at me. "Not the campground image that usually comes to mind, is it? We used to camp as kids up in the Willis State Forest off of Route Five, deep in the woods. My sisters hated it."

"Well, lots of the campers were people who had lost their homes or were passing through in search of work. It was right after the recession of two thousand and eight."

I leaned over and grabbed a folded piece of paper from my backpack. I moved it in front of Dominic. "What I'm hoping is that you can get me two good photos. One of Lucia Alvarez, and then, if it's on file, a photo of the boy after he transitioned. I printed this at the library, but I took it off the internet and the quality sucks. Can you do that for me?" Nervously, I added, "And can you fill me in on anything the police have that hasn't been shared with the public?"

Dominic appeared uncomfortable as he glanced out the window.

"I remember you, at Karen's, the morning after Sadie was killed," I said. "I wasn't too with it, I know, but you said you were there to see what you could do. Well, this is what you can do."

He moved his chair back and stood up. "I get that this is something you want to do for Sadie. I get that. Your little sister was a wonderful kid, and she didn't deserve to die in that way. But there's a lot of bad stuff out there. Dark stuff that most people don't know about or ever see." He moved to the windowsill and turned around. "Let me go back into the files. I'll read through them again and see if anything else has been added. Then I'll share what I can. When are you planning on leaving?"

I gathered the markers, the chips, and the bingo card and put them all back. I erased the pencil lines from the table and looked over at him. "It depends, but as soon as I can. Because I came back to work pretty soon after Sadie's accident, they told me I could take time off if I needed to. I need to for this."

Dominic and I moved to the hallway and started to walk back to his grandmother's room. I said quietly, "My main focus is meeting up with Carson's father to tell him he has a son and to persuade him to terminate his parental rights. But, like I said, I'm also going to ask around about the boy, with or without whatever you can give me."

AS I WAS SLOWLY DRIVING past the entrance to The Pines, I heard my name being called. I stopped and watched Dominic walking at a fast clip towards me. "Yeah?" I replied, rolling down my window.

"When I said 'bad stuff' back there, I should have been more explicit. Hate crimes involving the LGBQT plus population are on the rise, and…" He stopped.

I waited.

"And Black and Brown kids go missing in percentages that are disproportionate to their race in the general population. It's out of whack. A lot of them become victims of exploitation. Kids in state care tend to run away in high numbers, too. They're just as vulnerable."

I looked up at him with alarm. "Do you think that's the case for the boy?"

Dominic leaned on my car window. "I don't know his situation, but Hispanic and transgendered? Really tough to be out there on your own and not be exposed to bad elements."

He was right; I didn't know any of this stuff. Maybe it'd be better if I only went down to confront Ron Warren.

Dominic straightened up, looked back at the nursing home, then down at me and said, "I have comp time I never took when I left being a trooper and became a detective. I could come with you. It'd have to be under the radar. I'm not on this case anymore, and I have no business taking it any further. But finding out about the boy was important to Sadie, I know that. And, I kind of believe that she'd actually want this — us going down there ourselves to see if he was okay. Again, not in any detective role, only to informally help you out."

"No authority over me, your badge off, fully equals?" I asked.

"Yes. Just two people — acquaintances, finding out about a boy who meant a lot to someone who meant a lot. Does that make sense?"

I thought about it for a moment and replied, "Nah. This is my deal, Dominic. Besides, I don't do well with people in general. But I appreciate the offer."

He nodded and replied, "Maybe we should exchange numbers just in case you change your mind."

"I won't." But it would be good to have a way to get ahold of him if I did have questions about the boy. "Yeah, okay. Having your number isn't a bad idea."

He nodded, and we both took out our cells and passed them over to each other. Once we were done plugging in our contact information, I said, "I'll head out as soon as I make sure Carson is covered. My father might not like any of this. Telling Brother Ron about Carson and hoping he signs away his rights could backfire. But I can't keep going on like this — expecting the worse every day."

Dominic stepped back and looked at my Honda. "What year is this?"

I grew defensive and replied, "It's over ten years old, but it'll have to do. Not all of us can afford new cars."

He nodded then started to walk back to The Pines. I called out, "Can I have the photos? And any new information?"

He didn't turn back around, only said, "I'll text you."

Chapter 7

Two days later, Finn put down the hood of my car and said, "I don't know, Kate, I've done all I can to tune her up and fix what I see, but she's up there. How many miles?"

"A hundred and thirty-two thousand," I replied.

"Can't you rent a car?" he asked.

I was already using the money I had stowed away in case we needed to leave town. I'd budgeted for gas and staying at a motel. But the tune up, along with a new radiator hose and thermostat, were eating into a chunk of it. To rent a car, plus miles, was way over what I could afford.

"No, I can't rent a car." I looked at him and said, "It's about a thousand miles each way. Come on, she's good to go, huh?"

"I can't guarantee that at all. The water pump, the timing belt — all those things play into a car with this much mileage. You could drive on over to Thurston's and trade it in. There's a red Crosstrek out front that I've had my eye on. I think it's a two thousand and twelve."

I couldn't afford the monthly payment, but I didn't tell him that. Instead, I asked for a receipt for the work he'd done and left his shop.

As I stood outside and watched the cars zoom by on Route 131, I wondered what to do. I didn't have a credit card or roadside service. "It sucks being me," I said out loud and walked over to my car.

By the time I reached Tabor Road, I was doubting this whole trip of mine. *What was I thinking?* But I had to go. Every time I looked at Carson, I knew he deserved more than a mother who was constantly on high alert, waiting for the other shoe to drop. I had to take this all the way through to the end or I'd never be free of the fear. And Sadie's boy? He was becoming emblematic of my failure to be there for her, to keep her safe. No, it was just the question of the car. Would it make it there and back?

Dominic Sousa texted me later that night: *"I've got a better photo and more information. Putting it out there again — I could come with you."*

I hesitated then texted back: *"What do you drive?"*

"2014 Volvo, with great tires — it's a smooth ride."

"Going as equals, no bullshit cop stuff?"

"Right. I could get in trouble if I went as a detective since I'm no longer assigned to the case."

Carson was asleep on the little bed in the corner of my room. I got up and walked to my dresser and grabbed some lip balm. I looked at my reflection in the mirror. For someone turning 24, I looked tired.

Carson coughed and turned away from me, facing the wall. His covers had fallen off, exposing his little bare back. I moved over and covered him. Sitting on the edge of my bed, I weighed whether to drive the Honda and pray it made it there and back or take Dominic up on his offer.

A new text came in. *'It's about 17 hrs — we could split the driving.'*

I needed to be smart here and let go of my pride. I wavered for a moment then responded: *'I need one more day. Tues a.m.?'*

'4 a.m. too early?'

'No, I'll be ready.'

THE NEXT MORNING, after I took Carson to school, I found my father in his tool shed sanding the top to an old table and blasting Led Zeppelin. He looked up and smiled. I motioned for him to turn down the music. The song "Good Times Bad Times" was playing. The irony in that wasn't lost to me.

"Can we chat?" I asked as I moved to a stool, the one I used to sit on as a little girl. It was high and wobbly and scary to spin around on. Sadie loved the thrill of it, too, and then along came Carson. He didn't want to spin, instead he'd use it to climb onto the work table to see what the old man was doing up close.

The tool shed grew quiet when my father turned down the music and stopped sanding. He smiled and asked, "Little one get out okay this morning?"

I nodded. Carson and I were butting heads on just about everything these days.

He wiped his hands while I stayed perched on the stool. My father's sorrow had manifested itself into his incredible shrinking body. I didn't know how much weight he'd lost since March, but it was pronounced. His shoulders, already stooped, looked even more concaved. If somebody were to guess his age, I bet they'd pin him at 65, maybe even older. But he'd just gotten his 35th high school reunion notice in the mail. That made him 53 years old. Karen had told me that the old man had once been the spitting image of a young James Dean. "Only an athletic James Dean, if you can imagine." He'd been on the small side as a star second baseman at Langdon High. He could have played college ball, they said, but there was nobody guiding him, giving him any advice. He'd joined the Army the summer after he'd graduated.

"Some bad times, Kate. Some really bad times, uh?" my father said, referring to the Zeppelin song just finishing up. He crossed his arms and leaned against the work table. His left eye seemed milky — was it the start of a cataract? I knew what that looked like from the residents at The Pines.

"Yeah, the worst of times, Dad." I didn't turn from him like I usually did when we were going there about Sadie. We tended to tiptoe around our grief, avoiding all talk of the devastation caused by her passing. But now I needed to be straight with him and explain why I was going to Tennessee.

Clearing my throat, I started, "My way of handling losing Sadie has not been good. We both know this, and Carson is definitely feeling it. The rut I was in before — now I'm in it really deep. You...you've like risen to the top for him. Thank you."

My father moved closer and replied, "Katie-girl, look who you're talking to. How many times have I been there in that same rut and you've been the one to pull me out? So, I get it. The only thing I'd say to you now is to be careful. Sometimes there's a point of no return when the bottom of a bottle is your solution."

I nodded slowly and said, "That's why there's something I got to do that you might not agree with. But it has to happen to help me move on, move through this."

A road crew had started grading our road. Their trucks were loud out front, but I forged ahead. "There's a form called 'Voluntary Surrender of Parental Rights.' I printed it out at the town library. Tuesday morning, I'm heading to Tennessee to tell Brother Ron about Carson and to get him to sign it. I'll threaten to tell Darlene and Father Ray if he won't. Dominic Sousa is coming with me. We're going to try to find out what we can about Sadie's boy, too. You know Sousa, he's a professional." I didn't tell him that Sousa wasn't going down as a detective because I knew he'd be more apt to be okay with it if he thought he was.

Dad was looking at me intently now. I quickly added, "My worry over that asshole taking Carson dominates my life. I want to settle it, Dad. I need to."

His face seemed to soften for just a moment, but then he turned away. I reached for his hand and took it. "Do you understand...at all?" I asked.

This time when he turned back around, he had tears in his eyes. "There's so much at stake, Kate. He could fight you hard on this. But if you're set on going and confronting him, then be that goddamn ferocious girl I somehow raised, okay?"

I reached out quickly and wrapped my arms around him. My hug couldn't have been any tighter.

THE LAST THING I NEEDED to do was tell Karen and ask her to keep an eye on my father and Carson. I was in Karen's kitchen, an hour later, lifting the top of her cookie jar when she walked in. The difference between my father and her was striking, even though they were the same age. They looked decades apart. Plus, Karen was dressed to the max in a beautiful tailored blue suit with a pale purple silk blouse. Her bank had recently merged with a bigger out-of-state one, and she was up for a promotion. She smiled and sat down across from me.

"I cannot tell a lie. This is my third cookie. There's two left for you." I said, smiling as she glanced at the cookie jar. "And you look great! Like I'd give you all my money if I had any."

"About the cookies, Kate...I was about to throw them out. They've been there for over a week."

"Nice try, "I replied.

"No, I'm serious, they're well over a week old."

I stood up and moved to the cookie jar. "Then I'd say that this is one hell of a cookie jar."

Karen motioned for me to come back and added, "One of the big-wigs is flying in. It's my interview today."

Sitting back down, I turned to her. "They'd be fools not to promote you."

Karen smiled again and glanced at the little blue clock on her coffee maker.

She needed to get going, so I spilled it all out. "I'm going to Tennessee to tell Carson's father about him and get his signature to surrender parental rights. Carson will be five at the end of the month. For so long, I've been scared, planning to run if his father ever came up here to Vermont. But I have to stop. I have to confront him and go from there."

Karen slowly nodded and asked, "And your father says what?"

"That he gets it, that he understands," I replied.

Karen stood up and walked over to her sink then turned around, leaning against the counter. "What if he wants full custody?" she asked.

"I've been reading up on it — unless I'm an unfit mother, that won't ever happen."

"You've been drinking a lot since Sadie…" Karen said softly. She never held back.

"I know, but that's going to stop. I've got a plan for how to deal with Sadie's death better."

"Oh, yeah?" she asked. "Share that with me."

I held back, though, unsure how much she knew about Sadie and the boy or the detectives who came to the trailer back in January.

Getting back to the subject of Carson's father, I said, "If he won't sign away his parental rights, then I'll let him know I plan on telling his family he has a kid from an affair. If he still won't sign, then I'll get a lawyer and we'll figure it out."

"This is a huge decision, Kate." Karen walked back and sat down once more across from me. "But it's one I understand."

"Thank you," I replied. We both stood. "I'm leaving tomorrow at four in the morning and hope to be back in a couple of days. Will you keep an eye on them while I'm gone?"

Karen nodded then walked me to the door and asked, "You got enough money? Is your car up for the long haul?"

"Yes, to the money. And a friend is driving. So, we're all set."

We moved to her porch. Karen's daffodils, all along the side bank of her yard, were done blooming. We both stood looking at them. She put her arms around me and whispered, "Nine weeks and two days. It still seems impossible."

I didn't reply, instead I hugged her and then walked off the porch.

Chapter 8

Dominic was parked at the end of our place with lights off but his car was running. It was pitch black out. The peepers in the swamp across the road were loud. The night sky was overcast.

"You're a light packer," he said, quietly, when I opened the door.

I threw my backpack in the back seat and climbed in, keeping my shoulder bag up front with me.

"If we're lucky with traffic, we should be there by about ten tonight." He started back down Tabor Road. It was awkward as hell being with him, but the bucket seat was incredibly comfortable.

"We should call ahead for rooms. What's the name of the motel in that block you showed me?" he asked as we picked up speed through Langdon, heading for the interstate.

"Moody's. It's not very nice, but it's right smack dab where we want to be. I'll call in a couple of hours."

"And I'll fill you in once we stop and get coffee. In the meantime, if you want to sleep, go ahead," Dominic replied.

I'd tossed and turned most of the night in anticipation, imagining worse case scenarios about Ron hearing he had a son. Would he rant and rave that I'd kept it a secret for all these years? Would he threaten me with wanting full custody? Even though we'd had an affair for four months, I didn't know how he'd take it. He had been secretive, making sure that no one found out about us. He was a pro too, knowing just where to meet and what time was best. Our eventual confrontation seemed far off, even though I was in a car, finally going back to Tennessee.

I carefully moved the seat back, lightly pulling on the seat belt. "I'll drive, too, but if I could sleep now, that'd be good."

Dominic nodded. I turned away from him. I hoped I wasn't going to snore or drool — two things I often did.

"It's mostly interstate ninety west and then seventy-one south," he said. "But sure, you can give me a break at some point."

"When my father drove us down six years ago, we had to avoid major roads because he had unpaid tickets. It took us forever."

That was the last thing I remembered saying for a while. The smooth hum of the car, along with the super soft leather seat, lulled me to sleep.

It's the dream again — Sadie walking away from me. The air is warm and humid, with the wind kicking up. The sky's dark, and off in the distance, there's a rumble. "It's going to storm, get out of the road," I call to her, but Sadie turns and smiles then shakes her head. The rumble grows louder, a flash of lightning above the trees. "Take the path along the honey-suckle to Karen's porch and wait for me!" I yell. My voice is angry now. "Do it, Sadie, or else…" I begin to run after her, but my legs feel heavy. I finally reach her, yanking on her arm, angry that she's ignored me. But her arm breaks away. I stand there holding it. The rumble becomes a roar, and she's gone.

"HEY, WAKE UP." Dominic touched my shoulder. I slowly sat up and wiped my mouth. We were stopped. Two large tractor trailers were parked in front of us, their engines idling. It was light, a grayish pink out my window. The land was flat, and there was a river across the highway. Mist was rising above it.

"I've got to use the bathroom and grab coffee," he said. "It's seven twenty. You staying here or want to come in?"

I pulled my seat up and unfastened my seat belt. "I'll come in."

Walking behind him, I took in his outfit. He couldn't dress like that when we got to the part of Goodlettsville we were going to. He looked too cop-like, and I knew he'd stand out.

In the little shop, I grabbed some trail mix and coffee. 'I love New York' signs were all over, including on the sweat-shirts and t-shirts on a rack in the corner. Dominic walked in, caught my eye, and ordered coffee. He wasn't a talker, which suited me.

We fell in step as we walked back to the Volvo. *Should I bring up his clothes?* I didn't. Instead, as we pulled away and took the on-ramp, I asked, "You ever been to Tennessee?"

"Went to Nashville for a bachelor's party a few years back. One of my college roommates. But I don't remember much."

I glanced at him. He didn't fit being a 'Nicky' like his grandmother called him. He seemed way too reserved. He drove sitting straight up with his sunglasses already on, even though the sun hadn't come out yet. Some women would like his darkness, call him handsome. I noticed it but couldn't really appreciate it myself. I hadn't really thought about anybody in that way since Sadie's death.

He added, "I was a big drinker, had to outdrink all the other frat boys. But that doesn't work when you become a state trooper. The two don't mix."

I thought about Drew and the girl he had hung out with at Pete's. He was definitely sick of me. Truth be told, I was sick of me. "It doesn't mix well with relationships, either, even when they suck to begin with," I replied.

Dominic nodded and then replied, "I was almost married once."

I didn't say anything, not sure how to respond. Eventually he said, "If you're ready, reach back and grab that green file. I'll go over the important stuff. I've read through it a few times."

Soon, I was thumbing through the pages.

"There's a sheet with your name on top. I typed that up for you. It's a summary with the most important updates. A lot of the information in there is written in language meant for us in the field — full of law enforcement jargon."

The sheet had a picture of the missing child — here as Lucia Alvarez — clipped to it. The quality was much better than the one from the library's printer. The lady behind the counter had mentioned that the ink cartridge needed to be changed. She'd been apologetic.

I began to read. Lucia Alvarez had disappeared from her home in 2006, at the age of 16. She was from Shelby County, just outside of Memphis. Before that she'd lived in New York City. There was a big asterisk by that notation. "What's the asterisk by New York for?" I asked.

"Glad you saw that…Lucia Alvarez had been a Fresh Air kid in Vermont, and more specifically, to a family in Bridgewater. For three summers, she came to stay with the Hillard family. Lucia and their two girls went to the day camp at Farm and Wilderness."

"Holy shit!" I whispered, remembering my own experiences with a few Fresh Air kids at the Langdon Rec swimming hole. The inner-city kids tended to be shy at first, but by the end of the summer, we all played together. Mostly Black and Brown kids getting out of the city and experiencing life in the countryside.

I held up her picture and studied the dark-haired girl with the even features. "She looks sweet. This must have been taken when she was younger," I said, glancing at Dominic.

He replied, "There's a photoshopped picture of what he possibly looked like after he transitioned. I wish I could have shown Sadie the photo so she could have told us if it was a fair rendering of the boy."

I found the second photo and held it alongside Lucia Alvarez's picture. "Did Sadie describe the boy to you in any detail? Anything that stood out about him? Like piercings or hair?"

"Just that he was skinny. He was about five seven, and weighed… What's it say there?"

"One hundred and twenty-five pounds." I shifted in my seat and began to read more of the summary he'd written for me.

The DNA, extracted from the items in the car, had been uploaded into the national database and was a match for Lucia Alvarez. By the summer of 2009, Lucia was identifying as Lucas Alvarez. He'd been hired in Davidson County as a census worker for the Goodlettsville area and had been carrying out preliminary work for the 2010 official census the following spring. He had also been volunteering in various youth programs and was cited as one of the young, positive role models for Goodlettsville's growing Somalian population. Lucas Alvarez had even met the mayor at a community outreach dinner.

I looked over at Dominic and said, "He was living and working openly as a male, that's great."

"Read on about his family." Dominic motioned to the folder.

There were interviews inside the file, but I relied on Dominic's summary. After the DNA match, the police had returned to question the Alvarez family. No one knew of Lucas, and his parents didn't accept this new development. A close friend, however, had said it didn't surprise her that Lucia had transitioned. "A big heart and lots of dreams. I'm sure he left to get himself squared away."

Dominic continued, "After the night Sadie witnessed him getting beat up, Lucas disappeared. He didn't report to work that Monday or anytime thereafter. His roommate, at the apartment he was subletting, never saw him again. No hospital reports, no forwarding address, even his last paycheck wasn't picked up. The police in Goodlettsville issued a missing person's bulletin. Nothing."

I thought of Jeannie holding onto Sadie's last paycheck. *People don't leave money behind unless something happened.*

There were copies of our depositions given back in January. I'd never heard all of the details about what Sadie witnessed in the station wagon because I'd always cut her off. Now I read what had happened.

"Thank God those men didn't see her," I said when I got to the end.

Dominic glanced over at me. "I've had that same thought, too."

His handwritten notes were tucked in the back. I read what he'd written after Sadie's initial request for him to check on the boy. Across the top it read: *'Sadie Wade, Shay's, January, 2016,'* and what she'd given him to go on. At the end, he'd written, *'Sweet Kid!'* On the call Sadie had made when she'd raised the possibility that her boy was Lucia Alvarez, the missing girl, there were a series of asterisks with: *'Is Sadie's boy Lucia?? Call TBI, get forensics.'*

I turned to Dominic and asked, "Is there any place in here explaining why it took so long for the Tennessee authorities to want to question my father — six years almost — about the girl? We were back on Tabor Road within two days of leaving Tennessee in two thousand and nine."

"Apparently, Lucia Alvarez's debit card was used twice in The Diamondback that summer. The second time, a witness named Ben — I can't remember his last name — was overlooked. When they discovered that, they tracked him down. He mentioned your father, said the two of them had been tying one on. The address he gave was 'someplace up in Vermont.' Tennessee law enforcement got ahold of us eventually, and I drove out to Tabor Road, but no one was home. So, I stopped at Shay's. I knew Sadie worked there. Our paths had crossed a couple of times already."

I looked out the window at the whirling landscape. My father's assurance that Ben, his buddy from the service, didn't know where we were from had been bullshit, after all.

"They assumed the debit card had been stolen since no one in the bar recognized Lucia Alvarez's photo. They had no idea that they should have been looking for a boy, a young man, using a fake ID under the name Lucas Alvarez."

I was just about to close the file but saw one more handwritten note. *'In car on Tabor Road: Sister ripping mad. Her son — custody issues. Sadie's afraid of her.'*

We drove for some time in silence. Dominic asked if I was hungry, and I shook my head. Then I asked if he wanted me to drive, and he shook his head. '*Sadie's afraid of her*' — I couldn't get that out of my head. My insides felt like a giant pit opening up. I leaned against the car door, watching the landscape speed by. *Had I been that intimidating or overbearing to her?* For a few seconds, I wondered if I was going to be sick to my stomach.

After some time, I said, "Had a chance to look up stuff on missing children. The numbers for children of color are high, like you said."

Dominic replied, "Sometimes, kids who are thinking of running just need more support. Whatever their situation is, we need a multi-prong approach. Youth programs, counseling, drug and alcohol rehab, vocational education. Way more than what law enforcement can do after the fact."

A fleeting thought came: *Having Sadie in my life kept me grounded, kept me from ever thinking of taking off.*

IN SOUTHERN OHIO, we stopped to fill up the gas tank and take a walking break. I was hungry and said I'd drive after I ate. We were on I-71 south now and following signs to Cincinnati. I bought a salad and, at the last minute, a package of Twinkies.

It was warmer outside than in the car. I pulled my sweatshirt off and ate the salad leaning against the car. Dominic was still inside the rest stop. Just as he walked out, I took a bite of the Twinkie and looked up. A jet, barely discernible, was leaving a streak across the blue sky. '*Happy fucking birthday to me.*' What were the odds of having a Twinkie for a second time on May 9th in southern Ohio?

As I adjusted the mirrors and the car seat, I glanced at Dominic. He was watching me.

"What?" I asked.

"You a good driver? Should I stay awake?"

"Nah, you can sleep."

He reclined all the way back in his seat.

"Maybe keep one eye open," I said, pulling out and pressing down on the accelerator to join the southbound traffic.

But he never responded. Within minutes, he was snoring. I turned the radio up and rolled down my window a little bit. The highway stretched out before me. We had about 400 miles to go. Again, I was glad Dominic Sousa wasn't a big talker. Moody's, the shitty motel near the campground, had two rooms reserved for us.

Chapter 9

As we walked out of the office at Moody's, I held up my room key. "So, I'm on this first floor, right there." I pointed to a room three doors down from the office. "And you're up there. What number?"

Dominic held up his key and said, "Twenty-seven, and that would be…there." It was up the stairs and down the balcony, the second to the last door on the right.

I glanced around. "This place looks better than I remember — fresh paint and nicer landscaping. I don't remember those shrubs or all these perennials. I used to cut through here walking to work."

We grabbed our bags from the back seat and Dominic locked the Volvo. I watched him glance at my room and then at his.

"Would you rather have the second floor?" he asked. "Not be on the ground level with the cars coming and going, lights shining in, people walking by?"

"No, I can handle it." I turned past his car and pointed. "There's Rita's — see the blue neon sign? The 't' is still broken. I'm going to wash up and walk over for a beer."

Dominic looked at me and then up towards his room. "Baseball's on. I'm pretty beat. We'll meet up early, make a plan?"

I nodded. "Yeah, just not at four a.m."

"It's safe around here?" he asked.

I shrugged my shoulders. "Probably not. But I'm a big girl."

IT WAS THE SAME DIVE — full of young people, including the two guys taking turns hitting on me. I hadn't paid for a draft since I'd walked in. The bartender put another one down in front of me.

"That's from the big, rugged guy standing over there with the pool stick. My money's on him."

I didn't like how that sounded and said, "Oh yeah, what are you betting on?"

The bartender shook his head and moved further down to the other end of the bar.

Just then I felt someone lightly touch my shoulder and call out my name. "Kate, it's late. Let me walk you back to your room, okay?"

I swiveled around in my barstool and smiled. "Hello there, Dominic Sousa. So glad you decided to come. What'll you have?"

Dominic shook his head and said, "It's past one o'clock. Can I walk you back?"

He looked different wearing a gray sweatshirt and blue jeans. Much more casual and 'under the radar.' I leaned into him and whispered, "You're looking under the radar, for sure."

The guy to my right said, "Hey baby, I can get you home."

Dominic looked briefly over at him and then handed me my purse. "She's fine, thanks. Goodnight."

I ROLLED OVER and opened my eyes. The room was dark except for a sliver of light where the drapes didn't quite meet. It was early, just dawn, but someone was leaving, slamming their car door. They revved the engine. "What an asshole," I moaned.

A man coughed to the right of my bed. Dominic was sitting in the chair, his bare feet resting on the other bed. He'd pulled the bedspread over to cover his legs. He opened his eyes and looked over at me. "Is drinking a problem for you?" he asked.

The air conditioning was on high. I wasn't sure I'd heard him right.

I sat up and smoothed down my hair. "What did you say?" I'd felt worse. On the floor, in front of the TV, were my jeans and flipflops.

"Is drinking too much a habit of yours?" he asked, this time louder. He looked pissed.

"Only for the last nine weeks and three days. Don't look." I stood up and walked into the bathroom.

When I came out, Dominic was long gone. I wasn't thrilled about him feeling like he had to babysit me last night or saying what he had this morning. But then, as I pulled my hair back and washed my face, I thought drinking down here probably wasn't a good idea. It didn't bode well for talking with Brother Ron, and I didn't want Dominic's judgment.

I texted him, *'I'm walking over to the autobody shop. Ron Warren — Carson's dad — hangs there. Maybe the owners can get ahold of him.'* I didn't get a reply back, but I could see that he'd read the text.

Before I left, I scooted to the office and asked for a pair of scissors. I came back to the room and laid a second, clean pair of jeans out on the floor. I cut the legs off and threw them into the wastebasket. I found my purse with my sunglasses on top of one of the dressers. He must have put it there. The walk back from Rita's was fuzzy — I didn't quite remember it.

I locked my room door, returned the scissors, and crossed the parking lot. The autobody shop was on Sixth Street, one block up. With each step, I felt my chest constrict and my breathing slow down. If Brother Ron was there then this was showtime. *"Be ferocious,"* the old man had said. I clutched my shoulder bag close. I had checked — the form was there, ready for him to sign. *My whole world was at stake.* Only thing was, I didn't feel so ferocious.

THE TWO BAY DOORS WERE OPEN, and a truck was up on one of the lifts. An older, well- dressed man was talking to one of the owners. I moved closer, stepping into the garage, and waited. The owner glanced my way then turned back to the man. But he pivoted to me again and said, "Hiya, darlin', can I help you?"

It was one of Ron's buddies, but I didn't remember his name. I replied, "Wondering if I could have a minute to ask you something."

The older man quickly said, "Lloyd, I'll give you a call later in the week. Once the auction has a date, we can move."

The name Lloyd sounded familiar. He nodded, and the gentleman left. Lloyd turned around to me and said, "I know we've met…a pretty thing like you." He took a hankie out of his back pocket and wiped his face. "Couple of scorchers next few days."

"I worked the car wash a few years back," I replied. "You came by most every day. I'm looking for Ron Warren. Is he going to be around today, or maybe tomorrow?"

Lloyd slowly answered, eyeing me somewhat suspiciously now, "Ron's at some work thing till Friday. I remember you. You're the girl he ran around with one summer. Right when they got their twins."

His friendliness was all but gone as he added, "Ron's a total family man now. Doesn't drink or fool around anymore. I don't think he'd welcome seeing you."

"You're sure he's gone till Friday?" I asked.

"I know so," Lloyd replied, glancing at someone I couldn't see further in the garage.

"Is he going to come by here when he gets back? I need to see him."

Lloyd shrugged his shoulders and didn't say anything.

His silence didn't stop me from saying, "I need you to tell him that I've come back to Goodlettsville to meet with him." I stepped back out into the sun. "My name's Kate. Tell him I'm the Kate from the campground. It's important."

When I reached the corner across the street, I looked back. Lloyd was on his cell. His partner was standing there beside him, watching me. Maybe he was the one who had been listening to us. His name came easily to me — Cal. It was always 'Lloyd and Cal.'

Even though Ron Warren hadn't been there, I was still nervous. My palms were sweaty and the relief I felt was palpable. The plan I'd conjured up that afternoon I'd walked through the woods and fields back home had just been set into motion. I squared my shoulders and turned the corner. *Next time I'd better be ready.*

Chapter 10

Dominic was sitting outside my motel room door, in one of the cheap chairs scattered about the motel's ground level. It was getting hot now, nearing 80 degrees. He stood up when I unlocked the door. I wasn't in the best mood.

"I found out Brother Ron — Ron Warren, the asshole — is out of town till Friday. That sucks!"

"Okay. Today's Wednesday. So that gives us time to focus on Lucas Alvarez, right?"

Dominic's tone was calm and matter of fact. I took off my sunglasses and plopped on my bed. "God, I hate it here. All the memories of that summer are lousy. Apparently, Ron has turned into a good family man."

"He's got a wife and kid now?"

I looked over at Dominic, hesitating for just a moment. "Oh, he had a wife back then, and they'd just adopted twin girls. Considering he was a deacon in the tent church and his father was the pastor, he did a lot of picking and choosing around when to be virtuous. His time with me — not the virtuous part."

We sat quietly for a few moments until I asked, "What have you been up to?"

I got up to turn the air conditioning up.

Dominic leaned forward and replied, "I started showing the photos of Lucas and Lucia to people in the shops and businesses along Fifth Street, working my way toward Sixth. Nobody recognized either one. And I put a call into the census bureau — it's a federal agency, so I'll probably never hear back. I want to know what Lucas Alvarez's job was ahead of the twenty-ten census. I also called the number I found for his roommate back in the day. It just rang and rang."

I pulled the drapes open to let the light in. "I've got to get something to eat."

"I saw a diner over on Fifth. Let's go."

"O-kay," I replied, somewhat sarcastically. "So this is how we're going to do it down here? Like we're joined at the hip?" It was a shitty thing to say, I knew that, but I couldn't help it.

He looked over and said, "Of course not, sorry." And then he left.

"SHIT," I SAID OUT LOUD and hurried after him. The curtains were still open — anyone could see into the room. *Screw it. I don't have anything anybody would want.*

When I caught up to him, I said, "I can be a bitch."

He didn't say anything, just slowed down for me.

"How'd you score that?" I asked, indicating his shirt. It was a Tennessee Titans t-shirt.

"Thrift store, also on Fifth." He was short with me, but I didn't blame him.

"I may have to check it out for a pair of shorts. It's hot, isn't it?" I wished I'd shut up.

Dominic pointed to the other side of Fifth Street and said, "The store's there, and the diner is two doors down." He crossed the street, and I followed.

WHEN THE FOOD ARRIVED, I dived in. I was starved, realizing the salad and Twinkie yesterday on the road were basically all I'd had since the cookies from Karen's amazing cookie jar two days ago. Dominic had an appetite, too. We got more coffee, and I ordered a second orange juice. As I was finishing up, using my last bit of toast to wipe up the yolk on my plate, Dominic said, "Sorry about my comment this morning. I was pissed I hadn't slept well. That's all."

I pushed the plate away and wiped my mouth. The girl came by and took the dishes. "More coffee?" she asked, her hands full.

"Sure." I smiled. She reminded me of me: kind of plain and kind of tough.

I looked at Dominic and said, "You're not here to babysit me. I needed a better car and your help to find out what happened to the boy." I glanced out the window onto the street. "But don't worry, I'm not going to have a repeat."

Dominic was about to say something, but then stopped. He motioned for his cup to be filled, too. After the girl left, he said, "I was thinking it'd be good to walk on over to the campground, then through the fields and past the tent church to check out The Diamondback. You could show me where the station wagon was parked, where you found Sadie that last morning. You guys left after that, right?"

"We stopped and grabbed our clothes from the camper. I want to say Sadie ran to say goodbye to Hetty, and we picked her up there."

"Hetty who?" he asked.

I looked around the diner, hoping to see a woman who looked a little like Hetty. But there was nobody who came close.

"Hetty was — is — this cool lady who lives in the campground. Sadie spent her days with her before meeting up with my dad at the tent church. Hetty was about the only good thing down here. She's kind of an old hippy."

We split the bill and paid. A walk would be good after that big breakfast. I hadn't thought of Hetty since we'd left. I hoped she was still there, parked on the corner, at the end of one of the lanes.

"THE SMELL'S THE SAME — like rotten eggs. Not the smell of the woods or the fields in Vermont, huh?" I asked Dominic as we scooted down the path behind the gas station. It was a shortcut to the campground and one I'd taken daily when I'd worked at the car wash that summer.

"Could be from the trench drain at the gas station. An EPA violation, maybe."

"Just up this incline, and we'll be there," I called back to him. It was growing even warmer. *I should grab a swimsuit from the thrift store and swim later.*

LIKE THE MOTEL, the campground looked upgraded, too. There was a new configuration for traffic flow, and an actual sidewalk had been built, stretching all along the entrance way to the back lots. The mailboxes, once corroded and chipped, were now painted black, and a wooden flower box filled with red and pink impatiens was hanging below the information board. I even noticed the new flag on the pole — it was bigger.

"We lived in a fifth wheel parked down that way." I pointed toward the sidewalk and said, "Let's go." Part of me wondered what Dominic thought of all this — us living like that. But I didn't care really.

Dominic held up his hand. I waited, watching him walk over to the water fountain beside the information board. He took a long sip of water.

"It never worked back then. This is incredible," I said.

"Doesn't take much to wow you, does it?" he replied.

"Well, I mean, you know…" But it was funny, and I stopped being defensive and joined him. I took a sip of the cold water.

We walked along, and the parked campers seemed bigger and newer than I remembered. Each site had its own personality — some with colored lights, outside mats, and flags. We reached what had been our spot to find a shiny Airstream was parked there now. Two bikes leaned against the front, and a small dog was lying on a mat in the shade.

"I swear people must have more money now. Back then it was depressing." I pointed further down the lane. "Hetty's is on the corner."

Hetty was hanging sheets out on a line. Her permanent site was always festive with tomato and pepper plants in big pots, hanging glass globes, brightly painted outdoor furniture, and wind chimes. Her camper was painted a pastel pink, with a bright yellow awning. There was a mural of daisies painted on each side of her door.

She turned when she heard us approach. She looked at me, then at Dominic, and then back at me. *She's got no clue who I am.* I smiled and said, "Hetty, it's me, Kate Wade. Sadie's big sister."

"Jesus, Mary, and Joseph!" she exclaimed and held out her arms. We hugged, and she stepped back, holding onto my hands. "You've grown up!" To Dominic she said, "She's a beauty. Does she smile enough?"

I suddenly realized that Hetty was going to ask about Sadie. The news of her death would be devastating. They had shared a special bond.

Her small deck held a rocker and two chairs. "Hetty, let's go sit down. I have to tell you something." I quickly glanced at Dominic. He was leaning against the post, watching us.

Hetty sat down in the rocker and looked at me with concern. Her age was hard to determine; her hair was often covered in colorful scarves — like it was now — and her face was deeply lined by the sun.

I reached for her hand and said gently, "Sadie died. She was in a horrible accident. It happened almost ten weeks ago." Hetty's hand, wrapped in mind, fluttered. I held on tight.

Instantly, tears came to her eyes. "My Sadie, my little Galen," she whispered.

Some minutes passed, and no one spoke. Hetty rocked slowly back and forth. The campground was quiet; most everyone was off at work.

When I felt she had absorbed the terrible news and we had both stopped crying, I said, "She loved you so much. Every day she spent with you was an adventure."

Hetty glanced at me. "It was a hard time for you, I remember. The tent church has a way of pulling people in or pushing them away. For Sadie, it pulled her in. I would tell her to choose the bits and pieces that spoke to her, that the teachings of Jesus were the most important."

"She did that, Hetty, she took all that good stuff in and lived her life in a kind, giving, full-of-faith way. It was just cut way too short."

I looked over at Dominic. There was something tender in his eyes as he took in Hetty.

"And your father, it must be devastating for him," Hetty said.

"He's trying to manage. He's got a grandson, my boy. That keeps him busy."

Hetty looked surprised and turned to Dominic. "A child — what a blessing!"

I quickly replied, "Oh, Hetty, no — he and I — we're not together. It's not his child."

She nodded and rocked then stood up. "I have something for you, Kate. Give me a second."

We watched her go into the camper. I asked Dominic, "Should we show her the photos? It's a stretch, but maybe she's seen one of them."

Just then Hetty came back out and handed me a notebook. It looked vaguely familiar. I looked up at her and asked, "Is this Sadie's drawing book? The one she always carted around?"

"That last morning, she ran here to say goodbye and asked me to keep it for her. She said something had happened and you had to leave. I've kept it, hoping to see her, and you, again."

I held it to my chest. "Thank you." I hugged Hetty and turned to Dominic. He looked ready to leave.

As we started to go, I turned back and called out, "Why did you call her that, Hetty... Your little Galen?"

"It's Greek for healer. Look."

She pulled up her long skirt. I covered my mouth and said softly, "Oh my gosh, Hetty."

Her legs were riddled with bulging blue and purple veins. It looked beyond painful.

"For the months we spent together, Sadie would rub aloe onto these veins most every day while she prayed. All this disappeared. One of the tent church ladies asked if she would do it to hers. The same thing happened. Sadie had the touch, the healer's touch."

Chapter 11

A re you okay?" Dominic asked as we walked down through the second field on our way to the tent church. The land was dry and cracked — so different than the fields I'd just walked in at home. And it was getting hotter. I needed water.

I held up Sadie's notebook and replied, "This is going to be hard to look through. She was always drawing — at least until she started to crochet stuff. She still sketched after that, but not as much."

"What'd you think of Hetty's claim that Sadie made her veins all better?" Dominic asked. He was dripping in sweat. He lifted his shirt up and used it to wipe his chin. I tried not to look at his stomach. He was pretty confident in his masculinity — just like he was in everything else.

I replied, in a harsher tone than I meant to, "That's the tent church's bullshit. People being cured by the laying on of hands and praying."

Dominic nodded. "Reminds me of the patron saints I grew up with in the Catholic Church. You'd pray to the saint in charge of whatever ailed you, and you'd get better. We learned about intercessors in my catechism classes, too — people who prayed on behalf of others. They'd get God to intervene."

I glanced over and asked, "You believe in all that?"

Dominic shrugged. "I did, at one point."

The tent church was just past the edge of the field. I stopped. You could see its dull white canvas and the peak in the middle. Two cars were parked near the opening closest to us.

"Let's not get too close. We'll walk over that way." I pointed to the bank along the road, parallel to the tent. "If we walk up there, we won't have to acknowledge anyone."

Dominic replied, "They recruiting?"

"Always," I answered. The site of the church made me uneasy. At first, I'd fallen right into the nightly gatherings, going along with Sadie and Dad. There'd been nothing better to do, and I hadn't known anybody in town. But then the women had started to ask me to come to their morning prayer groups and offered me dresses to wear, suggesting I tone down my 'seductiveness.' What had they said? *"Pure thoughts begin on the inside, and dressing modestly keeps you pure on the outside."* Little did they know — or maybe they did — that some of their men folk had eyes for the girls in town who didn't wear modest dresses.

DOMINIC AND I CROSSED THE FIELD and climbed the bank to the top of the road. It was surprising how quickly the area just past the campground became countryside. Here, traffic was at a minimum and small rolling hills were dotted by a few houses.

My flipflops weren't good on the shoulder of the road. Little stones kept sliding in and bothering me. I stopped to wipe the bottom of each foot and said, "The bar is just past that next bend. This heat is unbearable. I'm going to swim when we get back."

Dominic waited until I was ready to go again. We passed the last house before the bend. Suddenly, a scrappy looking German Shepherd mix came charging down to the edge of the driveway and started to bark loudly. It wasn't friendly; the hair was up on its back, and its teeth were bared.

"Cross over to the other side of me, please," Dominic said, "and then we're going to move to the shoulder on the other side. Don't run but don't stop, either."

I crossed in front of him slowly and tucked myself in on his other side. The dog came at us, right up to the back of our heels. I could hear its growling and feel the heat of its breath on my legs. I took hold of Dominic's arm and whispered, "I hate mean dogs, I hate 'em."

Dominic steered us to the center of the road and then to the shoulder on the opposite side. The dog stopped and stood still on the solid yellow lines.

"Wish a big Mack Truck would come and flatten him," I said as I let go of Dominic's arm and glanced back.

Just then a woman whistled out the front door and yelled, "Sorry!"

Dominic waved to her, and we continued on. He'd been calm as hell. I was still shaking.

"You probably like dogs, huh?" I asked, a little snarky and embarrassed at how scared I'd been.

"I do, but not that one. My heart was pounding." He shook his head and gave me a half smile.

My face was feeling burnt, and my feet ached from walking on the pavement. But I didn't say anything. Instead, I walked slightly ahead of him, proving I wasn't a wuss. The heat was way hotter than anything we had in Vermont. Back during that summer, the campground had set up a sprinkler for the little ones. Sadie would sprint through the water, her mouth wide open and her hair dripping wet. Once, she'd tried to pull me along with her. I'd resisted but then finally gave in, and together we'd raced through the swirling water, holding hands and screaming "Geronimo!" The water had surprised me by how cold it was. The memory felt heavy against my heart. I pinched the side of my thigh, the pain replacing my sorrow.

THE DIAMONDBACK LOOKED BEAT, its siding a dirty gray and the porch along its front sagging. A couple of motorcycles were parked out front. "What time have you got?" I asked Dominic.

He glanced at his phone. "Just past eleven. The station wagon was out around the side and in the back, right?"

"Yeah. But I need a drink before we go look." I quickly added, "A Coke or water, or else I'm going to die for the second time in six minutes."

We walked inside, and I was immediately hit with the change in temperature. The air conditioning was on high. It was dark, too. There were no windows, only lights and beer signs around the bar and pool tables. Two guys and a woman sat at a table, just to the right of the dance floor. Their helmets were on the chairs next to them.

"Buy you a Coke?" I asked Dominic.

"Sure," he replied as he sat down next to me. He wiped his forehead with the back of his hand.

The bartender smiled at us. I fished in my pocket for some money.

Both of us drank our Cokes down fast, then Dominic asked for another round.

"You didn't walk here, did you?" the bartender asked.

"Oh yeah, we made that mistake," I replied. "Forgot how hot it gets down here. And we had to get past the Shepherd who almost tore my leg off."

"My leg, too," Dominic added, and the girl nodded knowingly.

"That would be Dutch. He's formidable, but he can be bribed. I sometimes ride my bike here, and a little bit of beef jerky goes a long way."

Dominic said, smiling now, "I'd like to buy his favorite kind for our return trip."

"I'll give you a piece of jerky on the house." She motioned to the bikers at the table. "They had a little trouble with him, too."

"Dutch scare you?" I called out to the table.

One of the guys responded, "He ran out to us, chased us some."

"He can't be good for business…right?" Dominic asked the bartender.

"Well, he's better than the tent church people. Sometimes their signs are pretty off-putting. 'Specially when the girls in their long dresses show up with them on a night we have a band. 'Repent Now, Sinners' is one we could do without."

"Do they have a good-sized following?" Dominic asked.

She shook her head. "Definitely less than a few years back. People tend to prefer the churches in town, the ones that are more moderate. Not just a tent plopped down in the middle of a hay field with a couple of porta potties."

"Do you know if Father Ray is still preaching there?" I asked.

She hesitated then replied, "I don't think he is. I want to say he had a heart attack and stepped down."

I asked reluctantly, "Did his son take over?"

"Don't know, sorry," she responded.

As Dominic took the beef jerky from her, she said, "Your accents are pretty strong. I've got an aunt in Boston. You're not as bad as her."

"No, we're not as bad as Boston," Dominic replied. "Thanks for this." He held up the jerky, and we both walked to the door.

WE STOOD IN THE EMPTY BACK PARKING lot under The Diamondback sign. It was hot and dusty. Already I missed the air-conditioned bar.

Dominic surveyed the area and looked over at me. "It's tough to imagine a kid having to stay here in a car for two days."

There was so much I already felt guilty about with Sadie. I hadn't even come to terms with this: that I'd been with Brother Ron and had only started looking for her on that second night. But I couldn't dwell on it — not now. Finding out about the boy and what had happened to him was something concrete I could still do for her. Even if he was dead, I needed to know. We all needed closure, for Sadie's sake.

I pointed and said, "The car was parked there, facing the road, but Sadie was in the third row, looking back at the ramp. In her deposition, she said the two guys started to push the boy at the bottom of the ramp, then he began to run towards her to get away. The guys kept hitting him all the way past here, beyond the car's back window."

Dominic turned around and looked back at the building. "That camera right there, on the back of the building facing us — it wasn't working. Footage would have captured the whole thing. I bet it's still not working."

"And," I said, looking at him, "I doubt the parking lot was crowded. We would have seen it all play out. It was late at night on a Wednesday. I remember because I had Tuesdays and Wednesdays off, and I'd been at the lake that day."

A woman came out of the back kitchen door and lit up a cigarette. She smiled over at us and called out, "There's fresh pulled pork for lunch. You should get some."

Dominic walked back to the ramp, and I followed. "Hi," he said. "We actually ate a late breakfast. Could we ask you a question, though?"

The woman was about my father's age. "Depends. You a cop? I'm not fond of them, at all." She wasn't smiling anymore.

"I am, but I'm not on police business now. We're on a road trip. My name's Dominic, this is Kate."

She shifted and leaned against the railing of the ramp. "You're from up north, I can tell. I'm originally from upstate New York — Binghamton area. But that was way back, in the eighties. Been down here ever since. It suits me better. Hate those winters."

"They can be tough, for sure. You been the cook here for a while?" Dominic asked.

She took a long pull on her cigarette. When she exhaled, she answered, "I've been cooking at The Diamondback for eight years. The owner is somewhat decent."

"Somewhat?" I asked.

"Yeah. Let's me decide the menu, treats his wait staff good. He could put more money into sprucing up the place, but he's getting up there in age."

Dominic nodded and asked, "We're wondering if you remember an unusual situation — a little girl coming in to use the bathroom, and you giving her free fries and Cokes.

She was young, like nine. Her father was inside drinking, but she stayed out here most of the time, in an old station wagon — a Chevy. This was about six years ago.”

“You already had your one question answered,” the cook replied, looking out past both of us.

I glanced at Dominic then moved closer to her. “A sweet kid, blond and small for her age.”

The woman looked at me but said nothing. Just as I turned away from her, she replied, “Sadie W.?”

“Yes, yes, Sadie W.” My pulse quickened. Dominic was watching her carefully.

“I got a drawing from her. It’s hanging in the kitchen. Cute kid. I almost called child services.”

I held Sadie’s drawing book closer to me and glanced over at Dominic. He seemed to understand that I didn’t want to tell her about my relationship to Sadie — or anything else.

“Sadie saw a kid get beat up the second night she was parked here,” Dominic said. “Do you know anything about that?”

“Lots of fights happen out here, but no, I don’t know anything about that one.”

Dominic reached into his back pocket and took out the two photos of Lucia and Lucas Alvarez. “Do you recognize either of these young people?” He walked up the ramp and handed the cook the pictures. She studied them closely and then handed them back to Dominic. “Same kid, aren’t they? I spoke to him — right out here on this ramp.” She took a final drag of her cigarette and dropped it.

“Can you share what that conversation was about?” Dominic was in full cop mode. He needed to dial it back a bit.

“Maybe it’d help to know why Sadie W. and this kid are of interest to you? Maybe I got to weigh if telling a cop

benefits them. Never had much good things to say about
the police, you know?"

I liked this lady, this tough cook. I jumped in and said,
"We're trying to find out if the kid ended up being okay. It's
that simple, I swear."

She hesitated then replied, "He was pretty vulnerable. I
mean, just look at him. Young, wanting to live his true,
authentic self, but the assholes — they don't put up with
anyone different. I suggested he go into Nashville, to a more
welcoming bar. He must have had a fake ID. He was clearly
underage."

"What did he say to that?" Dominic asked.

"Not much. Just that he was meeting someone."

"Did he seem nervous? Happy?"

"He was nervous, said it had something to do with his
job. That's it, basically. I should get back to the kitchen
now."

She started to make her way back up the ramp, but then
she stopped and turned back to us. "I do kind of remember
the girl and him being here at the same time. I like my
breaks — smoking out here with no worries. But that night I
had the little girl in the car to keep an eye on and then
him."

"Did you see who he eventually met?"

"I did not," she answered. "As for Sadie W. — she gave
me her drawing the last time she used the bathroom for the
night. Bertram, the bartender, pointed out which asshole
was her father. When I left later that night, I walked around
the car. I could see both of them inside sleeping. If it went
on for a third day, I was definitely calling child services."

"You've been really helpful. Thanks," Dominic said.

The cook nodded then replied, "Just so you know, the
cops came by here asking about the boy. Said new

information connected him to a missing girl from the other side of the state. It wasn't that long ago."

"Did you tell them any of this?" Dominic asked.

"Nah, remember, I don't like cops." She turned away from us.

"Well, thanks again!" I called out to her.

When we got to the end of the parking lot, I stopped and looked over at Dominic. "Can you wait a minute? I need to go back — but here, hold this." I gave him the notebook and ran back up the ramp.

I opened the kitchen door and saw the cook at the counter, starting to cut up a bunch of potatoes. "Any chance I could see the drawing Sadie did?" I was out of breath.

"Sure, it's right over here on the wall." She moved across the kitchen and pointed.

Above the clock to punch in was Sadie's drawing. It was one of the cook with wide hoop earrings; puffy, big black hair; thick dark eyelashes; and red, red lips.

She touched it and smiled. "I love it. She made me look young."

I ran my fingers over the big, flowery signature in the top right corner of the drawing. *Sadie W.* "It wasn't hard to remember her name, was it?"

The woman shook her head and said, "Nah, she was a doll. Do you know what she's up to, where she is now?"

I hesitated and then replied, "No, no clue."

Chapter 12

W e turned at the bend, and there was Dutch lying in wait. Dominic said, "Let's see how much the old boy likes this jerky." We were on the opposite side of the road, walking along its shoulder.

"Nope, not at the risk of scarred legs for life," I said, scrambling down the bank onto the field before the tent church. "Rather face the wrath of God than Dutch again."

Dominic caught up alongside of me. "It's got to be close to ninety-five degrees now."

The sweat was dripping down the back of my neck. "At least that."

"Question — the morning you came to The Diamondback to look for Sadie, you said it was dawn?"

"I think so — it was light enough to walk the fields. Why?"

"Trying to establish a timeline of that night. That's all."

I COULDN'T SEE UP ON THE ROAD anymore to
judge if we were safely past the dog and its boundary line.
The tent church was in front of us. Four cars were parked
near this end.

"Listen, if anyone calls out to us, let's just keep walking,"
I said. "They'll be real friendly, welcoming. Maybe even
offer us something to drink. But that's how they suck you
in."

I had just finished telling him that when a woman called
out, "Hot, isn't it?" She was walking towards us with
purpose, a smile firmly planted on her face.

"Rude doesn't come naturally to me," Dominic said. He
was still carrying Sadie's drawing book.

I reached over and took it. "Then watch me."

I turned to the woman as she approached. "We're not
interested," I said curtly. "Just passing through. Goodbye."

Young and pregnant in a long dress, she fell right in step
with us. Dominic looked over at me, his eyes growing big.

"We can see you're just passing by. But if you'd like to sit
a minute in the shade with a cold drink and listen to Father
Tim practice his sermon tonight, you're more than welcome
to."

I stopped and looked at her. "Father Tim?"

"That's right. Please, it's hot out in the noon sun. I'm
not sure how far you're walking, but you look like you could
use a break."

"Sure, that sounds wonderful." I veered toward the tent.

"What's going on?" Dominic asked. The woman had
stopped back at one of the cars. We could hear a child
crying.

"I need to see who this Father Tim is…make sure it's not
Brother Ron."

"Can I have a drink if they offer me one?" He was
looking at me seriously.

I laughed and replied, "Don't worry. It won't be deadly, and they won't hold us against our will. I may even have one, too."

FOR THE NEXT TWENTY MINUTES, we sat and drank very cold iced teas and listened as Father Tim, a man I vaguely remembered, practiced his sermon. Threatening Ron Warren by telling his wife and father about our affair was still in play if need be. Maybe it was even more potent, especially if his father was in poor health. I snickered, betting nobody in the history of this congregation had ever had these kinds of thoughts while listening to a sermon.

Dominic leaned over and asked, "What's so funny?"

But I shook my head and whispered, "Shhh, let's listen."

The topic was on forgiveness and the power of letting go. Two women were tidying up the tent church: carrying baskets of flowers to the altar, moving the benches, and sweeping the mats down the center aisle. They let us be, even the young woman who had first approached us. She was rocking a small child in the corner of the tent. We could hear her singing softly.

As we thanked them and said goodbye, I looked back at the tent. Sadie had loved it here — the community of people, the sermons, and the lessons for the young children. I'd been turned off by it all, and I'd rebelled against their practices, especially how women were delegated to be subservient. Yet these women didn't seem to be suffering or unhappy. I wondered, for the first time ever, if maybe these women lived more in peace than I could ever hope to live.

I followed Dominic along the path of the last field bordering the campground. He knew the way back to the motel. It wasn't hard — just a straight shot through the countryside, the campground, and then up behind the gas station, and we'd be once again in the part of Goodlettsville that wasn't as appealing as its tree-lined downtown with its high-end shops.

Just before we started to cross the parking lot to the motel, I stopped and took off my flip-flops again. Dominic waited patiently. As I wiped the tiny stones on my feet away, I looked longingly over at the pool. "I think I've got to go in, like right now."

"I didn't bring a suit, did you?" Dominic asked.

"No," I replied as I moved across the walkway and opened the pool's gate. I didn't care that I had no suit. I took off my t-shirt and slipped into the deep end. Two girls looked over at me but then turned back around.

Dominic followed me. "Nice?" he asked.

"Oh yeah. It's cold and feels great."

"The sign says suits only." He pointed to the *No Running* sign and the small print underneath.

"Well, unless you're wearing tighty-whities, I doubt anyone will notice. Besides, it's not the Ritz." I dove underneath to the bottom of the pool and picked up two rings. When I swam back up, I looked for him. He was already in the pool, swimming towards me.

"Yeah, this is great," he called out.

We both reached the side of the pool. He shook his head and wiped away the water running down his face. He looked younger. I could see the boy he once was, the 'Nicky' Mrs. Lake loved. He looked less standoffish, too, like just a normal guy.

"Now what should we do?" I asked, treading water.

"We should keep showing the pictures. It's encouraging — what the cook remembered. Other people might remember, too."

"Okay. My cell phone is in the room; I've got to check it. I'm getting out and going in to change." I climbed up the ladder and grabbed my t-shirt and put it on. My room key and Sadie's notebook were beside it. "Meet you outside my room in a few minutes?"

He nodded and pushed off, swimming the length of the pool. He was only wearing black boxers. No one would have ever noticed it wasn't a suit. But that wasn't quite true. One of the teenage girls watched him swim away and then quickly turned to me with a look of approval. I thought of the old man's often-used expression: passing muster. *Dominic just passed muster with the 15-year-old girls of Moody's.*

Did he pass muster with me? I watched his muscular arms slice through the water. Maybe, but I couldn't think about that kind of thing right now — I needed to stay focused on why I was here.

Plus, someone like Dominic would never be interested in me anyway.

WHEN I GOT INTO MY ROOM, I saw that I had a text from Karen. *'All good here. Anything new?'*

The text had come in late this morning, about the time we were seeing Hetty.

'No, Carson's father is out of town till Friday. Then I'll meet up with him. There's not much to do. How's Carson?' I was about to send it but then added, *'And how did the interview go?'*

I sat down on the bed and wondered what would come out of the meeting with Ron Warren. I'd done some research, just in case he refused to sign the form and my blackmail threat didn't work. The parental rights for fathers in Tennessee rested on whether the parents were married at the time of birth. If not married, then the mother had most, if not all, of the decision-making power. That was to my benefit, but Ron could require a paternity test and then ask the court to establish visitation rights or even joint custody.

The fact that I'd kept his child from him didn't put me in a good light. Unless I claimed that he wasn't the only man I'd slept with and I hadn't known who the father was. It would be a lie, but maybe a necessary one.

Right off, Ron Warren needed to understand that I wasn't after financial support. All I wanted was to tell him of Carson's existence and then stick that paper in front of him to sign. But before any of that, I needed to know that he was willing to meet.

Outside my door, Dominic was sitting in the same chair as before. We both wore jeans and clean t-shirts. "Ready to go?" I asked.

"Yes," he replied, standing up. Our cooling down in the pool was history.

THE TWO CITY BLOCKS — Fifth and Sixth Street — had been as far as I'd ever ventured back in 2009. When Dad and I had realized that Hetty was more than willing to have Sadie with her during the day, I'd started knocking on doors for some sort of employment. Not many places had been hiring at the time, but between a laundromat on Sixth and the car wash, there were some hours available. I'd chosen the car wash. Because there wasn't much to it, I was soon managing it for the dead-beat manager who came around once, sometimes twice a day.

There was a small Somali-owned coffee shop next to the car wash. Sometimes, in the late mornings, I'd make my way over to get a cup of chai and a buttery crisp cookie with cinnamon to go. After a while, a girl about my age and dressed in a long dress and wearing a hijab had started to poke her head around from the kitchen to say hello. At times she would add a phrase or two like, "How old did you say your sister was?" or "The dental floss is on the shelf behind the toothpaste." She'd been practicing her English, and I'd repeat the phrase slowly back to her and she'd say it again. It'd been our special little thing all summer long.

Lloyd and Cal had introduced me to Ron early on at the car wash, and he'd made a move on me almost immediately. I had just turned 18, and he was 30. It's not like I was 15 and still in school — although I bet he would have still gone after me, even then. His wife was dealing with two newly adopted babies they'd prayed for forever. He felt neglected and said I made up for that.

Our relationship had proved to be good for Sadie — trips to the diner and afternoon matinees at the Multiplex Cinema down I-65. We saw *Up* and *Where the Wild Things Are* and more — all on him. He'd give Sadie a twenty-dollar bill and tell her to get whatever she wanted at the concession stand. "Just remember to sit closer to the screen, away from us." He wasn't interested in the movies, ever.

IT WAS EVEN HOTTER NOW. Dominic and I were just passing the second-hand store when I stopped and said, "Let's go in. I need lighter stuff to wear; I'm dying in these jeans." The bank sign on the corner read 96 degrees.

Dominic looked further up the street then back at me. "When I was showing the photos around this morning, I only got to the dry cleaners. If we want to canvas the rest of the block and move on to Sixth Street, we've got to do it before businesses close at five."

I nodded. "We still have tomorrow, right?"

"Yeah, but I was hoping to drive out to the place Lucas Alvarez rented back then. It's just west of here, in Franklin."

"I can be really fast — just shorts and a swimsuit. I could get you some swim shorts, too?" I asked. Very few people were on the streets, but some construction was going on up behind us. We could hear the drilling and hammering.

Dominic reached into his wallet and took out a ten-dollar bill. "Sure, that works. I'll be on the other side of the street. Come find me."

Once inside the thrift store, I got busy. For two dollars, I could fill a plastic bag. Between the hammering above the place and the elevator music being piped in, it was loud and annoying. Just as I was walking up to the register, I saw a yellow sundress on a hanger. I grabbed that, too.

"Any chance I could try the dress on?" I asked the woman.

She hesitated then smiled. "We have a big dressing room, but with all the construction upstairs, we put our cat in there since she's afraid of the noise. Can you try it on with her in there? And make sure she doesn't get out?"

"Yeah, sure." I nodded.

The changing room was out the back of the store and down a narrow hallway. Near it were stairs leading up to the floors above. I could hear men calling out to each other and more drilling.

As soon as I opened the door, a black cat scooted out. "Shit!" I said, quickly dropping my bag and the dress to run after it. The cat darted up the stairs. *She isn't that afraid,* I thought.

Once I was on the second-floor landing, I saw her go out the fire escape door that was propped opened. I quickly followed, almost running into a big guy sitting on the stairs.

"Oh, hey, sorry," I said. The cat was already in his lap, and he was petting it.

"This your cat?" he asked. He wore a hard hat and a tool belt. He was dripping in sweat.

"No, it's the thrift store's cat downstairs. She just escaped from the dressing room. Supposedly she's afraid of all the construction."

He scratched her ears and said, "There's a lot going on up here. New second and third floor apartments. We'll be here for some time, so she better get used to it."

"I'm going to take her back down now," I said, smiling. He held her up to me, and I took her, surprised how light she was. Just as I turned to go back in, I looked out past the landing and down to the street level. We were facing the autobody shop's back door. Discarded truck beds and fenders, trash barrels, and metal scraps covered the back area. But it was organized, with a clear pathway that reached almost all the way to us.

I put the cat back in the changing room. I didn't bother to try on the dress, instead I stuffed it in the bag and paid the two dollars.

Dominic was easy to spot. He was across the street, standing outside a shop and nodding as a tattooed guy with purple hair gestured to where I'd just been — above in the construction zone. I quickly crossed the street.

"Hey, looks like you had some luck," Dominic said, indicating the bag I was carrying. "This is Murphy, Murphy — Kate. He remembers Lucas well. He runs this music shop, and Lucas came in a lot."

Murphy smiled over at me and replied, "Like I said, he was a good kid, not sure why he took off, or where he went, or even what he did for work. He liked Bob Marley, that I do recall."

Just then my cell rang. The caller ID showed it was 'Jeannie from Shay's.' I excused myself and stepped away.

"Hi Jeannie. Sorry I didn't stop by for the check."

"No, no, that's okay. I'm calling because I wanted to tell you about a strange conversation I had with Mathew, our linen guy, at the restaurant. It's about Sadie."

"I'm not in a place I can talk. Could I call you back later? I'm actually down in Tennessee."

There was a pause then she said, "You are?"

"I'm here with Dominic Sousa. We're trying to find out what we can about the boy, and…" I hesitated, unsure if I wanted to say more. But I continued, "I'm finally going to tell Carson's father about him."

"Wow, Kate. What I have to tell you can wait. You're with a good guy — just stay safe."

Murphy was gone, and Dominic was waiting for me. We spent the next two hours showing the photos to people along Fifth Street as we made our way to Sixth. No one else remembered Lucia or Lucas.

I was tired and told Dominic I was going to walk over to Rita's to pick up a pizza and bring it back to my room.

"I'll get one, too." But he stopped and said, "Sorry, I'll go after you."

"No, don't be ridiculous. Come now, if you want."

As we waited at a table near the kitchen, the bartender from last night walked by and said, "Hey, birthday girl."

I gave him a shitty look — he was being snarky.

Dominic stopped drumming his fingers on the table and asked, "Yesterday was your birthday?"

I nodded.

"So that's why… I wish you had said something," he replied.

I shook my head and said, "It didn't matter that it was my birthday. I've been drinking almost every night since Sadie was killed. I even drove off the road not that long ago. Drinking is how I've been coping. Get shitfaced, pass out, go to work, repeat. Birthday or not — I still would have come here last night. And right now, I'm already thinking I'll skip out later and get hammered again."

I left the table, feeling fed up with myself, and found the bathroom. Standing at the sink, I looked in the mirror. *Sunburnt and burnt-out.* My hair was wild, my nose was a bright red, and there were dark circles under my eyes. The t-shirt I wore was dirty and drooped at the neckline. I had ruined the flip-flops I'd bought for the trip. I glanced at the door, realizing how awful and ugly I must be to him. Not that it mattered — he wouldn't look at me anyway. *Sleep is what I really need.* I left to go back to the table.

Our pizzas were ready. Dominic was standing at the register.

"Here, let me get mine," I said, reaching for my wallet.

He motioned to the cashier. "I got it."

"Dominic, cut the shit, I'm buying my own food." The thought of at least two more days down here — not to mention the long drive home with him — seemed over-whelming. I was too miserable to be around anybody, most of all him.

But as we got to my motel room door, I felt bad for how abrupt I'd just been and said, "This whole bag was just two dollars." I reached into the plastic bag and took out the swimsuit and the pair of men's shorts I'd bought for him. I also gave him back the ten-dollar bill. The sun and walking that much in the heat had done me in. I wanted to eat and watch a movie and try to sleep. I couldn't wait to be free of him. "So, um, see you," I added.

Dominic hesitated then replied, "If you feel like you want to grab a drink later, call me. I'll go with you, buy you a birthday beer." He turned and started for the stairs.

"Hey," I called out.

"Yeah?" He stopped at the foot of the stairs to the balcony and looked back.

"You like the suit? Will you wear the shorts?" I asked.

He held them up, one at a time, and replied, "Yes and no, in that order."

A LOUD KNOCKING ON THE DOOR woke me. I had no idea what time it was. I'd fallen asleep at the start of a movie. The banging stopped but now someone was standing in front of my window, peering in. The cheap motel curtains sucked, and I could see the outline of a man. I quickly dialed Dominic's number. He answered right away.

"There's somebody outside my room. He was just banging on my door," I whispered.

"I'm coming."

A moment later, I heard Dominic call out, "Hey, that's my room. What are you doing? What do you want?" He sounded pissed.

I moved to just behind the door and heard a man — more like a kid — reply, "You staying with the girl in here?"

Something changed in Dominic's voice; it was deeper, more menacing. "What's it to you?"

"Ron will meet her at the lake Friday morning. She'll know where. Ten o'clock."

"Piss off," Dominic replied. And then to me through the door, he said, "Babe — open up!"

"Babe?" I asked, looking at him curiously as I stepped outside. The kid was gone.

"Tried to sound like a thug I arrested in Barre last week. How'd I do?" Dominic asked.

"Surprisingly good. Thanks for coming so fast."

Dominic walked in and closed the door. "Did you tell Lloyd where you were staying?"

I stood in front of the curtains, trying to remember the exchange we'd had just this morning. Today felt like the longest day ever. "No, I'm sure I didn't. My plan was to go back to them tomorrow to find out what Ron had said about meeting up."

Dominic sat down on the other bed and looked pensive.

"I'm really going through with this, aren't I?" I asked, feeling queasy.

"You can always change your mind and not show up. That's your prerogative, but if you do go — you're not going alone. I'll give you space, I promise. But I'll be close by. There's something about this that doesn't feel quite right."

Chapter 13

It was 11:20 p.m. I'd slept for almost four hours before the banging had woken me up. There was no way I could go back to sleep. Dominic had run up to his room to fetch his laptop, and now he was on it, sitting in the chair he'd moved in front of my door. He said he'd stay until I fell asleep again. That was reassuring, even though I'd acted like he didn't need to, that it was no big deal.

I channel-surfed but couldn't find anything interesting. Rita's had a band; you could hear it across the way.

He must have sensed how restless I was because he said, "I'll walk over with you, if that's what you want."

I stood back up and moved to the curtains again. It was a clear night. "Carson hasn't seen much of me since Sadie died. The old man has taken over, been the responsible one. That's something I never, ever thought I'd see." I paused then added, "Sadie would never believe it, either." A tear escaped, and I quickly brushed it away.

Dominic closed his laptop and looked up at me, "Her death and the grief must be unbearable for you, Kate."

I didn't look at him — I couldn't because I knew I'd lose it big time. A woman was leaning against a car in the parking lot, talking on her cell. I finally turned to him and said, "Sadie was starting to pull away. I could feel it, and that bothered me. It was like she wasn't buying into my dysfunctional stuff anymore. Working at Shay's did that — it was opening up her world. I've always been the opposite. Thinking we've got to hunker down, get through today because tomorrow could be worse. I've always thought the worst of everything and everyone. She rejected that. And then…a plow truck killed her. It should have been me, the fucked-up big sister."

Dominic quietly replied, "They say our outlook, how we perceive the world, is formed by our experiences. And our emotions are determined by what we think. At least that's what I learned from my criminal psychology classes."

I nodded and asked, "More nurture than nature?"

"I think so, but I'm not an expert, at all. We're all shaped by the early experiences we have with our parents, and…"

I shook my head. "My mom left me. The first eight years it was just me and my father, out on Tabor Road."

"Okay, so it was just you and your father, kind of isolated but together."

"Right. She was long gone; she had alcohol and drug problems."

Dominic slowly nodded.

I quickly added, "And my father — PTS and other issues, for sure, but he mostly managed okay as long as he could stay put."

"Gotcha, so you and your dad hunkered down and carved out a life. Then Sadie comes along and you do the same with her, but she experiences even more love because she not only has her father, she has you. Maybe that leads her to trust more," he said, looking up at me.

People were walking by my room. One of them had a basketball and was bouncing it along the cement walkway.

I looked over at Dominic and replied, "Our time down here, with Hetty and the tent church… That was a pivotal time in her life. It sucked for me, but Sadie really took it all in."

We sat quietly for a little while. Finally, Dominic asked, "Did you bring any other shoes besides the flip-flops?"

I bent down to the other side of the dresser and held up the pair of sneakers I'd worn in the car. "Yes, why?"

"Want to take a walk? There was a time when I decided to stop drinking. Getting physical helped me get through it." He held up his hands. "But I'm not suggesting one thing over another."

I glanced at my wallet then over at the sneakers. There were socks in my backpack. "Give me a second."

When I came out of the bathroom, I glanced at Dominic waiting at the door and said, "About the nature versus nurture — I could be prone to addiction from both my parents."

It looked like Dominic was about to say something, but he didn't.

THE PARKING LOT LIGHTS obscured the stars, and the pavement still held the heat of the day. Back on Tabor Road, even down in Langdon, a starry night was easier to see, easier to feel its vastness.

"Want to head to the campground?" I asked, glancing over towards Rita's. I felt a shift — maybe it was the start of some resolve, finally.

He was walking slightly ahead of me, but he stopped and smiled. "You decide." He had a pronounced dimple in his chin and a shadow of a beard. I wondered if he normally shaved at night or first thing in the morning.

Once we dropped down behind the gas station, we felt the cooler air, but the smell from the swampy area stunk. It had been 96 degrees today, and tomorrow's weather was supposed to be more of the same.

We walked down through the lanes at the campground. It was late and very quiet. We stopped across from Hetty's camper. The colored lights strung along her small deck were still on, and her wind chimes moved slightly in the breeze.

Dominic asked me to wait; he needed to use the communal bathroom. I stood, looking out past the corner of Hetty's lot, down towards the entrance. The sound of her chimes took me back to that summer. Sadie had finally learned to ride a bike, and when I wasn't angry at the world, I'd walk, sometimes even jog behind her as she wove in and around the campground.

Outside the communal bathroom, along the side of the stucco building, was a poured cement area with a hose. Sadie would wash her bike with dish soap and polish it dry there.

Hetty's chimes tinkled again. At night the sound was haunting — so different than the sound during the day. I looked at the cement block then back at Hetty's. I turned around and faced the campsite behind us.

Dominic was crossing the lane to meet me. "What is it?" he asked.

"Maybe nothing. I'm just remembering that I came here looking for Dad and Sadie that last night. I thought Sadie might be sleeping at Hetty's. Not as many campers were here, and those two spots were empty." I pointed behind us. "I cut through, and just before I crossed to Hetty's camper, I saw Sadie's bike leaning against the bathroom wall. I was going to grab it. But a truck stopped and backed onto that cement slab. It was the autobody shop guys — Lloyd and Cal. I almost called out to ask them what they were doing, but I held back. They started to wash out the back bed of the truck. It didn't make sense — they always came to the car wash and used their big discount because of the amount of business they gave us. But I stayed quiet and waited for them to leave, and they eventually did."

"Okay, is there anything else?"

"See the barrel out front of Hetty's with the dragonfly on it?" I asked Dominic, pointing to it.

He nodded and turned back to me.

"She's an artist, and she had two barrels out front for trash," I said. "That one has the dragonfly, but the other one had a blue monarch. I watched them load the blue monarch onto the bed of the truck before they left."

"You mean they stopped at Hetty's and just took it?"

"No, they already had it over on the slab while they scrubbed the truck out."

"Kate, were they washing or scrubbing? You've used both words, but which was it?" he asked.

"Oh, I'd say they were going to town on the bed — definitely scrubbing."

"Which direction did they come from?" he asked.

I indicated the corner near Hetty's.

"Were these lights here then? Or is this another improvement?" He pointed at the lamps along the lane.

"Want to say they were here — or lights of some sort were."

"Can you remember what you did after they left?"

"I woke Hetty up. She didn't know where Sadie was, said she hadn't come to her house at all that day. That concerned me, so I left and grabbed Sadie's bike."

Dominic walked back over to the cement slab and looked out. He came back to me and asked, "What time would you say it was?"

"About midnight, at the latest," I answered.

"But that doesn't make sense. You walked through the fields to The Diamondback at dawn and found them. Right?"

"I went back to our camper and waited, hoping they'd show up. I must have fallen asleep until first light. Then I walked through the fields, past the tent church, and made it to The Diamondback. That's when I found them." I held up my hand in the direction of the bathroom and added, "I'd forgotten about coming here."

Dominic nodded and said, "Let's get back to the motel. I have an idea."

WE PASSED SOME KIDS hanging out near the main office, talking quietly and smoking, then we stopped at my room for Dominic to grab his laptop.

"I've got chart paper and markers left over from a career day I presented at. They're in the trunk. We need them." He handed me the laptop and took the other things out of his car. We made our way up the stairs and down the balcony to his room.

Once inside, he asked, "Can you make a map of this area, kind of like the one you made for me back at The Pines but with more detail?" He tore off a piece of chart paper and handed me the markers.

"Sure." I moved to the table and said, "A pencil would be better, though, instead of these markers."

He handed me one, and I glanced at the time on my cell. It was 12:40 a.m. I got busy.

At one point, Dominic looked down and said, "That's good, really good. Can you draw in the station wagon, the cook with the boy on the ramp, Sadie in the car? And then add in Hetty's place, your camper, and the bathrooms across from her site? That will reflect where everybody was before midnight. Then we'll color code it and look at where the movement was, including Ron Warren leaving the campground, you, the autobody guys, Sadie, and your father. I got a hunch that wherever Sadie's boy went, the answer may be some place in here."

"Okay," I said, bending back over the chart paper. "But it's going to be pretty simple. I'm not that good."

When he came back over to my drawing a little while later, he looked at it carefully and pointed to Fifth Street and the building that bordered the back of the autobody shop.

"Murphy, at the music store, told me that this whole block between Fifth and Sixth Street had a fire. I've just been reading about it, how it went up in flames on the night of September tenth, in two thousand and nine. You left Tennessee on Thursday, September fourth."

"Okay. Just a coincidence?" I yawned, covering my mouth.

"I'm not so sure. A local census worker is beaten up and isn't seen around again, followed by a huge fire — what they determined was arson — all within a week."

I was losing steam and not quite following him. "Maybe I could finish this tomorrow?"

But Dominic remained focused and asked, "What was Lucas Alvarez doing ahead of the twenty-ten census? Did he know something that he shouldn't have? Murphy said that these apartments above here — " Dominic pointed to the little buildings I'd drawn adjacent to the autobody shop — "were sketchy places. I asked him what he meant, but he couldn't say why. It was just a gut feeling he had."

I stood up, yawning again. "They're redoing all of them now. Listen, I'm sorry, I know this is important, but I've got to get some sleep; it's almost three o'clock."

Dominic looked tired, too, and replied, "Give me a sec, and I'll walk you down."

Just before I fell asleep, I realized Karen had never answered the text I'd sent earlier in the day.

Chapter 14

I was woken by the sun streaming in through the curtains and the sound of kids out at the pool. I had a missed call and a text from Dominic. He was off to Franklin to see what he could find out about Lucas.

At this time tomorrow, I'd be meeting Ron at the lake. His boat was moored at the Old Hickory Lake Marina, Slip 12. It was where we sometimes met back then, usually after the tent church services on weekday nights. It was also where I'd spent that whole first night my father had decided to drink again while Sadie was set up in the station wagon.

Ron Warren had been manipulative, but he'd never forced me into doing anything. I wasn't a victim; we'd both gotten things out of our arrangement. A son, nine months later, hadn't been one of the things I'd wanted. Now, though, I couldn't imagine a life without Carson.

I debated calling Karen's cell. She'd be at work and probably wouldn't mind. But instead I sent her a simple text: *'Everything okay? Hope to be on the road tomorrow by noon.'*

She responded, *'Yes, yes, so sorry — work's been crazy. Carson and your dad had dinner with me last night. He misses you. Your dad is on pins and needles, waiting to hear how it goes. Call or text us as soon as you can after you meet. Of course, Carson has NO idea. Interview went well!'*

That made me feel better, and I responded with a red heart and a fingers-crossed emoji. I got up and found the bag from the thrift store. The woman at the counter had said, "Just so you know — all the clothing and bedding have been washed. Pillows and stuffed animals have not; they've just been spot cleaned."

It would be smart to wear a dress tomorrow when I met Brother Ron, especially if he was still associated with the tent church. I hung the dress up behind the bathroom door then slipped into the black one-piece suit and the pair of shorts I'd bought.

It felt good to be free of Dominic, to be able to relax while he was gone. We were better, or, more accurately, I had been better toward him last night. Overall, though, he made me uncomfortable, and that feeling only amplified my insecurities.

The girl in the motel office smiled as I stepped in. "Anything left of the muffins and donuts this morning?" I asked.

"Yeah, come back here and take a look." She was friendly and sweet, maybe a couple of years younger than me. The name on her shirt read *'Rosie.'*

The back space was small. Rosie pointed to the wrapped breakfast items on a tray on the back counter. "I can make you hot or iced coffee. And we have orange juice."

I looked over at a large container of cranberry juice. "Is that a choice, too?"

"Sure, it can be. It's actually mine from home. I've got a UTI, and I'm taking an antibiotic. But I might stop; it's killing my stomach."

"Ah, that doesn't sound like fun. I had a kidney stone not long ago. That sucked."

She nodded and said, "Life sucks, then you die."

The table by the pool was the perfect place to sit and eat my breakfast wrap and look through Sadie's drawings. I wanted to do that now that I was all alone. The kids splashing in the pool were far enough away for me not to worry about anything getting wet.

At first, I was hesitant to open the notebook, but eventually I did. Immediately, I was drawn into Sadie's little world of rainbows, flowers, butterflies, and houses. She'd loved to draw those over and over. She'd also loved faces, and there were plenty of mine, Dad's, Hetty's, and her own. I laughed at one of my faces — the one where she'd exaggerated my scowl and had written at the bottom, "Don't crash!" Her specialty had seemed to be eyes, while her noses were definitely lacking — just straight lines with half circles on each side. She'd liked colors and had given us all colorful shirts, eyebrows, hair, and earrings.

Other drawings were of her on the bicycle, the old man holding a hammer, the sun behind the altar in the tent church, and Hetty's vegetable pots with labels — peas, tomatoes, and peppers. When I reached the end, I closed the pad and rested my hand over it.

The kids were playing 'Marco Polo' in the pool. A little girl was It. I watched her as she called out, 'Marco,' then lunged for one of the kids who'd responded, 'Polo.'

The water looked inviting. I covered the notebook with the bath towel I'd taken from the room. The cold water was refreshing as I waded in then dived under to retrieve the rings at the bottom of the pool. I held them out to another little girl who took them and said, "Thanks."

"HEY, YOU'RE GETTING RED," Dominic said. He was standing over me. I'd fallen asleep, stretched out on my stomach with a *People* magazine spread open under my lounge chair. It had been left on one of the chairs near me.

"What are you, the burn patrol?" I sat up slowly, feeling disoriented and hot. "I'm sorry. My default setting is to be defensive. I need to work on that."

Dominic sat down near me and said, "I had some luck. The neighbors in the apartment building next to where Lucas lived remembered him. I have to go back in a little while. They both had doctor appointments. Mr. Blake — the neighbor — said Lucas told him a few things that might be of interest to us, especially about where he might have gone."

I nodded and replied, "That's good."

It was as hot as yesterday. Dominic was eying the pool. "I'm ready for a quick swim and then lunch."

I shielded my eyes and looked up at him. "Just wondering — if we find out Lucas had plans to leave and these folks think that's what he did, do we quit after that?"

Dominic's cell rang, and he reached to answer it. He stood up and whispered, "It's the regional census bureau office. I can't believe they're calling me back."

He turned and moved out of range. I dipped my toes back in the pool and dived in again, swimming the length of it.

Dominic met me coming out at the shallow end and said, "Lucas might have been canvasing the area for legitimate residences. There'd been some failed attempts at getting landlords' information. While the woman on the phone couldn't be specific about Lucas's work, she said it's quite common to send out field people ahead of the actual census."

I squeezed the water from my hair and walked the rest of the way up the stairs. "This might complicate things," I responded.

Dominic took a step back, his eyes sweeping over me.

"Take a picture, it'll last longer," I said in a sarcastic tone.

He looked away briefly then turned back at me and replied, "It's your burn — that's gonna hurt." He turned and walked through the gate.

I almost called out after him that my burn was on my backside, not my front. But he was already crossing the balcony along the second floor. Him checking me out like that was surprising, but it was a surprise I kind of liked. I tried not to think too much about why that was.

Within minutes, he was back, holding the rolled-up map. He wore the trunks I'd gotten at the thrift store and was carrying a bath towel.

"Just one more minute," he said as he placed the map down on one of the tables then moved to the deep end and dived in. Once out of the water, he called me over.

I could feel the burn, so draped the bath towel over my shoulders. I looked as Dominic pointed at certain parts of the map and said, "What if Lucas discovered something he shouldn't have? It could be in this street block, in the apartments Murphy pointed out. Maybe he was going to report it, but the guys Sadie saw beat him up didn't want him to. What if something illegal was going on? What if Lucas went to The Diamondback specifically to meet them?"

"That's a whole lot of 'what-ifs' and speculation," I replied, glancing at Dominic. *"Wild what-ifs,"* I wanted to say.

He sat down and seemed to be mulling over things. Finally, he said, "You're right. It'd be enough just to find out who those guys were and somehow get their DNA to the lab at the Tennessee Bureau of Investigation. They'd do the rest to figure out what really happened."

"But isn't getting DNA without a warrant against the law?" I asked. "Back at the trailer, we voluntarily said yes to being swabbed. But most times, don't you need a warrant?"

Dominic ran his hand across his stomach and looked up at me. "Sorry. That was my stomach growling, I'm starved." He had a swirl of black hair just below his navel. I quickly looked away. *He's probably a real player. Probably why he never got married.* All the more reason to stay away.

Still looking down at the map, he replied, "Actually, anything that's put in the garbage — discarded items — aren't protected by the Fourth Amendment. You give up your right to privacy when you place your crap in a bin out on the curb. It's a warrantless search and seizure, and it's done all the time."

I volunteered to run and grab grinders for us since Dominic wanted to sit by the pool and swim some more. I'd had enough sun.

It didn't take me long to walk to the Sixth Street sandwich shop. On the way back, I watched two spiffed-up restored trucks leave the car wash and turn back towards the autobody shop.

Back then, I'd ordered all the soaps and waxes. The cars and trucks had glistened when they were done. Everybody had been happy with the automatic car wash and with us, the girls who washed and polished them clean. The autobody shop had always used the automatic wash — but they'd tipped us generously in their 'Quality Classics' trucks.

I stopped in front of the window of the coffee shop and glanced in, wondering if the Somali girl was still there. It looked really busy inside. Some kid was stapling flyers to the bulletin board just past the entrance. I walked on by and then paused and looked back. One day that summer, a young guy had been doing that same thing. I'd walked right into him, causing him to spill all the flyers. Apologizing, I'd helped him pick them up, reading something about a community outreach program. *Could it have been Lucas?* In the summary Dominic had typed up for me, there'd been something about him volunteering in the Somalian community. I began walking again, realizing this was my own crazy 'what-if.'

ONCE I WAS BACK, I took the map into my room to finish it and eat while Dominic stayed by the pool. Soon, though, he was knocking at my door, telling me he was heading back to Franklin. He asked if I wanted to come.

"Nah, it's nice in here with the air conditioning on. I'm finishing the map."

"You sure? I'd love your…" But he stopped and said instead, "Got it, see you back here."

"Maybe later we could drive out towards the lake where I'm meeting Carson's dad. There's ice cream and little shops. You could buy something for that special someone in your life," I said, being a wise guy. I imagined his type would be a petite blond, someone who adored him with his good looks and confidence.

Dominic didn't seem amused, and instead of responding, he ignored my comment and left.

When I'd done as much as I possibly could on the map, I sat back and looked at it. It was a fair representation of the whole area. Nothing was to scale and it was basic, but it was still useful to see where we had all been that last night.

I stretched out and grabbed Sadie's drawing book again. I found it comforting as I turned the pages slowly.

The last image was a drawing of a truck: a bright blue one with big lights and a thick front bumper. I looked at the license plate. On it, she'd written in small neat lettering: *Quality Classics*. She'd fit it all in and spelled it correctly. I'd missed that detail out at the pool.

That puzzled me. As far as I knew, Sadie had never gone near the autobody shop in the months we were here. She'd spent her time at the campground, the tent church, and with me and Ron. Once in a while, she'd go play with the girls at the building site Dad was working at. At nine years old and just out of the third grade, she was never allowed to walk or ride her bike alone on the path behind the gas station leading to the busy streets. Hetty never went in that direction either, and especially not on foot. Any grocery shopping we did was out toward the interstate at the big Walmart. I even remembered driving with Hetty to shop there.

The second to last page she'd drawn on was torn out, but a little part of the 'S' in her big flourishing signature was left up in the top right corner. I was sure it was from the drawing Sadie had given to the cook, the one taped in the kitchen at The Diamondback.

I turned back to the beginning of the pad to figure out if her drawings were done in chronological order. Her bicycle pictures didn't appear until midway through the notebook. Dad had bought the bike sometime during that summer at a flea market. Hetty's plants were fully grown, with big green leafy stems, on the pages towards the end. And, on the last page, she'd colored the sky above the truck all black with funny little marks. That last night, before Ron had dropped me off, we'd been on his boat. The night sky out on the water had been incredible.

I moved back to the map and looked at The Diamondback. It was far enough away from the lights of Fifth and Sixth Streets to see the night sky. Once you left the gas station and scooted down the path along the smelly swamp, the whole topography changed. Instead of concrete and buildings, it became the campground with trees and bits of grass. Further out, it turned country: rolling hills, open fields, and big sky.

Was Sadie in the station wagon when she'd drawn this on that last night? There were no more drawings after it. Was it because she'd fallen asleep and the next morning had given it to Hetty to keep?

Lloyd or Cal could have parked one of their restored trucks at The Diamondback in full view of Sadie in the third-row seat of the station wagon. But was it the same truck I'd seen them in outside the campground's bathroom?

The color of the truck was throwing me off. The bright blue she'd chosen might have been her choice, though, and not entirely accurate. Sadie loved those glow-pens.

I wondered if either Lloyd or Cal had been questioned about being at The Diamondback that last night — the second time Lucia Alvarez's card had been used. Dominic could log into the files of the investigation and find out. I dialed his cell, but it went straight to voicemail.

My back was feeling hot from all the sun earlier in the day. There was aloe cream in the bathroom. As I turned to look in the mirror at the redness on my shoulders, I saw the yellow sundress hanging behind the door. Its bright yellow color had faded, the cotton felt thin against my hand. *Something about this yellow…*

The aloe was helping, and I began to rub some onto my face. I stopped and looked back at the dress again. Lloyd had wiped his face with a thread-bare yellow bandana yesterday, outside his shop. He'd taken it out of his back pocket and brought it to his brow.

My pulse quickened. There was something about a bandana in Sadie's deposition. Was it in the forensic report, too, from the items found in the station wagon? I never saw what the detectives took that day out behind the trailer, and I'd only skimmed the report on the way down here.

The possibilities Dominic had outlined earlier, the crazy speculations? I pictured Lloyd and Cal in them now. Had they been involved in something illegal? Was Lucas meeting them at The Diamondback? When I'd retrieved the cat on the fire escape landing, I'd seen how close the back door of the autobody shop was to the back of the buildings along Fifth Street.

If they were the ones who'd beaten up Lucas, it felt way too easy. Aside from the tent church men, they were the only guys my father's age I'd known down here. The cops must have checked them out when Lucas Alvarez went missing. *But how much time did they spend on trying to find Lucas when they had so many younger missing kids?*

I stepped outside. It was still warm, but clouds were rolling in. Dominic said it'd be enough just to get DNA samples from the people who'd beaten up Lucas. That the Tennessee police would figure out the rest if they had a match.

The autobody shop on Sixth was just a stone's throw away. *How hard could it be to snag a couple of things from their trash?*

I tried Dominic's cell one last time, but he didn't pick up. I waved to Rosie in the motel office as I walked by. *Just an item or two…*

The shop, Parker's Classics, was busy with people. Lloyd and Cal were there — I could see them showing a couple of guys the engine in one of their refurbished Chevy trucks. Today, Lloyd had a red bandana poking out of his back left pocket. It matched the color of the truck he was perched over.

The whole front of the shop — the paved part outside the two big garage doors — was full of other parked trucks that were being admired by the people milling about. They all had 'Quality Classics' license plates. Balloons were tethered to a big cart holding tires, and someone was grilling hot dogs and burgers to the right of the parking area. It must be Customer Appreciation Day or some sort of big sale.

It was shockingly hot, but I smiled at the sight. It'd be easy to slip into the garage, past the trucks in various stages of work, and into that back office. I stood on the sidewalk across the street to wait. As soon as Lloyd and Cal had their backs fully turned from the garage, I'd go.

I didn't have to wait. They left the hood up on that truck and moved to a second one parked at an angle, further away from the garage. Cal lifted the new hood, and the men gathered around to look. Lloyd was laughing, his head thrown back. It was the perfect moment to cross the street and scoot inside.

It took my eyes a moment to adjust to the darkness inside the garage. It was quiet, and no one was around; all the action was out front. I moved quickly, passing auto body parts and tools neatly positioned along the wall. When I reached the back, I smiled again. The office door was wide open.

A circular fan was swirling from the ceiling inside the room. Two old wooden desks faced each other. A whole lot of papers and files were scattered about. Above a large filing cabinet was a framed picture of both men shaking hands with some celebrity — a Nashville country western singer. On the opposite wall was a gallery of pictures — Playboy centerfolds — their poses obscene.

Near an old, dirty coffee maker, I saw two cups that were grimy and chipped with a 'C' on one, and an 'L' on the other. Dominic had said that only discarded items could be taken. I paused over the trash can by one of the desks. It was mostly filled with paper. I moved to a second bin near the other desk — mostly papers, too. My eyes returned to the two coffee cups — they'd be much better items to take. In a split-second decision, I moved one of the trash cans along the edge of the countertop and used a pencil to nudge each cup into it. There was still a bit of coffee in the 'L' cup, so I swirled the trash bin around until the cup tipped and coffee spilled out onto the papers. I scanned the room some more. A half-eaten hot dog was on one desk, and a partially-smoked cigar was in an ashtray on the other one. As gross as they were, I nudged them into the bin, too. A tattered plastic bag was lying on the floor near the filing cabinet. I swiped that and whispered, "Time to take out the trash." I quickly picked out the four discarded items from the larger bin and placed them into the smaller plastic bag. I made my way to the door but then looked back to see if there was anything else that needed to go out with the day's trash.

"The papers are in the office. It's a bit messy, but I'm sure…" It was a man's voice coming towards me. It sounded like Lloyd was fast approaching.

I ran out and took a hard right down the hall and out the back door. He must have seen me, or at least the back of me, because he let out a loud, "Hey!"

As the door slammed shut, I heard a deep growl, then a chain being dragged across concrete. I looked down, to the right of my leg. A thick, boxy-looking black dog wearing a thick studded collar and with a face full of scars was baring its teeth, definitely upset with my sudden appearance. For a split second, I considered throwing him the hot dog from inside the bag. But it was too late. He jumped up, his nails raking my ass as he chomped down. The pain was excruciating. I pivoted quickly, kicking him hard, and then I tore away, running down the path, the plastic bag hitting against my leg with every step I took. I heard a loud whelp — the dog had reached the end of its chain.

Someone let out a whistle, and I looked up. It was the hard hat guy on the fire escape. I ran to it and climbed the stairs, slipping past him to a spot just inside the doorway.

Lloyd was following me, and he hollered up at the man, "You see someone come tearing out this back door?"

I stayed hidden, catching my breath. The bite was painful and possibly bleeding. My hands were shaking.

The construction guy called down, "Your dog went nuts over this cat I'm holding. He must have eagle eyes."

"Could have sworn somebody darted out here."

"Like I said, it was this kitty that got him so riled up."

When the big guy stepped back inside, still holding the black cat, I thanked him.

"That's got to hurt some, let me take a look."

As best I could tell, the bite was just below my right buttock. The shorts were torn; the flap of the pocket was hanging by a thread. I covered my cheek with the pocket and turned around.

"Yeah, you're gonna want to clean this all out and watch for infection. You can run, girl, I'll give you that."

He started for the stairs and said, "Got to put the cat back now." He pointed down the hallway in the other direction. "If you take the opposite set of stairs, you'll be on

Fifth Street across from the music store and even further away from the truck place."

I nodded and weighed whether to change into something from the thrift store's pile of clothes in the dressing room below but then decided against it. As I climbed down the stairs, I glanced inside the plastic bag. One of the cups had broken, but the other cup, along with the half-eaten hot dog and the smoked cigar, was still intact. Limping, with my hand holding my pocket in place, I turned toward Moody's. I couldn't wait to show Dominic.

Chapter 15

Rosie was deadheading the petunias in the window box in front of the motel office. She turned as I shuffled by. "Oh my God, what happened to you?"

"A dog bit me. It hurts likes hell. I need to clean it out."

"We've got a first aid kit inside. It's got sterile gauze and cream. I'll bring it to you."

I managed a smile and said, "That'd be good."

SOON I WAS STRETCHED OUT on the bed, the gauze was in place. Rosie was going to come back with two of her antibiotic pills. "That's nasty. I'd take one pill now, then the other one in twelve hours." She started for the door.

At the same time, Dominic arrived. "Your girlfriend needs you," she said, scooting past him.

He appeared confused and stepped inside the room. "What happened?"

I propped myself up. There was a clean bath towel under my leg. "I got nailed by a dog. It's not that bad, but it hurts. I've got a lot to tell you."

"Was it that dog, Dutch, out by The Diamondback?" he asked as he moved to my bed.

I was wearing a pair of boxers that I'd stuffed into the two-dollar bag at the thrift store. I turned on my side and carefully peeled back the taped gauze. "He chomped down hard just below my butt. See?"

Dominic winced and stepped back. "Was it Dutch?" he asked again.

"No, this dog was Dutch on steroids. God, I hate surprises."

Rosie had left the door ajar, and now she knocked lightly. Dominic looked at me questioningly.

"Can you grab a twenty-dollar bill from my bag right there and give it to her? She's got two pills she's giving me. Tell her thanks and to buy a pizza on me."

Dominic seemed even more confused but did as I asked. Along with the two antibiotic pills, Rosie gave him a couple of Advils.

"I think a drug deal just went down," he said as he placed the pills on the stand next to me.

"How about you? Did you get any more info on the boy?" I asked, swallowing three of the pills with water. I stowed the last antibiotic pill in a plastic cup to take in the morning.

"Yeah. More to confuse us than anything else. You go first, though."

Dominic studied Sadie's drawing of the truck and listened as I floated the idea that Lloyd and Cal could have been the two guys after Lucas. That the yellow bandana Lloyd had used yesterday might be a clue, and how their shop bordered the back of the new apartments being built — the ones that had burned.

When I finally pointed to the plastic bag on the dresser and told him how I'd gotten the stuff from the autobody shop's trash, Dominic immediately got up and looked inside the bag.

"That was a crazy, dangerous thing you did, Kate," he said, turning to me with an incredulous look. "You should have run it by me, first."

"I tried, but you didn't pick up!" I could feel the defensiveness rising up inside of me. "At least now we have something to give to the police. That dumb dog wasn't my fault!"

Dominic moved to the door and angrily replied, "Yeah, they could be the guys, you're right. And they could have caught you and hurt you. You took a huge risk." He opened the door and said, "I need to go." His face was beet red.

"Wait! You didn't tell me what you found out in Franklin." I swung my legs onto the floor.

Dominic hesitated and then came back in. Sighing, he replied, "The elderly man, Mr. Blake, said Lucas was planning on leaving Tennessee. That he was expecting some big money, and he was moving to California."

"Really?"

"Lucas asked them to take his cat, and they did. It's a tabby. I saw it."

"Okay, so..." I replied, feeling confused.

Dominic sighed again and said, "He brought the cat over on the afternoon of September third. The same night Sadie saw him. They never saw Lucas again but didn't expect to. *'He's in California,'* Mrs. Blake told me."

I stood up and walked towards the bathroom. "So, maybe the meeting went wrong, but he still got the money and left. Or something worse happened. Man, this is hard to figure out."

Dominic added, "The Blakes never called the police when they saw the missing person's bulletin. They liked the kid a lot and wished him well, even though they thought he could have been involved in something shady."

My ripped shorts were on the floor. I picked them up and held them out for Dominic to see where the dog's teeth had torn through.

"Shit!" he exclaimed. "Now I'm pissed at you all over again." He closed the door and left.

BETWEEN THE SUN I'd gotten earlier and the bite, I was pretty tired. I crawled back into bed and got under the covers. But I just lay there, replaying my trip to the auto-body shop. Besides the bite, it didn't feel good lying to Dominic about the so-called 'trash items.' But since he didn't know the truth, he couldn't get in any trouble. I turned carefully on my side and thought some more. *Was snatching the stuff — stealing the DNA — making the argument that the end justifies the means?* I didn't have an answer.

I MUST HAVE FALLEN ASLEEP, because I never heard Dominic come back until it was almost dark. The rain hitting the tin roof of the motel and the wind blowing through my motel room's open door woke me.

"Get up, Kate, now. We've got to get out of here!" He was zipping my backpack and putting it on over his shoulders.

"What are you doing, Dominic?" I asked, sitting up slowly. The dog bite was on fire.

"I found out some things. I'll tell you once we've left. Just trust me." The panic in his voice alarmed me. "Get your shoes on and grab the map. It's pouring out."

Doing exactly as he told me, I followed him out to the Volvo, which was already running. He threw my stuff into the back and jumped in. I barely had my door closed before he took off. The wind and rain had plastered his hair and clothes to his body.

"Man o' man, this weather is intense!" Dominic said as he drove down Sixth Street.

"What's going on?" I asked, watching him take the sign for I-65 South to Nashville. "Why are we going into Nashville?"

"Lloyd knows you're here to see Ron Warren, but he's found out we've been asking around about the boy. And guess what? Lloyd is Hetty's nephew! Her brother owned all the land between Fifth Street, the campground, and on down past the tent church, right up to The Diamondback. He died and parceled out the properties in his will. Lloyd got the buildings that Lucas was doing preliminary census work around. I bet he's one of the landlords who didn't comply with the census."

I was trying to follow him, trying to discern how we were in danger, and I said, "My brain isn't quite working."

We merged onto I-65 South. We'd be able to see the lights of Nashville soon. "You got the cups? My phone, my purse?" I asked, suddenly panicking.

He nodded, took a deep breath, and let it out slowly. The wind gusts were moving the car; the windshield wipers were on high. "Let me back up."

"Yeah, why'd we have to leave like that?" I asked, looking at him pointedly.

"When I came back to your room, you were asleep. I reread Sadie's deposition. The bandana the man wrapped around his knuckles after he hit the boy had been a light color as she'd stated, and the bandana found in the station wagon and sent to forensics was a faded yellow. Also, there were traces of acrylic lacquer found on it, in addition to Lucas Alvarez's blood and someone else's. Acrylic lacquer is a common old-school paint used in autobody shops to give cars that glossy, real shiny look. And get this…in Sadie's deposition, she stated that the bandana looked familiar. She never said that to me."

There was a blast of horns, and then the cars in front of us slowed down. Lines of rearview red lights and dark streaks of rain were all I could see as Dominic switched lanes.

He inched the car forward and said, "It got me thinking. Did Sadie know Lloyd back then? Maybe she couldn't identify him from that night because it was too dark, even though the car was parked under The Diamondback sign. I decided to walk on over to Hetty's to chat, ask her about Sadie possibly knowing Lloyd.

"She was ready for a visit, so we sat out on her little deck. Pretty soon, she mentions that she has lifetime rights to live in her camper on her site scot-free. She told me Lloyd is one of her brother's kids, that he inherited the land the autobody shop is on and the buildings along Fifth Street. Two nieces split up the rest — the campground and the land the tent church is on.

"I asked her if Lloyd ever met Sadie. Hetty didn't think so. At one point, she shows me how spacious her camper is, including the sunroom she had built on the side. Did you know Hetty hand sews a lot of gifts, like scarves, bunting blankets, and hankies on that sun porch? And guess what? Her hankies are cotton paisley print. I saw lots of colors, including yellow ones. Then…" Dominic paused and looked over at me. "I left and made my way over to The Diamondback to check out things there again. I was interested in how well Sadie could see out of the station wagon at night, with the lights on in the lot. I was planning on staying there until dark to figure it out."

The traffic congestion was breaking up, and we picked up speed. Dominic kept his eyes on the road, glancing in the rearview mirror often.

"But as I was checking things out, the cook saw me and called me over to the ramp. Told me Lloyd Parker had been by earlier and asked if a couple of northerners were showing a picture of a boy around. She lied to him and said 'no,' but she didn't think he bought it. Then Parker asked her about me, specifically if I was an undercover cop and if she thought I was carrying — like as in a firearm. 'Be careful,' she warned me, 'Parker thinks he can get away with any- thing around here, including making people disappear.' That's when I took off back to the motel — and you. The rain and wind kicked up just as I crossed the fields."

"Holy shit," I replied.

"Yeah, Lloyd definitely knows we're trying to find out about Lucas Alvarez. You're sure he didn't see you run from his back office?" Dominic asked.

"He saw someone run, but I don't think he knew it was me."

"I bet he knows just about everything that goes on in that stretch of his, including us staying at Moody's. He's worried. He's either guilty of an assault that was never reported or... he's guilty of way more. Cal, his sidekick, is probably involved, too."

We were nearing the city. Everything he'd just said was scaring me. "I can't believe we're piecing all this together and the police here haven't," I replied, shaking my head.

Dominic quickly answered, "Remember, this started out as a missing child's case, one case out of almost three hundred missing kids in Tennessee alone. They're over- whelmed and understaffed."

"It's still not okay, Dominic." I looked out at the city lights. As we drove closer to the exit, I asked, "What happens tomorrow morning when Lloyd and Cal go to make…" But I caught myself and said instead, "Meeting up with Ron Warren just got more complicated, didn't it?"

Dominic nodded but didn't reply immediately. Finally, he glanced my way and said slowly, "We've got to talk about that."

I didn't like how that sounded. No matter what had just happened, I had to follow through on my plan around Carson. It was the whole reason I came down here. Dominic didn't have kids, so how the hell could he understand?

I turned to him and said, "I'm going to the marina. I need Brother Ron to sign off. I have to!" My voice was strong, but my stomach was all knotted up.

"Let's talk when we're not driving in all this rain, okay?" he replied. His voice was measured as he put on the blinker and made his way onto the exit.

Chapter 16

We checked into a hotel north of Broadway in downtown Nashville. It was where Dominic had stayed a few years back for the bachelor party he'd told me about on the way down to Goodlettsville. He used his credit card and called me Mrs. Sousa. I looked at him strangely, but he just smiled and signed for the room.

As we entered the elevator, he quietly said, "The room has two queens. Sorry, but I think this is what we have to do to stay safe. We'll drop off the items from the autobody shop at the Tennessee Bureau of Investigation on the way out. I've already googled the address. Then we'll ..." His voice trailed off.

The hotel room had a sitting area separate from the bedroom and bath. It was a huge upgrade from Moody's. Dominic closed the curtains and spread out my map on the table near the flat screen TV. We had already called for room service and placed an order for two burgers right before the kitchen closed.

Keeping my cool and not flying off the handle — like that time on Tabor Road — was the way to go here. I needed to be rational and calm. I sat down in the side chair near the couch and took a big, deep breath and began. "Dominic, it's more complicated now. I get that. We don't know if Ron Warren is also involved with Lloyd and Cal in some illegal crap and maybe even in the disappearance of Lucas. We've also heard Lloyd can be dangerous. But I've got to see this through. My whole life is wrapped up in that little boy of mine. If I don't get the asshole to sign off, or at least try to get him to sign off, then I'm forever trapped in limbo — in this sucky place called my life." *Did I sound as desperate and as pathetic as I felt?*

Dominic had been standing with his hands in his pocket, listening intently to me. Now he moved closer and took the chair opposite me. He leaned forward and replied, "Maybe I do get it, Kate, the sucky life part, more than you know. But it's too much of a risk. You could be ambushed by these guys and I've got no back up or — absolutely worse-case scenario — no weapon to threaten them with. We can brainstorm another way to do this, to get you free of him."

The anger came fast, pooling out of that reservoir of mine just below the surface. I was suddenly back at the trailer with him, the other two detectives, and the old man as they talked to me like I was the village idiot. I stood up abruptly and moved towards the door leading out into the hallway. Turning back, I yelled, "Screw you! I can take care of myself and get to the marina. I don't need you!"

But Dominic was quick and got in front of me, blocking the door. He held up his hands and said, "Jesus, Kate, don't be dumb about this!"

I wanted to scream that everything I'd ever done in my life had been dumb but that coming here to Tennessee with him was the dumbest thing of all! Instead, in a cold and calculating voice, I whispered, "Get out of my way, or I'll scream so bloody loud it'll wake the whole place up."

He stepped away.

Just then, there was a knock. It was room service. Dominic opened the door and grabbed the tray, placing it down on the table near the map. He reached into his pocket and slipped a bill to the waiting kid. He did it all in a matter of seconds.

It was awkward — both of us still standing near the door as it closed shut. But the interruption had given me a chance to cool down some. We glanced at each other.

Dominic nodded toward the food and asked, "Could we at least eat?"

Looking at him and hearing his sincere plea, I replied, "Give me a minute."

In the bathroom, I reached for a washcloth and ran it under very cold water. Sitting on the toilet, I washed my face slowly and then glanced in the mirror. "Do not give up," I whispered. But my heart was crushed. "Don't be dumb," he'd said. *That's how he sees me — as some dumb, poor-ass hick.* I blew my nose and walked back into the sitting area.

About half way through eating our burgers in silence, Dominic said, "So, tell me about this trip of ours to the marina." He was serious as he looked over at me.

"You mean it?" I asked hesitantly.

"It's not a move I'd make, but I get that it's important to you, even more than Sadie's boy was to her. And it's why you really came down here."

I nodded and felt relief, glad to be done arguing, to almost be done with this whole mess.

Dominic moved his plate and silverware around, including the little packets of salt and pepper and ketchup. "Can you make me a map of the marina?"

"Oh no, not this again…" But I smiled and knelt down on the floor, reaching for the things he had near him. I lightly touched his knee, looked up, and said, "Thank you." It was a simple gesture and totally out of character for me. I wondered if he knew that.

The fact that the marina was below the parking lot, giving Dominic a panoramic view of the docks, seemed to satisfy him some. Finally, I described Ron Warren and stood up. "Do you mind if I shower first?"

"No, no, go right ahead," he replied, still studying the floor.

As I showered, I wondered how it would play out, how would Ron react. He'd been arrogant back then, full of himself. But something told me he wouldn't have gotten involved with this kind of illegal shit. Younger girls, yes — but not murder or violence.

When I came back out, my hair was up in a towel and I was wearing the last clean over-sized t-shirt from my backpack. Dominic smiled and said, "Kate Wade, you've never looked better."

Was he flirting with me? A minute ago, we'd been ready to duke it out. I grew serious and said, "I'm not going to do anything dumb tomorrow. Just get him to sign."

Dominic quickly replied, "That was a bad choice of words I used back there. I'm sorry."

Climbing into the queen bed furthest from the bathroom, I felt his apology taking some of the sting out. I fluffed the pillows to get comfortable and then paused. *When did I start to care so much about what he thought?*

Before sleep finally came, I called out to the sitting area where he was still pouring over the maps, "What if he won't sign, no matter what, and wants full custody?"

Dominic walked into the bedroom. "Then you'll fight it, right?"

I nodded and turned away.

SOMETIME IN THE MIDDLE OF THE NIGHT, I woke up and walked through to the sitting room. Dominic had picked up the stuff from the floor and was sleeping on the couch in only his running shorts. He was spread out, with his feet hanging over the edge. He looked different, almost vulnerable. His mouth was slightly open, and I could hear his little breathing gasps. A wet towel was on the rug, up near his head. His dark hair was still damp; he must have taken a late shower and shaved. His hands were clasped across his stomach. I watched the rise and fall of his chest as he slept peacefully — especially compared to my tossing and turning in the bedroom. I wanted to adjust the pillow to keep it from falling, but I didn't dare.

Instead, I moved to the map of that last night at The Diamondback and studied it. I'd forgotten to draw in the swamp beyond the parking lot.

SLIP 12 HAD A BIGGER CABIN BOAT moored compared to Ron's boat from six years ago. This one was a Sea Ray: sleek, new, and beautiful. I stood on the dock, unsure if I was supposed to board it. There wasn't much relief from the heat and humidity, even down here. The blue-green lake water was still, with barely a ripple in it. Turning back to the parking lot, I saw Dominic standing near the Volvo up on the second tier and scanning the area below. He was in full cop mode. This time, I welcomed it.

'Don't give up' had been my mantra last night. I squared my shoulders and felt as ready as I'd ever be.

I turned and looked down the wharf. Ron was walking towards me. He looked a little older and had definitely put on a few pounds. He reached me and said, right off, "Okay, Kate. Not sure why you're wanting to see me, but here I am."

He was blunt and appeared impatient, so I jumped right in and replied, "You've got a son. I was pregnant when I left here. He's almost five, starting kindergarten in the fall. His name is Carson."

Ron took off his sunglasses and looked hard at me. He started to say something but then stopped. Two young girls were skipping down the wharf in our direction. They were holding hands, and one of them called out, "Daddy, Daddy!"

He quickly moved in front of me as if he needed to protect them from me. "Darlene's mother just had emergency gallbladder surgery. There wasn't time to find a sitter. I'll get them settled on the boat. Hold on."

They were little whirlwinds of energy, talking and laughing. They kept asking questions: Could they eat their penny candy, could they watch more of the video they'd started, how soon would they be going out on the lake, was it time to get on their life jackets, and who was that pretty lady in the yellow dress. I listened as Ron got them settled into the bow of the boat. He was patient and loving. Finally, he moved to the stern and stepped off.

The girls had quieted down. I waited for some sort of reaction to what I'd just told him.

He ran his fingers through his hair and turned away from the boat. "Listen, Kate. I'm sorry about back then. That I started things up with you. Besides being married and a new father, you were too young — though maybe not as young as some. But the boy's not mine. I can't have kids on account of having mumps as a teenager. Our girls were adopted."

"He's yours, Ron. He even looks like you." I'd brought a picture, and I fished it out of my bag. "Look."

He reluctantly took it and put his sunglasses back on. He glanced at it briefly then handed it back.

I quickly said, "I'm not looking for any financial support at all. That's not what this is about. I just need you to sign this paper here." I reached into my shoulder bag again and brought out the voluntary parental rights termination form I'd found online, as well as a pen. "If you sign this release of parental rights paper then that's it — we're done."

Ron reached for the paper. When he was done reading it, he began to shake his head slowly and replied, "I got a solid life down here. Darlene and me — we're in a really good place, and the girls are my world. We've switched churches, even moved to a better place for the kids' schooling. You coming here, trying to disrupt it — that's bullshit."

He took out a cigarette and lit it, inhaling deeply.

I needed to tread carefully here. "That's not my intention. I've been scared you'd find out somehow and take him. Coming down to have you voluntarily sign off your parental rights is a way for both of us to put it to rest."

Ron scowled and replied angrily, "You probably screwed other guys that summer. You were slutty, I do remember that. No way the kid's mine, no way I'd want it to be mine."

"So just sign. This makes it so I can never come back and make any claims. It's in your best interest to sign it."

He dropped the cigarette onto the wharf and stepped on it. "If I sign, you'll never come anywhere near here, ever again?"

I replied, "Never."

He looked back at his boat then down at the paper once more. I flicked the pen's point out and handed it to him. I was about to say, *"And Darlene never has to know,"* but I didn't. I waited.

One of the little girls giggled loudly. It jarred him out of whatever he was thinking because he quickly signed, looked at his watch, and dated it. "Here," he said. "Now go."

He turned and stepped back onto the boat. I looked down at the cigarette. It had burned out.

I COULDN'T GET OFF THE WHARF quickly enough. Not because I was scared of him. I was thrilled. *"No way I'd want it to be mine."* It sounded pretty convincing that Ron Warren would never, ever come up north to take my child.

As I made my way up the hill towards the parking lot, Dominic gave me a 'thumbs up' sign. I nodded vigorously then pointed to the bathroom in the dip below the lot. I was feeling giddy but needed to pee before we hit the road.

When I walked around the corner, just before entering the ladies' side, a man's hand grabbed ahold of my arm. "Lloyd needs to see you. He's at the shop. Let's go."

It was Cal. I looked up at him and said, "Take your frigging hand off of me."

Gripping me tighter, he replied, "You been snooping around, getting into stuff that don't pertain to you."

He was hurting me, forcing me to turn toward him, and I cried out in pain. But then I saw his twisted, ugly grimace. He was nothing but a nasty old man. I felt a rush of adrenaline, and I moved quickly, kicking him hard in the knee.

Cal let go and dropped down onto the concrete floor. "You bitch!" he yelled.

Free from his grasp, I took off, running back around the bathroom and up the hill. Dominic saw me coming and got into the car. He pulled out and stopped just as I reached the top of the stairs. I jumped in and we sped away, but not before I saw Cal standing in the middle of the parking lot.

DOMINIC ASKED, "Were you a track star in school, like in the hundred-meter sprint?"

We were wedged between two state cars, drinking Cokes we'd gotten from a drive-thru window two blocks over.

"No. I just hate surprises," I replied. My arm had a red mark where Cal had grabbed it. One of my flip-flops was somewhere back at the marina on the hillside. I wore my sneakers now. I was anxious to finish all this Tennessee stuff. I missed home, I missed Carson. I'd never been away from him for more than a day before.

Dominic handed me the plastic bag. Neither of us had touched it or anything else inside. "Ask for Detective Ellis. He's the agent on Lucas Alvarez's missing person's case. I'll sit tight and make sure Lloyd and Cal don't interfere. If I see them, I'll keep them occupied. But this is the last place they'd want to come."

I entered the large atrium on the main floor of the Tennessee Bureau of Investigation building. People were scurrying about. I walked up to two women manning an informational desk and asked if I could speak to Detective Kevin Ellis.

"Is he expecting you?" one of them asked.

I lied, "Yes, he's been calling me most every day, asking me to come in. You can tell him that the woman with the hard evidence in the Alvarez case is here."

She nodded and picked up the phone. I turned and watched the bank of people sitting in the reception area. Security was tight. No one moved towards the elevators unless accompanied by someone who wore a lanyard and worked here.

"He'll be down, take a seat," the woman at the desk said. Suddenly, I didn't want to meet with any cop. Dominic was the only cop I trusted. Plus, this place was crawling with law enforcement. *How dumb was I to swipe that stuff?* It was illegal! They could arrest me on the spot! Where would that leave Carson and me? I looked back at the woman and asked, "Do you have a pad of paper and a pen?"

Finding a seat, I started to write furiously for Lucas Alvarez's sake. I wanted to give Detective Ellis our best speculation based on what we'd found out, and I hoped he could figure out the rest without the DNA I'd stolen. All those missing kids, like Lucas, full of hopes and dreams — getting caught up in bad stuff because they'd been dealt a lousy hand. I could have been one of those kids with the mother I had. The old man had been the only thing keeping me from that. Lucas — Sadie's boy — deserved to have someone fight for him.

I glanced out the window. I couldn't see Dominic, but I knew he was still parked in between the state trooper cars, waiting for me.

The last thing I wrote down was something I hadn't yet ran by him. *'Lloyd Parker could have put the body of Lucas Alvarez in a barrel with a blue monarch butterfly painted on it and dumped it in the swamp behind The Diamondback.'* That last drawing of Sadie's — I assumed it was drawn before the boy got beat up. But what if she had drawn it after I'd seen them scrubbing out the back of their truck? Sadie had drifted in and out of sleep in the car. They could have gone back.

I signed it: *Kate Wade, Tabor Road, Langdon, Vermont,* and then I added my cell number. I walked back to the receptionist's desk.

She looked up at me and said, "The detective isn't ready for you yet."

Shaking my head, I replied, "Can't wait, but here's everything. It's all spelled out for him. Oh, and this cigarette butt in here..." I held up the discarded Twinkie's wrapper from the side pocket of the Volvo. "Have Detective Ellis take it to the forensic lab to check it against any statutory rape cases in the Goodlettsville area involving Ron..." I stopped and said, "His name's in there, too." I gestured to the papers already in her hand.

A guard in uniform opened one of the large atrium doors for me. Smiling, I walked through it then paused. As soon as his back was turned, I crammed the plastic bag into the garbage can to the right of the exit door. The cups clinked as they hit the bottom.

The air didn't feel as humid as it had before.

"Did it go okay in there?" Dominic asked as I climbed in.

"Yeah. Let's head home." I reached for my seatbelt and turned his way. He was already backing out. I texted Karen: *'Carson is safe; we're on our way back.'* I couldn't wait to hug the little guy.

Chapter 17

In northern Kentucky, it started to rain and soon became a torrential downpour. Cars on I-71 slowed to a crawl, some pulling over onto the shoulder to wait it out.

Dominic glanced my way and said, "I'm going to stop, too."

Minutes later, he pulled off to the side of the road. The rain pounded the car's roof. We couldn't see anything — it was a gray wash-out. The clicking of the yellow flashers was eerie, yet it felt strangely intimate inside the car.

Dominic reached in front of me and opened the glove compartment. He brought out a granola bar and a small bag of chips. He reached in further and pulled out a pack of Trident. He held them up. "My offerings to you."

It struck me how all alone and isolated I was from the rest of the world at this moment. Yet, here was this man, a stranger not too long ago, who'd come all this way with me for Sadie's sake. He'd stuck by my side, making sure I was safe. No one had ever done that for me before.

I smiled at him and reached for the gum, but just as I took it, I felt this incredible sense of sorrow rise up from somewhere deep within me. It was wrapped in self-pity — for all I'd been through and everything still wrong and insurmountable in my life. I started to cry for the girl I once was, with a baby on my hip, and then for the woman I'd become — guarded, going nowhere. I wept for that teenage girl sitting up behind the trailer who had no say, no self-determination. I couldn't stop, and I covered my face with both hands.

I turned away from Dominic and whispered, "Sorry, sorry," as my tears flowed, streaking down my face. I took deep breaths to try and stop. But then I saw my precious boy, Carson, and I cried even harder, my shoulders heaving. His awful father had rejected the mere idea of him.

Dominic sat quietly, his hand lightly resting on the headrest above me. I was sure he didn't know what to do. I didn't know what to do.

When I was finally done, I looked over at him and apologized again. He nodded and replied, "Want to talk about it?"

I was drained and wiped my face and then my hands against the skirt of the sundress. Short little gasps escaped me as I tried to pull myself together. The rain had let up, but Dominic didn't seem to be in a hurry to start driving again. He sat, looking at me with his dark, kind eyes.

"It's good that he doesn't want anything to do with Carson. It means I can finally stop worrying. But the way he dismissed him? Like Carson wasn't good enough to be his son? That, that…" My voice was breaking; I was going to start crying all over again. But Dominic took hold of my hand in my lap and held it tightly.

"You've got a great kid, and you're a great mother. Don't let anybody, least of all him, make you feel otherwise," he replied.

Eventually, he let go of my hand and opened the bag of chips. He took one then held the bag out to me. I dipped my hand in, smiled, and took a chip, too. I swished around what was left of my Coke from hours ago and drank it. When we finished the bag, he whispered, "You good?"

"I'm good. And thanks for coming all this way with me." I adjusted my seat and smiled again.

"We found out a lot in three days, but man, was it stressful," he replied as he pulled back out onto the highway.

I'd felt the edge of the dog bite when I'd moved my seat. It was swollen and warm to the touch. I hadn't taken the second antibiotic pill. In our hurry to leave Moody's, I'd forgotten it on the nightstand.

A little later, I asked, "What's your story, Dominic?" It was monotonous looking out the window. We had hours to go.

"My story, huh?" he asked. He started to speak, slowly at first. It was nice to hear his steady voice. "Well, I grew up in a house with three older sisters. Slamming doors and fighting over clothes is what I remember most. Marilyn, Margaret, and..."

"Melanie," I replied quietly. "I've met them all, and your gram has told me lots about them, and you."

"Oh, I'm sure she has. I was the first and only grandson. She spoiled me."

"I've met your mom, too. We all love her at The Pines. What I want to hear is the 'almost married' story."

He raised his eyebrows and replied, "It's a long story."

I lifted my head from the headrest. "It's a long drive."

"Okay then." He pulled down his visor. Already, the sun was back out. "Let's see…I dated a girl in college and after we graduated, we lived together just outside of Boston. She was getting her master's in speech language pathology while I was working at a brokerage house."

"Is speech pathology helping kids talk? And what does a brokerage house do?" I was too curious to pretend to know what either was.

"I really couldn't tell you much about her degree. Just that you need all sorts of classes to eventually work in a school district. As for the brokerage house I was at — it's a firm for buying and selling stocks for clients in the stock market. At first, I was just a glorified mailroom guy and a runner for the brokers. They had to decide if I was a worthy candidate for their training program."

"Living in Boston must have been fun," I replied, glancing at him.

"Yeah, it was for a time. Delaney — that's her name — and I started making more money and enjoying the night life, especially in the North End. But things started to get out of hand, like lots of my nights back in college. I was drinking more and more. When Delaney got a position in Newton and I got my stockbroker's license, I kept it up. We met people our age without kids and plenty of expendable income — young professionals, I guess."

Dominic grew quiet, and I patiently waited. There was no hurry whatsoever. I took out a piece of the Trident gum and offered the pack to him, but he shook his head.

He began again and said, "We decided, like a lot of our friends, to get married, and that pumped everything up even more. Engagement parties, stag parties, work parties, weddings — you name it. Every time I turned around, we had parties on top of parties. But the thing was, I couldn't remember one party from the next, because I was drinking so much at every single one. Delaney was better at holding her liquor, but still, there were times in the morning she felt just as lousy as I did."

Closing my eyes I imagined Dominic, this Dominic, out of control. I couldn't.

"My sister, Margaret, was the one who finally said it was okay to get off the party boat. She actually said that when we were on a party boat in Boston Harbor, celebrating our mother's retirement. I was, as usual, drunk and trying hard to be the life of the party. The way Margaret looked at me and said that… I'll never, ever be able to thank her enough."

"So what happened then?" I asked.

"Basically, everything. I broke off our wedding — we were only six weeks out — and took off. After staying in a rehab facility in upstate New York that Margaret found, I drove out west. I stayed away for seventeen months. It was what had to happen. But I was a complete asshole for doing that to Delaney."

I'm not sure exactly when I drifted off, but it was sometime after Dominic said he'd been an asshole. I did remember thinking that he could never be an asshole.

MY FATHER WAS PULLING ME by the arm and saying, "Wake up, Kate. You've got a fever. We've got to get you seen."

I didn't want to wake up. *This time, in my dream, Sadie heard me and was taking the shortcut up along the honeysuckle like I'd told her to. She smiled back at me and turned towards Karen's porch. Just as she stepped up, a big crack of thunder sounded above. I screamed and collapsed onto her. We shim-mied up against the house, under Karen's window, and started laughing. Another flash of lightning, followed by booming thunder. She pulled my arms tightly around her. A big gust of wind blew the rain in sideways, drenching us. We giggled,*

*wrapped in each other's warmth, feeling the wrath of the
summer storm.*

DOMINIC'S VOICE WAS CLEAR, yet persistent. "Kate,
you've got a temperature. It's the dog bite. Come on, wake
up."

Both of them walked with me through the Langdon
Clinic doors. "Where's Carson?" I asked Dad, feeling
awful.

"Karen came to the trailer to watch him. It's Saturday
morning. Dominic called me. Besides an antibiotic, you
need a tetanus shot."

Chapter 18

For the next two days, I moseyed around the trailer in my pajamas and Carson hardly left my side. When Monday rolled around, he argued about going to pre-school, but I told him I would pick him up early and we'd go for a cookie or a cupcake at the bagel shop. He was happy at that but still clingy.

Dad was mostly quiet until we found ourselves alone mid-morning. I had already told him about Ron Warren, but now I gave him Sadie's drawing pad.

"Where did you get this?" he asked before opening it.

"Sadie gave it to Hetty to keep. It's really sweet. Take your time looking through it."

I heard him chuckling then grow quiet as he turned the pages. He refilled his coffee. When he sat back down, he sipped from his cup then shook his head and said, "I can't drink. I know that. I lose all ability to reason. What guy leaves his daughter, his young daughter, out in a car while he goes on a bender?"

I reached over and covered his hand with mine. "I slept on the bathroom floor and woke up to Carson standing on top of me to wash his hands. I'm never going to forget that he saw his mother like that, ever. But I'm done with drinking, and so are you. We can help each other, Dad."

Then I told him about trying to find out about the boy, including the crazy speculation that Lloyd and Cal from the autobody shop could have been the ones who beat him up.

He listened and turned to the last page again. "I bought her a little flashlight and glow-in the-dark pens at the Dollar Store. I was bribing her."

"What set you off? You'd been sober for almost four months."

"Who knows — it could have been anything. Thank God we had you. You brought us home."

LATER IN THE DAY, I joined him as he was raking the winter debris that had blown across our yard. Back home it was cooler; spring was still unfolding.

My father stopped raking for a moment and called out, "Dominic — he's a good man, Kate. I think he has feelings for you. I saw the way he looked at you, took care of you, even when I was there at the clinic."

Standing, with a handful of sticks, I scoffed at that idea and replied, "Do you know how far I am from his social circle, or whatever you call it? A high school drop-out who..."

My father interrupted me, "Who earned her GED and is about to start her seventh year working in a place his grandmother lives. He told me how much his family appreciates you, how much you mean to his grandmother."

I didn't want to hear anymore. The idea that Dominic would be interested in me in that way was ludicrous. Besides, he'd made it very clear how he viewed me with his 'don't be dumb' comment.

As I left the yard to go in and shower, he called out, "I don't expect you to live here forever. You gotta have a life, Katherine Elizabeth. Even Sadie said that."

I closed the outside door and leaned against it. *Even Sadie said that.* She'd already had more of a social life at Shay's than I ever did.

Chapter 19

A lot happened in the next forty-eight hours. Carson and I picked up his tee-ball schedule and his shirt and ball cap at the Rec building. He was on the Orioles team. Then Darcy, my co-worker, left work at her usual time, but she came back less than an hour after to talk with me. She'd gotten an urgent call that her mother had fallen and was en route to the hospital. Darcy's mom lived in Arizona with one of her sister's — Darcy's aunt. She needed to fly out immediately.

"Can you and Carson move into the house and watch Alfie? You're the first person I thought of, and you guys know him, know his quirks. There's plenty of food in the fridge; I shopped this weekend. I have to go, Kate."

It was a no-brainer, I told her. I'd go right after work tonight, and Carson and I would move into the guest bedroom. She hugged me and left.

Then my supervisor made the decision to move me to the day shift since Darcy was leaving. I was the most senior staff member, familiar with the daily routines and all the residents. It suited us better, too, since my father was at the trailer, twenty miles away. It'd be too much for either of us to shuffle back and forth during the evenings with Carson in tow.

Darcy's old house was big, with lots of wood trim; a large, leaded-glass entry door into a vestibule; and a long, screened-in back porch. Similar old houses, with shady trees and uneven sidewalks, lined the street. Carson and I soon discovered the small neighborhood elementary school and its playground not far down from the house. Alfie was his usual low maintenance self, and I liked the close proximity to The Pines. Driving Carson to pre-school was the same distance, just in the opposite direction.

About a week after moving into Darcy's, I saw Dominic sitting with his grandmother in her room. We had texted each other a couple of times. He'd asked me how my leg was healing, and I'd texted him a picture of Mrs. Lake winning at bingo. Seeing him was surprising, even though I'd been half expecting it. We chatted and made small talk. The very next morning he was back. This time he came to see me first, by-passing his grandmother's room.

"Can we talk?" he asked.

I motioned down the hall, and we went into the community room. Turning on the light, I asked, "Is there news about the boy?"

"No, no. That's not why I wanted to talk to you. I'm, um…" He seemed flustered, something I'd never seen him be.

"What?" I asked, searching his face.

"I miss you," he replied, lifting his shoulders in a self-depreciating way.

"Dominic, come on." This was not what I was expecting. I felt my face redden.

"No, I mean it. I've thought about you a lot, more than I want to admit. Which is exactly what I'm doing — admitting how much I've missed you." He didn't look away. His eyes were intense.

"Well, believe me, that's a waste of time. I'm a nobody," I replied. My pulse was racing. I quickly looked down at the floor then back up at him. Somewhere a phone was ringing.

He moved closer and said, "I'm a nobody, too, Kate. An absolute nobody." He was smiling, but his eyes remained serious.

"Get real," I whispered, wondering if this was really happening.

"How about one date, maybe dinner?" he asked.

I shook my head. "All my focus right now is on Carson. I've moved into Darcy's house down here in Colton to pet sit while her mother is sick. My schedule just changed, too. Between pre-school, tee-ball, and work — that's all I can handle." I side-stepped him and turned off the light, leaving him standing there.

But that didn't work, because he followed right behind me and said, "I love tee-ball. Does Carson need somebody to practice with him?"

Paula, the registered nurse on duty, walked by us and gave me an amused look. Dominic Sousa was sometimes a topic of conversation for the day staff. *How old do you think he is?" "Is he with somebody?"* And the one that always got a chuckle: *"Imagine being arrested by him!"* No one knew we'd gone to Tennessee together, and I wanted to keep it that way.

I turned back to him. "Really? You'd do that?"

"I'd like to, yes," he answered.

The fenced-in yard off Darcy's porch would work, but I hesitated, not sure if this was a good idea. For Carson — yes. He'd love the attention. But where did that put us? Would it be weird, spoil our friendship?

"I can teach him the game, you know, at his level," he replied in that self-assured way I was used to.

Carson was still clingy with me. I knew part of it was losing Sadie, but he was also starting to question everything. Having another man — one I knew and trusted — spend time with him would be a plus. "He'd love it," I replied. "Let me get the stuff — some balls and a bat and that tee stand. He already has a glove."

"Nah, don't bother. I can round up everything. How's tomorrow after work? It's going to be nice weather."

Paula raised an eyebrow at me when I walked back by a little later with clean bedding for one of the residents. "Looks like Dominic Sousa wants your number, Kate. Lucky you."

"No, no, he's just going to play a little ball with Carson," I replied.

"Yep, the sure way to his mama's heart," she said, smiling.

Leaving work that afternoon, I couldn't help but think that more change was coming our way. Besides moving into Darcy's home and working daytime hours, Carson was growing up. He'd soon be on a team, learning rules, and listening to a coach…and Dominic Sousa.

"WHEN YOU SAID you were pet sitting, I didn't think it'd be for a dog. You and dogs…" Dominic's voice trailed off. He had pulled into the driveway at Darcy's and was now watching me. Alfie would not climb the steps to the front stoop. He was half sitting, half lying on the sidewalk. As an overweight English bulldog who was eight years old,

Alfie had quirks that tried my patience. I was tempted to pick him up, but Darcy's last words, written in a note to us, had said, *"Don't spoil him."*

"This is bullshit, Alfie," I said, pulling on his leash. I couldn't even entice him with a treat. He was six pounds overweight.

Carson stepped out onto the front stoop and waved shyly at Dominic. He was wearing his Orioles shirt and cap, and his glove was on the wrong hand. Dominic forgot about us and said, "Hey, there Carson! I'm Dominic, want to play ball?"

Carson scrambled down the steps and replied, "In through here." Dominic flashed me a quick smile and followed Carson through the gate to the backyard. I knew the first few minutes would involve Carson showing off — maybe a cartwheel, some somersaults, throwing the ball wildly. But I was confident that Dominic could reign him in and redirect him. Finally, I got Alfie to move.

I had promised Carson that he could have dessert for dinner if he was a good listener to the man, the 'coach' coming over. He said he would be, no matter what. Now I stood just out of view on the back porch, watching and listening to their banter. Dominic was showing Carson how to make the 'T' when he threw the ball, and Carson was constantly asking, "Like this, like this?" Pretty soon Carson said, "Want strawberry cake for dinner?" They'd been at it for almost an hour.

The back screen door was shut but I opened it and called out, "We're having strawberry shortcake for dinner. There're extra biscuits and plenty of strawberries — just have to whip the cream."

Dominic smiled and said to Carson, "I think your mom is inviting me to stay and eat."

Carson let out a "Yes!" and threw down his glove and ball and came barreling into the house.

Dominic passed by me and said, "You see that last hit of his? He's got promise." My heart just about burst from pride. I didn't care what Paula had said, Carson needed this.

After Carson had fallen asleep, Dominic and I sat talking. Darcy's back porch was comfortable with a big, droopy couch, a small kitchen table with four chairs, and an old radio next to a lamp on a crate turned upside down. Her husband, Jack, had died years ago when Alfie was just a pup. The porch had been his favorite spot in the evening, and she'd never changed it. A pair of his old boots still rested near the screen door.

Dominic looked over at me and smiled. "Thanks for letting me get to know your little guy. He's a good boy."

"You made his day. I should be thanking you," I replied, glancing at Carson's glove on the old Formica table. I'd been flooded with all this self-doubt — how could Dominic be interested in me? But then he'd done something so sweet and natural with Carson — gave him a piggyback ride up the stairs to his bed — that I wondered why I wasn't throwing myself at him. Drew hadn't liked Carson, and the feeling had been mutual. I stood up from the kitchen chair, and, without planning to, asked, "What is it you see in me, Dominic, really?"

He moved further down on the couch and patted a place for me to come and sit. The old couch squeaked as I grabbed a pillow for my lap and sat down. I turned toward him and waited.

He cleared his throat and paused then said softly, "I'll tell you — I see a mom who's fierce and protective, raising a wonderful, happy kid."

I smiled and started to get up, but he reached for my hand. "Wait, I'm not done. I also see a woman who has lost someone very dear to her, and she's trying to deal with that loss every single moment."

He squeezed my hand and added, "And I see someone who has no idea how beautiful she is. I like that about her. Plus, she can run like hell. That's impressive."

I didn't move, but he did. He gently pulled me back down, leaned over, and kissed me. Then he put his hand under my chin and said, "I've been wanting to do that for a long time."

"Oh yeah?" I whispered. "How long?"

Dominic smiled. "Since the first time we met on Tabor Road. Your cursing is impressive, too."

I turned away, and he asked, "What's wrong, what did I say?"

"Your handwritten notes in the file... You wrote that Sadie was afraid of me. I never wanted her to be afraid of me. I loved her. We were sisters, above everything else. Now she's gone, and I can't tell her that."

Dominic reached over, pulled me in, and held me. We sat like that for some time. He had a way of slowing me down, of helping me still my thoughts.

Finally, he said, "I don't think she was afraid of you, but she was afraid of losing you, your love, by opening up about the boy. You told me she'd been pulling away from you, but I think that was normal. You gave her the security to start to do that. What's the expression — 'roots to grow, wings to fly?' Sadie was starting to fly because of you, the constant in her life."

My head was against his chest. What he was saying in his deep, reassuring voice was comforting. Yet in one brief moment, our relationship had changed, had become something entirely different. I was feeling nervous and excited at the same time.

I whispered, "The moment I saw you differently — not as the detective, the stuffy kind of guy I cringe from — was at Moody's."

"Oh yeah?"

I shivered. The temperature was dropping. Dominic reached for the afghan from the back of the couch and wrapped it around me.

"When you were checking me out at the pool. I remember being surprised."

Dominic threw back his head and laughed. "I let my guard down. All the way back to the room, I was kicking myself for openly admiring your, um…physique. You didn't get creeped out by it?"

Turning to him, I shook my head and replied, "Getting that kind of attention from someone you find attractive isn't creepy, it's nice."

"Wait, so you were already attracted to me?" he asked. "Was it my black boxers?"

It was my turn to laugh. "You wish! How old are you, by the way?" I asked.

"Thirty last July. It's always a surprise when I see this stuffy, cringe-worthy guy in the mirror with another gray hair."

"Oh yes, I see some gray right here, and along there, and more here," I exaggerated, smiling and touching his thick, dark hair.

Dominic caught my hand and replied, "When you smile… Oh my God, Kate, you're even more beautiful."

"Just stop it, okay?" I whispered, secretly loving what he was saying.

He shook his head and pulled me close. "Hey, don't go getting defensive on me. You'll have to get used to me saying things like that. I can't help it."

We made small talk as we listened to the night sounds of Darcy's neighborhood. Someone was calling out, "Kitty, kitty," and beyond the fenced-in yard we heard the neighbor's garage door go down. I liked being wedged in close to other houses. It was the opposite of our desolation out on Tabor Road.

Dominic and I kissed again. He was gentle and that made me hold back some. Usually, I was all in, with no finesse.

He took my hand and looked at it in the soft light of the porch.

"What?" I asked, curious to know what he was thinking.

"No nail polish. Do you do trips to the salon?" he asked

"Never," I responded, pulling my hand back, suddenly feeling self-conscious.

But he gently reached for my hand again and ran his fingers over my fingers. "My sisters painted my nails and my toenails all the time. If they got a new color, they'd paint mine first to see if they liked it. I started to get teased about it. My sister, Mel — she's the toughest of us all — told me other kids were just jealous. I even used that line the next couple of times someone said something."

"And when did they stop? Or you stopped letting them — or wait, maybe they still do your nails?" I asked, grinning.

"Haha, wise guy. It was over by about the end of fourth grade. Kids were starting to call me gay. It was a different time."

"I hope Carson avoids all that, you know the name calling, the put downs, the bullying."

"Unfortunately, I think it's inevitable," he said as he adjusted the afghan around me, making sure it still covered my shoulders.

"What made you decide to be a cop?" I asked, looking at Dominic's profile, wondering how I'd missed just how handsome he was.

"Well, I..." But he was interrupted.

Carson was just beyond the kitchen, calling to me. I got up and walked through to the dining room. He was naked from the waist down.

"Mommy, I did it again. And is that my coach? Is he showing you how to throw and hit?" Carson asked, standing on his tippy toes, straining to see through the kitchen to the porch.

I carried him up the stairs and put a pull-up diaper on him. Since moving into Darcy's, he was trying hard not to wet the bed. Even though I limited what he drank in the evenings and woke him up in the night to go, he still had accidents. I quickly changed the sheets on the cot, and he climbed back in. Alfie never moved from his dog bed near Carson.

"You good? Can I go back down?" I asked.

Carson's hand was resting on Alfie's head. "How long, Mommy?" he asked.

I kissed his forehead and whispered, "I'll be up in ten minutes, promise." For some reason, this seemed to satisfy him and he could fall back to sleep.

I left the light on in the hallway and turned to go back down, but not before I told Alfie he still had one more trip out. "So don't get too comfortable."

When I returned to the porch, I half expected Dominic to be gone, but he wasn't. He was right there, waiting for me. *Just like in Tennessee.*

Sitting down again, I faced him and whispered, "So this, with you, maybe…" But I didn't finish, because I had no idea where I was going with my thoughts. Instead, I kissed him with a lot of vigor and absolutely no finesse.

When we pulled apart, he raised his eyebrows and said, "You kiss like you run; it's a wonderful thing."

I reached for his arms and wrapped them around me. "That, Coach, was me thanking you for having my back when we were in Tennessee."

Dominic laughed and said, "I heard Carson say 'my coach.' Was everything okay just now?"

"He still wets the bed sometimes," I answered. "We're working on it."

"Ah, I did that into my early twenties."

"Wait, what?" I looked at him questioningly.

"I told you — I drank a lot in college and for some time after. I was a belligerent drunk who was always the last one standing." Dominic lowered his voice and said, "We've talked enough about me. Kiss me again, just like you did."

It was many more times. He left a few minutes after midnight. Dominic managed to coax Alfie out and then back in.

"For the win," he bragged as I stood on the front stoop, wrapped in the afghan.

Chapter 20

Darcy kept me updated on her mother. It was going to be six weeks at least, and even then, her returning was iffy because her aunt wasn't in the best of shape either. Her mom was 84, her aunt 80. She mentioned that she may have to call it quits at The Pines. "It's crazy that I'd leave her to go help someone else's mother when mine still needs me." I assured her that Alfie and the house were fine, that she should do what made sense.

The thing going on with Dominic and me was taking shape in a way I'd never had with a guy. It wasn't my usual method of hooking up at the bars after a lot of drinking or meeting someone when my 3-to-11 p.m. shift was over. No, this was different, like having a best friend crossed with a lover: suppers together, trips to the grocery store, Carson's tee-ball games, stolen kisses, and calls to say goodnight.

But there was so much more — layers of family interactions that I flubbed or didn't understand at all. The first time his sister, Marilyn, came to The Pines to see her grandmother after our night out on the porch, she took hold of me, hugged me, and said, "Kit, that brother of ours needs you to keep him level, on an even keel." I'd smiled and walked out of Mrs. Lake's room, unsure what that meant. Then Melanie had arrived and said, as she was casually walking past me in the hallway, "Dominic grabbed our tee-ball stuff but forgot the bases. Remind me when I leave to get those for you. That kid is never organized." Upon seeing me, his mom had whispered, "Oh Kit, he needs a girl who doesn't expect everything all at once, you know? Have patience."

Finally, I went to his gram and asked, "Mrs. Lake, what is the deal with Dominic? I can't figure out what everybody in his family is saying. To me he seems pretty solid."

Before she began, she said, "Speak to Margaret last. She'll explain Nicky to you best, plain and simple. She's an elementary teacher."

I sat and listened to Mrs. Lake describe how Dominic, her Nicky, had grown up in the arms and laps and eventually the shadows of five distinct women, herself being one. She mentioned how his fiancée had been the sixth woman. Then when he'd canceled his wedding, his friends had disappeared and frat brothers were no longer supportive. Nicky had done some traveling and a whole lot of soul searching. When he'd returned, he'd entered the Police Academy. He'd realized he was an alcoholic who finally understood his limitations.

"And his father?" I asked. "What about him?"

Mrs. Lake sighed and said, "Dead at the age of thirty-four. Drowned while ice fishing. He'd had too much to drink. He left three young girls and a baby boy. Of all his children, Nicky needed him the most."

For the rest of my shift that day, I went over that night in my motel room and how I'd told him my mother had left me, that she was an addict. I'd felt sorry for myself, and I was sure it had come across that way. Yet, Dominic had kept quiet about his own father.

IN BETWEEN ALL OF THIS, he and I managed to carve out 'alone' time. Dominic owned a 'new build' — what he called his house further south of Colton. On our very first night when we were totally alone, we'd planned on going out to dinner. But then we settled on a 'pizza to-go.' To be free of the little guy, no matter how sweet he was, was a gift.

When Dominic opened up his kitchen cupboard to reach for the plates, I wrapped my arms around his waist and asked, "Just how hungry are you?"

Our lovemaking was slow and deliberate. I'd never come close to making love before. What I had experienced in the past was always induced by alcohol and a healthy sex drive. I didn't know how Dominic was feeling, but my own thoughts were a revelation to me. When he fell asleep afterwards, I lay there in his bedroom. My mind was racing. Sleep wasn't going to happen.

I found his flannel bathrobe hanging on a hook and quietly left the room. I walked around his house with a cup of coffee I'd made in his Mr. Coffee Maker. He also had an espresso machine, but I'd never had an espresso and had no clue how to make one.

I ran my fingers along the kitchen's shiny surfaces — the new appliances and countertop — and then walked along the hardwood floors that glistened. The floorplan flowed from the bright, white kitchen into a living room with a bank of windows and skylights. The hallway, leading to the two bedrooms and bathroom, had framed photographs of his family, his graduation from the Police Academy, and vintage posters of Larry Bird, Joe Namath, and Jackie Robinson. Above the flat screen and under recessed lighting was a large, wrought-iron piece of art. There was a finished basement somewhere, but I didn't look for its door.

Instead, I quietly unlocked and opened the slider to the deck. Stairs led down into a sloping yard. It was very early in the morning and still dark, but I could see the outline of the woods beyond. I inhaled deeply and closed the door.

A sinking, depressing feeling started to wrap itself around me. It had everything to do with me and Dominic. He existed in a different world than mine: a college degree, good job, money, and a functioning family. There was no way he could ever be serious about me. I was a high school drop-out, earning below the poverty line as a nursing home assistant, and I had a kid. I lived with a father who had issues. My sister had witnessed first-hand violence and was then tragically killed. All this shit was stuff that happened to people like me, not to people like him.

I found my clothes on the floor in his room and tiptoed out. Once dressed, I sat in his living room in the morning light and waited for him to wake up. Birds were starting to flutter at the bird feeder on his deck. I watched them peck at the seeds, some falling onto the deck's floor. They were determined to get their share.

I would ask him to take me home and tell him what a mistake our getting together had been. There was no way this was possible. It was crazy to think we could have something significant.

Dominic finally came out of the bedroom an hour later and walked down the hallway. When he reached me, he bent down and we kissed. I looked up at him and said, "That was nice. The whole night was nice."

He sat down on the arm of the chair and touched my sleeve. "Then why are you in a hurry to leave, Kate Wade?"

Looking up at him, I quietly replied, "This, you and me, we're not being realistic about our relationship. We have very real differences. Our attraction to each other — it's based on those crazy days in Tennessee. But that can't carry us, Dominic." Saying all this to him was breaking my heart. With a tremor in my voice, I added, "I've got to think of Carson, too. He can't become attached when…" I didn't finish my thought.

Dominic moved over to the couch next to me and asked, "What do you perceive our differences to be, Kate?"

I opened my mouth in awe and then stammered, "You… you've got to be kidding."

"No, I mean it. What do you see?" he asked again.

"Okay, I'll rattle them off if they're not so obvious to you." I was growing angry, so I took a deep breath to slow down. "For starters, I'm poor and you're not. Also, I've never even walked across the stage in high school, while you have a college degree. My father has mental issues that tie me to him, you have a functioning family. The biggest thing — I have no way to get out of the fucking rut I've been in for years. You, though… It's smooth sailing." I sat back smugly and glared at him.

"Ah, I see a return of the girl from…" But Dominic stopped. It was clear he was referring to the bitch I'd been when we first got down to Goodlettsville.

I made a 'come on, let's have it' hand gesture to him, but he smiled instead. It was a disarming smile, but I wasn't falling for it.

Shaking my head, I responded, "Be honest. You see all this, too."

"No, I don't, and I'll tell you why. Between the mortgage, car payment, and paying down my college loans on what I make as a new, low-ranking detective, I have very little money left at the end of the month. But I do pay my bills, and I know you like to pay your way, so we're alike in that. The college degree I hold in finance is totally useless. Except for the two years in the brokerage house I told you about, it'll never come into play again. I regret walking across that stage. One of my sisters is bipolar. My whole family is tied to her diagnosis because we're all involved in her treatment plan. Like you, I feel it's important to be there for family. As for the rut you're in… I'm not going to compare my rut to yours, but mine was pretty significant. I'm an alcoholic, and I deal with what that entails every single day. No alcoholic would ever characterize it as smooth sailing." He stood up and moved in front of the sliding doors before turning back around. "If you're in a rut, climb out, Kate. Figure out how and do it."

I sat quietly. The birds were chirping even louder now. Everything he'd just said countered my argument. I leaned forward, wanting to respond, but I didn't know what to say.

Dominic moved in front of me and knelt down. "I spent thirty-one days detoxing and dealing with my addiction. You stopped in one night. Whatever's holding you back, I know you can deal with it."

"It's not that, it's just…"

He reached up and touched my hair. "What, what is it?"

I felt the tears, but brushed them away and whispered, "Going to Tennessee, getting him to sign off on Carson was supposed to be the big game changer for me. It's not enough, though. I want more for Carson and me. But that would…" He waited, his eyes never leaving my face. "That

would involve me going back to school. And school, Dominic, was a total disaster for me." I'd never been this honest
with anyone.

Dominic nodded and thought for a few moments before
replying, "The girl you were at fourteen isn't the woman
you are at twenty-four, right? Most everybody who goes
back to school after working in the real world has more
direction, more drive. What is it you want to study?" he
asked in his patient, gentle voice.

"That's part of it. I don't know because I blew out of
there before..." My voice trailed off.

"Okay, so, maybe you could go into the community
college down in Peddan and ask questions. If you start by
breaking everything down into smaller steps, it won't be so
overwhelming." He stood back up, his eyes still on me.

"Just ask questions?" I repeated.

"Sure. People do it all the time. They have handouts
outlining career paths and what classes to take for all the
degree programs they offer. It could be the start of finding
out what's out there."

I sat for a moment longer then nodded. When I stood up,
Dominic reached for me and whispered, "So, Kate Wade's
going back to school."

Leaning in to him, I brought my fingertips up to his lips.
"Shush... First, she's going back to bed with her man."
Desire had totally replaced my depression.

MARGARET, HIS SISTER, showed up unexpectedly a
little while later. We were eating cold pizza and drinking
orange juice. I was wearing Dominic's bathrobe again and
was embarrassed to see her in the doorway. She apologized
for not calling and said, "I just need your bike rack from the
garage."

While Dominic walked out the side door to open the garage, Margaret looked over at me and said, "You've got a great guy there, Kate. It's been a long time since he's made a move. Hope you're sincere."

"I know what I've got. I just can't believe it," I replied seriously.

She touched my hand and smiled. Her eyes were as kind as her brother's.

Chapter 21

I was passing the chicken-shit smelling farm when my 'Check Engine Light' came on. At the same time, I heard a clunk and then another clunk in the Honda. I pulled over onto a patch of farmland. It was a wide-open space leading up to an old farmhouse to the right and a big barn to the left. I sat there and hit the steering wheel in frustration.

I'd been coming from dropping Carson off at my father's and was in a hurry to get back to the house. Dominic was having dinner with me and staying the night. Carson still considered Dominic just 'our coach.' I was apprehensive to explain anything else to him because of the negative experience he'd had with Drew.

My dad had held out his arms to Carson earlier and hugged him, saying, "I've missed your voice and your energy!" I knew his missing Sadie was mixed into all that, too, just like her absence was mixed into everything of mine.

Now, stranded, just off the side of the road, I got out of the car and tried my cell. "No service, of course," I moaned.

Just as I turned to figure out how far from Colton I was, I heard a loud neigh and looked back. *This can't be real* — a big guy on a big horse was riding this way, bareback and bare-chested. It looked like something staged for a movie. Then it hit me: This was Sam, Sadie's Sam.

When he reached me, I stepped back, intimidated by the horse. It was one of those working horses like the Budweiser Clydesdales, but this one wasn't clean or combed pretty.

"You got a phone I could use? Or know where I can get cell service out here?" I asked. The way he'd broken Sadie's heart didn't endear him to me any. I gave him a cold, hard stare.

He slid off the horse, held on to the reigns, and pointed. "See that dip down near where the fencing meets? There's service there. You'll see some cigarette butts, maybe a cooler. My father calls his brother at that spot. He's in Nebraska."

I understood the lack of cell reception. Out on Tabor Road, our best spot was standing in front of the window above the kitchen sink, the phone held between two cactus plants.

"Is my car okay right here?" I asked before turning to walk toward the fencing.

He nodded and said, "It's fine."

"*Screw you,*" I really wanted to say but didn't.

Soon I heard someone behind me, and I turned back. The mammoth horse was eating grass near my car, its reigns tied to some old, rusty farm equipment. Sam had put on a dirty gray t-shirt, and he said, "Just making sure you find the exact place."

I was walking backwards, facing him, when I suddenly called out, "I know who you are. You treated my little sister like shit."

"What I did was awful. You're right."

I stopped and waited for him to reach me. "You know I'm Sadie Wade's sister?"

"Yeah, saw you at her funeral. What happened was horrible. Sadie didn't deserve that. She was…"

But I cut him off and replied, "A lot of people went to her funeral, most didn't know her or care about her."

We made it down to the fence. I checked and had three bars. I dialed Dominic and when he picked up, explained where I was and what had happened. His last words were, "Don't talk to anyone who looks the least bit sketchy, okay? I'll be there in twenty."

"My friend is on his way," I said, putting the cell away. "I'm going to go back and wait at the car. We'll get a tow, just don't know how soon they'll come."

Sam walked back with me. I glanced over at him. He was a giant, maybe kind of a gentle giant because of the way he was looking at me.

"I was…it was, ah! I don't know how to explain it to you, what I did to Sadie. I believed some asshole buddies. It's like the biggest thing I've learned this senior year. Don't go against your gut, don't believe the bullshit," he said, clearly frustrated.

"She really cared for you, and you hurt her." I reached the Honda's car door.

The big, old, ugly horse snorted, making me jump. I quickly got in the car and closed the door. I wanted to roll up my window, but it was too warm. Plus, my engine wouldn't turn over.

The kid didn't move. He just stood there then scrunched down, resting on his haunches. "Here's the thing, Sadie's sister…"

"My name's Kate."

"Here's the thing, Kate. That night we met may go down as one of the top five, no, maybe the top three best nights I'll ever have in my entire life. And I screwed it up."

His face was streaked with dirt, and his fingers, resting on my car door, had bitten and cracked fingernails. He hesitated then continued, "Zoe, Sadie's best friend from the restaurant, and I have this thing. Sometimes when we see each other we talk about an imaginary alternate universe. Zoe started it one day after school when she and I were having a hard time, you know, about Sadie. In it, Sadie and I get married. Zoe describes that day — the colors of the bridesmaids' dresses, what Sadie wore, and even who got drunk at the party after. I've added to it — like I was playing for the Raiders, and we were living in California. But we came back here because we wanted to live on the farm more than anywhere else in the whole-wide world. Right now, Sadie and I have four sons, they're all named Z something — that's from Zoe. Like Zillow, Zenith, Zilch, and I can't remember the last one. I don't want to sound disrespectful in telling you this. I just want you to know Sadie was a big deal to me, and I know I blew it." He stood up and backed away.

It was quiet; no one had driven by. I climbed out of the car and leaned against it. For once, I had nothing to say. What was there to say?

"My mother says the best thing I can do is learn from it," he said, glancing over at me.

"I think she's right," I replied.

We heard a car. It was Dominic. I introduced him to Sam. A tow was already on its way. As we pulled out, I said, "Maybe those little boys of yours could have super powers."

Sam raised his eyebrows ever so slightly and smiled. The kid had a great smile.

THE DROOPY COUCH on the back porch turned into a bed. Dominic wondered why the springs squeaked so much and looked underneath. "It's an antique," he laughed, looking over at me. "Let's sleep out here tonight."

It wasn't much wider than the couch, but I smiled and replied, "It's your call."

We made up the bed with sheets from the linen closet on the second floor. We had to double them over, and I grabbed my pillows and quilt from the guest bedroom. As soon as we climbed in, we felt the bed sway. I laughed and said, "Is this supposed to rock?"

He pulled me close, my back tucked up against his chest. We faced the backyard. All we could see was the outline of the apple tree and the roof line of the house beyond the fence. The night was cooler; August was almost over.

"I'm going to keep you warm and safe, right here, nestled into me all night long. I won't let you fall out," Dominic whispered.

Alfie padded out to us and flopped down on the porch floor. The only light on was the little light above the stove in the kitchen.

I reached down and patted the top of Alfie's head. "My father missed Carson. I think we can do more of these little sleepovers."

Dominic didn't respond; he seemed deep in thought. Finally, he said, "My grandmother has told you plenty of stories, but I bet she never told you the one about her son-in-law, my old man — that he died a drunk. He wasn't

a full-time drunk, but he drowned with an empty bottle of
Schnapps in his ice fishing shanty. It's the big joke about the
Sousa family — my sisters were sometimes called the
'Peppermint girls.' Probably most of the kids calling them
that had no idea why, but a few did so…yeah. We were
Italian, fatherless, and lived with my grandparents. My
mother was the bookkeeper at the local hardware store for
thirty-seven years. The rumor, when I was finally old
enough to understand it, was that my father wasn't even my
real father."

"That must have been hard. At least, though, your
family had money, Dominic."

"You're right. My grandparents did. Now, it's a different
story. It's why I go to The Pines to do my gram's finances.
Between what my grandfather left of his estate and my
grandmother's care, she's just about tapped out. But Violet
Lake will stay put, however long she has."

"I had no idea," I whispered.

He shifted and moved down, wrapping me in his arms
again.

"Your father, Kate, even with all his issues, was mostly
there for you. Mine wasn't, ever."

We were quiet for some time then Dominic moved to
kiss me. Our kissing had changed — I was leaning more
toward his gentleness while he'd picked up my vigor. When
we pulled apart, I asked, "What did you think of Sam?"

"The farm kid? He's a giant."

I described the alternate universe Sam and Zoe sometimes played out. Would Sadie be okay with it? I wanted to
hear his opinion.

Dominic thoughtfully replied, "She was always serious
with me, so maybe I'm not the one to ask. But wait, that's
not exactly true. The first time we ever met was at the
kitchen door at Shay's. I was there to see Stephen, one of

the cooks. Sadie was eating those bright worms — gummy worms — in the kitchen. I watched her hide some in the cooks' garnish containers. She was being very mischievous."

I smiled, picturing Sadie doing that. Alfie let out a series of little yelps as he slept.

"They're kids trying to deal with a friend's death — an incredibly hard thing — as best they can," Dominic added.

Earlier in the evening, as I'd tossed the salad to go with the pasta Dominic had been making, I'd pieced together that the last time Sadie had seen Sam was the morning of the day she'd died. She'd never had her blood drawn after seeing Sam, even though I'd watched her walk in to the clinic. When we hadn't gotten her results back, the old man had finally called. There was no record of Sadie Wade ever coming in that morning. It was another thing that didn't make sense on that last, horrible day.

"Sam was Sadie's first and only boyfriend for about two weeks. I kind of think she'd be okay with him and Zoe doing that, maybe even amused."

Dominic whispered, "I think she would be, too."

We moved further down on the day bed, and he climbed gently on top of me. "There's not much room, but this thing was made for us."

I lifted myself up and kissed him slowly. We had all night.

"STOP!" I WHISPERED. "We're too loud, Dominic, the bed, it's too loud!" A light in the house beyond the apple tree had come on. I could see someone in the window. Alfie had moved into the house, away from us.

"What?" he asked, straddling me.

"Oh my God, get off of me, now!" Somehow, I managed to roll out from under him and onto the porch floor. I grabbed the quilt and wrapped it around me. Crawling to the kitchen door was difficult, but once I was there I stood up and scooted in. Dominic, completely naked, followed me. He was laughing.

I stood by the sink and saw the person, a man, move away from the window. Dominic walked up behind me, rearranging the quilt around us both. "It's way too dark to see anything on the porch. But I get that we were loud." He grinned.

"It was that damn bed! Those springs!" I whispered.

"And us, too." He kissed my neck, and I turned to him.

"When do I become more than just a coach to Carson, Kate?" he asked as his dark brown eyes searched mine. "I'm in love with you. I want you and Carson totally in my life."

I didn't have the words yet to tell him I felt the same way. Instead, I took his hand and led him up the stairs.

Chapter 22

Seeing Sam and talking with him nudged me into finally stopping at Shay's to see Jeannie the next afternoon. I'd been avoiding the restaurant because it held so much of Sadie — all the times I'd stopped to pick her up, the Christmas party, and the painful time right after her funeral.

It was early, before dinner was being served. Jeannie hugged me and left for a moment to go get Sadie's last paycheck. I apologized to a woman who had been sitting with Jeannie on one of the stools.

"Oh, that's all right. I rent the upstairs apartment from her. We see each other all the time. You don't need a job, do you?" she asked, smiling.

"Here — no. I am, though, looking to go back to school. I'm just not sure for what."

She nodded. "I work for the state, trying to recruit good people for Family Services. My division is working with at-risk youth. I'm Allison, by the way."

I walked closer to her and asked, "Like some kids in state care?"

"Yes, exactly." We both turned to Jeannie as she came back through the kitchen door. The woman stood up, ready to go.

"What kind of degree do you need for Family Services?" I asked out of curiosity.

"There are all sorts of levels. Here, in this area, I have spots for trainees. You don't need a degree. You just have to pass all sorts of background checks and have at least four years of experience working in human services."

"Is working as a nursing home aide considered human services?" I asked.

"It definitely could be if trainings have been provided," she replied. "Of course, you need a high school degree."

Jeannie handed her a take-out container. "Thanks, luv," Allison said. "Here's my credit card."

Just as she was signing for it, she looked back at me. "Where was I? Oh, yes, a high school degree or its equivalent, like a GED."

"So they train you?" I was growing more interested.

"Absolutely, for about eighteen months. It's over twenty dollars an hour to start, with benefits and insurance. A lot of people go on from there and get their degree in human or social services. Are you...? Sorry, first I should ask, who are you?"

Jeannie jumped in and said, "My bad, Allison this is Kate Wade."

I smiled and added, "I work at The Pines in Colton. I've done lots of trainings, and I'm starting my seventh year there. But I'm interested in how to keep kids, adolescents, safe."

Allison nodded and said, "I'd love to give you my card, and we could talk further."

"Yes, definitely." I tucked the card into my pocket. *Karen could tell me more, too.*

"WOULD THAT BE SOMETHING you'd like to pursue?" Jeannie asked once we were alone and she'd given me Sadie's last check.

"I'm not sure. Maybe. Yes, I think so." Lucas Alvarez and what might have happened, along with all the things I'd read since coming back from Tennessee, still bothered me. Family conflicts, abuse, and neglect led to a lot of teens running away. Once on the run, they were susceptible to a whole bunch of other things like substance abuse, self-harm, and exploitation. Law enforcement everywhere seemed to be short staffed and incapable of providing enough resources to find missing kids. The focus, the experts said, needed to be on preventative measures and support put into place early on. I could easily have been considered at risk. Dropping out of high school was one of the major indicators.

Jeannie brought me back by commenting, "You look great, Kate."

One of the cooks came out and smiled at me while he filled a glass from the soda gun. I remembered him from sometime back. Jeannie waited until he left and said, "Dominic stopped in here a few days ago. He looks pretty good, too."

"Did he say something?" I asked, trying to read her expression.

"Well..." She rolled her eyes slightly. "He mentioned he'd fallen hard for someone but wouldn't tell me any details. I knew you were in Tennessee together, so…I'm happy for you guys."

"It isn't weird?" I replied, searching her face, trying to detect if she thought Dominic was way out of my league.

"No, it's not weird, it's wonderful. Sadie would be happy; she liked Dominic."

"I'm still wondering what he sees in me."

"Kate, did you not see how Eugene just looked at you?" Jeannie asked, then she moved behind the bar and started to put wine glasses away. "Hey, before I forget, Mathew, our linen guy, would like to meet with you. He's been wanting to tell you something about Sadie for a while. That's why I called you down in Tennessee. Can you come by some afternoon and talk with him?"

"Sure. I usually pick Carson up from pre-school between three and four."

"Any chance it could be tomorrow? We're getting linens."

"Tomorrow I'm actually with Dominic at that time. My car's having major work done. It's fine as long as he can come, too."

MATHEW WAS TALL AND THIN, about fortyish. Jeannie, Dominic, and I were in the kitchen, and we had just been introduced to him. He seemed a little uncomfortable, but he smiled and said, "I'm just going to plow through this. Sometime in January, I had to come here to pick up a delivery of tablecloths and napkins. It was a mistake. It was early, about three o'clock, and Sadie was just starting her night. I think maybe Eugene was prepping. I came in the kitchen door and asked her for the linens. Right before I left, though, Sadie took hold of my arm and asked if she could see my hands. It was awkward, and I asked her if it was going to be some kind of prank."

Mathew stood up and moved until he was in front of the cook's station.

"But she didn't do anything funny. Instead, she just held onto both of my hands like this…" He reached for Jeannie's hands and held them out in front of her. *'You should feel better real soon,'* Sadie said, and then she let go."

He continued, "At first, when I left, I was pissed off at you, Jeannie, for telling Sadie I had Crohn's and that it was getting worse. That's what I thought about all the way driving back to Brattleboro. I was going to ream you out for telling people my personal business."

"I didn't tell her, Mathew. I've told no one," Jeannie replied.

He nodded and said, "I didn't think you ever would. The thing is — I did feel better, and it started then, like right then. The inflammation in my GI tract has subsided, and my symptoms have quieted way down. I've had more energy.

"When my gastroenterologist did an intestinal endoscopy, he was surprised, no, shocked is more like it. This past April, I was scheduled to have surgery to have part of my intestines removed. But there was no need for the surgery because there was no longer any infection. My Crohn's disease and all of its complications have just about disappeared."

He moved to the dishwasher, touched the knobs, and brushed his hands over the sink's faucet. "I'm forty-two and was diagnosed with it ten years ago. I don't ever remember feeling this okay. I know it sounds batshit crazy, but I think Sadie had something to do with it. Has anyone else had a similar experience with her, you know, before?" Mathew looked at us for a response.

I spoke up. "I'm glad you're better, that you didn't need surgery. But don't people with Crohn's experience lulls in their inflammation? I thought that was normal. Am I wrong?"

"No, you're not wrong. But this is more than a lull between flare ups. The damage in my intestinal lining — it's gone. It's unexplainable."

Pushing in the stool he'd sat in moments ago, Mathew looked at us all and said, "I just wanted to meet you and tell you this. You knew Sadie, knew what a doll she was." He moved to the kitchen's door. "I actually think she was incredible."

Once he was gone, Jeannie motioned for us to follow her through to the bar. We watched as she put a fresh pot of coffee on. "That was something, huh?" she said as she placed three cups down.

Dominic glanced over at me and replied, "Actually, it's the second time we've heard that Sadie healed somebody. Hetty, a woman in Tennessee, said something similar. "

The phone rang and Jeannie excused herself. I got up and moved around the bar to grab the coffee.

When Jeannie returned from taking a reservation, she handed me an envelope. "I forgot to give this to you when I gave you the check yesterday. It was in a drawer at the hostess stand. It's addressed to you."

I read it out loud, "To the family of Sadie Wade, in care of Shay's Restaurant." It looked like a sympathy card. "It's from Somerville, Mass. I have no idea from who."

Jeannie poured herself a cup and replied, "Sadie *was* incredible. You know, when she first snuck into the restaurant, I thought she was going to be nothing but trouble."

Just then one of the cooks brought out two freshly baked pies: a Boston Cream and a mixed berry. He brought them over to us with a flourish. Dominic pointed to the chocolate one and smiled.

"Wait, what did you just say, Jeannie?" I asked.

But she was already cutting into the Boston Cream and asking for plates. Dominic held up the envelope and asked me, "Mind if I open this, maybe snoop around and find out the connection?"

I shook my head and took the plate Jeannie extended to me as I repeated my question to her, "What do you mean about Sadie sneaking in here?"

As Jeannie cut a piece for Dominic, she replied, "Sadie showed up at our kitchen door all wet. Said a boy she'd been with was drinking and driving. It scared her, so she got out and walked here in the freezing sleet. You didn't know that?"

I shook my head again, feeling perplexed. Sadie hadn't been honest with me about that first night here. Swiveling in the bar chair, I glanced at the fresh linen Mathew had left, still in its plastic wrap near the bar's door. *Had Sadie kept other things from me, too?* Like her laying on of hands besides just me and my kidney stone?

The piece of pie was good, but I only took a couple of bites. After a little bit, Jeannie leaned over and said, "Just realized how much you and Sadie have similar profiles, like from your nose down." She moved her hand to the bridge of her nose to show me exactly where she meant.

Nodding slowly, I smiled. We'd never seen the old man's full profile because of his thick, coarse beard. We'd shared something of him, after all.

The house reminded me of Dominic's new build — new but on the modest side, with a fenced-in front yard perfect for small children and a foundation for a detached garage already poured. I turned off the Honda and started to climb out. They knew I was coming. I'd texted Ellie last night. Her quick response was, *'This is what Karl needs, TY.'*

On the back of one of their vehicles was a sticker in the shape of Vermont and underneath it read, "Best place on Earth." I thought about that for a moment, realizing I'd never ever once thought about leaving the state. Yes — to changing up my life, but never of moving to another region of the country. But that wasn't true, was it? If Brother Ron had tried to take Carson, I'd have gone all the way to Mexico, or even to Alaska, to be safe. Now, with that scare gone and Dominic in our lives, my whole attitude had changed. Plus, the call I'd gotten from Allison at Family Services had been positive and encouraging. We were going to meet next week.

Without the fear, hope and calm were vying for first place.

Karl opened up the front door and stepped down the stairs. He was a big, burly guy now, though in middle school he had been small, slow to mature. I was sure I'd scared him back then as I'd stopped every teacher dead in their tracks when they'd tried to teach because I hadn't liked their "no" to my requests to leave class again. My M.O. was to walk the halls as much as possible.

Ellie came out, too, and we stood, kind of awkward, unsure of things. She finally said, "Logan is napping. He's grown out of naps, but I think he's got the beginning of an earache. Would you mind if we sat at the picnic table?"

I smiled and replied, "Sure. Is he starting the first grade already?"

Karl, looking apprehensive, nodded and said, "Yep. Ellie and I are going to have a girl. We just found out. We're starting to tell people."

Ellie smiled at me as we all sat down. I looked at Karl who was still looking glum. I reached over and touched his hand. "Congratulations to you both. A baby girl... When Sadie was a baby, sometimes I'd just stare at her for hours as she slept. I'd never seen such an angel before."

Tears filled Karl's eyes, and he tried to wipe them away. I needed to say what I'd practiced this morning and say it right now, right out.

"That last day of Sadie's life, a lot of the things she said and did didn't make sense. My dad and I could list them. But from both of us — we hold no ill will toward you. We know what she did — stepping out like that — you couldn't have stopped in time. I'm here to show you, possibly, why she did it, though. Look."

I pulled out the little Superman crocheted hat from my shoulder bag and placed it on the picnic table. "Sadie was making this for Logan. I think she finished it, although if you look on this one side here, I'm not so sure it's done."

Ellie exchanged glances with Karl, but neither one of them moved to pick it up. They both just sat and stared at it. Then Karl touched it and replied, "This makes sense. Logan and I asked her to make hot chocolate after I plowed Shay's not too long before, you know, it happened. He was wearing a Superman shirt."

I watched Ellie lift the hat and carefully hold it.

Slowly, and in a measured voice, I replied, "Sadie was probably excited when she heard you go by, even though she wasn't feeling good. She'd been up early that morning, and by the time you came through, she was probably going stir crazy. And she had a fever. The main thing, Karl, it wasn't your fault. Please understand that."

Ellie mouthed, "Thank you" to me. Karl gazed out toward their road. I wasn't in a hurry to leave. This was important, especially for him.

Finally, he looked back over at me and said, "I don't know what's real or not real about those moments anymore. I think about 'em, I dream about 'em, and I cry about 'em. You coming to us, it means a lot. Thank you." He glanced at Ellie quickly and added, "In all my memories of it, Kate, your little sister had this look of, well, it wasn't alarm or even dread, it was different. It was like she'd been half expecting it."

Ellie jumped in and added, "The best advice Karl's gotten about living through this was from our minister. It's to greet each day as a blessing, because it could be our last."

Karl spoke up. "And sometimes, no matter how hard we try to make sense of stuff, there isn't a way to do that because we're only human and subject to limitations. For some reason, when he said that it made sense to me."

I smiled and replied, "No, I think I get it. Sadie might have tried to say something like that to me on her last day."

We sat a little while longer, then I stood up. They followed me out to the driveway. Ellie was holding the hat, and Karl reached over to hug me. When we broke apart, I nodded, wondering how best to end this. All I could say was, "See you around, guys. Take care, and congratulations."

On the way back through Langdon, it felt good that things had gone as best they could with Karl, and that Sadie's hat, twenty-six weeks and one day later, had finally made it to Logan.

As I passed the hardware store, I pulled over. We needed something for that squeaky couch.

Chapter 24

I reached for my cell and said, "Hello?" A young man's voice asked, "Is this Kate Wade from Tabor Road in Vermont?"

"Yes." I smiled at Carson. He was holding the wrench for Dominic.

"My name is Lucas Alvarez and..."

"Hold on, hold on, please," I pleaded. Dominic was just starting to take off the training wheels to Carson's bike.

"Dominic, come here, come now!" I called through the screen then opened the door and motioned for him to hurry. "Sorry, Lucas. Can I put you on speaker so my friend can hear? Would that be all right?" My voice was shaking.

There was a slight pause, then he replied, "Okay."

I covered my phone and yelled to Carson, "I'm letting Alfie out to play while we take this call. So go play!" I opened the door again and pushed Alfie out.

Dominic ran up the back steps and asked, "What's going on?"

I shook my head in disbelief and whispered, "This." Into the cell, I said, "Lucas Alvarez, my friend, Dominic Sousa, just came to the phone."

Dominic's eyes grew big as he looked at me and said, "Hey, Lucas."

"Hello. I'm calling because Detective Ellis thought you'd want to hear from me, especially since Lloyd Parker was brought in on suspicion of murdering me. But I'm not dead, as you can tell. He did try to kill me, though."

I didn't know what to say. Dominic jumped in and asked, "That night at The Diamondback?"

"Yeah. Lloyd and Cal beat me to a bloody pulp. But why do you care, what's your deal in this?"

Dominic looked at me tenderly and answered, "There was someone who saw it happen. I'm a detective, and that someone wanted us to find out what we could about you."

There was another pause, then Lucas asked, hesitantly, "The little girl in the station wagon?"

I did a quick intake of breath and replied, "Yes. She was just nine years old. Her name was Sadie, Sadie Wade. She worried a lot about you."

"Are you her mother? Her sister?" he asked.

"I am. I was, kind of both," I replied, glancing over at Dominic.

"They left me for dead. At first, though, they loaded me onto the back of their truck, but I was bleeding too much. It bothered Lloyd, getting the truck all bloodied up, so he dumped me back out and split. That's when the girl — your Sadie — came. She tried to stop the bleeding, she even prayed. We both thought I was a goner.

"I couldn't stay out in the open like that, too afraid they'd come back or somebody else would finish me off. I'm

trans, if you didn't know. I tried to crawl, then the girl
— she half rolled, half dragged me the rest of the way under
her car. She washed away the blood as best she could. Lloyd
and Cal did come back, but they didn't see me.

"I hope it didn't like traumatize her. I had broken blood
vessels in my eyes, and it must have been scary. Plus, they
stomped on my legs pretty bad. I remember telling her it
was all just a bad dream.

"Way before the sun came up, I crawled out from under
the car and took off with the flashlight she'd given me.
Weirdest thing…I felt okay by then and could walk. I
cleaned up at a friend's place and left town, left the state. I
had something on Lloyd. It was just a matter of time before
he'd come after me again."

"Can you tell us what that was?" Dominic asked.

I quickly handed the phone over because Carson was
trying to pick Alfie up, but I heard Lucas say, "Suspicious
activity in his apartments had been reported by one of the
shop owners. Lloyd quickly accused some Somali gang
members in the area of using his apartments to run a sex
trafficking ring. But really, it was Lloyd setting them up to
take the fall to shield the guys who really were. Lloyd was
getting a kickback from them. The auctions he went to all
the time — it was a front for that shit."

Carson scooted by Dominic and went into the kitchen. I
mimed eating a popsicle. He moved a kitchen chair to the
freezer and took out a purple one. He sat down trium-
phantly and began to lick it.

"You had proof of this?" Dominic asked.

"Yes, pictures on my phone of Lloyd's involvement and
the real guys running the show. I was doing field work and
thought the arrests at the time were bogus. Somalians tend
to stay within their own culture, their own people, not

associate with old white dudes like Lloyd. But Lloyd and some Nashville guys fabricated evidence."

Lucas paused and said, "Sorry, I'm walking and someone just yelled to me. Hold on."

Dominic reached over and touched my shoulder. "Are you okay?" he asked.

But I didn't answer because Lucas came back on the phone and continued talking. "Lloyd Parker was in the Rotary, and a member of an upstanding family who owned a lot of land — nobody doubted his integrity, questioned his claims. And it was easy to blame the Somali community. It got traction, and a bunch of Somali immigrants were indicted as part of a three-state sting. It was all bullshit. Lloyd was meeting me at The Diamondback, said he'd buy the photos and my silence. I'm not proud to say I wanted the money and took the bait. It almost cost me my life.

"The apartments going up in smoke a few days after? I bet he set the fire 'cause he didn't know what happened to me, where I was, or what I was going to do. Now, almost six years later, I finally did what I should have done back then. I gave the police all I had and told them what happened."

I glanced at Carson then replied, "I hope you're safe now and that you've found good people, Lucas."

"Thank you. California was my goal, but I didn't quite make it. Things are okay, though, where I am. Hey, when I was young, I spent summers in Vermont. It's a beautiful state, peaceful and… green," he laughed.

Hesitantly, I asked, "Crazy question, but did you ever staple flyers to the Somalian coffee shop's bulletin board on Sixth Street?"

"All the time that summer. Why?" he replied.

"Do you remember a girl running into you once and your flyers going everywhere?" I held my breath. Dominic gave me a quizzical look.

                    SPRING & SUMMER 2016

"No, can't really say I do," he answered. "But maybe."

It grew quiet. Lucas lowered his voice and said, "Your little sister saved me. Will you tell her that?"

"Yes," I whispered and ended the call. I turned away so Carson couldn't see my tears.

Dominic put his arms around me and whispered, "Finally, we know."

I wiped my eyes and walked to the freezer. I took out an orange popsicle and sat down next to Carson. Dominic joined us. He chose red.

ON SUNDAY, four days after the call, Dominic was carrying his laptop onto the porch and called out, "Kate, listen to what I found in *The Tennessean!*"

I sat down beside him.

"*'A federal judge in Nashville has dismissed all charges against eleven people accused in what officials called a multi-state sex-trafficking organization connected to Somali gangs.'* It goes on to say that the Sixth Court of Appeals cited concerns over the evidence in it. Somali immigrants and refugees who had been incarcerated since two-thousand and ten were released. This was what Lucas was talking about, the bogus claims Lloyd made."

"So, what about him, Lloyd Parker?" I asked.

"I'm going to find out. Lucas Alvarez's information and proof that Lloyd fabricated evidence should be the least of his problems. That's a Class C felony, and it carries a prison term. The more serious charge — human trafficking — carries at least twenty years. Attempted murder is a first-degree felony. Lloyd Parker is going to be put away for the rest of his days."

"Don't forget the charge of arson, too." I thought for a moment and added, "Lucas Alvarez coming back set those people free."

Dominic, still reading, replied slowly, "Yes, no doubt."

Carson had practiced all afternoon on his bike without the training wheels. Now, he was washing the bicycle with soap and water. Dominic had torn a towel in half for him to dry the bike when he was finished. Alfie was lying under the apple tree.

I stood and grabbed the leash hanging from the hook near the porch door. I needed to go for a walk and digest all this. Carson was starting to dry the handle bars, but he saw me and asked, "Can I come, too?"

Dominic read my mood because he called out, "Let's you and me practice some more, down street in the school parking lot."

Alfie resisted getting up, but I pulled, and he finally did. We walked out through the gate and turned in the opposite direction of the school. Our Tennessee trip felt like it had happened in another world, in another time, yet that summer down there with Sadie and Dad felt like yesterday.

Darcy's street was quiet, and Alfie stopped and peed, lifting his leg often. For the umpteenth time, I replayed the call from Lucas Alvarez. He was alive and well. Sadie had not only seen Lucas get beat up, she'd helped him stay alive. She had blocked out the worst parts, but those parts had still been there, buried in her subconscious.

Alfie was refusing to walk any further. We turned around. The big green house, the one I'd grown to love, was going to be home for a while longer. Darcy had called and asked if I'd consider staying through the year. Her mother was doing well, but she wanted to stay put and enjoy her. "She's eighty-four, and I'm not sure how much time she has left. Same with my aunt." I hadn't hesitated when I'd said yes. My mind had immediately started churning, figuring out what I'd need in order for Carson to start kindergarten just down the street instead of at Langdon where he was already registered. Darcy seemed to have thought it all through — suggesting I pay for half the utilities and that she'd draw up a simple renter's contract to show the school we were legal, renting residents. "The utilities aren't bad once the upstairs is closed off. You and Carson could bunk in together downstairs. Alfie would love that since he hates to climb the stairs. And I'll send you money for his food. He'd never make it here on the plane."

I hadn't told anyone yet, most of all my father. While he said he was doing fine, I felt guilty. It wasn't just because I'd left Tabor Road to house sit and had taken Carson with me. It was because of Dominic, too. I had a life now, beyond him. *But he wanted this for me.*

It was just past 8:00 p.m., and houses were starting to turn on their porch lights. Someone in the upstairs window of the brown brick house next to ours turned on a light.

I leaned against the chestnut tree in front of Darcy's and thought about all the dark stuff going on that summer in Tennessee. Girls, probably my age and younger, were experiencing horrible things. Walking by those apartments back then, I'd had no clue. Could I have done something? Anything?

It had felt surreal speaking to Lucas. We'd been key players in a chain reaction. Dominic and I had gone to Tennessee and snooped around. We'd passed what we'd found out on to Detective Ellis. That must have led Ellis to investigate Lloyd Parker's possible involvement and ultimately the state of Tennessee to file suspicion of murder charges against him. And that had brought Lucas Alvarez back to tell the truth. Now, innocent people who'd been behind bars on bogus charges were set free.

As I bent down to untangle Alfie's leash from his back legs, a fleeting thought came to me. It had been Sadie's refusal to forget about the boy that had started the entire chain reaction.

"KATE, LOOK AT THIS KID GO!" Dominic yelled to me as he jogged alongside Carson in the road. I couldn't help but notice the pride in his voice.

Carson's wobbling was all gone as he headed straight for me, looking fearless and determined. When he reached me, I quickly helped him stop and held the handle bars while he put a foot down. We both turned to wait for Dominic.

"I'm in love with you, too," I blurted out when Dominic reached us. "Just so you know," I quickly added and smiled.

"That is a good thing to know, Kate Wade," he replied, catching his breath.

Carson yawned — it was almost dark and past his bedtime. Dominic centered him on the bicycle and pushed him off toward the front stoop of the house.

"You coming?" he asked, turning back to me.

I nodded. Alfie raised his leg again. *I'd been wrong — it was happiness, pure and simple, in first place now.*

DRIVING BY THE TRAILER and not turning in felt weird. I parked just beyond the turn-around. The overgrowth was thick with pricker bushes, and the trees formed one big, leafy canopy.

For once, I didn't see any evidence that high school kids had been here fooling around. I walked further in on the trail and found a place to sit near the base of the logging road. The afternoon sun was warm. Bees were darting in and around the bushes and the mammoth ferns. Their deep green was a colorful contrast to the white bark of the birch trees.

We hadn't had any recent rain, but the layer of leaves underneath me felt damp. I thought better of it and stood back up, wiping the seat of my pants off. The dead maple tree Sadie had been thrown against was long gone. Dad and Chet had used a chainsaw to cut it down.

I looked back. No one was walking or driving down Tabor Road. Both the trailer and Karen's house were quiet. Now was as good a time as any. Sadie's final resting place, near Lynn's house in Rutland, was pretty, but here was where I chose to come. This was her stomping ground, and the last place she was alive.

I cleared my throat and began. "Hey, Sadie, the boy — your boy — is okay. I spoke to him. His name is Lucas Alvarez. He wanted me to tell you that you saved him that night at The Diamondback. You must have suppressed a lot of what happened because it was so frightening. But you helped him and he got away.

"Other people say you've helped, even healed them. Like Hetty. She's still right there on the corner. You believed in all the tent church stuff, and your faith was strong. I'm sorry for discouraging you because I didn't believe." I stopped. Black crows were making a racket in the trees above.

I waited a moment then continued, "But I'm rethinking everything now. It's clear you understood way more than me." A light breeze, passing through the trees, ruffled the loose strands of my hair. I quickly brushed them away from my face and kept on. "Things overall are changing. I've even been happy — that's crazy, I know. The stuff that made me angry? I was scared. Scared to lose you, and then scared to lose Carson. I was scared to confront what scared me. Or to trust others who wanted to help. And I resented Dad for the way he was."

Something scurried behind me, and I glanced back. It was nothing. I shifted my feet and said, "But I'm working on all this, especially at letting go of the anger and fear.

Laying low, expecting the worse — that just robs you of a life worth being in."

The culvert across the road was all dried up. The bank where the hat had been frozen in the snow melt was covered in knotweed. Was it a fever or her wish to give Karl the hat that had propelled Sadie here that night? Would we ever know for sure?

A hummingbird hovered over the wild honeysuckle nearby then shot off.

The sun's rays, filtering through the canopy, cast everything into bits of pinks and golds and yellows. Fine little particles swirled in the afternoon light. It was beautiful.

I glanced down the road then turned back to the clearing. I imagined Sadie, right here beside me, and said, "We didn't have it so great out here on Tabor Road. No friends or boyfriends knocking on our door. Skimping to get by, you sleeping on the couch, and Dad hardly ever going anywhere. But we had each other. We always had each other. The old man — he did that for us. He kept us together."

A flashback came of me holding Sadie in my arms as her mother drove away. I began to twirl slowly, like I had that day in the doorway. I tilted my head way back and stretched my arms out, reaching for the sun's warmth. The sunlight danced above as the tall pines stood watch.

"Always remember, Sadie Rose," I whispered, feeling an incredible love settle over me, "we were sisters, most of all."

EPILOGUE

Fall 2016

Elaina

We *need to take this slow, Timothy,* I thought as I handed him over to his father. Terrance looked awkward, but I half expected it. I'd never seen him with a kid, let alone a baby before.

"He's up to nineteen pounds, that's a good size. I'm not sure how long he is now. Only breastfeeds a little at night, and that won't last too much longer. He likes the bottle, and he's starting a little pureed carrots and peas now that he can sit up on his own. He's due for a bottle soon. I can show you how to feed him one."

Terrance smiled and looked over at me. "He's solid, isn't he, Elaina?"

It was the first time he'd ever seen his son. He'd moved out two weeks before my due date. Said he couldn't handle the idea of a baby with a heart defect and an unknown future. I didn't think I could either, but I had no choice.

His lawyer had called me a week after Timothy's birth and set up the monthly payments, stating they were more than what the Commonwealth of Massachusetts' child payment calculations called for. I'd suspected he wanted me to think Terrance was some sort of great, upstanding guy, instead of what he was — a deadbeat asshole leaving his girlfriend just days away from having a newborn with extensive medical needs.

All my thoughts and feelings around Timothy's birth came rushing back to me as Terrance stood and walked with the baby in his arms around the dining room table, through the living room, into the kitchen, and back again.

I remembered thinking he must be really struggling if they're taking this long to bring me to him. A decorative sign, 'I'll love you to the moon and back,' had been above the baby's dresser. I had whispered it then as I'd waited, "I'll love you to the moon and back no matter what, Timothy."

The doctor had finally come and reached across the side bars of my bed, "Elaina, you have a beautiful baby boy who weighs nine pounds, six ounces, with an Apgar score of nine and a half. I'd give him a ten, but I've never given a baby a perfect ten––not to say your baby boy couldn't be my first."

The nurse had helped me by pulling back my hospital gown, and the doctor had placed him against my breast — "Skin to skin," she'd said. I saw my baby's perfectly shaped head, his coloring, and his little hands.

I'd looked up at Dr. Rosen, scared and confused. "I don't understand… I saw the imaging. The left side of his heart is underdeveloped. It could be fatal. Please, my baby needs immediate intervention."

Dr. Rosen had nodded and, in a serious tone, replied, "Your baby appears to be fine. I'm the pediatric cardiologist on call since Dr. Asmati is ill. The assessments of this little guy's cardiac structure and function were wrong, possibly due to equipment failure. Another doctor and I have thoroughly examined Timothy and performed not one, but two echocardiograms. He has no cardiac malformations or anomalies. There's no diminished size or capabilities on his left side. His heart is good and strong."

I'd reached up and taken hold of her arm. "Could…" I had hesitated. I'd been perplexed and still frightened that they had missed his diagnosis. With more confidence, I had said, "I would like the second cardiologist to come in, please. It's not because I don't believe you. I just want it confirmed that…" I had stopped speaking — too afraid to complete my sentence for fear it'd ruin what she'd just told me.

"Absolutely, I understand, Elaina. Let me page Dr. Davis," Dr. Rosen had responded, smiling warmly. "I know it's a bit of a shock to find out he has no heart issues, but it's a good shock, right?" She'd left the room. I'd held Timothy as close as I'd possibly dared.

The nurse, who'd been moving things around in the room, had come over to the bed. Peering down at my son, she'd said, "All births are miracles. Maybe, though, Momma, yours is an even bigger one."

I LOOKED UP AT TERRANCE now and said, "I'm sorry, what?" I'd been remembering and hadn't heard him ask me a question.

"If you're okay with it, I'll feed him while, you know, you stay close by and make sure I'm doing it right."

Terrance followed me. "Nice place you got here, Elaina. It's bigger. You guys need that."

While I measured the formula out and put a nipple on the bottle, Terrance leaned against the refrigerator. Timothy was ready, his eyes following me. Two uncomfortable minutes passed while I waited for the bottle warmer's light to go off.

"How did they get it so wrong, Elaina, how?" He followed me back into the living room.

I showed him how to keep the baby upright but back enough to take the bottle. I put the burp cloth right up under his chin and said, "Give him four ounces then burp him, and he'll take another two to four ounces after that."

"Okay, like this?" Terrance asked as he started. He seemed to be more at ease. "I mean, my God, the appointments right before we left for Vermont. It was a lot of heavy stuff they were telling us. You know — eating problems, failure to thrive, and open-heart surgery down the line. But look, he's okay, right? I don't get it. Dr. Asmati showed us the scans. Things weren't right."

I sat back in the easy chair and looked around the living room as the afternoon sunlight played on the hardwood floor and settled on the basket of baby blankets and the pictures above it. Timothy's six-month photoshoot had had so many great ones to choose from. Suddenly, I felt all my anger towards Terrance ebbing away. I understood his fear, his anxiety, and why he'd bolted. In this moment, I realized I didn't need him — Timothy did.

"The cardiologists at the delivery said that it was a case of the assessments being wrong, maybe equipment failure. Or it was — " I looked at Timothy, happily drinking the bottle, his eyes fixed on Terrance — "a true miracle."

Right before Terrance put on his jacket to leave, he picked up a large gift bag and placed it on the dining room table. "My mom and sister kind of went crazy. It's stuff for a nine-to twelve-month-old. It's good for him now, isn't it? "

I nodded and said, "It is."

"There's something else I got. I ordered it." He reached into the bag and brought out a small Louisville Slugger baseball bat. He held it up and turned it over. On the other side of the wooden bat was carved, *'Timothy Hanley, March 1, 2016, 7:50 p.m.'* "That's right?"

I nodded again. "It is."

"Okay, cool."

He came over and lightly touched Timothy's head. "Can I see him sometime soon? Maybe bring my mom?"

"Sure. We can work this all out. I want him to know you, Terrance. Your whole family."

At the door, he turned back around, and said, "You should hate me, Elaina, for what I did."

I shrugged my shoulders. There was nothing to say.

After he left the apartment, I watched his car pull out of the parking spot and onto the street. I told Timothy to wave and held up his little dimpled hand. I let the curtain fall and walked with him in my arms to the framed children's placemat on the wall in his nursery. It was a map of Langdon, Vermont with The Mountain and ski runs, Shay's Fine Dining and then other stores. I'd drawn a circle around the Rite Aid store. On the bottom, right hand corner of the placemat, I'd written the date: *January 31, 2016.*

I replayed the girl stepping out of the passenger side door of the old truck and approaching me. Terrance and I had just been arguing in the parking lot. He'd been going into the liquor store. I had bought Tums and a heating pad. I'd been firm in wanting to return to our rented condo instead of going back out to the bars, desperate to head back home to Somerville the next morning.

The girl hadn't been more than 15, maybe 16, at the most. She'd worn a maroon Langdon sweatshirt over baggy, flannel bottoms. She'd been pale and thin, with her hair pulled back. "Can I touch your belly — real quick?" she'd asked.

I could see her breath and had wondered if she was on something. I'd ignored her, thinking I should get back to the car and lock the door.

"Please," she'd pleaded, and there'd been something in her voice that had made me stop. I'd turned back around and looked at her.

I'd hesitated then unzipped my North Face coat and said, "Okay."

She'd reached out and spread both hands carefully on my shirt, across my belly. "Is it a boy or a girl?" she'd asked.

"A boy," I'd replied, feeling slight pressure from her hands and possibly a tremor, but it hadn't been at all threatening. "I like the name Timothy," I'd added. That had surprised me because, until that moment, I hadn't dared speak his name to anyone.

The girl had looked up at me then whispered, "I relinquish all my fear, Timothy."

"What did you say?" I'd asked. We were standing under the parking lot light and I could feel the cold, winter air on my stomach.

"I relinquish all my fear," she'd said again. That time, I'd heard her clearly. She'd taken her hands off of me and added, "Your baby's going to be just fine."

She'd walked back to the truck. Our exchange had lasted no more than ten seconds.

                                          FALL 2016

I PLACED THE BIG GIFT BAG of baby items near the dresser and put Timothy down on the rug. I moved the big pillow up behind him and his stuffed animals out in front. Lifting out the gifts from Terrance's family made me smile. Each outfit was cute and something I would have chosen, too. The costume, a little lion, was perfect for him to wear on Halloween in two weeks.

The small, wooden bat would go on his shelf. I hadn't told Terrance that the exact time of Timothy's birth was wrong on the birth certificate. "Those long minutes you were being poked, prodded, and scanned are ours, Timothy, only ours."

He looked up at me and then, in a determined move, reached for his little monkey. He immediately brought it to his mouth and started to babble. I began clipping the tags off of the new outfits and dropped them into the hamper to be washed. Flashes of my baby boy all grown up hit me. *He'll look so much like Terrance* — today's visit made that very clear.

Sitting by him now, on the floor, I pointed to the placemat on the wall of Langdon again. I leaned in, brought him close and whispered, "See that mountain, see that circle I drew right below it? A miracle happened there, baby boy."

TEARS CAME EASILY as I remembered watching the truck with the girl leave the parking lot. An old man had been driving. He'd worn a bright orange hunting cap, pulled down low, and he'd had a thick gray beard. She'd been sitting in the passenger side looking straight ahead, but, when they'd passed by me, she had turned and looked me squarely in the eyes. She hadn't looked afraid — instead, maybe tired. I had seen a trace of a smile, but I wasn't positive. Now, maybe, that's what I wanted to believe.

A detective, Dominic Sousa, had tracked me down at my new address. He'd explained that he was calling to find out about my connection to Sadie Wade. I told him I'd seen the obituary posted on the restaurant's Facebook page and had recognized the girl. That I'd wanted to send my condolences. I was reluctant to tell him my story. But he'd been kind and patient and had said, "Elaina, you're not the only one who may have been touched by Sadie. And I say 'touched' in the figurative *and* literal sense."

It was then that I'd described our meeting outside the drugstore — what Sadie had said and did. I'd explained how bleak things were for me: the baby due in four weeks, with a congenital heart defect, and a partner who was unsupportive and looking for a chance to bail. How I didn't know what was in store for us or even if my baby would live.

He'd asked me Timothy's date and time of birth. "March first at seven-fifty p.m." I'd paused then added, "But that's not accurate."

That's when he had replied, "March first at six fifty-four p.m. is Sadie's official time of death, but, like your baby's birth, it's wrong, too."

I'd hesitated for just a moment. "Timothy was born one hour earlier, at exactly six fifty p.m." I'd heard his quick intake of breath. "Is it Sadie's real time of death?" I'd asked.

"Yes," he had whispered. "And the heart defect?"

"He wasn't born with one."

I BENT DOWN, kissed the top of Timothy's head, and whispered Sadie Wade's words once more: "I relinquish all my fear." An overwhelming sense of calm enveloped me. *We were going to be just fine.*

Do bad things happen for a reason?
Is it to make the good things come even sooner?
Maybe it's all a well-laid plan or
is it just random steps, one leading to the other?
What do you believe?

I never imagined all this, here and now.
Good people and a place I belong.
God at the helm, guiding us all
on this incredible journey through time.
What do you believe?

I look all around and see
your kindness and compassion.
You move through our lives and drop
beautiful pebbles of love,
for us to touch and hold.
This is what I believe.

If tomorrow never comes,
if the sun never rises,
if this is all we have, it will be okay.
Because pebbles of love are never gone.
They just settle deep into our being.
This is what I believe.

With Gratitude

Thank you to Rachel Carter, my editor, and to Jen Payne of 'Words by Jen,' my book designer. You've both been invaluable to me and a joy to work with!

To my readers ~ thank you for reading *Relinquished*, my third book about the people of Langdon, Vermont. If you liked it and haven't read my other two novels, *Rectified* and *Redeemed*, please check them out at pollyannaporter.com.

All three of my books are 'stand-alone' stories, yet, like people in our own lives, my cast of characters pop up from time to time across novels. To name a few: the little girl mentioned in the shopping cart at the check-out with her angry father in *Redeemed* is Sadie. Jackson Larson, the oldest brother from *Rectified,* is Sadie's cousin and warns her of black ice. Karl, the man who snow plows in *Relinquished* is Tom Dunne's buddy who spends the morning playing hide and seek in David's barn in *Redeemed.* Jeannie Ricco, best friend of Sara Scott's from *Rectified*, appears across all three novels.

I hope I've conveyed in my writing that each one of us has a back story and that story often shapes who we are, and what may lie ahead. Yet, we do not have to be tied to our past, especially when that past hasn't served us well. Change and growth, forgiveness and letting go are within grasp for all of us. It may seem daunting, but it is never impossible.

Thank you once more for reading my work. Vermont winters, along with a great dog at my feet, provided me the perfect setting to imagine.

— Pollyanna Porter

www.ingramcontent.com/pod-product-compliance
Lightning Source LLC
Chambersburg PA
CBHW030913300726

48970CB00001B/139